R0201323482

08/2020

D0841641

BLACKOUT
A PETE FERNANDEZ MYSTERY

PALM BEACH COUNTY
LIBRARY SYSTEM
3650 Summit Boulevard
West Palm Beach, FL 33406-4198

ALSO BY ALEX SEGURA

SILENT CITY
DOWN THE DARKEST STREET
DANGEROUS ENDS
MIAMI MIDNIGHT

BLACKOUT
A PETE FERNANDEZ MYSTERY

ALEX SEGURA

POLIS BOOKS

The following is a work of fiction. Names, characters, places, events, and incidents are either the product of the author's imagination or used in an entirely fictitious manner. Any resemblance to actual persons, living or dead, is entirely coincidental.

Copyright © 2018 by Alex Segura
Cover and jacket design by 2Faced Design
Interior designed and formatted by E.M. Tippetts Book Designs

ISBN: 978-1-947993-54-9
eISBN: 978-1-947993-30-3

Library of Congress Control Number: 2018932409

First trade paperback edition July 2019 by Polis Books, LLC
221 River St., 9th Fl., #9070
Hoboken, NJ 07030
www.PolisBooks.com

POLIS BOOKS

For Eva and Guillermo, always.

"*I felt so heavy with love. I could feel it packed inside my chest.*"
—Vicki Hendricks, *Miami Purity*

"*In the light of eternity, is it better to sell out and ride or stand up and walk?*"
—Elmore Leonard, *Gold Coast*

PART I: WOLVES

PROLOGUE

She was always running.

She was a few paces ahead of him, her blue dress dirty and torn, the sky a dark, cobalt gray. His heart pounded in his chest as he ran to keep up with her. She looked back, her eyes wide with fear. *Was she running from him? Or were they both running from the same thing?*

He smelled the ocean, and felt the sand grow rough and rocky under his feet as he raced away from the shore into a cluster of trees that he hoped would provide them with some kind of refuge.

She was screaming now. He heard her as he got closer, picked up speed. She turned her face and looked back at him—*behind him?*—her eyes red, her face tear-streaked and smeared with makeup. Her long brown hair was tangled and dirty. She was barefoot, the cuts and scrapes visible along her legs as she stumbled from exhaustion.

If he could reach her, he could help her. Pete was certain of this.

His leg cramped. His body ached as he pushed himself. The branches grabbed and scratched at him, clawing at his face and tugging at his shirt and pants as he struggled to keep up with her. He needed to reach her.

She made a sharp right turn, deeper into the trees, humid and dank, a malicious rain forest consuming them. Everything was sleek and wet and dirty. Pete turned, too, and suddenly, they were face-to-face. Yet, her eyes were panicked and agitated, her back pressed against a massive, jagged rock that blocked her path like a stone gatekeeper. She was cornered—and afraid.

Of what? Of me?

She gripped his shoulders and he got a good, clear look at her, the trees seeming to close in around them. She hadn't aged at all, her features still soft and smooth, her eyes coal black and in stark contrast to her pale, paper-white skin. Whatever bumps and bruises she'd collected during her run had disappeared, whisked away by a force that Pete didn't want to understand. She was here, just as he'd known her. Like she'd just stepped off the graduation stage, fist clenched around her diploma, raised high as the crowd roared.

Except Pete knew that had never happened. And as the fleeting thought crossed his mind, like a whisper in a loud, crowded room, she changed. Her form flickered out of focus, as if viewed through a blurred camera lens. Her face was heavy with a mundane, aching sadness that Pete found all too familiar.

She pulled him close, and he could feel her warm breath on his cheek as she spoke, the last words of the dream. The dream he would dream again and again.

"Remember me."

Before Pete could respond, a fast-moving darkness swallowed him, pulling her away and down into a blackened void that seemed to stretch on forever.

CHAPTER ONE

Miami, Florida
April 11, 1998

"Pete Fernandez, troublemaker. How is that even possible?"

Pete whirled around and looked down the long, cavernous hallway that connected the second floor of Southwest Miami High's A and C wings. He yanked out the headphones that were blasting Oasis' *Definitely Maybe* album. He'd hoped to get through his Saturday cleanup duty unnoticed. But here was Patty Morales, ace softball pitcher, plucky newspaper editor, and Pep Club president, walking toward him, all smiles. He tried to avoid her eyes. They were friends, sure—they'd shared a few laughs in class, worked together on the school paper, hung out with some of the same people. But it ended there. They didn't hang out after school and Pete still felt a grating embarrassment when he relived their last conversation. The painful jumble of words continued to echo in his brain as they escaped his lips, stilted and slow, like a production assistant wheeled onto the anchor desk seconds before on-air.

Hey, um, Patty, prom's coming up, and I, uh, just wanted to see …

He could still feel the sheen of sweat on his hands. The dry, cottony mouth that prevented him from saying the words he'd practiced in front of the mirror just that morning.

Girls like Patty Morales didn't struggle for dates. She carried herself with a calm and ease that belied her true, potent mix of smarts, confidence, and beauty. She was out of his league, and Pete knew it. But he had to try.

She'd responded to Pete with a soft, warm smile that felt more like a dagger to the stomach. It wasn't so much that she said no, Pete realized later, as he replayed the exchange in his mind. It was the look of pity lurking behind the smile that made him feel like shit. Like a fool. He'd slinked away to his next class—his head down, eyes buried in his European history textbook as he sat in the back row of Ms. Delgado's class.

"I'm on garbage duty until graduation," Pete said as Patty approached.

Patty Morales and the prom were Pete's biggest concerns a few months ago, but that seemed like a distant car in the rearview mirror now. He was dealing with a set of problems that would have seemed unimaginable at the start of his senior year. For kicks, Pete and his now-former friend Javier Reyes had tried to make off with some forties of Olde English from a bodega in their suburban Miami neighborhood of Westchester. They'd failed in spectacular fashion. Instead of pulling off a daring, if somewhat moronic, act of resistance, Pete narrowly avoided being arrested—only to be placed under 24-hour surveillance by his father. His dad, Pedro Fernandez, dropped him off at school. He picked him up. If his dad had to work late, Pete was forced to sit in his airless office at police headquarters, the constant chatter and buzz of activity making it impossible to do anything beyond making tedious small talk with Carlos Broche, his father's burly and gruff partner, in the homicide department of the Miami PD. This was the new world order for Pete, at least until he graduated and left home—and his father—for good.

The incident had made the gossip rounds at Southwest, but Pete gained no currency in the eyes of his more rebellious peers or even his fellow bookish, shy types. It made him seem dumb. Because, well, it had been dumb. Pete still wasn't sure what had driven him to do it, aside from a desire to spite his father and impress Javier, a popular kid who had no reason to be driving around town with a likable but not popular guy like Pete. He wanted to show his friend he was tough, too, that he could hang with him and his kind. But he'd just shown Javier that he was a coward and fraud.

Though the infraction happened outside of school, the administration still felt the need to levy some kind of punishment on him—a move that came with his father's full support, Pete knew. All things considered, the punishment was mild, if tedious: school cleanup duty every Saturday morning until he graduated. Pete wandered the school grounds, tossing cigarette butts, plastic cups, fast-food containers, and an occasional condom into a clear plastic bag that he dragged behind him.

"Well, that's only two months away," Patty said, a polite smile on her face. "How long are you stuck today?"

"Until two."

"I'm working on some layouts for next week's issue of *The Lancer*, if you're bored," she said, giving him that sad smile again. "I could use your help. You're always good at coming up with those zinger headlines."

She felt bad for him. Pete's stomach lurched at the thought.

Pete was conflicted. He wanted to run, to leave this punishment— real and imagined—behind and seal himself away for as long as it would take. He didn't want to be tangled up in the pull of her sympathy. Yet her concern, which Pete could happily misinterpret as interest, beckoned him. He wanted to be near her. To smell her too-sharp perfume and listen to her breathy voice and to think, just for a moment, that he was part of her story. But what was left of his pride won out.

"No, thanks," he said. "I gotta head home after this. I'm on house arrest."

"Oh, okay," she said, a slight sadness creeping over her smooth features. She understood. Even a girl as friendly and warm as Patty knew how the social hierarchy of high school chugged along. They moved in different circles, only interacting for fleeting moments as they whizzed along their divergent paths.

Pete turned around, but then felt her hand on his shoulder.

"You know, Pete, I meant to tell you this before," she said, her words steady and unhurried. "When you asked me about prom."

About prom.

"It's not you, okay? I hope you know that," she said, taking a step closer, her hand still on his shoulder. "It's not that I wouldn't have had fun with you. But, I mean, I don't think of you like that, you know."

Like *that.*

"When you asked me, I wasn't in a good place. I'd just gotten fucked over by my ex—that guy from Columbus, Danny Castillo," she said. "And I had already told Mari and Illiet that we'd go together, you know, as friends? Single girls not needing a dude, right? So, I couldn't change it up on them at the last minute."

Heat spread over Pete's face and he knew his cheeks were red. He clenched the half-full garbage bag tighter, the plastic burying itself in the creases of his palm. He wanted to be anywhere but here. Even the musky, humid holding cell they'd thrown him into after the robbery, which smelled of urine and sweat, with its chorus of low, menacing voices paired with the methodical ticking of a clock, seemed preferable. The last thing he wanted to hear about was Patty's private-school ex-boyfriend.

"But it meant a lot that you asked me," she said, meeting his eyes. "I just wanted you to know."

She moved her hand away and gave him a languid wave. "So ... I'll be in the yearbook room if you want to stop by, okay?"

She smiled and then turned toward the student media room, glancing out the large, fingerprint-clouded windows that overlooked the patches of unkempt grass between the school wings.

Pete felt a surge of euphoria spread through him, like an energy drink kicking in. He made a mental note to ditch his garbage detail early so he could have a few minutes to say hi before his dad pulled up in front of the school.

But Pete never saw Patty alive again.

CHAPTER TWO

Patty Morales turned right off the breezeway and walked toward A200, the student media classroom where the Southwest yearbook and newspaper set up shop. She didn't like coming in on the weekend, but it meant the office would be quiet and she could get work done. It also got her out of the house, away from her parents. She knew her dad would leave. It was only a matter of when. Her parents fought daily. The arguments never got physical, but the tension and anger permeated everything around the house. Terse exchanges in the morning as the three of them bustled through the kitchen. Snide remarks from her mother as her dad tried to make conversation over a rare family dinner. Tiny fissures in their daily lives that would continue to grow into a bottomless canyon that would swallow them all. Patty knew her mom was difficult. Loud, brash, opinionated. It was what had drawn her father to her when they were first dating, she guessed. That attraction was gone now, replaced by anxiety and resentment, a silent battle fought under the cover of long, painful silences that seemed to stretch for days. It meant her father came home late and left early, if he came home at all.

It was the nights spent elsewhere that sealed it. Patty wasn't stupid. She lived in the same house with her parents and heard the arguments, even behind closed doors. Patty felt the disdain that festered between them, replacing the warmth and love Patty had once thought immortal. Her father was spending most of his time elsewhere—and while her mother hadn't discovered a smoking gun in terms of his fidelity, it still had created an irreparable rift between them, and Patty took the brunt of the collateral damage. Yet Patty wasn't mad at her father. She loved them both and, even at the age of eighteen, understood that life was loaded with large swaths of gray. Her parents weren't perfect. Neither was Patty.

Patty used the key the media advisor, Mrs. Vazquez, had given her and walked into the classroom. She flipped the lights on and moved toward a bridge-like workstation set up near the back of the room for the newspaper staff's main editors. She sat in her usual seat and powered up her computer. As she waited for the Mac to awaken, her thoughts returned to her parents. She sighed deeply. Her house seemed forever altered—a place once bursting with memories of *Nochebuena* celebrations, birthdays, and anniversary parties had become simply the place where Patty slept.

Patty heard her beeper vibrate and grabbed her purse, sliding her hand inside the small brown bag. The pink pager's thin display revealed a familiar—but unexpected—phone number: Danny Castillo.

Patty wasn't sure if she could even count Danny—the tall, brooding Columbus High quarterback—as her ex-boyfriend. It started and ended in a brief and blinding flash of activity. From first kiss to drudging conclusion, the totality of their relationship felt more like a slapped-together TV montage than a true romance. They met at her friend Soraya's party a few months back. Mild flirting at first. His hand grazing hers as they sat on the long black couch. A lingering look as the conversation lulled to a stop. Shared sips from a lukewarm bottle of Corona. An ironic, awkward dance to Semisonic's obnoxious earworm "Closing Time" as the host ushered the stragglers out. Then the buzzed, zigzagging drive home, during which he hadn't tried a thing—no weaving lean-in for a kiss, no clumsy hand in her lap. Ever the gentleman, she mused.

The all-night phone calls started next. After dinner, she'd scurry to her room and close the door, knowing her parents were too caught up in whatever personal turf battle they were waging to think about her. It all seemed so frivolous now. But it had felt to Patty like she and Danny really talked, communicating on a deeper level—not just about school gossip or the music they were listening to or *90210*-type bullshit, but things that felt substantial: what he wanted to do with his life, college, his family.

It seemed like a relationship, Patty thought, as she dropped the beeper into her purse and wheeled the creaky chair back toward the screen. She wasn't exactly super-experienced when it came to dating, having spent her high school years thinking about college and doing the things that would get her there. Patty wanted an Ivy League school, but she'd settle for anything that guaranteed her ample distance from the sweltering summers and family drama of Miami.

They'd gone on dates, they'd hung out with his friends, and spent time together at his house while his parents were away. Not time-time, but they did stuff. More stuff than Patty had done before. The bristle of stubble against her cheek, his hungry mouth on hers, the heat that seemed to radiate from him. It had all been new, passionate, and special. It made Patty wonder whether the heat and her parents' problems were good enough reasons to leave Miami, if Danny was going to stay.

The first doubt crept up on her like a toothache, more overt and bothersome as time passed. He'd invited her to go to church with him to some off-the-grid congregation she'd never heard of. Patty wasn't religious, but she was Cuban, and that meant she was Catholic. She couldn't remember the last time she'd been to a church service except for Christmas Eve, Easter, or a funeral. It wasn't part of her routine.

The church—or, God, in some form—had become a significant part of her father's life, though. From what little she picked up from the wall between the rooms, she knew her father spent his time away from home doing something spiritual, which her mom did not approve of or think much of. She still worried her father was having an affair, but there was little evidence to back that up. The truth—that her mild-mannered, humble father had strayed from his wife to embrace God—was much more bizarre to Patty than an extramarital indiscretion.

With all that background noise going on at home, Patty didn't have room for much more. So, she passed on Danny's church outing and he seemed okay at first. Easy. Patty had enough to worry about, anyway, what with her entire home life crumbling before her eyes. She thought that'd be the end of it. It was—but not in the way she'd envisioned.

She opened PageMaker to mock up the next edition of *The Lancer*, Southwest's somewhat monthly newspaper. She was the editor-in-chief, a fancy title that just meant she was stuck finishing up the things the editorial staff didn't get to: copyediting stories, writing headlines, making sure the final proofs were delivered to the printer, and, on release days, lugging and dropping off stacks of newspapers to classrooms before school started. But she loved the work and enjoyed her staff—most of them, anyway.

Thinking about the newspaper's core editors—news, sports, features, opinion, and arts—pulled her mind back to Pete Fernandez. She liked him. Not like-liked, because that spark just wasn't there, but he was funny, smart, and focused when he wanted to be. He could have made a case for himself to be editor of the paper, but for whatever reason, he didn't—allowing Patty to take over, unopposed. Not a bad guy, even if he'd made stupid decisions.

The prom thing had been strange, but not all that surprising. Patty could tell that Pete had the crush of crushes on her. The mixtapes slipped into her locker, how he'd turn away when she'd catch him staring in class. The occasional, not-so-surprise run-ins between periods. He was a sweet guy, but Patty wasn't attracted to him. Didn't dream of him as she doodled in her notebook or as she listened to the tapes he made her—which were a little heavy on the Beatles and Billy Joel and thick in terms of the message he was trying to send. He was her friend, and she was sad they'd graduate and part ways before they could become closer.

"It's for the best," she said to herself as she sent the double-page interior spread to print. It was a forward-looking piece on graduation, with updates on who'd been accepted where and some quotes from notable "student leaders" about how much they'd miss the purple-and-white building that made up Southwest Miami High.

Her beeper buzzed again and Patty groaned. *What the hell did Danny want?* It'd been almost a month since she'd broken it off and he'd seemed more than happy to never talk to her. Another buzz. The first message was Danny's number, the next said 911. Emergency.

Patty picked up the phone next to her computer. She dialed 9 to get an open line and then Danny's home phone number, from memory. It rang once before he picked up.

"Hey."

"Hi," Patty said. "What's up? You beeped me 911?"

"Yeah, I need to talk to you," he said, his voice drowsy like he'd just woken up from a long nap. "I need to see you."

"I don't think that's a good idea. I'm busy."

"At the paper?"

Patty didn't answer.

"I can come pick you up," he said. "I have stuff to talk about. Big stuff. It's important."

She pinched the bridge of her nose and closed her eyes. *Be strong.*

"Look, Danny, no," she said. "I have shit to do and I haven't heard from you in weeks. You didn't even respond when I left you a voice-mail about that cop—who, I swear, has been showing up all over the place. It's creeping me out. So, yeah, I get it. We're not friends. Which is fine. I told you I needed space, but you can't have it both ways, okay?"

She heard him starting to respond as she hung up. But she put the receiver down firmly. She was done with the drama. *The cojones on this guy, using 911 like that.* She'd been worried for a second. Patty went back to work.

P atty finished up later than expected, but she felt satisfied. The sections were laid out and edited—only missing a game story on that night's girls' swim meet. Ryan would have the recap written in the morning and then Patty would figure out how to get the proofs to the printer so they could have the paper out by Tuesday. *Not bad, Morales. Not bad.*

She shut down her computer and grabbed her purse, looking around the large classroom to see if she'd forgotten anything or if she had to bring anything home. She grabbed a large binder from Mrs. Vazquez's desk. It contained the proofs for the upcoming 1998 yearbook. The editor of the book, Hannah Aclin, a girl that Patty didn't know well but was friendly with, had asked her to give the pages a once-over for style and consistency. She'd work on it tonight. Patty locked up behind her and walked down upper A wing, away from the breezeway. She didn't hear the footsteps until she'd reached the middle of the hall, close to Mrs. Dymond's classroom, where she took AP English. The steps seemed slow and hesitant, the person unsure they wanted to be seen. Creeped out, Patty turned around quickly to try to glimpse whoever was behind her. But the hallway was empty, and she felt stupid.

"Been here too long," she said. She was right, too. It was almost six and the Miami sun was fading into darkness, an orange smear sinking into a pink sky. She'd just gotten caught up in the work, she thought, and now it was time to go home and see what new spectacle awaited her. She made it to the stairs at the end of the hall. Then she saw it. The body. It was on the landing that separated the first half-flight of stairs from the rest, near the school's south exit. The man was lanky, crumpled and moaning, sounding like a trapped and wounded animal aware its time is up. He had his hands wrapped around his head, knees in his chest in the fetal position as he rocked back and forth. Patty realized she knew who it was, and took the stairs down two at a time to reach Danny Castillo. She didn't see any injuries, but it seemed like he'd taken a nasty fall. The black-and-blue marks might show up later.

But I didn't hear anything fall.

She reached for Danny's shoulder. He hadn't noticed her yet.

"Danny! Jesus," she said. "Danny, what happened to you?"

She rolled him over and saw his eyes flutter. The middle of his white Columbus High T-shirt was soaked with a dark, spreading stain of blood. His anguished sobbing stopped, and he seemed to freeze, his eyes locked on a distant object past Patty.

This can't be happening.

But now the footsteps she thought she had imagined were back—louder, more confident. As she followed the sound, her eyes drifted down toward the hallway that lead to the first-floor A wing classrooms. That's when she saw him, looking up at her and the fallen Danny. She let out a relieved sigh.

"Oh, thank God," she said. "Help—help me with him? We need to get him to a hospital—I think he's dying."

CHAPTER THREE

Three quick knocks sliced through the silence blanketing the dark bedroom.

Pete Fernandez's eyes fluttered open. It was well before ten in the morning on a Sunday. Even his hardnosed father usually let him sleep in on a Sunday. It was the least he could do, Pete thought. The man had taken everything else away.

Now he was knocking on his door—and talking through it, too. Pete rolled over in his bed and checked his alarm clock. Eight o'clock. What ... the ... fuck?

"Pete, get up."

Pete didn't respond. He sat up and tried to rub the sleep from his eyes. The only light in the room poked through a crack in the blinds—a small sign that there was a world outside.

"Pete, I won't ask again," his father said, his voice calm but forceful. Pete sighed. He knew this tone too well. Something was wrong. Unease settled over him.

"Hold on, gimme a sec," Pete said.

"Hurry up, okay? Carlos is here."

Carlos? Why was he here this early? Pete stood up and changed out of his pajamas. He checked his reflection in the mirror above his dresser. He looked tired. Bored and tired. He winced as he opened his room's sole window. The beaming Miami sunlight busted in and lit up a room in disarray—textbooks tossed in a pile near the door, clothes strewn along the floor like some kind of confused breadcrumb trail, and leaning towers of CDs stacked around a massive stereo system. He'd fallen asleep to Elvis Costello's angry, driving *Blood & Chocolate* album. Music was one of the few things that seemed to lift Pete's spirits. These days, Pete found the darkness and chaos comforting, the feeling of floating in an empty void more soothing than he cared to admit. Pete knew it was dangerous to romanticize the dark monotony of his life, but he found it hard to muster the motivation to stop.

Carlos Broche, his father's partner, had been part of Pete's life as far back as he could remember. Basically an uncle to Pete, he'd stepped in to help Pete's father with the challenges of being a single parent after the sudden death of Pete's mom. He admired Carlos, and he was over often, but never this early.

More knocking. More forceful.

"Pete, get out here," his father said, louder this time. "It's about your friend, Patty."

Pete's father sat in his usual maroon recliner as his partner paced around the living room, hands in his pockets, brow furrowed.

"He'll come out in a second," Pedro said, motioning for Broche to sit down. He did.

"What's taking him so long?"

"He's a teenager, Carlos, *tu sabes*," Pedro said. "Plus, I'm his least favorite person. I'm the bad guy who makes him go to school and not steal."

"You're such an asshole," Broche said with a smile.

"What do we know?"

"Not a lot," Broche said, rubbing his eyes. "It's not even a missing persons case. Hasn't been twenty-four hours. But her parents—well, her mom—is in a panic. Screaming that her girl would never just disappear like this without calling or letting them know. Most of the time, that's bullshit, but I did some digging and I think it fits here. Girl's an A student, member of every honor roll you can think of, ton of extracurriculars, editor of the school paper—you name it. Not even a tardy notice on her record."

Pedro slid a hand over his tired face. It'd been a long week, and he was hoping to just unwind today, his one day off. But when his partner had called and explained what was happening, Pedro told him to come right over. That was a cop's life, detective shield or not.

"Solid intel, but that doesn't lock it down for me," Pedro said, lowering his voice to a whisper. "Good kids can do bad things, *compadre*. You know this. Look at *mijo*. Quiet, studious, next thing you know, he's trying to steal malt liquor from some shithole—"

Their conversation was interrupted by a clearing throat. Pedro turned his head and saw Pete standing a few feet away in a ratty Pearl Jam T-shirt and a pair of faded black jeans. He didn't look like a kid who'd just slept for ten hours, Pedro thought. In the morning light, Pedro could see the dark bags under his son's eyes, and noticed the loose way his clothes seemed to hang off his thinning frame.

"You got me out of bed," Pete said. "What's up? What about Patty?"

"Sit down," Broche said.

Broche had always taken a tougher stance with Pete than his dad had. It was his nature with everything—attack it head on, don't give an inch. Pedro tended to take a more diplomatic approach, and, while stern, couldn't hide the affection he had for his only son.

Pete took a seat at the other end of the sofa, not looking at Broche.

"Is anyone going to tell me what's going on?"

"Patty Morales is missing, kid," Broche said. "And no one's seen her since she went to school yesterday to do some work. You were at school yesterday, right?"

"What, do you think I took her or something?"

"Don't get defensive," Broche said. "Calm down. No one is in trouble here. We need to know if you saw her and when. That's all."

Pete nodded. He looked to his father, instinct trumping any resentment he had.

"Did you see her yesterday?" Pedro asked.

"Yeah, but for, like, a minute," Pete said, palms up. "I was walking through the breezeway—"

"The what?" Broche asked.

"The upstairs hallway, it connects A and C wings," Pete said. "I was cleaning up—picking up any trash I saw—and was cutting through the breezeway to get to lower C wing, where the, uh, where the class was."

"Class?" Broche asked.

"Not really a class. Detention—they make him pick up trash around the school," Pedro said, saving Pete the embarrassment. "He's got to do it every weekend until graduation."

Broche waved Pedro off.

"Did you talk to her?" Broche asked.

"A little bit," Pete said, trying to think back to the conversation. "She was on her way to the media room to work on the paper. She asked if I wanted to help her."

"What time was this?" Pedro asked.

"I'm not sure, around noon?" Pete said. "I was finishing up the first half of my, uh, work. She said she would be there until at least two, and when I was done, well ..."

"What, kid?" Broche said.

"Well, I thought about going by, but then I changed my mind."

"Why?" Pedro asked.

"I didn't want to explain to you why I'd be staying later," Pete said, looking down. "I figured you'd think I was lying or something. It was easier to just wait for you to pick me up."

Pedro and Broche were silent, waiting for Pete to continue.

"But I walked by," Pete said. "And the room lights were still on. So she was still there when I left."

"This is helpful," Broche said. "It gives us a sense of what ..."

Broche trailed off and looked at his partner. *What she was doing before she was taken.*

"Are you friends with this girl?" Pedro asked his son.

"Not really, not close," Pete said. "We were friendly. We had a few classes together."

"I heard a little different," Broche said, scratching his chin.

"What?"

"Her mom said you asked her to the prom," Broche said, his eyebrows popping up for a moment. "But Patty said no because she'd made plans with her girlfriends to go stag together."

Pete looked at his father, but Pedro was staring at Broche. Pete's face flushed.

"I did, so what?" Pete said. "She said no. Big deal. I'm not going to prom anyway."

"Pete, I'm not your enemy here," Broche said. "Trust me, this is a walk in the park. If you ever get interrogated by the cops—and Jesus Christ, I hope you don't—this will feel like a trip to Disney World. So, just hear me out. I know you, your dad knows you. You're not a bad kid. You did something stupid, so that puts you on the police radar. You also got slighted by this girl—"

"I didn't get slighted," Pete said, spittle flying out of his mouth. He stood up and started toward his room. "It happens all the time. People ask other people to prom and sometimes they say no."

"Sit down, *hijo*," Pedro said. Pete complied.

"Sure it does, you're right," Broche said. "But do the girls that reject the guys go missing? No, rarely. I'm just saying, you have to tread carefully. Be helpful and also look out for yourself. You don't want anyone to pin this on you, and it's not a stretch to think about that, okay? You have a strong alibi—your dad, a respected Miami homicide detective, picked you up from school a little after two, right? But that's not foolproof."

"I can't make up stuff that didn't happen," Pete said.

"No one is asking you to," Pedro said. "Just be honest. Can you tell us anything else about this girl? About her life? Was she dating anyone?"

"She'd just broken up with someone, some Columbus jock," Pete said, trying to remember the guy's name. He'd met him once, at a party. He was your typical athlete. Built, tall, close-cropped black hair and a perpetual smirk. "I knew they'd broken up, which is why I even asked her out."

"Danny Castillo?" Broche asked.

"Yeah, that's him," Pete said. "Have you talked to him?"

Pedro let out a slow breath.

"We can't, kid," Broche said. "Danny Castillo is dead."

The Miami Times
April 12, 1998
SW Dade Teen Found Dead, Another Missing
Darryl Forges, Miami Times Staff Writer

The halls of Southwest Miami Senior High School were jarred out of their usual weekend lull yesterday by a bloody scene that seemed more suited to a teen slasher flick than a serene suburban place of learning.

Police have confirmed that Daniel Castillo, a senior and star quarterback for neighboring Columbus High School, was found dead on the Southwest premises, apparently shot twice in the chest, his body splayed out at the bottom of a school stairwell.

In addition, police have listed Southwest senior Patty Morales as missing. Morales, an honor student active in many school extracurricular activities, including the newspaper and pep club, was last seen on school grounds yesterday afternoon, working to meet a deadline for the high school's monthly newspaper, *The Lancer*.

* * * * *

ALEX SEGURA

The Miami Times

May 5, 1998

Still No Leads on Missing Teen, Police Say

Steve Vance, Miami Times Staff Writer

The family of Patty Morales, a Southwest Miami High School senior who has been missing for almost a month, is begging the community for help in finding her and asking that neighbors and friends remain vigilant.

Morales has not been seen since April 11th, the day her ex-boyfriend, Daniel Castillo, was found shot dead at Southwest High. Police sources have confirmed that while Morales is not a suspect in the crime, they are anxious to gauge how much she knows about the Castillo slaying.

"We are praying and praying for Patty to come home to us," said her father, Roger Morales, a hospital administrator in south Dade. "If anyone knows anything, or saw anything, please reach out. If you have Patty, please look inside yourself and realize it's not too late to let her go. And, Patty, if you are reading this, know that we love you and are waiting for you to come home."

The Morales family is offering a $15,000 reward for any information that would lead to their daughter's safe return home.

Patty, a well-liked and active student at Southwest, was last seen the afternoon of April 11 on school grounds, working in the high school's media room to meet a looming newspaper deadline. That evening, having not heard from her in hours, her parents drove to the school to find Morales's 1993 Toyota Corolla abandoned in the student parking lot. They then called police, who discovered Castillo's body in the school.

BLACKOUT

*****

The Miami Times
February 9, 2013

15 Years Later, Morales Family Still Holding Out Hope for Missing Daughter

Lonnie McQueen, Miami Times Religion Writer

Roger Morales lives in a cavernous three-bedroom house on the edges of Homestead in South Dade. Inside the home, which Morales has only occupied for a few months, is a collection of mismatched furniture, half-empty moving boxes, and stacks of takeout containers. He lives alone if you're thinking of actual, in-the-flesh roommates. But there is a constant presence in his life: the memory of his daughter, Patty. Morales, whose once thick black hair is now wispy and white, spends all of his energy, when not working as a hospital administrator at nearby Homestead Hospital, on the search for his daughter.

Patricia Morales has never been officially declared dead. Though families who have not heard from a loved one for long stretches of time usually petition for that classification in an effort to claim any financial death benefits, Roger Morales is not ready to accept that his only daughter is gone.

Patty Morales, who had just turned 18 when she disappeared, was last seen working on the school paper at Southwest Miami High on a weekend afternoon. Morales refuses to consider death as a possible outcome. In his mind, Patty is alive, and her reasons for disappearing, or for being taken, will be revealed when she returns.

"I think about what she's doing now, or what she would be doing if she stayed here," Morales said.

"She might have a family, a career, some kids. She was always so driven and smart."

There have been many private detectives and many heated conversations with the police, who long ago filed Patty's case as "cold." Endless trips by Morales around the country chasing the thinnest of leads: The man in Charlotte who claimed he saw Patty working at a restaurant. The family in Pensacola who assured Morales that Patty was the proprietor of a bar, the Spanish Trail. Those exchanges at least offered a flicker of light, a sliver of hope for Morales to feed on. It's the cranks and critics that cut deeply, he says. The ones who blame him and taunt him for his quixotic quest.

"We live in a very cruel time," Morales said, sitting in his self-made war room, pictures of Patty plastered on the wall, a map of Florida littered with blue, red, and green thumbtacks. "People like to tear things down, make you feel bad for believing. I know I haven't lived a perfect life. I've already put myself on trial in my own head. I don't need them to do it for me. But it still hurts."

Morales won't elaborate further, but based on conversations with former colleagues, friends, and family, a picture emerges of a man enthralled by religion late in life, immersed in the sermons of a tainted celebrity guru. Morales won't comment on whether he currently is or ever was a member of La Iglesia de la Luz, a church that cropped up in downtown Miami during the mid to late 1980s and disappeared under a cloud of legal problems before the turn of the century.

The organization was led by the bombastic and charismatic Jaime Figueras. Figueras, often draped in white and known for his deep, booming voice, founded the church in a ramshackle storefront in Little Havana and appealed to working-class and poor Cubans—mostly new arrivals courtesy of the Mariel boatlift in 1980—with promises of a better life and the tools to lift themselves out of poverty.

Figueras offered things that these "shadow people," ignored by the government and sometimes without a network or family, couldn't get on their own: help navigating the complex and byzantine world of city bureaucracy to resolve simple tasks like getting food stamps or questioning an inflated telephone bill. For those in more dire straits, Figueras' followers provided a no-questions-asked cafeteria serving warm food. The church asked those who could give a dollar or two do so, to help their less fortunate "brothers and sisters."

Soon, Figueras began collecting celebrity patrons, including City Commissioner Arturo Trelles and original Florida Marlins shortstop Miguel Sawaya. Donating to and visiting the church became *de rigueur*, a way for stars and politicos to step back from the glitter and celebrity excess of the 1980s and show that they really did care about the little guy and his *familia*.

The organization—or cult, as it's often described by critics who liken it to a mob family run by Figueras, his top lieutenants and his two children—downsized drastically in 2000 amidst allegations of tax fraud and unsubstantiated rumors of violence against former members, Today, Figueras and his remaining followers, can be found on a chunk of farmland in Key West.

PART II:
DOWN BY THE WATER

CHAPTER FOUR

April 6, 2013
Homestead, Florida

Pete Fernandez took a long pull from the Poland Spring water bottle. He winced as the vodka slid down his throat. He snapped the car stereo off, silencing Paul Westerberg's anxious plea to be taken down to the hospital. He stepped out of his car and onto the street, the muggy Miami night coating him in spongelike heat. The air was thick and moist, and even though the sun had been down for a few hours, its damage remained.

He was looking at the house tucked into 152nd Court in Homestead, off Kingman Road and SW 304th Street. The house was new, bearing the faux-elegant markings of recent South Dade architecture: brick driveway, Spanish-style roof, and decorative shutters that wouldn't do much against an actual storm. Pete could see the living room light was still on.

He stumbled as he crossed the street. He tried to straighten up as he got closer, the swig of vodka hitting him harder than he'd expected. His vision blurred, and there were two houses. He felt light-headed and grimy.

Pete didn't know Homestead well. The city was the last stop in South Florida before you hit the Keys and the ninety miles of water that separated the United States from Cuba. He wasn't even sure this lead made much sense—but after a few hours of research, spent while knocking back a half-dozen vodka sodas at the aptly named Fat Monkey Bar on Krome, Pete felt like he was onto something. But he'd been wrong before. He'd been wrong a lot. This whole case felt wrong.

After a disastrous year that included the death of his best friend Mike, his unsurprising dismissal from his position at the Miami Times newspaper and the realization that his onetime fiancée Emily would never be more than a missed connection, Pete had taken on a few private investigator jobs to make ends meet in the wake of what might have been his fifteen minutes of fame—the unraveling of the urban legend known as the Silent Death—a contract killer used by all facets of Miami's various mobs—Cubans, Italians, Albanians, Colombians. The gun for hire was also Pete's old high school friend, Javier Reyes. He'd kidnapped a woman Pete had been hired to find: Kathy Bentley. The story ended with Javier dead, Pete mildly famous, and Kathy the closest thing he had to a friend.

The dizziness grew stronger and Pete struggled to stay upright. He tried to take a deep breath and let out a barrage of hacking, heavy coughs that forced him to bend over, a knee on the wet asphalt. His limbs felt heavy. His head throbbed. Moments like these had become all too common for Pete, the days of drinking a few beers for pleasure now replaced with week-long binges that were guaranteed to end in a blackout. His life felt unhinged and rife with doom, like a driver pumping the brakes as his car careened down a steep hill into a widening chasm. In his darkest moments, which were growing more frequent, one thought bubbled to the top: *I will die this way.*

For a while, Pete strangled the voice, convinced he could live like this. Maybe not thrive, but survive. He tried to taper off the drinking. After the Silent Death business, he'd been down to a few beers a night, sometimes one. But it didn't last. It never did. Counting drinks; scheduling his binges; drinking at home, alone, the lights off and the air conditioning turned to frigid levels, a safe space for self-destruction—none of it worked. Once Pete picked up that first drink, any vestiges of control were gone and it was off to the races.

While spiraling out, he'd met Jackie Cruz—a sharp, sexy, and energetic lawyer—and fell for her fast. They weren't a good match. She knew what she wanted from the world and how she would get it. Pete was still wondering why he was on the planet at all. The potential romance turned into a series of awkward sleepovers, yelling matches, and missed calls. He was a mess and acted like a fool, showing up at her place reeking of booze, clothes in tatters, clinging to anything good still within his reach.

When Jackie dumped him and tried to reconcile with her cop ex-husband—some lunkhead named Mario Delacruz—Pete interrupted a few dates. It ended in a messy encounter that could have featured a jail cell if Mario hadn't actually been a reasonable guy with a truckload more patience than Pete. Somehow, Jackie forgave Pete. Their relationship now centered around Jackie asking him to run errands that fell under "investigation," but amounted to sifting through someone's garbage. It was a living, he told himself. Barely.

This case was different, though. Patricia Morales, Jackie's niece, was the stuff of local legend. She'd been missing since 1998 and presumed dead by most, including the police. Pete had gone to high school with Patty, and had sported a huge crush on the smart, friendly, and well-liked girl. The case had gone cold despite the gory, TV-friendly details that surrounded Patty's disappearance—her ex-boyfriend was found shot dead at the school, where Patty had been working on the newspaper over the weekend. Despite months of searching and endless investigative hours, the Miami PD—including Pete's homicide detective dad and his partner, Carlos Broche, both dead now—had scored a goose egg.

Initially, Pete hadn't realized that Jackie was connected to the girl he'd pined for, fifteen years prior. That changed when the Miami police discovered a new, unexpected lead in the frigid Morales case: a man named Kenny Sampson, who hinted that he knew where Patty Morales was buried, and who killed her. The revelation, which was leaked to the press with the speed of an inside job, electrified a city clamoring for closure. Similar to the tragic cases of Adam Walsh and

Shannon Melendi, the Patty Morales saga remained a lingering stain on South Florida—a reminder that the wide-open tropical paradise was rife with dark, sinister corners.

Then Sampson had disappeared as fast as he'd popped up, like a shadow dancing across an alley. As time passed with no leads on Sampson, the PD slowly lost interest, lacking the funds and energy to pour into an ice-cold case with plenty of live ones to chase after. But Jackie was interested, and when she latched onto something, something that involved her family, she would not let go. So, while the easy task would have been to sic Pete on the AWOL Sampson, she did the opposite. She opened her checkbook and asked Pete to investigate the case—from top to bottom. He had special insight, having known her niece, the daughter of Jackie's much older half-brother Roger, which made Jackie the aunt to a girl who, if alive, would be a year or two younger than Jackie's thirty-six.

It sounded like Pete's kind of case, and he needed the money. He hesitated at first, but then dove in as best he could, considering the shakes and his need for a vodka wake-up call and a noon chaser.

Over the last twenty-four hours, since taking the case, Pete had become reacquainted with Patty Morales. Patty had wanted to be a magazine reporter, or TV news producer—maybe a lawyer. She did community service not as a box to check on her college admissions application, but because her heart became fuller from the work. She loved her family, but didn't turn a blind eye to their problems. Pete could hear his father's summation of the evidence in his head: "Good student, no record, decent home life." But that still left room for mischief and secrets. Everyone had secrets.

He shoved a hand into his front jeans pocket and came back with a roll of mints. He popped two in his mouth and stepped toward the house. Left. Right. Left. Right. Once he got the rhythm going, he was fine. He didn't see any movement in the house as he reached the front door. The porch light flickered on, then off. The front yard was covered in faded grass, more brown than green, a byproduct of hot weather and poor upkeep. Low hedges bordered the left side of the house. Something caught Pete's attention around the corner. A shape that didn't seem right.

Pete rubbed his eyes, like a child just waking up from a long doze. He wasn't seeing double anymore, but everything was surrounded by a hazy glow, and he wasn't sure he could count on his sight much. But in the darkened night, the corner of the house looked off. The earth around the low-cut hedges appeared indented and disturbed.

Pete walked toward the corner of the house, his feet crunching on the dead grass. He closed his eyes for a moment, hoping to regain balance. He took in a long breath and let it out through his mouth before opening them again.

As Pete moved closer to the corner of the house, he noticed a branch had grown wild at the bottom of the hedges and stretched out, like something reaching out from underground, struggling to pull itself over and into the world. Pete shook the morbid thought from his head. Yet, as he got closer, the form seemed less and less like a branch. By the time he got to the corner he realized it had nothing to do with the foliage at all. It was an arm. Rather, it was an arm bone. Part of one, at least. The humerus. The memory from high school biology flittered into his brain like a small bug.

The arm bone was connected to a small pile of remains. Pete fell down on his knees next to it and swallowed hard, the mint residue mixing with the liquor to make a medicinal taste. Pete could make out the form in the moonlight. He felt certain this was Patty, though he had no basis in reality to confirm this. *Had once been Patty.* Pete pulled out his cell phone and let the dim display light shine over what he was sure were the remains of Patty Morales. This had once been the girl he spoke to in that breezeway at Southwest High. The blue-green light hovered over the scene, shaking along with Pete's shivering hand, giving the remains an unnatural glow, like some kind of radioactive metal, toxic to the touch. This shape, this pile of broken things was no longer a girl. The remains were old, and whatever evil thing happened to Patty happened years ago, when Pete was a petulant teen, picking up trash after a huge fuckup, oblivious to the world. Patty probably hadn't lived much longer past that moment they shared, Pete realized as he gagged, trying to keep whatever small morsel he'd had for lunch down. The sight of Patty's remains, the noxious, chemical smell rising up from them, and Pete's own pickled insides propelled him to his feet. He stumbled back, turned and threw up, the vomit liquid and clear, hot as it barreled through his throat, burning his insides on the way out. Whoever killed Patty wanted her to be found here, now, outside her father's new house—a house Patty never knew. This was a message.

He heard someone behind him.

"Who's there?"

Pete turned around to face Roger Morales. Morales stopped abruptly, his eyes glaring, mouth agape. A slow, high-pitched sound seemed to radiate from the air around them. Pete realized it was coming from Morales, now on his knees, his hands buried in the pile of bones and cartilage, his fingers sifting through the earth, grabbing at the pieces of Patty's skeleton, bringing them up to his face, to his lips, kissing them with a hungry, manic desperation, like a lost man reaching fresh water for the first time in days.

"My baby," Morales said. "Oh my God, you found my baby."

CHAPTER FIVE

September 15, 2017
Spring Valley, New York

Fernandez Investigations was nestled in a strip mall off Route 59 in Spring Valley, a short drive from Nanuet and about fifteen minutes from Pete Fernandez's quaint three-bedroom house in neighboring Chestnut Ridge, close to the New Jersey state line. Spring Valley was at the lower end of middle class when compared to other cities in Rockland County, the less sexy cousin to Westchester County. But Pete liked the blue-collar town, and found the chain stores, gas stations, and mediocre Mexican restaurants comforting in contrast to the blazing rainbow of lights and clanging orchestra of sound and people that was Manhattan. Here, people kept to themselves unless they needed something. That was fine by Pete.

The storefront consisted of two rooms—a sparse waiting area and Pete's office. It was tucked between a Panera Bread and a Starbucks, with a huge Barnes & Noble nearby to cap off the collection of stores. He didn't mind his neighbors much, and downright loved them when he could pinch their Wi-Fi. On dull afternoons like today, Pete needed any distraction he could find. He was sipping his fourth cup of coffee in his back office and scrolling through the baseball postseason scores on his phone when the door chime sounded.

Pete waited a moment before hopping out of his chair. He didn't have a receptionist. The last person to do the job, a teenage stoner named Franco who spent most of his idle time streaming porn from his phone, hadn't worked out. After dismissing the kid, Pete needed to save some cash and just handled it himself. Business was slow.

Fernandez Investigations specialized in missing persons-slash-pets, catching cheating spouses, and vetting candidates for jobs when employers needed more than a routine background check. When they wanted to know if the guy they were about to make their VP of marketing liked to do a few bumps off a hooker's ass on his way home from work. It was fine work, when he could get it.

He heard the door open and rustling in the waiting area—footsteps, hesitant, and a low, confused "Hello?"

Pete moved down the short hall that connected the two rooms. He was dressed in his usual frumpy gray suit, his dark hair cut close and a few days' stubble setting up shop across his plain face. The waiting room was pristine and spartan, more clean than stylish. There were a few mall-bought paintings on the walls and an IKEA couch for those who might have to wait to be seen, which didn't happen often.

The woman appeared to be in her late fifties, fit, and well put together, her dark blonde hair tied back, her face sporting a dry, impatient smile. She wore a beige business suit and had set her leather carrying case down on the small coffee table, atop a handful of old magazines—*Cosmopolitan, Teen Vogue, Sports Illustrated,* and a solitary *Ellery Queen.*

Pete stepped toward her, his hand outstretched.

"Sorry to keep you waiting," he said as she took his hand. "My assistant is out to lunch."

"It's close to three," the woman said, smugly.

"She likes to eat after the rush," Pete said. "Can I help you?"

"Well, I hope so."

Pete motioned for her to follow him into his office.

"Do you know who I am?" the woman said as she took a seat across from Pete's desk.

"Should I?" Pete said as he took his chair.

The woman seemed uncomfortable, as if she were in the midst of doing something distasteful or tacky, which Pete supposed was true. She'd clearly never had to hire a private detective, but he could imagine how it felt.

"My name is Ellen McRyan," she said. "My husband, Trevor McRyan, is a well-known man."

Pete nodded. Trevor McRyan was indeed a well-known man. He was a rising-star Florida state senator with political aspirations—equal parts Bobby Kennedy and Jeb Bush: a good ol' boy with a liberal streak that made him beloved by the Southern elites and MSNBC. A rare mix that created a challenging balancing act, Pete thought. He skipped the fawning and got to the point.

"What brings you here, Mrs. McRyan?"

"We'd like to—discreetly, I might add—hire a private detective to do something for us," she said. "And we discovered that you might have some, well, expertise in this area."

Pete let the words of the serenity prayer weave through his mind as she finished. This would not be a direct conversation, and Pete was rarely in the mood for the indirect.

"Well, you came to the right place," Pete said. "I happen to be a private detective and I'm also free to take on new assignments. So, now that we've determined our goals are aligned, we can—"

"Spare me the glib patter, Mr. Fernandez," McRyan said. "I am not here because of your sterling record, which, based on my research, doesn't involve much more beyond catching cheating husbands with their pants down or finding missing doggies. Not much aside from, well, your earlier scandals."

Pete stood up.

"I can spare you from everything, ma'am, all due respect," Pete said. "In fact, the door you came in through still works. You can walk out at any point."

McRyan sighed.

"I apologize," she said. "I'm—we're under a lot of strain. Can we start over?"

Pete sat down.

"Sure."

"I'll get to the point then," she said. "But it's essential that we keep this confidential, even if, after review, we decide not to hire you."

"Of course."

"My husband, Trevor, is planning his next move, beyond the state senate," she said. "We feel he's left a big footprint in local politics. It's time to spread out, and strive for the change we want across the state. We're still exploring how that might work, how he might play a part in the—well, how do I put it?—in the political discourse."

"I've read your husband is exploring a run for governor of Florida," Pete said.

Mrs. McRyan winced, as if this nugget of information was classified and Pete hadn't read it over his morning coffee, scanning the app of his hometown paper.

"Yes, well, that's not definite," McRyan said. "But if the time comes, we need the help of someone familiar with the terrain, if you will."

Pete gave her a polite smile.

"I don't take Florida cases, Mrs. McRyan. I don't take Miami cases. I'm happy to connect you with some Florida-based detectives who might suit your needs but—"

"We don't want another Florida detective, Mr. Fernandez," she said, her tone stern, like a daycare provider chastising a kid for eating paste. "Do you think I was just in the neighborhood? Driving over the Tappan Zee Bridge or going antique shopping in Nyack? No. I came here, to this state, city, town, to see you. My husband was specific in his desire to hire you, and, obviously, he can't come here himself. The press would pick up on it immediately. In case it needs to be noted, all expenses would be paid, you'd get a healthy—perhaps unwarranted—advance, and this is an assignment that should be simple to complete. That said, my husband is hell-bent on secrecy and tact, two things he claims you are capable of, according to friends of his."

"I don't know if I should thank you or kick you out of my office," Pete said. "But I'll just repeat myself: I don't take Florida cases. Been that way for a year now. I don't go down there. I live in New York. My license isn't even valid in Florida anymore. I wish I could help you, but if you're not willing to take a suggestion, then I think our conversation is done."

"Do you even want to hear what this is about?" McRyan said, incredulous.

"No, thanks."

He didn't walk Mrs. McRyan out.

Stiletto's was a subpar strip club down Route 59 on the fringe of Spring Valley. Like most dingy strip clubs, it had a faded, outpost-like quality, with no surrounding stores or businesses to take some of the stink off the place. The neon sign—a giant woman's shoe, with the heel making up part of the first T in the venue's name—was stuck in a permanent, seizure-inducing flicker. A gray pallor seemed to hang over it, especially during daylight hours, giving it an abandoned, cryptlike quality.

As Pete pulled in, he saw the five-car lot was half full. He parked his banged-up Honda Accord and walked into the club's murky main stage area, which consisted of a small bar positioned next to a dance floor that might accommodate two dancers on a good day. Today was not a good day, and one woman swayed to DJ Khaled and Rihanna's droning on about their wild, wild thoughts. The topless woman, her long, dark hair hovering around her face like a cloak, gave Pete a dazed smile as she zombie-walked through her solitary routine.

Aside from the dancer, a single mom of three with the stage name Ruby, and the bartender, a bulky Mexican guy named Roberto, the place was empty. It was getting close to prime hours, where dads and husbands would sneak in for a drink and a peek before heading home, smelling of hand lotion and peach schnapps. Then there'd be another lull before you got the drunks stumbling out of bars, blue-balled from failed dates or being shot down, looking to at least see a naked woman before passing out in their cars or beds.

Roberto nodded as Pete reached the bar.

"Jen here?" Pete asked.

"Round back."

Pete wove around the stage and pushed through a door that read EMPLOYEES ONLY. Inside was a snug, poorly lit dressing room that felt more like a broom closet. Sitting at the solitary vanity mirror, with every other bulb out of juice, was a woman about ten years Pete's junior, her dirty-blond hair was in a tight bun. She didn't have any makeup on and was wearing a faded black U2 T-shirt and yoga pants. She looked great, Pete thought.

Jen frowned and turned back to the mirror as the door opened and she saw Pete. Pete caught a glimpse of her livid expression in the reflection.

"What do you want?"

"Got a second?" Pete asked.

"I have to get ready, Pete," she said. "I'm on at the top of the hour. You know that."

"It'll just take a minute," Pete said, closing the door behind him.

She stood up in response, turning to face him, her body leaning back, a curious look in her eyes.

"I've got a lead on your dad," Pete said, pulling out a small, worn notebook from his back pocket. "Looks like he's holed up in a motel in Suffern, or Mahwah, depending on your loyalties. Place called the Oak Lodge."

Jen nodded. Her real name was Jennifer Ferris. Her stage name was much flashier—Destiny. She'd come to see Pete a month ago, looking for her degenerate gambler father, God knows why. It took some legwork, but Pete had found him the previous night. The man had set up shop in the motel with little to do but drink himself to death. Based on the photos Pete had snapped, he was getting close.

Pete and Jen had fallen into an ill-advised relationship. It consisted of Pete showing up at Jen's apartment late at night and leaving a few hours later, feeling more ashamed and depressed than he had when he reached her door, the brief pleasure soon replaced by a cloud of regret. Another bad decision in a year littered with bad decisions, like confetti on asphalt after a parade. The only saving grace, Pete thought, was that he hadn't picked up a drink.

Jen had cut things off with Pete the week before. She was young, but she wasn't dumb, and she could tell Pete was sleepwalking through something Jen saw as more than a hookup. Pete had taken it the same way he seemed to be taking everything these days: with a blank expression and a shrug. He couldn't muster a reaction—to Jen, to his job, to his life. That had made her even more furious. This was the first time they'd spoken since.

"You have an address?" she said, one eyebrow raised.

Pete tore off a sheet from his notebook and handed it to her.

"Thanks," she said.

Silence filled the tiny space for a few seconds too long.

"Look, I'm—"

"Just leave, okay?" she said. "I don't need the sympathy. I'm a big girl. You're the one I feel sorry for."

"It's not like that."

"Yeah? Please explain how it is, then."

"I'm not ready," Pete said. "I'm still dealing with—I'm not in the right mind-set for this. I can't be committed to anything—anyone."

She turned around and sat down in her chair, not looking at Pete as she began to apply her makeup, her hands possessing a compulsive anger, as if she could will him away with the right dab of eye shadow.

"Get out of here, Pete, okay?" she said, reaching for the eyeliner.

Pete turned around, but stopped as she wheeled her seat around to face him.

"I mean, you're fucking almost forty," she said. "Not for nothing, but guys your age would kill to get with someone like me. Seriously, what is it? Is it this?"

She waved her hand around the room, toward the stage and thumping music reverberating through the thin walls. Someone was singing about being stuck in the middle with you.

"Because if that's it, I feel sorry for you," she said. "I don't dance because of any repressed daddy issues or desperation. The money's good. I need money for school. Once that's done, so am I. If that's—"

"It's not that."

"Then what?"

Pete didn't respond.

Jen let out a frustrated groan before she swiveled around and returned her attention to the vanity mirror. Pete opened the door and walked out.

The All Souls Group met in an old church on Washington Avenue in Suffern. Pete made the meeting each week. Sometimes, if he had the time, he hit the morning meeting held in the same space. It was his home group and he had a responsibility to be there. His duties were integral: he made the coffee.

Pete was a drunk. A drunk who went to meetings a few times a week to not be a real drunk. He'd given up drinking twice. The first attempt fell apart during a case involving a Miami serial killer who had a hard-on for another, long-dead mass murderer. The psychopath had captured Pete's ex-fiancée, and Pete could have stopped it. The realization of his failure gave him more than enough runway to kick off a serious case of the "pour me" syndrome. He went on a blackout bender that reached its bottom in a roach motel in Little Havana. Pete couldn't remember much about that last, miserable night. Now and again he'd have flashes of things that happened—an empty jug of wine on his lips, the rough feel of a strange woman's skin in the back of a car, the smell of dirt and sweat that coated his every pore, the crumpled paper with his sponsor's cell phone scrawled on it—like electric shocks from another life. But it had been his life, and those shards of memory pulled him away, showing him just how bad things would get if he were to drink again. These infrequent reminders helped keep him coming back to the rooms.

Since then, he'd been sober for over two years. AA didn't fix all his problems, but it helped him stay humble and clear-headed. He'd be dead otherwise.

The night felt cool, the air crisp and dry. The brutal summer was ending and morphing into a chilly fall, which Pete was thankful for. The transitional weeks between seasons were his favorites. It was like the entire world was shifting together, becoming something else. Not too cold, not too hot.

He let the breeze wash over him as he walked down the street toward the church. It was ten to 8:00 and Pete was running late. His detour to talk to Jen had been brief, but still lingered, like a morning fender bender. He felt foolish for allowing himself to think—and leading her to believe—that the relationship might have legs. That it might be the kind of thing that involved sappy month-a-versary posts on social media, Caribbean cruise vacations, or date-night dinners at the Olive Garden. He'd been more honest with her for the five minutes they'd been talking in her dressing room than he'd been with her the entire time they'd been sleeping together. He wasn't ready for anything, serious or not. She was a beautiful, smart young woman. She'd find someone to appreciate her and she'd find other things to do with her time than strip. If that's what she wants.

These thoughts had ping-ponged around his brain as he drove around Rockland County, trying to figure out what he could do to salvage whatever they shared. Not romantically, but as people. The ride had ended with the realization that there was nothing to salvage. Jen didn't want to be his friend. She didn't want to share a bed with him anymore either. Some connections started with a bang and fizzled fast.

Pete approached the entrance to the church basement.

"You Pete Fernandez?"

Pete turned toward the voice. A tall, well-built man in a dark suit stood a few feet away from the doorway.

"Who're you?" Pete said.

"Mark Chadwick," the man said, stepping out of the darkness, his hand extended. "I'd like a few minutes of your time."

Pete shook the outstretched hand and then took a step back.

"That's just about all I have."

Chadwick looked around and nodded.

"Used to be in the rooms myself," Chadwick said.

His features were bland and almost soothing, but there was a sharpness to his voice that kept Pete on edge. *How did this guy know I was coming here?*

"Don't think you can graduate."

Chadwick laughed. A forced, empty chuckle.

41

"You pissed my boss off earlier today."

"Mrs. McRyan?" Pete said. "Well, I wasn't looking to piss her off. Collateral damage, I guess."

Chadwick moved in closer to Pete.

"The McRyans are important people," he said, a smirk on his bland face. "They want your help."

"Well, life's full of little disappointments, I guess. I don't take cases in Florida. There, I've said it three times. Does that mean it'll sink in?"

Pete saw the swing coming, so he had time to step back and watch Chadwick lunge into thin air, the punch's momentum almost knocking him onto the floor. Pete took the opportunity and jabbed Chadwick's ribs with his fist. That sent him down, clutching his midsection and groaning. Pete wasn't much of a fighter, but he knew one thing: most brawls were won by the guy that made contact first.

"What the fuck, man?"

"Pretty sure you swung at me," Pete said, standing a safe distance away.

Chadwick stood, inching up, his hands holding onto the church wall for support. He kept his eyes on Pete, his carefully combed gray hair now disheveled, a look of dubious anger on his face.

He's surprised I got the best of him.

Chadwick raised a hand.

"Look, I wasn't trying to get into fisticuffs here," Chadwick said.

"I'm happy people still use that word in the year of Our Lord, 2017."

"Cut the shit, okay?"

"You came to me," Pete said, his voice lowered.

Chadwick grunted as he finished standing up.

"Mrs. McRyan didn't want me to tell you this, but fuck it," Chadwick said. "It doesn't look like you're convinced. Guess money doesn't appeal to you. Maybe this will."

Chadwick pulled out his cell phone and pushed a few buttons. Pete noticed he was flipping through his iPhone's photo gallery. He stopped on one and turned the phone to face Pete.

"You know this guy?"

Pete did. The man in the photo was Robert Harras, an ex-FBI agent who Pete had run into a few times over the years. The first time they'd been at odds. Harras was law enforcement chasing a serial killer. Pete had been a pesky novice. The time after that, they'd been on the same side, mostly. Despite considering Harras a friend, he hadn't seen or spoken to him in over a year. The last time they'd talked had been tense, and the conversation ran parallel to this tête-à-tête with Chadwick. Harras wanted Pete to return to Miami to help him solve a cold case involving a dead girl. Pete had passed. They had shaken hands and parted ways. In his darker, lonelier moments, Pete was certain he'd never see Harras again.

The photo was recent. Harras was in full agent attire—gray suit, Ray-Bans and a well-trimmed beard. But he looked worked over—ragged and unhealthy. The photo had been taken without his knowledge, by someone shooting from a good range with a high-quality camera. Harras was under surveillance.

Even worse for wear than the coarse stressball Pete had seen in his old Inwood apartment shortly after he and Kathy had escaped Miami for New York, a heavy bounty resting on their heads. *Kathy.* He pushed her out of his mind. He didn't need to dredge up the muck, not before a meeting. Not right after talking to Jen.

"Where'd you get this?"

"So you know him, then?" Chadwick said, his face eager and alert.

"What does he have to do with your boss?"

"Your friend Robert Harras has made some dangerous enemies, pal," Chadwick said, the phone moving from side to side in a slow seesaw. "He's a dead man walking. He just doesn't know it yet."

Before Pete could respond, or press Chadwick for more information, the man stepped back into the shadows. A few moments later, Pete heard a car engine start, followed by the peeling sound of tires spinning over asphalt.

"**A**re you going?"

"I don't know," Pete said. He tossed another half-empty cup of coffee into the nearby wastebasket. "It feels like a bad idea."

"That's never stopped you before," Albert said.

The older, stocky Russian man was dressed in black—sweater, jeans, and scarf. The rims of his glasses were black. His hair was black. Pete would have guessed he was a poet even if he didn't know it already.

Pete scanned the room—the church basement was empty, chairs stacked on the walls and everything in order. The post-meeting cleanup took a handful of minutes. It gave Pete time to chat with Albert, his sponsor. Albert, who had been sober for as many decades as Pete had years in the program, served as a spiritual advisor of sorts—someone to help Pete work the program through suggestions and advice. Albert was the polar opposite of Pete's old Miami sponsor, Jack, but Pete found their talks just as helpful.

"True," Pete said. "But I can't ignore that all this is happening for a reason."

"Everything does," Albert said, pulling out a pack of Marlboro cigarettes from his back pocket. "That doesn't mean everything requires a reaction from you. That's your ego talking."

They took the stairs up to the first floor, shutting lights off and testing doors to ensure they were locked. This was their weekly ritual, making sure the space was secure when they left, avoiding a terse note from their church landlords. The room was nice, clean, and in a central location. They did their best to make sure the meeting would remain there for those who needed it.

As they stepped outside, Albert lit a cigarette and looked at Pete.

"You haven't spoken to this man Harras in a while, you say?" he said.

"Not for a year, maybe more," Pete said, scratching at the stubble on his face. "I didn't try to stay in touch, I guess."

"No, you didn't," Albert said. "Coffee?"

"Now that's a good idea."

Estrella's Diner, off Main Street in Nanuet, was a simple, no-frills homestyle restaurant. The place was never full, which Pete liked, though he doubted it helped the owners' bottom line. They took a table near the back, ordered two black coffees, and settled in.

"I hear they're closing this place down," Pete said.

"Guess so," Albert said, pushing his glasses up his nose. "Some kind of craft beer spot."

"Chalk one up for the hipsters."

"Such is life," Albert said, picking up the menu and giving it a quick once-over. "I'm assuming you didn't agree to get together because you wanted to talk about gentrification."

"Probably not," Pete said.

"Explain why you should go back."

"I shouldn't," Pete said. "At least not if I value being alive."

"So, case closed. Stay here. You have a comfortable job. A somewhat complicated social life and so on."

The waitress walked up. Albert ordered soup and fish tacos. Pete went for a corn beef sandwich.

"So, some stranger comes at you with a photo of a guy you used to run with, and you hop on a plane back to Miami?" Albert said before taking a swig of his coffee. "Does that sound smart to you?"

"Harras is my friend."

"So's Kathy, right?" Albert said. "How is she doing?"

"I'm sure she's fine."

Kathy.

They'd been playing this conversational tug-of-war for almost a year. Albert would ask how Kathy was doing, Pete would evade the question and they'd stew in silence until one of them changed the subject. Though Albert had never met Kathy, he knew how important she was to Pete, and also seemed to think figuring out what had happened between them was the key to getting him back on a track of forward motion, as opposed to the stasis Pete had been living in for over twelve months.

Kathy Bentley had been Pete's investigative partner for five years—dating back to when they lived in Miami. Pete's first case had been to find Kathy. Since then, they'd taken down serial killer Julian

Finch and Orlando Posada, a crooked ex-cop who was also the head of Miami's deadliest street gang, Los Enfermos. That last case was a big reason for Pete's move to New York. When you take down the head of a violent street gang, you still have to deal with the body—and the body was not thrilled with Pete Fernandez.

Kathy and Pete had hid in plain sight in New York for a few months. The battle with Los Enfermos had left Kathy in the hospital, recovering from a knife wound—an injury that took the life of her unborn child. Kathy refused to let Pete—or anyone—know who the father would have been. Once they left the Magic City, they'd found an apartment in Inwood—the northernmost part of Manhattan before you got to the Bronx—and defaulted to a comfortable domestic routine. Pete worked as an investigator in Westchester for a few local attorneys and Kathy pecked away at freelance writing gigs penning sordid true-crime tales for glossy magazines. Their more dangerous days seemed to be behind them. Except for the bounty on their heads.

Their friendship unraveled soon after the move to New York.

The first time it happened, it felt right, like a natural progression. They already lived together, sharing work, meals, and time. It was after one of those quiet dinners, Pete's *arroz con pollo*, while they shared the kitchen cleanup, that a hand grazed another. A glance was exchanged. Bodies moved toward each other. Pete leaned into Kathy, his mouth on hers, her hands sliding up his chest and grabbing his hair. By the time they reached Kathy's room, they were barely dressed, groping at each other hungrily, propelled by a passion neither of them expected. Their touches were rough, visceral, and desperate, two lonely people who'd been without this kind of feeling for too long—contact that crackled with emotion.

The next morning, their legs and arms still tangled together, Liz Phair's whitechocolatespaceegg on loop, they tried their best to not make it awkward. Playing it off with a few glib lines and a quick shift to their usual, platonic routines. But that only worked the first time. Soon, the sex had become as regular as any other part of their joined lives, despite their best efforts to ignore it. But before long, they couldn't.

They'd crossed a threshold, and it was impossible to go back to who they'd been before—just friends, partners but not lovers. You can't be that intimate with someone, someone who's ridden shotgun during the most traumatic times of your life, and not expect to feel anything. Or so Kathy tried to explain, a few weeks into the affair. She was ready for more. For something substantial. She didn't want to pressure Pete, but she also didn't want to wait. Pete, as always, was unsure. But patience was not a trait Kathy Bentley was known for. After an awkward week, Kathy made it clear she wasn't interested in having a roommate she sometimes fucked. Pete packed up and left. First to a seedy SRO in Manhattan, then up to Rockland County. They hadn't spoken since.

Albert took a long sip of his coffee before giving Pete a dubious look.

"You're sure she's fine?"

"I'd assume so, yes."

"When did you talk to her last?"

"It's been a while," Pete said. "But she'd reach out if she was in trouble."

Albert nodded.

"You know, a big part of our program is about trying to keep our side of the street clean. That requires willingness," Albert said, weaving his fingers together, forming a steeple under his chin. "That means, even after our initial step work is done, we still make amends to people we've wronged, as we realize we've wronged them."

"I'm not going to Miami," Pete said. "I'll make a few calls, make sure everything is okay, and go back to what I've been doing."

"Which is what?"

"Running my business," Pete said, brushing off a speck of lint from his sleeve.

"How's Jen?"

Pete let out a long, frustrated breath.

"Am I on trial here?"

"Pete, gimme a break," Albert said. "I have much better things to do than grill you for my entertainment. You're the detective, right?

Well, I'm trying to place enough clues in front of you, so you can see a pattern."

"I get it, okay?"

"Fair enough," Albert said as the food arrived. He poked at his tacos but kept talking. "So, walk me through this. Why would this McRyan flunky have a picture of your friend?"

"He didn't say, that's the problem," Pete said between bites of his sandwich. "The McRyans are shielded. They didn't make a threat. But this guy did. He's saying that if I don't help the McRyans, Harras will get hurt."

"Harras is a grown man—ex-FBI, right? I think he can take care of himself," Albert said as he dabbed at his mouth with his napkin. "And look—I'm not your therapist. But it is obvious there's a lot of, well, evading going on here. For whatever reason, you're not speaking to either Kathy or Harras, and you're not keen on going back home to Miami. Now, it's normal to want a simpler, safer life. But you're ignoring important elements that help make up who you are. Think about why that is, before it's too late."

"Too late?"

"Alcoholics can't let secrets or resentments fester for too long. They'll drive us to drink," Albert said, dabbing at his mouth with a napkin. "Maybe not tonight. Maybe not three years from now, but eventually. And that's a death sentence."

P ete dialed the number from memory as he got behind the wheel of his car. It rang through the Bluetooth hookup as he backed out of the diner parking lot. A familiar voice answered.

"Pete?"

"Dave," Pete said. "What's going on?"

Pete's greeting was met with silence. He'd -expected this. Though Dave Mendoza was one of Pete's dearest friends, they hadn't talked in close to a year—and not for lack of trying on Dave's part. A local Miami businessman with a shady track record, Dave had helped pull Pete and Kathy out of the fire on more than one occasion. His connections to the Miami underworld and his general street smarts had proven invaluable. He was also the kind of person you didn't want to piss off. The silence confirmed to Pete that Dave was, in fact, very pissed off at him.

"Let me explain."

More silence.

"Dave, you have to listen," Pete said.

That's where Pete was wrong. Dave didn't have to do anything. He hung up.

Pete decided not to go home. He pulled into an empty parking lot, turned the car around, and went back to the office.

He spotted the dark figure waiting near the entrance to Fernandez Investigations with ease as he closed his car door. Chadwick.

"What do you want?" Pete said, pulling out his keys. "I have work to do."

"I talked to my bosses," he said. "They're, uh, frustrated with my methods from earlier."

"You mean threatening a friend of mine?"

Chadwick rolled his eyes.

"Trust me, if I wanted to threaten—"

Pete raised a hand.

"I'm not interested in going to Miami, or working a vague case for people I don't know," Pete said. "So, unless your boss will come clean and tell me what she wants and why, then I'm not going to talk about this anymore."

"She'll come see you and share more of the details."

"All of the details, or there's no deal."

"She can do that," he said.

"Have her come by here at nine tomorrow morning," Pete said, opening the door and stepping in. "Then we'll talk."

Pete closed the door, leaving Chadwick outside, the frigid evening sending a gust of wind through the empty shopping center.

CHAPTER SIX

Kathy Bentley stepped out of the offices of *The New Tropic* and into the early Miami evening, the sky darkening to a muted purple. She walked toward her car, parked down the block. She'd been at the job on the outskirts of Wynwood for nearly a year and still marveled at how the neighborhood had changed. It was a trendy, gentrifying area of northwest Miami loaded with art galleries, fusion restaurants, and dark, hip bars that played all the right songs. A few years back, Kathy would have thought twice about walking down these streets after hours.

The *Tropic* was a daily local culture email newsletter and website that also featured community-focused news reporting and feature writing, mostly done by Kathy. She enjoyed the work, and appreciated the regular paycheck and non-vampire hours, but it was the first pit stop in her winding career that felt, well, like a job. It had nothing to do with the work itself, which was fairly engaging. Her bosses were fine, too—millennials looking to save the world with the enthusiasm and verve that one can only tap into before the age of thirty-five. For once, Kathy, much closer to forty than thirty, felt like the newsroom den mother.

After having been known as "Chaz Bentley's daughter" while working at Miami's still-flickering daily newspaper, the *Miami Times*, Kathy grew comfortable in the role of young, rising star. People loved her quick and witty remarks, fearless-slash-reckless reporting, and ability to drink them under the table. Now, when she asked her new coworkers to grab a few drinks down the street at the end of a stressful day, they stared back as if Kathy'd asked them to poison dogs around town. *Fine*, she thought. It was a paycheck.

After the last two years, Kathy was ready for a lull. She was okay with tedious and boring if it meant her rent was paid, she could sleep eight hours a night, and her biggest worry was getting hit by a car, not a stream of bullets.

You're not eighty years old, Jesus, she told herself. She wasn't a nun looking to lose herself in prayer. She had a life and career. It was just a little different. A little more settled.

Boring as fuck.

She laughed as she approached her silver Jetta and unlocked the car with the key fob. Tonight would not be a moping night, she'd decided. It'd been a year and change since she had come back from New York, and she was tired of spending any of her mental time there, waiting for Pete to realize that he might just be allowed to have a sliver of happiness despite whatever shit he pulled when he was a lush.

As she opened the driver side door, she saw someone approaching the car, or, more likely, walking down the block to their own car. Something about the figure made her doubt that, though. She slipped her right hand into her handbag and gripped the butt of the .22 she kept there. Kathy Bentley did not like being surprised.

Her hold loosened as the figure stepped into the glare of a nearby streetlight. He was familiar—*too familiar*. She repositioned her bag on her shoulder and closed the car door, looking at the tall older man from over her car roof.

"What do you want?"

"Guess I don't rate a hello anymore," Robert Harras said.

Kathy narrowed her eyes. The former FBI agent looked more faded and worse for wear than the last time she had seen him, over a year ago in the Inwood, New York, apartment she had shared with Pete. Harras had visited them to coax Pete to return to Miami—which would put his life at risk—to help solve some case that the FBI and Miami PD had botched years before. Kathy made it clear she thought this was A Dumb Idea.

"I'll give you a 'Hi' and we can call it even," Kathy said. "Were you following me?"

"It's not following if I know where you are," Harras said. "I was waiting for you."

"How'd you even know I was back?"

"I see your byline in my inbox each morning," Harras said. "Give me some credit, will you?"

Kathy felt a smirk forming on her face and tried to shoo it away. She had decided a while back that she did not like Robert Harras, and that was the way it would be, even if she found him attractive in a weird, Tom Skerritt way. There were other reasons, too. He knew them as well as she did.

"Credit duly assigned," Kathy said. "To repeat, in case you missed my question—"

"Look, I don't want to have this discussion in the middle of the street, okay? Can we get a cup of coffee somewhere? Someplace that doesn't treat coffee like ice cream."

"No, I will not get coffee with you," Kathy said. "You and I both know that's not a good idea. Second, your weird coffee thing is very mid-90s CBS sitcom and not at all funny."

Harras stepped around Kathy's car in a few quick motions, belying his age. In a moment, he was right in front of her. She could smell his sandalwood aftershave and get a good look at his face—the lines deeper than she remembered, a new darkness around his gray-blue eyes.

He opened his arms and took her into a short but genuine hug—at least from his side. She patted him on the back as he pulled away. They ended up closer than before.

"Was that so bad?"

"Yes, actually," she said. "It was terrible."

"We were all friends once, remember?"

"The past has a way of fading fast," she said.

The conversation stalled for a few long moments. Harras' eyes peered into Kathy's, a flash of desperation shooting through them, as if to punctuate what he was about to say.

"I need to find Pete," Harras said. "I need his help. Badly."

Kathy took a step back, bumping into the driver side door of the car. Harras' desperation was real, and it was unsettling. The man had always seemed buttoned-up and no-nonsense, even during rare moments of emotion and, well, passion.

"I, ah, I don't know how to find him," she said. "We don't talk much anymore. Honestly, we don't talk at all."

"What? What happened?"

"It's, ironically, not something I want to discuss out in the street."

"Follow my car," Harras said, backing up and turning to walk down the block. "It's that black Escalade a few spaces down. Let's sit down and talk. We're overdue."

I know your fucking car, she thought.

Kathy nodded, stepped into her Jetta, and waited for Harras' car to pull out onto the street.

"I thought you wanted coffee?"

"Changed my mind," Harras said as he wolfed a slice of Andiamo's Vesuvio pizza—an olive chunk splattering onto his plate.

In what was now considered Midtown Miami, or MIMO, Andiamo was an oddity in that it served good pizza in a town that wasn't known for its pie. The restaurant had a cozy interior dominated by a counter and a few huge pizza ovens and a bustling outside seating area that catered to the bulk of the restaurant's eat-in patrons. Harras had ordered for them and picked a table on the fringe, facing Biscayne Boulevard, the horns, tire squeals, and salsa music creating a buffer of sound around them.

Harras polished off his last slice and pushed the plate forward. Kathy had never known Harras to be a big eater—the detective seemed fit enough, from what she could tell.

You could tell. You liked to look at him.

She cleared her throat.

"Is it time for sharing?" she asked. Kathy had discarded her salad before Harras went in for a third piece of pizza.

Harras took a long gulp of water and leaned back in his chair.

"Someone wants me dead," he said. "And I don't know who. I have a few ideas, but nothing definite."

"What does that have to do with me?" Kathy asked. "I mean, no offense and all that, but—"

"Are you being followed?" Harras asked.

"What? No."

"Are you seeing things rearranged in your apartment? Stuff missing?"

"Again, no," she said. "Do you think it's Los Enfermos?"

Harras rubbed at his temples.

"Believe me, if Los Enfermos, or what's left of them, wanted us dead, we would be," he said. "This is different. Someone wants me gone, but they're not in a hurry, and they need to figure something out first."

"Okay, well, let's avoid the obvious pothole in your story—the fact that you're getting more paranoid as your gray hairs turn white or commit suicide," Kathy said. "Who would want you dead? And what do I have to do with it?"

"I'm not sure," Harras said. "I've worked lots of cases. Lots of people don't want me around. But most are dead or in prison."

"Fine, but what can Pete do that you can't? Did you forget you're in the FBI and Pete is a loser?"

Harras let out a humorless, machine-gun laugh. "It's complicated."

"Jesus, can you fast-forward past the Choose-Your-Own-Adventure portion of the meal and get to the point?" she asked. "What does this have to do with Pete? Or me? And what can I do?"

"Can we talk straight for a second?"

"I don't know what you mean," Kathy said, looking down at her hands, her fingers digging into her palms, the pain sharp.

She knew what he meant.

"Look, I'm sorry I wasn't there for you more," Harras said, his voice lower, the words coming out drip by drip, like a recording asking you to push 1 if you wanted to hear it in Spanish. "I can't imagine what it was like. I just didn't think you needed me around. Pete was there. I came to visit, and once you were up and out, I figured you wanted your space, I—"

"It was your fucking baby!" Kathy said, her voice cutting through the din of Miami traffic, the chatter buzzing over the tables around them and the sounds of Dean Martin warbling that everybody loves somebody sometimes. A few chairs squealed as customers turned to see what was going on.

Harras responded, but Kathy was already on her feet and yanking her bag off the third chair at their small table.

"You must have known," Kathy said. She felt her face going red, her hands gripping her bag so tightly that they hurt. She was shaking, her body pulsing with a rage she didn't know was there, as if it'd been waiting for this perfect moment to spring out and fight. Her voice had dropped now. "You could have asked, you asshole. I was dying in the hospital. I lost my baby. Our baby. Did you think I was fucking everyone in town? You knew as well as I did what we were doing and what it meant, then you let it go, okay? So fuck you and go to hell, Harras."

She darted out of the restaurant to her car, ignoring Harras' hurried words of apology as he stood up, her mind darkening to pitch black, the outrage tasting coppery and sweet in her mouth as a voice wailed in her skull. A voice that pleaded and hoped what this man said was true—that he was as good as dead.

CHAPTER SEVEN

September 15, 2017
Spring Valley, New York

"**L**ookit this fucking cocksucker."

Tony Persico nodded from the front passenger seat as Vincent Salerno motioned toward the strip mall storefront they'd been asked to stake out. It was close to eight in the morning, and their target, some newbie PI named Fernandez, was opening his office. The guy was carrying a venti cup of Starbucks coffee and a beat-up briefcase to accompany his battered black jacket and jeans.

"Prick doesn't know how to read a fucking calendar," Tony said, not looking up from his phone. "It's fucking September and this guy's dressed like he's takin' a summer stroll, you know?"

Vincent—Vinnie to his friends, Fat Vinnie to people he would eventually kill—smiled. Tony was always good for a laugh. The older gangster, a capo in the DeCalvacante family, had offered to keep Vincent company on the job. Now that he was close to seventy, Tony's days doing their thing were winding down and he was happy to relive some of the drudgery of his early jobs. Vincent was just glad to have someone around to shoot the shit with. He knew if he played his cards right, he'd be taking Tony's captain spot, assuming their boss was playing fair. That was a big assumption.

"I don't even get what we're doing here," Vincent said, his hands gripping the wheel. They were parked across the lot, the car facing the front door of Fernandez Investigations. The order had come through late last night and there'd been little explanation. Vincent was used to things being vague. That was their thing. But Vincent wasn't some *stronzino* just coming up in a crew. He'd been a made guy in the family for close to a decade, had a wife and three kids to support. When the boss called him in the middle of the night to do something, it involved cutting up a body, not parking in a Rockland mall watching a skinny shitbird sip his soy latte.

"You know as well as me," Tony said, wagging a finger at Vincent. "Boss says we come, we come."

"I hear you," Vincent said, a slight whine accompanying the big man's words. "It's just bullshit, and you know it."

"Boss said to watch this guy, we watch this guy," Tony said. "Then, when he gives the high sign, we stop watching and we hit."

Vincent took a long sip from his coffee and settled in.

Chadwick's light rap on Fernandez Investigations' glass front door notified Pete that his guests had arrived. He opened the door, stepping aside to let Chadwick in. He looked behind the older man but didn't notice anyone else with him.

"Where are your bosses?" Pete asked.

"They're coming. Car was a few blocks behind me," he said, scanning the small area that could barely be considered a waiting room. Chadwick frowned.

"Is this where you give me the terms?"

"Terms?" Chadwick asked.

"You know, the guidelines for the chat," Pete said. "I've been a reporter before. I know how these political types operate. Nothing is freewheeling. Especially when you're thinking about running for governor."

Chadwick rubbed his face. The man looked spent. Pete struggled to feel some kind of sympathy for him. "I got nothing," he said. "They have something they need your help with. That's all I'm paid to know."

"But it's not all you know, right?"

Chadwick shook his head. "You seem like a patient guy. Give it a few minutes and find out what they want."

It took less than that. Pete heard the door swing open before he turned around. Ellen McRyan and a tall, silver-haired man with dull blue eyes and a dark gray tailored suit stepped inside. The man's expression was blank as he nodded in Pete's direction.

"Thank you for seeing us, Mr. Fernandez," Mrs. McRyan said, a forced smile on her face.

Pete motioned toward his office.

"Don't mention it," he said. "Let's talk inside."

Pete's office was what some would describe as light on personality. A small desk was set up at the far end, with a forgettable black chair behind it and two metal folding chairs in front. The walls were bare aside from a Johnny Cash Hatch Show print behind Pete's chair and a poster of the Coen Brothers' *Blood Simple* to the left of it. Under the posters was a simple record player, with a stack of albums next to it—Lou Reed's *Transformer* atop the pile.

The McRyans took their seats with stiff, unnatural motions. Mr. McRyan looked the place over, his mouth settling into a curt, polite smile. Pete took his seat across from them.

"Okay, so let's get down to it."

"Mr. Fernandez," Trevor McRyan said, his face smoothing over, eyes brightening and smile sharpening. Politics in action. "I realize you and my wife got off on the wrong foot. I'm sorry about that. We have a sensitive issue to discuss. Not only for me, as a public figure, but personally, for us as a couple."

Mr. McRyan motioned to his wife. She held her large purse on her lap and took the move as a sign to reach into the bag and pull out a manila folder.

"My husband, as you guessed, is in the final stages of determining the, um, viability of a candidacy for the governorship of your home state," she said, sliding the folder over the desk to Pete. She held her hand up for a few seconds, as if to ward Pete off from opening the folder just yet. "He has been extremely successful on the local level, representing his district in the state senate. He has been a vocal advocate for the causes he believes in over those years. Now, we're thinking about what the next political chapter will be for us, and in what way we can best serve the people of Florida."

Pete's gave them his best shit-eating grin. "How amazing for you."

Mr. McRyan cleared his throat.

"I'll get down to it," he said. "Part of being a statewide candidate is being prepared to have every bit of your life—the good, the bad, the invented and salacious—out there for public consumption. Everything from my junior high school report card to my tax filings last year are fair game—"

"Maybe not your taxes," Pete said.

The McRyans blinked at Pete's joke. He motioned for Mr. McRyan to continue.

"As much as I've tried to live a humble, good life, no one is free of problems, or tragedies," he said, pausing for effect. "And we need some help—discreet, experienced help—to manage this situation."

Pete leaned forward. "I'm going to be honest, I don't have any other meetings today," he said. "But I'd really like to speed this along. Can I open this folder, or are we still setting things up?"

Mr. McRyan fidgeted, an annoyed huff escaping his mouth. Before he could form any words, his wife took charge.

"It's our son," she said, motioning with her chin for Pete to open the folder. "Stephen McRyan. He's gone. He's left us."

Pete put his palm over the folder, hesitating.

"Left?" Pete said. "Did he die?"

"Not that we know," Mr. McRyan said. "Jesus, I hope not. But he's gone. We haven't heard from him in about two months. Part of that time he could have just been ignoring us, but he usually needs something—money, a job, rehab."

Pete flipped open the folder, expecting to see an unfamiliar photo, perhaps atop a stack of personal papers—birth certificate, college transcript, driver's license—the things private detectives didn't really need. At least not this early. For a missing person's case, the first step was to run a basic skiptrace, and if that failed, retrace the target's steps, then zoom out and get a sense of their habits. For starters, he just needed a photo and a home address.

He didn't expect to get a roundhouse kick from his own past.

CHAPTER EIGHT

April 1, 2013
Miami, Florida

"I don't do that."

Pete Fernandez slid the dark beer a few inches away. Jackie and Pete were seated at the Kendall Ale House's crowded bar while they waited for a table to open up. Normally, Jackie hated this place—it was loud, generic and the food tasted like reheated T.G.I. Friday's. Britney Spears' "Toxic" blasted through the restaurant's speakers. But it was on Jackie's way home and Pete had suggested it, so here they were.

Pete was a friend of a friend of a friend. There was chemistry between them, Jackie would admit. They'd slept together a few times—if you could call drunkenly groping, getting naked and passing out before completion sex. She didn't recall much from those nights. But none of that mattered now. She needed his help, if he could help anyone.

"Do what? Talk with friends?" she said.

"I do that," Pete said, his eyes on the beer. He hadn't taken a sip, but had ordered it. "I don't do what you're asking. Investigate stuff."

"Dude, that is bullshit," Jackie said, looking around for any sign of their table being ready. It'd been twenty minutes. "You don't do the one thing you're good at anymore? Just when I need your help?"

"I quit," Pete said. He leaned over and pulled the glass to his mouth and took a long, thirsty gulp. He set it back down and slid it even farther away.

Jackie shoved him—a quick, playful push.

"Pete Fernandez, the man who discovered the secret identity of whatever the dude's name was, that mob killer," Jackie said. "You're retired? What do you do now? Sell insurance? You sure as hell don't work for the newspaper anymore."

Pete was a big deal. Or had been. A few months back, he'd blown the lid off the "Silent Death," a mob killer so notorious most people considered him an urban legend. In the process, he'd been fired as a newspaper editor and had found a missing woman. His life was complicated. Jackie had met Pete after it all went down.

"What else can I help you with?" Pete said. His stare was blank and glassy. *Still drunk*, Jackie thought. She pulled back, as if to put Pete into better focus.

"You mean what else can you help me with that doesn't involve finding Patty?" Jackie said. "That's the thing you won't do, Pete? Jesus, man. You'd think after all the bullshit you put me through you'd do me a solid."

"Right," Pete said. "Anything but that."

Jackie hopped off the barstool. She was of average height, solid build—she liked going to the gym—and was easy on the eyes. She'd had a boyfriend—an older guy—who used to say that to her all the time. He was an idiot. She tied her dark hair into a quick ponytail while moving toward Pete, who straightened up.

"Thanks for nothing, bro," she said. "I'll see you down the line, maybe."

"Oh, come on, Jackie. Don't be mad," he said, but Jackie was already heading toward the door.

I'*m an idiot*, Jackie thought as she slammed the driver side door of her Mercedes shut and backed out of the Ale House parking lot. Why did she think Pete Fernandez of all people would be of help? He was a mess. Reeked of alcohol even before they got their first round and seemed to be in a daze. Much worse than the last time she'd seen him. Slept with him.

Whatever. She was desperate. The emergence of Kenny Sampson had raised her hopes and she wouldn't let his sudden disappearance deter her now. She'd gotten too close to finding out what happened to Patty to let it drop. She knew what the cops wanted her to understand. She wasn't dumb. Patty was dead. She wasn't as dense as her half-brother Roger, who still acted like his daughter was just off on a long school trip. Patty was dead. But Jackie wanted to know why. Why did someone think it was their right to snuff out someone so bright? A girl who had nothing but good things in front of her. Who had a path out of the swarthy abyss that was Miami. Jackie couldn't let that be. She wouldn't.

Pete Fernandez. What a waste.

She took the long way home—she needed some time to clear her head. She felt stupid. Had she just wanted to see Pete? Nah. Maybe. Who knows. She felt bad for him—she wasn't sure why.

She tried to focus on Patty. Though she was only a few years older than her niece, a byproduct of having a much older half-brother, Jackie had felt a strong maternal energy toward the girl. She remembered long drives filled with conversation about life, work, goals and their dysfunctional family. Patty had looked up to Jackie, emulated her cool, gruff aunt and even hinted that she also wanted to pursue law if the journalism thing didn't work out. Jackie relished being Patty's aunt and confidante.

But today, most of Miami had moved on from Patty Morales. Celebrity and political scandals, street violence, other murders—there was always something new to distract from the case of that missing girl. Every few years, some reporter would "revisit" the crime with a feature-length story, and every few years the piece would become shorter and buried deeper in the already dwindling pages of the *Miami Times*. But Jackie hadn't moved on. Finding out what had happened to Patty kept her going, pushing harder. It got her through all-night law school study sessions and prepping for the bar exam. If no one else would help, Jackie would find her on her own. She would do it alone, without Pete Fernandez.

She realized that she knew why she'd met up with Pete. It was to avoid the next call she had to make. She pulled into her parking space outside her Kendall townhouse and dialed.

"Hey," she said when he picked up.

"This is a surprise," Mario said.

"Can you talk?" Code for "Do you have anyone at your place now?"

"Yeah, I'm good," Mario said. Her ex sounded smug. Maybe she was projecting.

"I need a favor," she said. "With Patty. Well, Patty's case."

Mario cleared his throat. Maybe he was expecting something else. She hoped not.

"Okay," he said. "Look, Jax, you know I can't get you any more files or shit like that. They'd have my ass."

"I know," she said. "I—I just don't know what to do. I was hoping I'd get some private help but that fizzled and—"

"From that Fernandez clown?" His voice had gone from familiar to professional. Jackie was glad for that.

"I just need an advocate, Mario," Jackie said. "Someone to speak for Patty. I know what happened with Sampson. He was a good lead."

"Well, he's gone, Jax," Mario said. "Nothing I can do about that. They won't reopen Patty's case without new evidence. As far as they see, from what I can tell, she's dead and not coming back."

"That guy knew something," Jackie said. "You said so."

"Maybe, maybe not," Mario said. She winced at how callous her cop ex could be.

"You know he did," she said. "Roger's checked out. Her mom is a mess. Patty deserved better than this. I'm the only person who seems to give a shit."

"You know I can't do anything, okay? We've gone over this," Mario said. He sounded spent. He didn't want to be on the phone with his ex-wife. "My advice to you would be to get on Roger and have him turn up the heat on the PD. Then, maybe, we can do something. Have you talked to him?"

"I've left him a few voicemails, but he might be traveling for his church again," Jackie said. She tried to remember the last time she'd seen her half-brother, but drew a blank.

"Lemme know what he says when he picks up his phone," Mario said, and hung up.

Jackie cursed and grabbed her bag. She stepped out of the car and headed for her front door, which was around the corner from her parking space. The tree-lined walkway was poorly lit and smelled of wet grass and duck shit. The perils of living in Kendall.

She didn't realize someone was waiting in her doorway until it was too late.

CHAPTER NINE

September 15, 2017
Spring Valley, New York

"**P**ete? Are you alright?"

Pete blinked a few times before looking up at the McRyans sitting across from him, confused—not concerned—expressions on their faces.

"I'm fine," he said.

He wasn't fine. The photo that rested atop the McRyans' documents seemed to stare back at him from another, more sinister time, a cursed, noxious relic. The picture took Pete back to another life—when his nights were fueled by drink, a blur of mistakes and near misses on the road to annihilation. His days hadn't been much better—throbbing, fuzzy and packed with shame and resentment. A garden-variety drunk's life.

Pete swallowed. His mouth felt dry and chalky.

"That's our son," Mr. McRyan said, hesitating for a second. "Stephen McRyan. Stephen Augustus McRyan."

Kenny Sampson.

That was the name Pete matched with the image of the man staring up at him. It was a family photo—two parents flanking their only son, forced smiles on their faces, a distant expression on his. The photo was from the shoulders up, but Pete could tell they were outside, perhaps in the parking lot of some high-end restaurant after a pricey meal. The McRyans looked younger, and their son looked identical to the man Pete had met under a different name. That gave him a ballpark time frame for the photo. Five years ago, give or take a year.

"What's the rest of the stack?" Pete said, sliding the photo to the side.

"Don't you want to hear what we want?" Mrs. McRyan said, incredulity simmering under her refined tone.

"You want me to find him, right?"

"Well, yes," Mr. McRyan said. "We do, but this is a complex issue, and we'd like to walk you through it."

Pete sighed.

"It's not that complex, Mr. McRyan, with all due respect, Let me guess," he said. "Your son has a rapsheet. You've tried to keep him at bay with money and rehab stints, and that's been fine. You've lived your life as under the radar as a rising-star politico can live. But just around the time you decide to throw your hat into the ring for governor, lil' Stevie goes off the grid, and you're left wondering when he will pop his head out of the water and say shit that'll ruin your chances. How am I doing so far?"

Mr. McRyan cleared his throat again before responding. "You're in the ballpark, but I don't appreciate your tone," he said.

"Is everything I need in the file?" Pete said.

"What do you mean?" asked Mrs. McRyan.

"I mean, can I just sit and read this file and know what needs to be done, or are there things you want to tell me?"

"You'll find we are very thorough," Mrs. McRyan said, her voice taking on a hiss-like quality.

"Okay, then I have some questions for you," Pete said.

He waited a moment before continuing.

"First—why did you choose me for this?"

"We needed someone who could be discreet," Mr. McRyan said. "And you came highly recommended."

"By whom?"

"They asked to keep their name out of this," Mrs. McRyan said.

"Tell me or I'm out," Pete said.

Mr. McRyan let out a harried laugh and leaned back in the chair, which Pete knew was about as comfortable as a piece of granite.

"Christ, do you even like making money?" he said, exasperated. Pete could tell the back-and-forth was getting to him, but he didn't really care.

Pete looked at him and waited.

"It was an attorney, Jackie Cruz," Mrs. McRyan said finally. "She's helping us … in Miami. If things go as we hope, she'll be our political director on the ground there. She said you were not only discreet, which I imagine is a prerequisite for any private detective, but also that you were used to—well, how did she put it?—'Sticking your hands into shit elbow-deep, if that's what it takes.' She doesn't speak highly of many people, as I'm sure you know."

Pete nodded. He'd last seen Jackie over a year ago, when he was working his final case in Miami. She was a high-powered attorney with a no-nonsense attitude and was a shark in the courtroom. But she had lost one of her earliest cases—defending Miami cop Gaspar Varela against charges he viciously murdered his wife—and it had haunted her for most of her career. When Pete and Kathy reinvestigated the crime, at the behest of Varela's daughter, who was hoping to find a sliver of evidence to exonerate her dad, Jackie proved vital to uncovering the truth. Jackie was one of the friends Pete had neglected to stay in touch with over the last few months. But the past has a way of creeping up behind you and whispering in your ear when you least expect it.

"That sounds like Jackie," Pete said, noncommittal. "Next question: where was your son last seen? When did you last hear from him?"

Ellen McRyan scrunched up her nose, as if she'd inhaled a fleeting, disgusting odor.

"Stephen was in Miami until a few months ago," she said. "He was staying in one of our apartments downtown. He was going through some financial trouble so we let him sublease the place."

"Is that address and info in here?"

"Yes," she said. "Stephen is a decent person. He has his troubles. His demons. But we want to help him. We need to find him so we don't have to deal with all this in, well, in a court of public opinion. You understand that."

"What kind of trouble could he cause for you?" Pete said, turning to look at Mr. McRyan. "What secrets does he have?"

Mr. McRyan shook his head, as if trying to ward off Pete's inquiry.

"Nothing factual, nothing real," he said, pausing, as if looking for his next words in the air around him. "He's had a hard life. He's out of his mind sometimes. Look, the kid is a wild card. We want him home, where we can help him and I can focus on this election, if that's what we want to do. But first and foremost, we want to know where he is."

Pete believed Mr. McRyan, mostly. The politician probably *did* want his son home, or in a secure rehab somewhere far away where the press couldn't reach him.

Kenny Sampson.

The name echoed in Pete's mind. Why had Stephen McRyan been in Miami under an assumed name? Could Pete be wrong? He knew he wasn't. If he'd learned one thing over the last few years, it was to trust his gut. Sampson and McRyan were the same person. The question was why. He knew who to talk to about that.

He pushed back from his desk and stood up.

"Five hundred a day plus expenses and I'll need a three-thousand-dollar deposit," Pete said. "If that works for you, I'll hop on the next plane down to Miami."

Fucking Miami.

The McRyans stood up. Trevor extended his hand. Pete took it.

"Pete, this means a lot to us," he said. "We appreciate your help. Obviously, if we could keep all this—"

"All confidential, yep," Pete said, ushering them out of his office, his hand placed on Mrs. McRyan's shoulder. "If you could messenger the retainer and any other info that might not be in the file, I'll get on it next. I'll call if I have questions."

"Thank you," she said, a sad smile on her face. "Our information is in the folder. Please keep us posted as things progress, in a timely fashion."

"Of course."

"Oh, and since you'll be around," Mr. McRyan said, pulling a folded piece of paper from his suit pocket, "come by Vizcaya this weekend. I'll be giving a, well, important speech."

Mr. McRyan gave Pete his shiniest political smile as Pete took the flyer. The orange piece of paper was light on detail—promoting a "Special Event Focusing on Florida's Future!" with special guest Trevor McRyan. Pete was all but certain the festivities would serve as his campaign kickoff event. It was the season for it, Pete knew.

"I'll be there," Pete said.

They turned and left. Pete closed the door to his inner office and took his seat.

He took a long look at the photo of Kenny/Stephen. He hadn't thought of the man in about four years. Even then, he'd been a marginal player in a bigger case.

Four years ago, Pete was a few inches away from what he'd eventually call his bottom—the lowest point of his drinking life. The desperate moment when he realized he couldn't beat back his demons alone. Soon after that, he'd walked into an Alcoholics Anonymous meeting and accepted complete defeat for the first time. In AA parlance, he'd admitted that his life had become unmanageable.

Pete had been floundering in the aftermath of taking down the Silent Death mob killer. No job. No prospects. He was living in his dead father's house and drinking himself to death. A beer with breakfast. Airline-size bottles of whiskey or vodka tucked in different hidey-holes around the house—just in case. Long nights wandering the city, stumbling into bars and creating trouble with the few friends he had left.

Four years ago, Pete's life was barely one, and he was the last person qualified to investigate one of Miami's most talked-about cold cases.

But that's what Jackie Cruz was now asking him to do. Again.

He pulled his cell phone out and dialed the number. She picked up on the third ring.

"Figured you'd crawl from the wreckage at some point," Jackie said. "I'd say it's nice to hear from you, but it's not. I'm pissed at you. But I'll let you work toward fixing that. What's up?"

"Looks like I'm coming down to your neck of the woods."

"You mean *your* neck of the woods? You're from here, Pete," she said. "Also, what the fuck? The only way anyone hears from you is by sending work your way?"

"How'd you know?"

"About the McRyans? I figured it was a matter of time. You saw the photo?"

"Yeah, Kenny Sampson."

"Stephen McRyan," Jackie spat out the name.

"What do you need me for?" Pete asked. "You saw the picture. You can track this guy down."

Jackie sighed.

"At some point, maybe in a decade or two, you'll realize you're good at this shit," she said. "Until then, take my word for it. I need you to look for him. And I need to find out what he knows about Patty before you hand him over to mommy and daddy. You owe me that much."

The words sliced into him from a thousand miles away. Jackie knew how to connect with Pete in a way that Kathy and his other friends had given up on. He was stubborn, instinctual and loyal, but his biggest weakness was an overwhelming sense of guilt. He was trying to work on it. Even in the program, wholesale life changes came slow.

"I'm putting my life on the line going down there."

"Maybe if you picked up the phone when Harras or your *novia Americanita* called, you'd find out that Los Enfermos isn't exactly thriving down here," she said. "You're as likely to get clipped up there.

So don't pull that 'wah, wah, wah, I'm so brave' act, okay? Get your ass down here and solve this case. I need to close the book on this. I need to find out who killed my niece."

Before Pete could respond, she'd hung up. He was about to dial her back when he heard something.

Footsteps. Outside his office.

At first, he figured it was the McRyans. Maybe they'd forgotten something. But he also knew his front door locked when it closed to prevent any casual pop-ins. No, this was a surprise guest, and Pete didn't like surprises.

He pulled out his Glock from a desk drawer. The gun had been his father's, back when he was a Miami homicide detective, before dropping dead twenty years too soon. Pete took a few quiet steps toward his door and waited next to the doorway. The door swung open, blocking Pete. From behind the door, Pete saw two men step into the room. One was large—six feet, well over three hundred pounds of padded muscle. The other guy was shorter but reedy, and older. They were both dressed in black and armed. The bigger man scanned Pete's office while the thin man stood about a foot away from Pete's hiding spot.

"Where the fuck is he?" Fat Man asked.

"Fuck should I know, Vin?"

"Unreal, fucking unreal," Vin said, taking a few steps toward Pete's desk and the open manila folder. "I knew this was a waste of time. Did you see him leave? Shit."

Pete stepped around the door and placed the muzzle of his gun at the base of the thinner man's skull.

"Don't move," Pete said. "Drop the gun."

The older man complied.

By then, Vin had turned around, his own gun pointed toward Pete and the older man. He didn't seem concerned that Pete was armed, or that he was holding a gun to his partner's head.

"There you are," Vin said. "I knew we couldn'ta lost you like that. Now, step back, let Tony move away, and we can talk about this all civilized and shit."

"Yeah, let's talk, buddy," the man named Tony said, turning his head a bit to get a look at Pete.

Pete pushed the barrel of the gun harder against Tony's head.

"I said don't move, asshole."

"Aw, shit, come on," Tony said, grimacing.

Pete moved his chin toward Vincent.

"Drop the gun, then we talk," Pete said.

Vincent sighed and did as he was told.

"Take a few steps back and sit on the ground," Pete said.

Before he could react, Tony turned around and grabbed Pete's gun hand, pointing the weapon up and launching a fist into Pete's midsection. The blow sent Pete stumbling backward onto the floor, gun still in his hand.

He could hear Vincent bending his cumbersome body down to retrieve his own gun. Pete waited a second, giving Tony the impression he'd taken the hit hard, then swung the butt of the gun into Tony's face as the older gangster got within range. He heard the soft crunch of metal on bone and the man let out a surprised, pained squeal as he stepped away, hands covering his broken nose. Pete grabbed the gun with both hands and set it on Vincent, who was still crouching down, picking up his own weapon.

"Kick your gun to me and sit down," Pete said, out of breath. He could see the older man on the floor now, blood dripping from his face as he emitted a low, muffled moan.

"Now why you gotta go do that for?" Vincent said, motioning toward his fallen partner. "We just wanted to talk to ya."

"So sit over there, away from your gun, and let's talk, okay?"

Pete tapped the older man's midsection with his foot. "Get up and join your friend over there."

Tony let out another long moan and stood up, shooting a scowl at Pete as he stumbled over to sit by his friend. After a moment, both men were staring at Pete, like two truant school kids waiting to hear their punishment.

"Who sent you?" Pete asked.

"Got nothing to say to you," Tony said, though it sounded more like *gob nuffin da saydjeu.*

Pete stepped closer to the men, gun trained on the bigger one. He motioned for them to raise their hands and patted them down. He didn't find any weapons, but he grabbed their wallets and stepped back to his previous spot. He opened Vin's and looked at the name on the driver's license: *Vincent Salerno*. The other read *Tony Persico*. Pete didn't need to be a student of organized crime to know who they were.

"One of you'd better talk," Pete said. "Someone needs to explain what two mobsters from the DeCalvacante family are doing up here in Rockland County, in my office. If not, maybe I shoot both of you and we call it self-defense."

"You wish, kid," Tony said. "We ain't saying shit. So let us go, or we sit here until the cops come and we get bailed out in a few hours. Your call."

"Again, who sent you?" Pete asked.

"You seriously got no idea, do you?" Vincent said. Tony shot him a dirty look but the larger man persisted. "You think we came across your little PI operation here and thought we'd say hi? Think about it. And if you think this is it, that we come at you once and call it a draw 'cause you got lucky, well … I got nothing else to say."

Pete felt his hand tighten on the gun. He knew he'd get little else out of the two men. He knew mobsters stuck to their code of *omertà*, though the blood oath had been watered down in the age of RICO and witness protection. But their mere presence proved one thing—and it sent a chill through Pete: even in New York, he wasn't safe.

"Get the fuck out of my office."

CHAPTER TEN

September 17, 2017
Kew Gardens, New York

The Mowbray was a six-floor, pre-War apartment building in Kew Gardens, Queens, just a few steps from where Kitty Genovese had screamed for help and—if you believed the original legend—was ignored by thirty or so people before being stabbed to death. Since then, that bit of lore had been debunked, putting New York City's reputation as an emotionless and cutthroat metropolis on the line.

Pete watched the building from across the street, huddled under an after-school learning center's faded orange awning. It was close to two in the morning and he was debating whether to take the direct approach and knock on Stephen McRyan's door, or wait a few more hours until the guy walked outside. Sometimes the latter got you better info—you could tail the target and see what his routines were, or who he communicated with. This intrigued Pete, but he knew it was of little interest to McRyan's high-powered parents. They wanted their kid tucked away and put on ice for a while.

Stephen McRyan, a.k.a. Kenny Sampson, was living under the name Sammy Wolven, working odd jobs around the neighborhood and doing sporadic Uber runs in his banged-up Toyota Matrix, which Pete saw was now parked in front of the building. Pete knew this background thanks to a few favors he'd called in, the first to a New Jersey detective named Francisco Rivela, an old friend of Pete's from before his PI days. Together they'd spent many a night getting blotto in cheap New Brunswick and Newark bars during a time when Pete still considered himself a sportswriter. The older cop was on the verge of putting in his papers and moving down south.

"To what do I owe the honor?" Rivela had said.

"I need a favor."

"Sounds about right. Haven't talked to you since that business with GG Garcia and the Donne guy."

Pete had made a return visit to Jersey a few years back to do Rivela a solid and help investigate a missing person's case. It was time to cash in that chip.

"Yup," Pete said. "I'm in New York, settled for a bit."

"I'm only hearing from you now?"

Pete cleared his throat. How did you explain to an old friend the difficulty that came with seeing him? The old feelings and habits that bubbled up? He'd spent most of his time with Rivela at bars, knocking back drink after drink, musing about the world, discussing old movies like *The Night of the Hunter* and *Out of the Past*. It was a hallway Pete didn't walk down much these days, for a reason. The fond memories brought back a thirst that Pete couldn't survive.

"Yeah, I'm sorry," Pete said. "Been keeping a low profile. I'm up in Rockland, too. No one likes coming there."

"What do you need?"

He'd told him. Rivela cut the guilt trip he'd been laying on Pete short and said he'd get back to him in a few hours. As promised, the older detective called up with an address—and instructions.

"You're damn lucky," Rivela said. "So do me a favor when you nab this guy."

"Sure, spill."

"Got a buddy, old source of mine, opened an Indian restaurant a few blocks from where your guy's holed up," Rivela said. "Throw him a couple bones and tell him I said hello. Hey, maybe even grab a bite there. I'm not one for Indian food—too spicy—but I hear good things about the place."

"Good Yelp reviews?"

"Excuse me?"

Pete laughed.

"Yeah, I'll do that," he said "Thanks."

"My pal's basically the town gossip. Sees everything, knows everyone. You're in luck. He says your mark keeps to himself, mostly," Rivela said. "Eccentric. Unless he's working, he only seems to come out for groceries or to catch a movie at the theater down the block. On off days, he says the guy talks to himself and just seems way weird. Something ain't right, is what he told me."

"Got it," Pete said. "I'll take him down easy."

"Nothing you do is easy, if I remember right."

"That hasn't changed."

"Now we're even, I guess," Rivela said, a twinge of regret in his creaking voice.

"I'll let you know how it goes," Pete said. "We can grab a bite when I'm back in town."

Rivela coughed into the phone, a wet, lingering noise. It didn't sound good.

"Yeah, let's do that," Rivela said. "Got lots to catch up on."

After Pete clicked off with the detective he was swallowed by a wave of anxiety, like a dark shadow falling over him on a bright spring day. He knew the cop was older, and cops didn't age gracefully. He'd have to make a visit to his friend once he returned.

Pete checked the time on his phone and waited. His thoughts veered back to earlier that day, and the DeCalvacante gangsters. Why would two New York made guys want to take him out? It was unlikely that they were under contract from Los Enfermos? Drugs and the mafia didn't mix, at least not officially. Pete knew of a lot of made guys who ran horse or oxy on the side, or put a little money into the cartels, but it was never sanctioned, so picking up a murder contract from a Miami drug gang seemed out of the question. Still, Pete had pissed off many people over the years. It could be anyone, he thought.

McRyan lived on the third floor, overlooking Austin Street and the Long Island Rail Road station. Pete noticed his kitchen light flicker on behind the curtains and he knew it was time to move. He walked into the building's foyer and pushed a few of the apartment call buttons. Eventually, an annoyed voice blared through the lobby intercom.

"Hello?"

"UPS," Pete said.

"It's the middle of the night, what the fuck?" the woman said, her static-loaded voice heavy with sleep.

"Urgent delivery, ma'am."

The door buzzed and Pete walked in, making a beeline for the elevator. He got off on the third floor and turned right. He felt for his Glock, nestled in a holster under his left arm. He hadn't seen Stephen McRyan or Kenny Sampson or whatever his name was in years. But what little he remembered was bad. Pete wanted to be ready.

He rapped on the door of 3H and waited. He heard rustling on the other side. Pete had hoped that by showing up so late he would catch McRyan off guard, and that surprise would allow Pete to not only talk to him, but convince him to return to Miami. At the very least, Pete could confirm where Stephen McRyan was holed up.

"Who is it?"

Pete took a step back. The voice coming through the door was drowsy, which wasn't surprising. What was surprising was that it belonged to a woman. Pete hadn't banked on McRyan shacking up with someone.

"I'm looking for Stephen McRyan," Pete said, trying to put on his best "official business" voice.

"Who?"

"He may be going under the name Sammy Wolven," Pete said.

The door opened a crack, still hooked onto the latch lock. Through the slit of space, Pete could see a dark-haired woman, with tan skin and curious eyes. She was a little younger than Pete, younger than McRyan, and beautiful. Her long black hair cloaked her smooth features and softened her questioning eyes.

"Sammy isn't here," she said. "Plus, who's asking?"

"My name's Pete Fernandez. I'm a private investigator. I need to speak with your boyfriend. What's your name?"

"Nancy. And Sammy isn't my boyfriend, okay?" she said. Pete had expected it to get a rise out of her.

"What is he?"

"We're friends," she said. "He lets me crash here when … when I need to."

"Any idea where he is now?"

"Gone," she said. "Long gone."

The apartment, a small one-bedroom, was light on furniture—a ratty couch and a small, rickety TV dinner table dominated the living room—and smelled of mildew and skunky weed.

Nancy hovered by the door, her body language suggesting she didn't want this to be a long visit. Pete wheeled around to face her.

"How well do you know Sammy?"

"Not too well," she said. "We hang out sometimes. Like I said, if I need a place to crash, he lets me stay here."

"Even when he's gone?"

"Even then," she said, her expression flat.

"Do you see clients here?"

"Fuck you."

Pete didn't press. He'd taken a risk and it had offended or misfired. Maybe both. He tried a softer approach.

"Sammy might be in trouble," Pete said. "That's why I'm looking for him."

"Did his daddy send you?" she said, a knowing lilt in her delivery.

"Yes," Pete said. He saw no point in masking the truth. Stephen McRyan had spilled to this woman, so any obfuscating on Pete's part would get him nowhere. "When was the last time you saw him?"

She twirled a strand of her hair with her left hand and took a few steps into the living room, bringing her closer Pete. She was dressed for bed—a loose-fitting tank and shorts. Here, in the light of the room, Pete could really see her. She was young, not much older than Jenny Ferris, with a similar blunt, street-smart air to her. Pete knew he would not be able to trick her into revealing where McRyan had gone. The direct approach might work better.

"How much?"

"Excuse me?"

"How much to find out where your pal Sammy went," Pete said, reaching for his wallet. "It's his dad's money, so don't let your sympathy for me stop you from upping the ante."

She considered him with a sly smile.

"Bingo," she said, motioning for the couch. "Let's talk."

For five hundred dollars—all that Pete had on him—she let him know the basics. Sammy Wolven, a.k.a. Kenny Sampson, a.k.a. Stephen McRyan had run back home to Miami, hoping to use some of his contacts to hide out from his parents. She also confirmed something else Pete had suspected—Stephen was trying to shop his story to the press, ideally whoever had the biggest bank account, so he could disappear on his own terms. He was desperate, more desperate than she'd ever seen him, Nancy said, and he'd hinted that some people were after him because he'd made them angry. The details of the story Stephen hoped to sell in order to go off the grid and where he was hiding out in Miami were not within Pete's budget. Nancy didn't take credit cards.

P ete pulled out his cell phone and pushed the saved contact number. His friend picked up on the fourth ring.

"You okay?"

"Yeah, sorry, I know it's late," Pete said.

"It's fine," Albert said, clearing his throat, as if to expel the sleep from his body. "Just surprised. You rarely call me during normal hours, much less in the middle of the night."

"I have to go back."

"Back?"

"To Miami," Pete said. "This case I'm working on—the McRyan thing. It's taking me back there."

"Are you sure it's the case—or something more?"

"What do you mean?"

"Pete, the last time I saw you, you were adamant you couldn't go back—that people down there wanted you dead," Albert said, now shifting into a professorial, methodical tone. "But now you're calling me and saying you *have* to go back. You told me about the McRyans before. So, I have to ask: what's changed?"

"Two things," Pete said as he reached his car and got behind the wheel. "One, I don't think I'm safe here. Two, there's more to this case than just a rising-star politician trying to track down his bad-boy son."

"Get rid of the ego," Albert said, "and ask yourself, 'Why do I need to get involved?' Why do you, Pete Fernandez, have to chase this down?"

Pete started the car and made a three-point turn on Austin Street, heading toward Union Turnpike and the Van Wyck.

"Someone wants me dead, and they found me upstate, which means they can find me anywhere."

"So what does that mean?"

"It's personal now."

CHAPTER ELEVEN

September 18, 2017
Miami, Florida

"You look like shit."

Pete grabbed his bag off the Miami International Airport conveyor belt and turned around. Jackie Cruz, dressed in a smart black business suit and wearing a pair of large, imposing sunglasses, smiled at Pete.

"You look great, as usual," Pete said. He leaned in for the standard Miami cheek-peck and hug greeting. She held it for a few moments longer than Pete expected.

"Figured you could use a ride," she said, motioning toward the parking lot with her chin. "Plus, MIA—improvements aside—still feels like a maze, so I didn't want you getting lost."

"I haven't been gone that long," Pete said, rolling his bag behind him as they walked through the sliding doors that lead to outside.

"I'm still surprised you came back," she said, giving him a once-over.

"So am I," Pete said.

They crossed the street in silence and reached the parking lot elevator. Jackie did look good—fit, tan and well put together. It reminded Pete that once, a lifetime ago, they'd almost had something. He'd been too far gone to appreciate it then, and now most of what he got from her, like what she showed the rest of the world, was a rock-solid exterior. She didn't let a lot of people in. A lifetime of hurt and betrayal will do that to you.

"What?"

"Just reminiscing," Pete said. "In my head."

"You sure you're still sober?" she asked, winking before summoning the elevator.

Pete responded with a quick chuckle before shifting to business.

"McRyan's kid is here, somewhere," Pete said. "That's all I could get from his friend."

"Nancy Artino?" Jackie said. "I looked her up. A few minor charges—soliciting, shoplifting. Nothing too terrible. Guess he was putting her up for a while. You bought her a few more weeks living in his pad."

They got to the car and Pete tossed his luggage in the backseat of Jackie's Audi. She turned on the engine and Shakira blared from the stereo before she jerked forward and shut it off with a laugh.

"So, let's get this out of the way, alright?" Jackie said, her hands wrapping around the steering wheel. "Kathy's living in Wynwood. She works at a newsletter thing called *The New Tropic*. Don't ask me what it is. I'm too old to get it. I think it has something to do with networking or Art Basel. Anyway, we've had lunch once or twice. She's good. She seems good. Harras—zilch. Haven't heard from him. The word is he's consulting for his old bosses, but that could be bullshit. Dave is, well, doing whatever Dave does. Good?"

"I guess that'll have to do."

"Excellent."

"What now, Ms. Cruz?" Pete said. "Do we strategize?"

"No," she said, backing out of the space, tires squealing. "First we eat and I get a few drinks in me. Then we plan. You should take a shower and clean up some, too, Mr. *Grajo*."

"**T**revor McRyan says you're working for him."

"I'm consulting," Jackie said as she handed Pete a can of Diet Coke. "I don't do it much, it doesn't net me a lot, usually, but this guy is the goods. If he offered me a permanent gig on the campaign, I might take it. We've had some prelim discussions."

"Yeah?"

Jackie plopped down next to him on the couch, a long hunter green chunk of leather facing the bay windows of her townhouse. She had changed out of her business get-up, downshifting to pajama bottoms and a plain black T-shirt. They'd opted for takeout, and it had been the right call, Pete thought. He was tired. After staying up all night and then hopping on a plane, he needed sleep. Tomorrow, refreshed, he could dive into the case.

"Yeah, he's no joke," Jackie said, almost surprised at her own lack of cynicism. "He's not a bleeding-heart liberal, but his policies are progressive. He talks like a working guy. McRyan came from a poor family and married up. He connects with people in a way I haven't seen in a long time. And it's not just charm, because any politician can wing that. No, he feels genuine. The whole 'I'd get a beer with him' thing is true, except this guy isn't a moron. It helps that he's handsome as hell and can talk theory and economics like a professor. Except he doesn't sound like one—he sounds like the guy who owns the grocery store down the street. Folksy but not too folksy, smart but not too smart, handsome and seems honest. It might all be bullshit, but I like him. I haven't believed in a politician in a long time. I hope he doesn't destroy my last glimmer of optimism."

"Same here, for all our sakes," Pete said. "But what does he need you for? I know what he hired me to do."

"He wants—no, needs—someone to introduce him to the major Miami players to help him fundraise and find the right people to be seen with, like the mayor, county commissioners, newspaper editors, celebs, you get the drill," Jackie said. "He's a nobody state senator with lots of support north of Broward, but zero name recognition here. If he wants to win against a Republican candidate—and probably one with a Latino last name—he needs to get in ASAP and work South Florida hard. Hence, the early announcement."

"And why he's paranoid about his son."

"Right," she said, cracking her knuckles. "The son could be bad for him, very bad. No one knows what Stephen McRyan knows, or will share, but people are sniffing him out. The last thing McRyan Senior needs is his kid's mug plastered in the *Miami Times* talking about who knows what, or defending his own rap sheet."

"But won't that come out anyway?"

"Sure," she said, stifling a yawn. "But it's less sexy if the only comment is micromanaged PR from the McRyan campaign, especially if it comes out this early. Once lil' Stevie is in the fold, they can leak the story to a friendly outlet and, if they're lucky, turn their family tragedy into a positive that paints him as a real guy—not some political drone."

Pete stretched.

"I need to figure out my hotel situation," he said, standing up. "It's getting late."

"Oh, shut the fuck up," she said. "You're staying here. I have a guest room. It's all yours. I know you have that McRyan money, but we're working on this together, basically."

"You sure?"

"Just don't take it the wrong way," she said. "I don't want to wake up and find you mewling outside my door, okay?"

Pete laughed, returning to his seat.

"I think you can do much better than a bruised and battered PI," he said. "So no worries on that front."

She reached over and rubbed his shoulder, her hand lingering a second or two, fingertips digging into muscle.

"Don't sell yourself short," she said. "I didn't say what I'd do if I found you outside my bedroom door."

Pete woke up with a jolt, one leg dangling over the edge of the queen-size bed in Jackie's guestroom. The mental cobwebs were beginning to dissipate, the dream disappearing, like a hand wiping a fogged-up window. But he could still hear Jackie's heavy, sleepy breathing in his head as he stood up and walked to the bathroom, his bare feet slapping on the cold, off-white tile. He closed the door and turned the light on. He checked himself in the mirror. The stubble was new, the dark crescents under his eyes weren't.

The dream had seemed almost real. Familiar. The day's mild flirtation with Jackie had spiraled into his subconscious and set up shop. *Still better than the times we got together in real life*, Pete thought to himself with a chuckle. Those long-ago moments with Jackie were blurry at best amid blacked-out chunks of time.

"Don't plan the wedding yet, okay?" she'd whispered in his vision, her tongue flicking his earlobe as she dragged him into bed, her mouth hot on his neck as he fell on top of her.

Too real.

He heard footsteps behind him and started the tap, washing his hands and splashing water on his face. He wouldn't be sleeping much tonight.

When he stepped out of the bathroom, she was there, her body covered by a thin blue robe, a knowing smile on her face.

"Poor Pete," she said. "Too much activity for one night?"

"Can't sleep."

"Oh?" she said, mock concern on her face. "Bad dream?"

The next morning, Pete awoke around nine to the smell of Cuban coffee and *huevos fritos*. He'd never known Jackie to cook, and that was reaffirmed as he walked into her immaculate and expansive kitchen. An empty takeout bag rested on the counter by the sink as she slid eggs, sausage and pieces of *pan Cubano* onto their respective plates. She brought the plates to a small breakfast nook that looked out on a man-made lake. She smiled as he walked in.

"*Cafecito?*" she asked.

"Yes, please," he said, taking his seat and unfolding the cloth napkin she'd placed next to the plate of food. It smelled amazing.

"Islas Canarias," Jackie said as she poured a shot of Cuban coffee from a Styrofoam cup into a small *tacita*. "There's one on 137th Ave. Figured you wouldn't mind waking up to some familiar food. I doubt you can get this in New York."

Pete had already started shoveling food into his mouth. He was hungrier than he had thought, and the flavors were delicious and comforting. He'd been gone too long.

"That's for sure."

Jackie took the seat across from Pete and sipped at her coffee. The food on the plate in front of her sat untouched. She was dressed in a sports bra, a loose-fitting gray top and yoga pants. Looking at her sent his mind back to the dream, which was not a bad thing, but also not something he wanted to worry about much at the moment, either.

"Are you okay?" she said, her eyes meeting his. "You have that weird puppy dog look I was hoping you'd outgrown."

"I'm fine," Pete said. "Just tired."

He swallowed a bite of food and took a slow sip of coffee. It was strong and he could feel it coursing through his veins, activating parts of his brain that had lain dormant.

"Good, because we have a lot of ground to cover," she said. "First off, I hope you realize your job is more complicated than the McRyans think."

"Oh?"

"Stephen McRyan," Jackie said. "You have that covered. You'll do your job there. But we need to talk about how he fits in with something else."

"Kenny Sampson," Pete said, biting into a greasy piece of bacon. "And your niece."

"Right," she said. She got up and walked into the living room. When she returned, she had a thick file folder under her arm. Jackie dropped back into her seat and opened it. She slid a finger over the top page, scanning for something.

"Kenny Sampson, who we now know is Stephen McRyan, popped up in 2013 claiming to know the truth about Patty—how she was killed, who did it, the works," Jackie said. Her tone was lawyerly and robotic, but Pete could feel an undercurrent of anger. "But he disappeared before he could be questioned by the police, before Patty's remains were—before, um, you found her."

"Do we have any sense of what Stephen claimed to know?" Pete asked.

"That's the problem," Jackie said. "I have the police file on Patty. This is part of it—the stuff from when they reopened it in 2013. And there's nothing on Stephen. It doesn't even look like any names in the file were redacted. And this is the real deal. My sources are good—hell, one of them was my ex-husband, another was that grumpy detective Brownstein that you got to know. But yeah, nothing. So, that tells me someone went to a lot of effort to clear all traces of Stephen from the case, and that someone has great connections and is fantastic at covering their tracks."

"His dad?" Pete said before polishing off his coffee shot.

"No way he has that kind of pull here, as much as he'd like to," she said, shaking her head. "No, this is bigger. And remember, back then, the elder McRyan was a fledgling state representative looking to cement his base up north and maybe run for state senate. The last thing on his mind, or within his grasp, was Miami powerbrokering. No, whoever did this was established and had sway."

"But why would anyone else cover Stephen's tracks?" Pete asked. "Is it proof of guilt? I'm not sure. But it's not good."

"It's not good, you're right," she said, her eyes still on the file. "It's doubly worrisome because Stephen hadn't even spoken to the police yet. Just popped up and made a lot of noise to the press. But any cop worth their salt would've noted his name in the file, and their efforts to find him and sit him down in a room. But you look at the file now, it's like he never existed."

Pete stood up, popping the last half piece of toast into his mouth.

"Where are you going?"

"First, I'm going to take a nice shower in that apartment-sized bathroom of yours," Pete said, walking out of the kitchen. "Then I'm going to get to work."

CHAPTER TWELVE

"Incognito" was the name of the game for Pete Fernandez. He pulled the Dolphins cap down, almost over his eyes, as he walked into the Walgreens on SW Eighth Street and Le Jeune Road. The hiss of the automatic doors and the store's white, blinding lights welcomed him as he walked down the central aisle at a good clip. Since coming back to Miami, Pete had tried to keep to himself. Well, as much as one could when you're a private investigator trying to track another man down. The last few days had been a flurry of settling in—checking into a nondescript hotel after spending his first night back at Jackie's, renting a newish looking Toyota that featured a dashboard out of *Deep Space Nine*, and trying to process his new reality, which included being targeted by not only a fading Miami drug gang, but by one of the five mafia families of New York. Everything was happening fast. He had an appointment with Jackie downtown the following day to discuss next steps in the hunt for Stephen McRyan.

Pete wasn't sure if there were any. It was harder and harder to disappear in the days of social media, cell phones and constant surveillance, but it could still be done. The fact that he hadn't found any strong leads on Stephen McRyan worried Pete. It brought him back to his conversation with Nancy Artino in Queens. McRyan was running scared. He'd done something that pissed some potentially powerful people off. Frightened people were the hardest kind to find, Pete knew—they'd cut any corner, do just about anything to stay out of sight. But who wanted Stephen McRyan aside from his parents? If he'd been on this merry-go-round of disappearing, getting paid, and disappearing again already, why would he fear his mom and dad now? It didn't synch up for Pete. If he believed his hunch, then it meant there was another, perhaps deadlier player involved.

Pete knew the case wasn't open-ended, either—the elder McRyans were getting antsy about their errant son as their big Vizcaya event loomed. They wanted results yesterday. They'd hoped to have the younger McRyan back in the fold before they made anything official. Something had to break, soon.

Pete walked to the freezer aisle and pondered a Lean Cuisine dinner. He'd subsisted on meals at Versailles, but having Cuban takeout a few times a day would all but guarantee a new, larger wardrobe in less than a month. He almost bumped into someone as he turned around.

"How long have you been back?"

Pete gave the man another look. Robert Harras.

"*Awkward Encounters in the Frozen Food Aisle,*" Pete said. "Or, *The Saga of Pete Fernandez and Robert Harras in Two Parts.*"

"Funny," Harras said. "For someone who's in hiding, you weren't hard to find. Or maybe you forgot I was once good at this job."

"How could I forget that, Harras?" Pete said. He stuck out his hand. Harras looked at it for a second before shaking it. Pete couldn't tell if he was trying to be funny.

Harras looked older, worn down. A few more gray hairs in his goatee and wrinkles around his eyes. He still had the posture and build of a Bureau man, his hair closely cropped and his stance rigid.

"Meet me at my car?"

Pete slid into the front passenger seat of the black Escalade Harras had parked in the far west corner of the Walgreen's lot. It was early afternoon. People were at work or prepping for a siesta. The Miami sun was all—consuming, a bright, looming yellow sphere that seemed to bleed out into the light blue, cloudless sky. It was a lovely sight, if you could hack it. But staring at the sun too long came with a price.

"I see you took my invite," Harras said.

Pete said nothing. He knew Harras would figure out he'd come back and rub it in—he just hadn't expected it so soon. A year ago, during his last visit, Harras had asked Pete to do the thing he was now doing—come back to Miami and help solve the murder of Patty Morales. But it was not as clear-cut then. Stephen McRyan wasn't yet connected to Kenny Sampson and Pete wanted nothing to do with Miami and all its baggage. Now he wasn't sure there was anywhere else he could go. He couldn't keep his mistakes buried any longer.

"Not quite," Pete said. He placed the bag of groceries at his feet and looked at Harras. "I'm here on a case. Not the one you wanted me here on, exactly, but here. You seem well."

Pete was lying. Harras looked jittery, on edge. Like a patient waiting for bad news from the doctor.

"I'm fine. And you look the same," he said. "Still dry?"

"Still sober, yep."

"So who's paying you? If you're not chasing the Morales thing, what are you working on?"

Pete sighed. Harras was never one for small talk.

"That's confidential," Pete said.

"So you're not here on the Morales case?" Harras asked.

"Not exactly, I said."

"What the hell does that mean?"

"Officially, I'm here on something else, but I'm here because of the Morales case."

"What, you speak in fortune cookies now?"

"That's all I wanna say, okay?"

"Are you kidding me, Fernandez?" Harras said. "After all the help I've given you?"

"Aren't you retired?"

"Semi," Harras said. "So what?"

"That's the problem," Pete said. "I don't know what that covers. If you're still working with the cops or the FBI, I have to play defense."

"You didn't hesitate," Harras said. "You were scared. Comfortable in your hideout. You'd sailed off into the sunset. What's changed?"

"Nothing," Pete said. "I don't know."

"What kind of an answer is that?" Harras said. "You gotta get your game up. You're home now. Stop acting like you just walked into this job."

"Fuck you."

Harras nodded to himself, looking out his window for a second before turning back to Pete.

"I deserved that, I guess," Harras said.

"It's fine," Pete said. "And, look, as nice as it is to see you, I need to finish my covert shopping. Can we cut to the chase?"

"Well, two pieces I want to discuss. On the Morales thing," Harras said. "There's stuff on it that only the FBI knows, that we could use your eyes on. You were there, at the scene, and I know you can look at it differently. That's why I came by your place in New York. We've worked together. I know I've given you shit before, but I meant what I said the last time I saw you. You're a good detective. We need that."

"The reason I'm here is connected to Morales," Pete said. "What's the other thing?"

"This one's a bit—well, personal," Harras said, grimacing at the use of the word.

"Are you sick?"

"No, no," he said. "Nothing like that. I just—I think I'm in trouble. I can't explain it well."

"That's a first," Pete said. "How do you know?" His mind jumped back to Spring Valley, and the photo on Chadwick's phone.

"I'm being watched, I know that for sure," Harras said. "It's not just me being a paranoid old cop. Someone's tailing me, and I don't know why. Or what the endgame is. I could use a hand figuring it out."

Pete frowned. He wanted to help his friend, but he needed more.

"Well, what can I do?"

"I'm not sure," Harras said, his voice hoarse. "I have a feeling that something's coming down. It's all catching up with me."

Pete had never seen Harras like this. His eyes were wild, desperate and …

Afraid.

"You're freaking me out here."

Harras waved him off. "Just remember to keep your eyes and ears open, will you?" he said. "I've got a bad feeling. Usually, those feelings point me to some kind of evidence, but so far I've got nothing."

"You got it."

"Alright, enough about me. What else can you tell me about this gig?" Harras said, looking more like his old self, like he'd shaken off the brief, fearful interlude. "Must be big if it got you to come back here."

"I'm on a missing person's case. I need to track someone down," Pete said. "The money's good. I couldn't pass it up. Plus, things got hot in New York."

"Trouble always finds you," Harras said, his voice distant again.

"Look, let me know what I can do," Pete said as he reached for the door, stopping before opening it. "That goes for everything. You, the Morales case, whatever. I'll be around for a bit. Maybe for a while."

"Have you talked to Kathy?"

The question threw Pete off for a moment. He settled back into his seat before responding.

"What? No," Pete said. "Why do you ask?"

"She's your partner, isn't she? You do these things together," he said. "I assume she's working with you on this, with an assist from that ex-con idiot Mendoza."

Pete wasn't sure he wanted to press it, but he did it anyway. Curiosity always won.

"I haven't talked to Kathy since she left New York," Pete said. "Have you seen her?"

"Jesus," he said. "You're acting like we just met. No, I haven't seen her. Why else would I ask?"

Harras' response seemed hesitant and defensive. *He's hiding something—but why?*

"Well, you're grilling me like some perp you pulled off the street."

"Forget Kathy, then," Harras said, waving a hand toward Pete. "Hell, forget everything I said. I'll give you the intel I have on Morales because you should know it before you go any further. Take it for whatever you think it's worth. I don't care if you help the Bureau or not."

"Fine."

"Just so we're clear—this case isn't just about a dead high schooler," Harras said. "It's a bigger problem, and I think the PD is avoiding it. I think the FBI might be avoiding it, too, even if they're telling me they want your help. I'm not sure why yet, but it ties into some other shit that's dragging the department down."

"Sounds familiar," Pete said. "The Miami Police Department is corrupt? Check. Been there before. Somebody hiring me because they think I'll hurt more than help? That's a bad rerun for me. But hey, you found me. You knew I was back in Miami. Tell me something I can use."

Harras reached into his sports coat pocket and produced a business card—it was worn and bent. He handed it to Pete. It read, *La Iglesia de la Luz - Salvation for Those Who Seek It.*

"This is where the information stops flowing," Harras said.

"La Iglesia de la Luz?" Pete said. "The cult?"

"Maybe it was, twenty years ago," Harras said. "They had storefront churches all over town—mainly south, Homestead, north Keys, areas around there. Guy running it—Jaime Figueras—was a kind of celebrity for a while. They boasted a few notable followers—B-list athletes, city officials, that kind of star power. Then something happened and it all imploded."

"Didn't he get locked up?" Pete asked. He vaguely remembered the story from his childhood.

"For a bit, but he got out fast—tax evasion," Harras said. "But they didn't get him on the real juicy stuff. There were allegations Figueras paid people to take down those who spoke out against the church, rumors Figueras was bilking his congregation—which was made up mostly of poor immigrants struggling to find some sliver of hope— of what little money they had. There were darker stories spreading around about him, how his whole setup was a sham, how he preyed on the young, female members of the church and what it took to make it into his inner circle. Harsher charges were filed—conspiracy to commit murder, assault and battery and money laundering, to name a few. He was arrested. But the witnesses dried up. Stories were recanted. The real, red-ball case died on the vine, basically. Even the financial stuff was glossed over. He had great attorneys."

"So what happened to him?"

"He went into hiding," Harras said. "He owns a chunk of land in the Keys—he and his remaining devotees live there, sheltered from the outside world."

"What does this have to do with Patty Morales?" Pete said.

"That's what I don't know," Harras said. "At least not in concrete terms. But I know there's a link. Her dad was involved in the church, but that's never percolated to the top. I haven't investigated this much beyond asking people an offhand question over the years. A few crumbs have pointed to the church, but that's all I have. Crumbs."

"It's a start," Pete said.

Harras grabbed Pete's shoulder.

"Ping me if you get anything. I'll try to help. No questions asked."

"Just like old times."

"Except we're older," Harras said.

"Not any smarter," Pete said.

He opened the passenger side door and walked out. Pete had to try and get a lead on the erstwhile Stephen McRyan. Maybe, after that, he'd connect with another old friend—and pray it went half as smoothly as his conversation with Harras.

A second after opening the door to her apartment, upon realizing it was Pete Fernandez on the other side, Kathy Bentley turned around and walked back into the confines of her Wynwood home. It could have been much worse, Pete thought. He'd expected at least one swing, definitely some expletives. But it was still early.

He followed her down a long hallway leading into a spacious, half-furnished living room. Even with a few lights on, the large apartment was dark and loaded with shadows. The curtains and blinds kept out the streetlights if not the noise, giving the space an otherworldly quality Pete found unsettling. It smelled of pine cleaner and Kathy's tart perfume, and the dim lighting paired with the apartment's spacious décor made it feel cavernous and hollow—like a vacant church sanctuary. Although Kathy had been back in Miami for over a year, the place looked to be in a transitional state, with her decorative flourishes serving as lynchpins of sorts—hints of what each area would look like when she made her way to them. In the living room, a Belle and Sebastian concert poster and framed photos leaned against the walls, waiting to be hung, next to a sectional couch and half-stocked bookshelves.

She walked over to a small table and turned off the stereo playing Stevie Wonder's *Innervisions*, which was just ramping into "Living for the City," as Stevie sang about a father working fourteen-hour days. She looked at Pete. Her face looked scrubbed and clean, free of makeup.

"Were you asleep?" Pete asked.

"I would hope so," Kathy said. "It's almost two in the morning."

"Sorry," Pete said. "I figured you'd be awake."

"I am, indeed, awake now," she said, hugging herself. "And you are, apparently, alive."

"I'm alive."

"I'm pretty sure you owe me many apologies for being a gigantic asshole," she said. "But don't let me influence your actions too much, I know how much you hate that."

The words came at Pete like daggers—in sharp, slinging bursts. Kathy had been waiting for this moment, and she would make sure each hit landed. Hard.

"I'm sorry," Pete said. "I should have called. Emailed. Anything. I just needed some time."

"Well, you got it," she said, letting her body fall down on the couch. "Also, fuck you."

"Look, I apologized."

"Oh, silly me, I guess that means we're all good?" Kathy said, standing up and taking a step toward Pete. "I guess that means we're besties again, because you're so sorry? Well, fuck you for thinking that being quote-unquote sorry is even your role. You have no fucking agency here, Pete—I left you, remember? Don't spin this like some pity post-breakup check-in. Like you left me sobbing on the kitchen floor because you couldn't deal, bro. I left you, Mr. I'm Too Emo and Weird to Understand How to be in a Perfectly Healthy Relationship with a Hot, Smart Woman. This is not something I dwell on, okay? Get the fuck over yourself. Please, get off your spaceship and stop acting like you're doing me a goddamn favor by coming here. You're lucky I don't kick you out right now."

"You're right."

Her shoulder slumped.

"Well, this is no fun," she said, her anger muted, a small smile starting to appear on her face. "I was hoping to at least get into a mildly heated discussion."

"That was pretty heated."

"You don't know me very well, it seems."

Pete took a step toward her. She raised her hand, as if to ward him off.

"Whoa, slow down. We're not at the huggy-reconciliation stage just yet, okay? What do you want, Pete?" she said, her voice cracking. "Why are you here?"

"I'm working a case," he said. "I need your help."

"How nice for you."

"Can we sit? Can I explain?" Pete said, moving toward the couch.

Kathy gave him a dismissive nod and sat opposite Pete on the couch's other section. The air felt calmer, less electric, like the morning after a heavy snow. Kathy looked deflated, as if Pete's willingness to accept blame undercut all her firepower.

"Okay, prodigal Pete, now you tell me why you came back to Miami," she said. "Though, I think I know the answer."

"Am I that predictable?"

"Well, for stuff like this, yes," Kathy said. She took a sip from a small cup full of a light red liquid that Pete assumed was vodka mixed with cranberry. "This is kind of what you live for."

"What do you mean?"

"You know exactly what I mean," Kathy said. "You do these things—coming back to Miami, investigating cases that uproot your life—to avoid reality. Or to avoid dealing with what's around you."

Pete decided to ignore the amateur psychoanalysis.

"Do you know Trevor McRyan?"

"Our future über-progressive governor?"

"Well, he wants to be," Pete said. "He wants me to find his son."

"That sounds… lucrative," she said. "Is he trying to avoid skeletons from jumping out of his closet? I wondered how he stayed scandal-free for so long."

"Something like that," Pete said. "But that's not why I took the case."

"Right, I forget you don't take jobs for stupid reasons like truckloads of lobbyist money," she said, rolling her eyes as she put her glass own on the floor and leaned back into a stretch. "So why did you take this case and come back? I thought you were scared Los Enfermos were still gunning for you. Not that you checked to see if I was okay under similar circumstances, but I'll drop that in the complaint box."

"I was—I mean, I am," Pete said. "But when I saw a photo of the McRyan kid, who's about our age, he looked familiar. Stephen McRyan used to go by the name of Kenny Sampson, at least four years ago. He claimed to know things about the murder of Patty Morales. Remember that case?"

"Yes, everyone who lived here then does," Kathy said. "Honor roll, A-student and all-around superstar teen goes missing. Her remains are found outside of her father's house fifteen fucking years later. Father is suspected, but the evidence doesn't pan out, then the case goes ice cold—again."

"That's most of it," Pete said. "Did you know Patty Morales was Jackie Cruz's niece? Well, half-niece? Her older half-brother, Roger Morales, was Patty's dad."

"The same Jackie Cruz who helped us with the Varela case?" Kathy said, her eyes narrowing a bit, her brain revving up. "The lawyer you had a fling with way back when?"

"Yeah," Pete said. "We dated for—but I was, shit, I was a mess. So that didn't work out."

"Your track record is sterling in that department, present company included," Kathy said, smiling. "I imagine she's as charming as the last time we saw her."

Pete ignored the jab. Kathy and Jackie not getting along was nothing new.

"Jackie was the cool aunt who was only a few years older than Patty," Pete said. "They spent a lot of time together. Jackie was just finishing college and thinking about law school. Short story, she was close to Patty. She thought of her like a little sister."

Kathy motioned for Pete to continue.

"So, time passes, the case grows cold and then this guy, Kenny Sampson, shows up out of the blue, claiming to know about what happened, basically pleading with the cops to interview him," Pete said. "But, in classic Miami PD fashion, by the time they get to Sampson, he's in the wind. So, they shrug their shoulders. Case was cold anyway, right? Jackie then comes to me and asks me to take the case and figure out what the hell happened to Patty Morales."

"I think I sort of remember this," Kathy said. At the time, Kathy and Pete were only hovering around the idea of working together. "But you said you passed on the case?"

"That's what I told Jackie," Pete said. "But I ended up taking the gig and looking for Patty anyway."

"Of course you did."

"I eventually found her," Pete said, fighting the urge to stop the story before it took him back to that yard, and Patty. "Well, what was left of her. Outside of Roger Morales' house."

Pete looked away from Kathy and toward the windows that faced the street. His life up to that point had felt like a series of failures—the death of his father, the sharp and sudden decline of his career, the shrinking taxicab that drove his fiancée and her bags away. Most of that could be chalked up—if he was in a dismissive mood—to other factors. But standing over a pile of remains that had once been a girl, a girl he knew and cared for, pulled him into a pit of darkness he'd never considered—a lower level of guilt and shame that threatened to drown him. He knew, logically, that it wasn't his fault. He hadn't seen Patty in over a decade, had only just begun to investigate her disappearance. But Pete also knew that he—a drunk, lonely shell of a man with little to look forward to aside from the next bottle—was alive, and she'd died before experiencing any of the things life had to offer. She would never graduate college. She would never fall in love. She couldn't list her favorite live shows, or reminisce with old friends about their high school days. She was gone, and she'd deserved better. Pete was alive and had squandered everything. It was a knockout punch from the real world, and it still stung, even after years of trying to rebuild himself.

I don't deserve to be alive.

"She was dead, not even a body anymore—a skeleton, basically. Whatever evil had been done to her had happened years before, and the remains were dropped by the Morales house to be found," Pete said. "The cops, obviously, had no idea where the murder took place and couldn't immediately tell from looking at a pile of bones what kind of murder it was. Her father was home when I discovered the, uh, remains. They arrested him. They claimed they were bringing him in for questioning, but he was the only thing they had resembling a suspect."

"Where's the father now?"

"Morales is around, somewhere. He was questioned, but eventually they dropped it. There was no evidence linking him to the murder, no motive, and enough evidence that he had no idea her bones were outside his house until I showed up," Pete said. "Jackie had the case file from back then and it omitted Kenny Sampson, altogether, though, which is curious, especially after he made so much noise about knowing what really happened."

"You knew this girl, right?" Kathy asked.

"Yeah, high school. We were friends, sort of," Pete said. "In the way you're friendly with people you barely see. She was a good kid."

Kathy leaned forward, picked up her glass and took a long pull. Pete had expected a quip, or some kind of zinger targeting his high school self, but instead was met with silence. Proof that things were still a ways away from being okay between them.

"Where's the motive, then? Why kill this girl, hide the body, then dump it on daddy's doorstep years later?" Kathy asked. "If her dad didn't kill her—who did?"

Pete didn't respond. He watched her talk. She seemed relaxed. Poised. Even in yoga pants and a T-shirt, she looked put together and present. She'd rebuilt a life for herself here in Miami. Meanwhile, Pete was living in an empty house in upstate New York, a mattress on the floor and a hot plate near the bathroom. He spent his days chasing deadbeat dads and cheating spouses and his nights reading library books and eating food out of a can.

"I don't know," Pete said, shaking himself out of his mental detour. "I'm not sure how much help I can be."

"Look, this is who you are. These are the cases you shine at. You know this. I'll spare you the free therapy," Kathy said. "Because it's late and because I don't think it'll do much."

"Why's that?"

"Because you need to realize this for yourself," Kathy said. "Not just this case, which is probably serving as a nice little distraction from you and your life and how you are. You had it all spread out for you—the stable living situation, good income, no death threats, meetings galore, the inkling of an adult relationship that didn't involve drinking to blackout to see where things go. But you couldn't handle it. And before you spin this in your little brain—this isn't about me. I'm a big girl and I can deal with rejection. But I can't deal with fear, and that's what fuels you now. Not fear of the dangerous— you dive into stupid shit all the fucking time. You're almost afraid of the normal, because it means you've accepted that this is what your life might be."

Pete waited a moment. "Are you done?"

"For now, yes," she said.

"Can I give you my side of this?"

"Sure."

"This case was on me," Pete said, straightening himself up on the couch to better face Kathy. "I was trying to fix something, but I was too broken to do it."

"It's not your fault the kid died, Pete," Kathy said. "She was probably murdered fifteen years before you even looked for her."

"Let me finish."

"Okay."

"I knew her," Pete said. "We were friends. I saw her the day she went missing. I sometimes think back on that day and replay it. If I'd just stuck around, or made a point of talking to her later—or, well, anything—she might be alive. And then, wracked with this weird guilt years later, I'm still not able to figure it out. I botch the whole thing."

That did it. Talking to Kathy, finally speaking aloud what he'd bottled up in the furthest, deepest corners of his mind, did it. Now, despite sitting in Kathy's living room, he found himself back in that moment, years ago. He could feel his head swirling from the vodka, his body off-kilter, struggling for balance as he made his way toward the house. He saw as the dark shape beckoned to him from the side yard, an evil portent that Pete refused to ignore. The odd, awkward pile that he couldn't make out until it was too late, until he made out too much—the faded, dirty bones clustered together in the soil like a campfire, what was once a human body now dumped in a heap like garbage. His foot catching on what used to be an arm, his body falling forward, his face close to Patty, one last time, the smell of her, microscopic bits of her sliding up through his nostrils, the flecks and pieces of a person Pete knew now just dust and bone.

"Maybe I could have stopped it," Pete said, the memory's aftershocks leaving him disoriented. "I knew something was off about it. I knew I could help."

"Who knows what could have been?" Kathy said. "You did the best you could under the circumstances."

"I was a mess," Pete said. His eyes were red. He didn't want to talk about this anymore. He didn't want to live with it anymore. "I should have been smarter."

"Jesus, she was already dead," Kathy said, sliding over to sit next to Pete, wrapping her arm around his shoulder. "Isn't your little program all about forgiveness and understanding? You were a raging drunk. I wouldn't have hired you to wash my porch, much less find my niece. You were in no shape to do that."

Kathy broke the embrace and stood up before the touch lingered too long.

"If this is a quest to right a drunken wrong, you're in it for selfish reasons."

"What if it's something else?" Pete said, looking up at his partner. "Like?"

"Finding out who killed an innocent kid, cut off her life before she could do the things she would do," Pete said. "And shutting them down."

"Attaboy," she said, smiling for the first time. "Now I'm in. You're still an asshole, though."

CHAPTER THIRTEEN

The Miami Times
April 2, 2013
Miami Attorney Attacked Outside of Kendall Home
Victim of vicious assault in critical condition

Lauren Zirulnik, Miami Times Staff Writer

Jackie Cruz, an up-and-coming local attorney known for helping downtrodden defendants unable to afford representation and for defending disgraced police officer Gaspar Varela in his losing battle against charges that he murdered his wife, was severely beaten by an unknown assailant on the front steps of her Kendall townhouse, leaving her with a broken jaw, three broken ribs and a fractured skull, according to family members watching over her at Kendall Regional Medical Center.

Authorities are asking for the community's help in tracking down the attacker, described as being of average height, stocky and wearing a wool-knit black cap and a black jogging suit, according to Cruz's neighbor, William Dunlop, who was walking his dog near her condo at the time of the assault. Dunlop said he did not get a clear look at the man's face.

"He was waiting for her," said William Dunlop, who lives a few houses down from Cruz. "The second she got out of her car, he was on her. It was brutal, man. I don't think he would have stopped if I hadn't yelled that I was calling the cops."

April 1, 2013

Pete reached the hospital room just as the nurse was exiting, closing the door behind her. She gave Pete a quick once-over and frowned. He knew he didn't look good. Probably didn't smell great, either, unless you were fond of the odor of stale vodka and sweat. His clothes were wrinkled and dirty—he couldn't really remember if he'd showered in the last two or three days. He was also hammered. The drive from his father's house—his dead father's house—in Westchester to Kendall Regional had been mostly a straight shot down Bird Road, but even that involved a few near misses he didn't want to think about.

He'd dozed off—*passed out*—on his dad's old recliner after their disastrous Ale House meeting, awoken by a call from a police detective letting him know his friend was in the hospital. He'd knocked back a few quick jolts from the bottle to get his head right after he got word of Jackie's condition.

"Can I help you?" the nurse said, concern setting up shop on her face.

"I'm here to see Jackie Cruz."

"I'm sorry, she's not seeing visitors now," the nurse said, still standing between Pete and the closed door. "Our visiting hours start at ten tomorrow morning, though. I suggest you come back then. Your friend's been through a lot and needs her rest."

Pete felt a hand on his shoulder and turned around. The hand was connected to the arm of a tall, rumpled-looking man with a well-trimmed beard and dark brown hair.

"You Pete Fernandez?" the man said. His voice was clear and authoritative. *Cop.*

"Yes," Pete said, mindful of how much he talked, not sure if his breath was a signal he was bombed. "Are you Detective Brownstein?"

Brownstein stuck his hand out. Pete shook it. The handshake was firm but not overly so. The nurse hurried off down the hall, shaking her head to herself.

"Paul Brownstein, Special Victims Bureau. You got a second to talk?"

Pete nodded. Brownstein led Pete to a waiting area with a small couch and table that was set up near the elevators. There were two cups of coffee on the table and Brownstein motioned for Pete to take one.

"Figured you could use this," Brownstein said. "You sounded like I'd roused you from a pretty deep sleep when we spoke earlier. It's late, too."

"I was asleep," Pete said, taking a chair next to the couch and sipping from the coffee. It was bitter, black and strong. It would help diffuse his drunkenness and mask his hobo breath. "Thanks for calling me."

"I don't normally reach out to friends," Brownstein said, folding his hands together. "But I know Jackie and she was pushing for it before she fell asleep. So, I figured I'd do her a favor, and then, as a bonus, I'd get to talk to you."

Even in his clouded state, Pete knew where this was going. Pete Fernandez was not a friend to the Miami police. While uncovering the truth behind the killer-of-killers known as the Silent Death, Pete had also unearthed some embarrassing and controversial truths about his father's ex-partner, Carlos Broche, a well-liked cop on the brink of retirement. Broche was dead, the truth about his work for the Silent Death added to the pile of allegations against the entire department. On top of that, the Miami cops weren't ecstatic a washed-up sports journalist had discovered the identity of the city's biggest urban legend before they did. Short version: Miami police didn't like Pete. Pete didn't give a shit.

"If this is about the stuff with the Silent Death, I'm not going to talk about that," Pete said. "And I will not sit here and get berated by another pissed-off cop. I came because my friend is hurt, and I want to find out what happened."

Brownstein gave Pete a dry smile and placed the palms of his hands on his thighs with a light slap. His eyebrows popped up.

"Great," he said. "Because I don't give a shit about you or your history with the department. I don't care about how the department looks or what it thinks. I care about closing cases. I care about that woman sleeping in that room, drugged to the gills because she's in excruciating pain. I care about why someone would attack her when she's done nothing but help people for years. In fact, as far as I can tell, all she's done lately is meet with you before she got pounded. A guy who's known for tripping into dangerous situations and sometimes figuring them out. That's why you're here. That's all I want to talk about. Is that okay with you?"

Pete felt a sharp pang of shame.

"Special Victims Bureau?" Pete said, shifting gears. "Does that mean the guy who attacked her knew her? Was it a sex crime?"

Brownstein was still smiling, humorlessly, but Pete could tell he was growing impatient.

"I understand you're not a cop," Brownstein said, tilting his head to the left. "But I do think you understand how investigations work. I know nothing about this crime yet, beyond what your friend—who is, like I said, drugged to the gills—told me. Or what that glory-hound neighbor said to me and in the fifteen interviews he did after that. I can't tell you if the guy knew her, no. I can tell you she wasn't raped, if that helps. I will murder you myself if I find that bit of news in the press tomorrow, though. That's all I've got, beyond a hunch I'm hoping you can help me with."

Pete was starting to like this guy. No frills, straight to the point.

"Have more of that coffee, too," Brownstein said. "I don't particularly like talking to drunks, but I may have to suffer through it with you."

Pete didn't like Brownstein much anymore.

Not because he was bad police—it was clear to Pete that he was a good detective. He was shooting straight. Too straight. Brownstein's brusque style was not doing wonders for Pete, and he couldn't shake the feeling that the detective enjoyed holding up a mirror to him, showing Pete what a mess he was to the world. By now, Pete had shaken off the drunk and downgraded it to a big buzz, so his synapses were firing better, but he knew he was off. Brownstein made it clear he also knew it with each question or subtle jab. Pete's responses were dull but not drooling, and he did his best to keep up with what Brownstein was trying to tell him—and what he could piece together wasn't good.

"You think this is tied to Jackie's niece?"

"It's a guess, with few facts to support it," Brownstein said, tossing his empty coffee cup into the trash and returning to his seat across from Pete. "But yes. This lady, Cruz, has no enemies. The most dangerous people she interacts with are her own clients. They love her. She's got a golden reputation when it comes to the bad guys, but for the right reasons. She feels like even the guilty deserve a shot at a fair trial. Hell, she defended Varela of all people. She keeps her nose clean, works hard, you know the type. So what changes? What does she do differently before she's attacked? She sniffs around her missing niece, years after the kid goes AWOL."

"Who wouldn't want her to find Patty?"

"You tell me, Nancy Drew," Brownstein said. "You're the expert. Didn't she hire you?"

"She tried to," Pete said. "I passed."

"You knew Patty Morales, right? Back when you were pimply and skinnier, yeah?"

"We were kind of friends in high school."

"'Kind of,' as in you messed around and stayed friends, or 'kind of' as in she didn't give you the time of day beyond a few pity hi's and 'byes?"

"The latter."

"Figured," Brownstein said, cracking the knuckles of his left hand. "So, answer the question. Why'd you pass? You're invested in this one. From what I can tell, your dad and his partner were looking into this when it happened, albeit unofficially."

This was news to Pete. From what he remembered, his father and Broche were officially on the case. Or maybe that's what they'd wanted Pete to think.

"I'm not an investigator," Pete said. "Not anymore."

"Yeah? That's funny, because it seems like that's what you were doing recently when you made the entire department look like a steaming piece of shit," Brownstein said, no malice in his voice, matter-of-factly. "What do you do now?"

"Nothing."

"Nothing, eh? Just sit at home, drinking your troubles away? Whatever works, I guess."

"I passed on the job," Pete said. He was tiring of this tennis match. "Next question."

"All I've been cleared to do is investigate who attacked your friend," he said, eyes drilling into Pete. "But even that has parameters. If I say it's linked to the disappearance of Patty Morales, one of the biggest cases this town obsesses over, then I need actual evidence. Unlike you, my solitary drinking friend, I have a stack of cases bigger than the pile of avocados in my backyard. I can only give this a fraction of my day, if I'm lucky. That means I can only focus on the evidence—which isn't much—and extrapolate from that. If only I knew a semi-competent investigator who might have a personal stake in this to help me out here, off the books."

Pete hated himself here, in this moment, sitting across from Brownstein, drunk, while his friend lay in a hospital bed, recovering from a savage beating. Had he taken the job, had he stuck around and talked to Jackie a bit longer, she might be fine. Instead, he chose an all-too-familiar oblivion. Maybe he could have prevented this. Well, maybe he could help fix it, at least. Right here and now.

"I'll see what I can dig up," Pete said.

Brownstein gave a relieved nod in response.

"Good, good," he said. "But don't spill that this is happening. If you do, I play dumb and you're dead. The last thing I need are my bosses finding out I'm working with you, even if it's unofficial."

"Right, God forbid."

"Don't get whiny, it doesn't suit you," Brownstein said. "In terms of the Morales thing, everyone wants it to be the dad. It's easy, tidy and makes sense. I don't think it's the dad—but I think he's somehow connected. See what you can dig up about him first."

"I said I'd look into it."

"Just do it, okay?" Brownstein said, showing a flash of frustration. "Can you shake the drunk off for a second and read between the lines? There's something here that I don't have the evidence to follow up on. Something involving her father. Get off your ass, Fernandez. Patty is probably dead. And now your friend is in the hospital. They both need you."

Brownstein got up and started to walk past Pete, toward the elevators.

"Get your shit together, man," he said, not trying to hide his disdain.

Pete never saw Brownstein again. The grizzled cop's words would come to haunt Pete, echoing in his brain and driving him toward Roger Morales's home, looking for answers, a few days later.

CHAPTER FOURTEEN

September 23, 2017
Miami, Florida

Pete let out a groan as he stepped out of Kathy's car, a thick, oppressive, waterlogged warmth enveloping them within seconds. Pete wore a blue polo shirt, faded black jeans and sneakers that had seen better days. As much as he wanted to downshift to shorts and a T-shirt, he had to look at least marginally professional for their first formal meeting with Jackie Cruz. Kathy, despite the subtropical temperatures, seemed light as air in a green summer dress. Pete thanked all that was holy as they stepped inside the building's lobby and the first waves of cool air conditioning hitting them. *Was Miami getting hotter?*

"Let's get this going," Kathy said as they approached the front desk.

Pete showed the security guard his ID and explained who they were. The man printed out nametags and pointed them toward an escalator that led to a bank of elevators on the second floor.

"Have you heard from Dave?" Pete asked as they waited.

"I have, yes," she said, checking her phone and putting it on SILENT before tossing it into her bag. "But he does not particularly want to hear from you, if you're dying to know."

They took the elevator up in silence and walked into Jackie Cruz's office. It was a small affair—a cramped waiting room with months-old copies of *Time* and *Newsweek* and a bored-looking assistant more interested in checking her phone than greeting guests.

"Can I help you?" the disgruntled millennial said, not bothering to look up.

"You could," Pete said.

The girl seemed confused by Pete's response, enough to look up, her big brown eyes resembling puddles of dirty water.

"We're here to see your boss," Kathy said. "The person you work for? The person who people come to see and you're supposed to welcome?"

The girl rolled her eyes and went back to her phone.

"Sit down and I'll let you know when she's free," she said, almost to herself.

"I'm Pete Fernandez and this is my partner, Kathy Bentley," Pete said as he pushed off the partition separating him from Jackie's assistant. "Thanks for your help."

They sat down. Kathy picked up a stray magazine and flipped the pages without lingering on anything.

"She's a real professional," she said. "You'd think we were just some randos."

"As opposed to people her boss has asked to see?"

"Exactly," she said, sighing and settling into her seat, her eyes scanning the small waiting area.

A few minutes later, they were led into Jackie's office—a spacious room anchored by a large oak desk and surrounded by bookshelves and a few tastefully selected art prints. It felt like someone's idea of a power office, right down to the jaw-dropping view of Biscayne Bay. Jackie didn't bother standing up to greet them as they entered, her eyes following as they took the two seats in front of her. She looked calm but focused, like a golf pro scanning the green before taking a swing.

"Let's talk," she said. No ceremony. "First order of business: the McRyans are fine with Kathy coming aboard. Spoke to them this morning. I let them know it's a best-case scenario for them. You actually get Pete to work, which is a plus. They're on edge and super-jittery about their kid being AWOL, and they haven't seen the kind of progress they want. So, I spun it as good news. And while I know that you're back, Pete, because of the McRyan case, there are a few other things we need to go over first."

"Oh?" Pete said. Jackie's demeanor was no-nonsense. It took him a second to calibrate to the meeting. He had to remind himself that while Jackie was a friend, she was also a cutthroat attorney, and they were now on the clock.

"Let's talk about Patty Morales," she said, irked. "What have you found?"

"Um, well, as you seem to know—I got looped into this bullshit last night," Kathy said. "Before that, I'd pretty much forgotten who the hell Patty Morales was. Then this stray cat over here," she motioned to Pete, "wandered into my apartment. This is all very new. So, please, humor me and get me up to speed before you go all 'Always Be Closing' on us."

Jackie pursed her lips, looking at Kathy and Pete for what felt like the first time.

"Look, I need results on Patty Morales, okay?" Jackie said. "I will go to any length to close this case. It's personal."

"Jackie, we understand, but I just got here and I'm supposed to be finding Stephen McRyan—you know that. And, let's face it, I've got nothing on him yet, so I'm not exactly his parents' favorite person," Pete said. "I'm not even officially working the Patty Morales angle."

"But that's why you came," she said, her voice a snap, like a briefcase clicking shut. "Not because some wannabe politician asked you to, but because it ties into something else, right?"

"Yes, you know that," Pete said. He could feel Kathy's eyes on him. "But this is an introductory meeting to get Kathy up to speed. Then we can get to work."

Jackie frowned. She was somewhere else. On edge. Tired.

"Okay, so, can you tell us what you know? That would be helpful," Kathy said. "But be warned, I've heard the intro—teen goes missing, years later, you get worried, Pete is drunk, remains of kid found at dad's house, dad charged but quickly exonerated and so on. I want to hear what's new and what info you might have to help us solve this case. I also want to know how the McRyans fit into this at all. Then maybe I can write a book. Then we can be friends. Big maybe on that last one."

Jackie stood up and turned to face them, smiling. Pete hadn't expected that reaction.

"You're such a bitch," Jackie said. "I love it."

Pete tried not to show any signs of relief that the border skirmish didn't turn into a full-on nuclear war between the two women.

"I aim to please," Kathy said, not returning Jackie's smile or warmth.

"What's new, okay," Jackie said, pacing behind her desk. "Well, Roger Morales wasn't convicted of Patty's death. The remains—because it'd been years since she was killed—didn't really hold much evidence that could help convict a murderer. But the DA pushed forward anyway, and the fact that his daughter was found dumped on his property didn't help her dad's cause, or his standing in the community. So, while the evidence was slight, it was clear the body had been moved, so the thought—from the district attorney's perspective—was something happened between Roger and Patty and she died, then Roger tried to cover it up."

"But that's not what happened?" Pete said.

"I don't think so, no," Jackie said. "I mean, look, I'm not close to Roger. That whole side of the family is like some weird fever dream my mom had before she settled down with us. It happens. So, we don't really talk, never did. But I knew his daughter. I know he loved her. I know he's a good man, hardworking, and is haunted by her death in a way I wouldn't wish on anyone."

"So then what?" Kathy said. "Someone killed Patty and dumped her on his lawn? Because that is some fucked-up shit."

"Did Morales have enemies?" Pete said.

"Like I said, we weren't close," Jackie said. "I'm sure he did. Do you remember anything from the time you spent working the case?"

"It was a few nights," Pete said, defensiveness creeping into his voice.

"Right, and you were a sad drunk, we know the soliloquy," Kathy said.

"The whole period's a blur," Pete said. "I worked the case for a few days, did some sniffing around Morales on Jackie and this cop Brownstein's direction, stumbled upon the bones. Then I got pushed aside. All I could get on her dad was he was a low-key guy who spent a lot of time helping his church and seemed genuinely surprised his daughter was not only dead, but that some sick fuck had left her corpse on his property. He seemed baffled, but also, I dunno, offended and resentful. The mom was hysterical every time I saw her—angry, confused, impossible to understand. They didn't seem to be supporting each other much, either. Maybe I'm remembering it wrong."

"No, I think you're on the right track," Jackie said. She looked at Kathy. "Anyway, once the cops took over, Pete was frozen out of the case. Which, honestly, was fine for me and for him, because he was in no shape to do much else."

She looked over at him, as if waiting for him to make a remark. When he didn't, she pressed on.

"Once the evidence surrounding Roger fizzled and there was no new evidence on Patty or her ex—Danny Castillo's—death," Jackie said, "they looked at other people who might have interacted with Patty before she disappeared."

"Didn't a certain Pete Fernandez also interact with Patty before she went MIA?" Kathy said.

"Correct," Jackie said. "But Pete's alibi was airtight. He was doing some kind of detention and then picked up by his cop dad."

"Detention?" Kathy said, a quick giggle escaping her lips. "Was someone a bad boy?"

Pete rolled his eyes.

"As I was saying, they questioned a few people," Jackie said. "One of the people they wanted to talk to was a guy named Kenny

Sampson. Seems like they knew each other, though they went to different schools. That plus the fact that Sampson reappeared just a few days before Patty was found, claiming to know the truth about the case, made him a prime target for the police. But then he was gone."

"This Sampson is the McRyan's son?" Kathy asked.

"That's what I think," Pete said. "It's too much of a coincidence."

"The resemblance is unreal," Jackie said. "I buy it. It could explain why the McRyans want to find him, too."

"You think?" Kathy said. "Might be bad PR if the son of a gubernatorial candidate is implicated in one of the biggest cold cases in Miami history. Just a guess, though. I could be wrong."

"Is that why you're working with the McRyans, then?" Pete asked. Jackie had taken a seat behind her desk now, checking something on her computer. She looked up.

"Not exactly," she said. "Like I told you, I actually like the guy. I buy his shtick. I had no idea they had an adult son. I mean, I know they're older, but they must have started young. When they talked to me about their son and I saw the picture, though, I knew it was him. And I knew you needed to see the photo. So, I put them on your trail."

"It worked," Kathy said. "Predictable Pete Fernandez."

Pete ignored her.

"McRyan's a good man," Jackie said. "Something about him, his platform, got me interested."

"How sweet," Kathy said. "Jackie's first political crush."

"Like I told this *sangano*," Jackie said, moving her chin toward Pete. "McRyan was a virgin when it came to Miami politics. Wouldn't know Versailles if he ran into it with his Dodge Ram truck. So, I reached out, offered to introduce him to the right people, get some money flowing into his coffers. Next thing you know, we discover that the exiles like this northern gringo who looks like a Kennedy but didn't drop the ball on the Bay of Pigs. He actually has fans down on Calle Ocho."

"Do you think he has a chance of winning?" Pete asked.

"He's announcing early, and in a big way," Jackie said. "Tomorrow, at Vizcaya of all places. Doesn't get more Miami than that. That'll scare off the other Democrats, and the Republicans haven't figured out their standard-bearer. Open elections with no incumbent are always a crapshoot. He's definitely a stronger candidate than Reno or McBride."

The mention of failed Democratic Florida gubernatorial candidates came from Jackie with such ease it brought a chuckle to Pete lips.

"Are we still invited to the big coming-out party?" Pete asked.

"Of course," she said. "You're on the list. So is your lady friend."

"Remind me again why I'm here?" Kathy asked, her expression flat.

Jackie ignored the jab.

"What do we know about Roger Morales now?" Pete asked.

"He worked in management at Homestead Hospital," Jackie said. "Dealt mainly with patient complaints, wrongful death stuff—that sort of thing. Seemed to have a good reputation. Gradually climbed up the ladder. Once the accusations hit, though, he was fired and, from what I could tell, couldn't find work after that."

"What about his relationships?" Kathy said. "Is he still with Patty's mom?"

"Divorced from Tere Acevedo, Patty's mom. She lives in Homestead now," Jackie said. "They were separated, not yet divorced, when Patty's remains were found. She filed for divorce after his arrest. No sign of any kind of reconciliation, either."

"What about Patty?" Kathy said. "Was there more to her under the perfect, A-student veneer?"

"Not a lot," Jackie said. "Mostly well-behaved. As much as a teenager can be. Great grades, involved in afterschool activities like sports and the newspaper. She was happy, even though there were problems at home. Her parents argued. Her dad was getting more into his church, her mom wasn't around much. But Patty worked hard, focused on her schooling. She was on her way to getting out of there, out of Miami, and to something all her own. I wish I could have helped her."

"What about you?" Pete asked.

"What about me?" Jackie said.

"The first time you asked me to look into this, when I brushed you off," Pete said. "You got jumped when you got home. What came of that?"

"That's a mild way of putting it," Jackie said. "But yeah. I was attacked that night. Ended up in the hospital. My jaw is still fucked up."

"That sounds, how do you say, relevant," Kathy said.

"Nothing came of it, really," she said. "The cops had no leads. The guy who did it was hard to identify. He was dressed in black, head to toe. He made some vague, threatening remarks—'Mind your own business, bitch, your brother doesn't need any help'—but nothing that told me or the police much beyond it being somehow tied to me poking my nose into Patty's disappearance. Someone knew I was trying to dig into it, and they wanted me to stop. And I did, for a while, because I was laid up. Then you found Patty and that took over everyone's attention, understandably."

"Do you remember anything else about the man who attacked you?" Kathy asked.

Jackie scrunched her nose for a moment, her eyes looking at the wall behind her guests.

"He was tall, almost lanky," she said, the words jumping out in quick bursts, as the thoughts formed in her head. "He seemed, I don't know, older. His voice was almost relaxed. He was angry and cursing but he didn't seem like a novice."

"I should have made sure you got home okay," Pete said.

"Oh, stop that already," Jackie said, looking at Pete. "As much as you'd like to, you can't take the blame for everything. I eventually had to go home, so I would have run into this guy then. I'm just frustrated they didn't catch him."

"What do you know about the church Roger was a part of?" Pete asked. "La Iglesia de la Luz doesn't exactly have a great rep here, at least based on what Harras told me."

Jackie nodded and opened one of her desk's bottom drawers. She pulled out a business card and tossed it to Pete.

"Talk to this dude," she said. "He's an expert on cult-y things. Used to be the reporter on the religion beat at the *Times* when the paper had the budget to have a religion beat. Now he teaches at FIU's north campus."

Pete looked at the card: Lonnie McQueen. The name rang a bell, but Pete didn't think he'd ever worked with the man. He slid the card into his back pocket.

"Done and done," Pete said.

Pete expected some kind of reaction from Jackie—a signal that the pain over her niece's disappearance and murder was still fresh. But she just she pushed back from her desk and stood up. Jackie Cruz was too busy to dwell.

"I think you have enough to get started," she said. "Let me know if you need money or whatever it is you two do to validate your work and I'll get it from the McRyans."

"Just like that?" Kathy said, still in her seat.

"Just like that."

CHAPTER FIFTEEN

"**H**ow the hell did McRyan swing this?"

Kathy's words were muted by the sudden gust of wind pelting her, Pete, Jackie and the crowd of people gathered around the podium, which stood at the top of the stairs that led up from the North Villa facade of the Vizcaya Museum and Gardens in downtown Miami. The museum rested off Biscayne Bay in Coconut Grove, as notable a landmark as you would get in Miami, and one that was not usually reserved for political speeches, much less those given by little-known state officials looking to run for higher office.

"Money, honey," Pete said, sliding a pair of reflective sunglasses over his eyes and giving her his best attempt at a winning smile. She stuck out her tongue in response.

He felt uncomfortable in his dark suit, the only one he'd packed for the trip, which was feeling more like a move. Pete, Kathy and Jackie were standing in a cluster of about twenty people that surrounded the podium, waiting for the candidate—or candidate-to-be—to appear and wow the masses waiting on the other side of the lush and sun-drenched garden with his populist words and Kennedy-esque phrasing. People were hungry for a candidate they could believe in, or at least try to, Pete thought. In this age of Twitter rants and viral scandals, voters seemed more frantic and desperate in their quest to find anyone who stood for something, even if it was only a ruse.

Decades before, Vizcaya had been the sprawling, ostentatious winter home of retired millionaire businessman James Deering. It was one of a handful of places that caused even the most jaded Miamians to pause and take notice—its rustic and elaborate Mediterranean Revival architecture stressing the landmark's patios, balconies and courtyards, creating a stark and welcome disconnect from Miami's congested highways and urban sprawl.

Pete gazed out toward the crowd, seeing an array of people—from the well manicured and spotlessly dressed to the more working class and, in surprising patches, the young. Teenagers, twentysomethings, male and female. For a moment, Pete felt almost hopeful himself. He was interrupted by a tap on his shoulder. He turned to see Jackie, in a slinky black dress, her hair sleek and flowing around her face, her strong features accentuated by a wisp of makeup. Seeing her up close took Pete back to his dream from a few nights before, and he tried to stay focused on the present.

"McRyan's coming out soon," she said, looking at Pete and Kathy, nodding toward the other side of the makeshift dais. "His wife is over there. She wants to chat with you if you have a minute."

Pete nodded and followed Jackie. He didn't feel Kathy behind him and realized she was staying back. Despite Pete's clearing the air upon his return to Miami, the tension between them hadn't fully washed away, and Kathy wasn't yet completely onboard with Pete and the case.

As Pete and Jackie approached, Mrs. McRyan smiled.

"Thank you so much for coming," she said, giving Pete her best First Lady-in-Waiting smile. "It means a lot to Trevor that you're here."

Jackie smiled and nodded. Pete took Mrs. McRyan's hand and shook it gently.

"Should be a great day for your husband," he said.

Mrs. McRyan drew closer to Pete, her smile unchanged, but her eyes hardening as she moved her face next to his, her mouth near his ear.

"Have you found him? Our son?"

"No, not yet," Pete said, matching her whisper. "I'm a night or two behind him. From what I can tell, he was crashing somewhere near Delray Beach."

That sign of progress didn't have the desired effect. Pete saw Mrs. McRyan's face go from faux-smile to a mix of dread and anger—then, as if by muscle memory, revert to her political smile.

"We need this resolved," she said. "As soon as possible. I hope you realize how urgent this is for us—for me—for the state."

Pete started to respond but stopped as the music began. The notes were familiar, and once the vocals kicked in, Pete turned his face away from Mrs. McRyan, unable to mask the smile on his face.

"Gloria Estefan?"

"Of course, bro," Jackie said. "What's more Miami than 'Get On Your Feet'? I think it's a great campaign song."

The music continued to boom, now challenged by the roar of the crowd, an eager, hungry cry that hit the podium in waves. He nodded toward Mrs. McRyan and followed Jackie back to their spot behind the podium and next to Kathy. Pete rarely did political events. It wasn't his scene. He was unprepared for a response like this, with such a range of people clamoring for a chance to get a glimpse of a politician Pete would have been hard-pressed to recognize just a few months back. He leaned toward Kathy and almost yelled into her ear.

"This is insane."

"People love this guy," she said.

For a moment, their eyes met, their faces inches apart. She turned back to her previous position hastily.

He didn't have much time to linger over it, as the sound from the crowd reached an even more feverish pitch and McRyan walked up onto the stage, stepping up to the podium gingerly, like a seasoned quarterback jogging to the huddle—polished, prepared, calm. He looked impeccable in a dark blue suit and sharp red tie. His hair, despite the wind and humidity, looked almost helmet-like, silver-gray and without a strand out of place. He didn't just look like the frontrunner to be the next governor of Florida, Pete thought, he looked damned presidential.

"Wow," Jackie said, her voice cutting through the clamor.

"Does he deliver?" Pete asked.

"Check it out for yourself."

"What a beautiful day," McRyan said, gripping the sides of the podium, smiling out into the crowd, a knowing grin on his face. "What a great day to be in Miami, huh?"

The crowd responded with a deafening cheer. Pete noticed a few handmade signs were popping up—McRyan's Our Guy! and Unido con McRyan!—billowing as the wind slapped the crowd and tried to ruffle McRyan's helmet of hair. The energy was electric. Pete felt like he was watching a killer rock band at the height of their popularity. *These people loved him.*

"My friends, *mi familia*," McRyan said, leaning forward, the cheers softening enough to allow for him to be heard by the teeming crowd. "Let's not dance around this: Florida needs change. Florida needs a new leadership—a leadership interested in you, especially, and not in special interests. A leadership that works for the working class, not in spite of it, lining the pockets of the already rich. A leadership that is about progress, not passivity or obstruction. A leadership that helps those in need without expectation or a price tag. A leadership that celebrates the diverse, beautiful culture of this state and doesn't pull us back into the Dark Ages."

McRyan slammed his fist down on the podium, startling Pete. The crowd screamed joyfully in response. Pete let his eyes dance over the masses. Young men and women shrieked without inhibition. People waved signs with a frantic fervor that he thought was only reserved for sporting events, and a smattering of older attendees clapped and cheered as if they were being transported back to a rally from 1968. Even standing where he was, a few feet from McRyan, Pete was having trouble making out what he was saying over the cheering. It got even harder when McRyan uttered the words all the people in the audience had come to hear.

"With that in mind, my fellow Floridians, my friends, *mis hermanos y hermanas*," McRyan said, yelling into the mic now, struggling to be heard, "I humbly announce that I will run for governor of the state of Florida! With your help, we can make great change together. I cannot do it alone, but—"

At first, Pete thought the sound had come from far away, a celebratory shot from some kind of military salute, or some drunks who thought shooting guns into the air was acceptable. But then he saw McRyan slump forward, his hands clutching the podium, trying to hold himself up, a dark hole in the back of his blue suit, blood spreading out of it, seeping into his clothes.

The screams of excitement were now a cacophony of panic, the sound of scrambling feet and mania building as McRyan struggled to stay upright, his head lolling forward, looking around as if to catch sight of the bullet that was now making its way through his internal organs. Pete felt Kathy's hand pulling him down, and he let himself fall into a crouch, Jackie now in front of him, moving toward McRyan, not bothering to duck. She forced past him, using her forearm to shove him back as the second shot—it was clearer to Pete now, a rifle, high-powered, from above and behind them—cracked through the pristine Miami day, taking a huge chunk of McRyan's scalp. Pete saw blood and brain matter spray out, and watched as the just-announced gubernatorial candidate was plowed forward by the gunshot's momentum, sending him and the podium off the stage, toppling down the long flight of stairs that led to the crowd, which was mostly gone now, the people charging away from the scene, like animals startled by a lion's roar.

Pete's ears were ringing, his eyes on the space where McRyan had once stood, now replaced by Jackie, her hands tugging at her hair, confused. Despite the noise in his head, he heard sirens, an endless echo of them, which was not an auditory trick—he envisioned a swarm of police cars and ambulances heading down Miracle Mile as the word spread: gunfire at Vizcaya.

Pete got up, shaking off Kathy's grip, and walked toward Jackie, who was stepping backward, each step hesitant and shaky. He reached out, his hand on her shoulder, and she turned with a start. Her eyes were glassy and dazed. Pete could see Mrs. McRyan on the far end of the stage, crying and screaming while a bodyguard tried to pry her away from danger.

"He's gone," Pete said, trying to pull Jackie back to them, to some kind of safety.

"No, no, how did this happen?" she said. With a burst of strength, she shoved Pete back toward the rear of the stage, taking a few steps toward him as he stumbled.

The next gunshot seemed louder, no longer muffled by the roaring crowd or McRyan's speech, booming over the fading screams. It was followed by the loud, dull thump of Jackie's body as it slammed backward onto the floor, her head snapping forward as she hit the terrazzo tile, a low cracking sound as she landed. Pete rushed forward, staying low, not sure if another shot was coming.

"Pete, no," Kathy said, her voice sounding like a garbled phone call, his ears still clanging from the shots. He ignored her. He had to reach Jackie.

She was flat on her back, her arms trying to cover the hole in her chest from the bullet that had entered from behind, blood bubbling under her hands. Jackie's eyes were wide with surprise, her shoulders shaking, her mouth already spitting up blood.

"No," Pete said, kneeling down next to her.

"No, no, no," he said, his hand on Jackie's shoulder, her body shivering on the ground, her eyes rolling back into her head.

"Jesus, Jackie, no," Pete said, on the floor now, trying to cover the wound, blood all over his hands and shirt and face.

She coughed—blood gurgling up and out of her mouth, her eyes cloudy and distant now, straining, trying to find something.

For a second, they met his—she saw him, and she tried to force a smile through the pain and shock. She was shaking more now, the blood pooling under her and around her, her face growing paler and her hands—gripping Pete's arms as he tried to stop the bleeding— loosened their grip. Pete could hear people around him, more sirens in the distance. He felt Kathy standing next to him, heard her cry, a low, jagged sound that made Pete think of his childhood.

"No," Pete said again, his words more a sob than speech.

"Oh, Pete, I wanted to ... I wanted to fix this for ... Patty," she said, each word a strain, like a wheezing breath, her mouth red, her teeth stained with blood, her face quivering. "It's on ... it's on you now ... I'm sorry."

PART III:
HELL IS CHROME

CHAPTER SIXTEEN

The trip to Mercy Hospital felt like a formality. Pete sat in the waiting room, his white shirt speckled with Jackie's blood, a blank, empty stare on his bruised face. Kathy sat next to him, her legs folded up on the seat, her forehead resting on her knees. The waiting area, which had resembled a war room just an hour before, was now eerily quiet.

The voice of the newscaster on the lone working TV set mounted above the nurse's station recapped the afternoon's events for what felt like the hundredth time. The thirtysomething brunette named Tatiana Ordoñez delivered the latest in a flat, dull monotone.

"A shocking, bloody turn of events today out of Vizcaya as rising star politician Trevor McRyan, a state senator who represented Florida's northwestern fifth district, was gunned down by an assassin's bullet just moments after announcing his plans to run for governor in the 2020 election. McRyan was rushed to Mercy Hospital but was listed as dead on arrival. **The Miami Police Department is not commenting on the investigation but a spokesperson confirmed there are no suspects in custody. McRyan was not the only victim of the attack, as well-known Miami attorney Jackie Cruz, who defended the recently exonerated ex-Miami cop Gaspar Varela, was felled by a final bullet a few moments after McRyan was shot.**

The screen flickered off. Pete looked up and saw Robert Harras enter the waiting room, looking even more haggard than the last time Pete had seen him. He made a beeline for Pete and Kathy. When he reached them, he placed a hand on Pete's shoulder, a sign of affection tantamount to a kiss on the cheek for the ex-FBI agent.

"I came as soon as I heard," he said, his voice clipped and cracked.

Pete wasn't sure what to say. He was pulling himself out of a state of shock, and what he discovered in its place was chaos: in less than five minutes, Pete had lost one of his closest friends and his client. His mind was filled with a jumble of images and moments that he felt would forever be seen through the prism of Jackie's death: her sly, conspiratorial smile; the sound of her cutting laugh; the dull look in her eyes that appeared before she had to share bad news. It was all past-tense now. She was gone, and all Pete was left with were questions: Who would want Jackie dead and why?

Kathy looked up for at Harras moment, shook her head, and returned to her previous position.

Harras motioned toward the empty seat to Pete's left. Pete nodded and he sat.

"You should both go home," Harras said.

"They said they might need to ask us more questions," Pete said. His voice came through sounding more like a plea than a statement of fact.

"They don't," Harras said, his tone sympathetic. "And if they do, just let me know where they can find you. There's no point sitting here. You're torturing yourself."

"What else is new?" Kathy said, still not lifting her head to face them, her voice sounding like it was coming through a tunnel.

Pete ignored her. He knew she was trying to manage her shock as best she could. Sometimes that came out as misplaced sarcasm.

"Did the cops say anything else?" Pete asked.

"Not really," Harras said. "I'm technically retired, and even when I was FBI, Miami PD wasn't keen on me sticking my nose in their cases. Now they can tell me to fuck off, outright, especially after the stuff with Los Enfermos last year."

Pete looked at his friend. Harras was sitting on the edge of the seat, his legs open wide and rubbing his hands together. He was jittery, anxious.

What else is going on with you?

"But I think you were wrong to come here," Harras said, eyes on Pete. "To Miami. I shouldn't have asked you back."

Kathy lifted her head.

"What the fuck are you talking about?" she said.

"The target was McRyan," Harras said. "That's obvious enough to anyone; you don't need a badge for that. But why Jackie?"

"She was helping McRyan with his campaign? I dunno," Kathy said, leaning back in the chair and letting out a long, exhausted sigh. "We can't solve this sitting here, on that point you're right."

"The cops told me what happened from their perspective," Harras said, still looking at Pete. "But that's not enough."

"What do you mean?" Pete asked.

"Tell me what you saw."

"McRyan went down, Jackie stepped up toward him, I moved towards her and she shoved me back," he said. "Then she got shot."

"Did you wonder why she pushed you away?" Harras said. "Why she stepped back?"

Pete's eyes widened. Harras nodded.

"Jackie Cruz was a tough attorney, and she handled controversial cases," Harras said. "But from what I can glean from my sources, she wasn't exactly on anyone's shit list. Everything she did was out in the open. You, on the other hand, don't fall into the same category."

Harras stood up.

"You think they were gunning for me?" Pete asked. The guilt he'd already felt over coming back and taking Jackie's case spread at an alarming rate, like a pool of dark blood on a faded linoleum floor.

"Whoever wanted McRyan dead wanted to take you with him," Harras said. "And they don't strike me as the types that shrug their shoulders and give up when they miss."

Kathy set him up on her couch with a blanket and a few pillows. After the hospital, Pete had made a pit stop at his hotel and gathered his small collection of belongings before returning to Kathy's place. Now wasn't a time to be sitting in a hotel room alone. He grabbed a pair of shorts and a shirt from his suitcase and went into the bathroom to change. When he returned, she was sitting in front of the television, a glass of white wine in her hand. She'd changed, too, into black pajama bottoms and a pink tank top. It was close to three in the morning.

Harras had left the hospital shortly after his ominous speech, but not before suggesting Pete request some form of police protection. Pete declined. If he'd been less exhausted, he would have found the idea of the Miami Police Department protecting him hilarious. He plopped down on the couch and watched Kathy scroll through her phone, as she sipped hungrily from her glass.

"Dave called," she said.

"Oh?"

"Yes," she said. "Don't worry—he asked if we were okay."

"I guess there's still hope for getting the band back together."

"Mild concern over whether someone was murdered is not synonymous with liking said person."

"Ouch."

She turned to face him, dropping the phone on the small coffee table that separated her from the couch.

"What are your plans?"

"I intend to sleep," he said.

"After that."

"Well, what do you think?" Pete said, anger creeping into his voice. "We have to find out who did this. We have to find the McRyan kid. We have to figure out how it ties into Patty Morales. I don't know where it ends, honestly. I don't know."

"Just checking," she said. "You've been extra waffly and weird lately, so I didn't want to assume. You're welcome to stay here, of course. I'll have to take some time off from work."

"Thanks," he said. "We can get down to business tomorrow. I just need to sleep and clear my head. I still can't believe she's gone."

Kathy nodded.

"I'm sorry," she said. "I should probably have something more meaningful to say, but I don't."

Kathy's phone buzzed on the table. She picked it up and looked at the display. Her forehead crinkled.

"Again?" she said. "Dave, did you butt dial me?"

Her expression went from confusion to concern.

"Wait, what?" she said. "That's not possible—we just saw … already?"

"What happened?" Pete asked.

"Okay, okay, calm down," Kathy said, still talking to Dave. "Let me talk to Pete and we'll go from there."

She hung up and put the phone back on the table. Her hand was shaking.

"They found the shooter," she said, running a hand through her hair as she looked at Pete, her brow furrowed in confusion. "They got the guy who killed McRyan … and Jackie."

"What?" Pete said, leaning forward. "Who was it?"

"Harras," she said. "They've arrested Robert Harras for the murder."

CHAPTER SEVENTEEN

Pete didn't think he could miss Jackie Cruz any more. But in this moment, he did. He was hamstrung, and the two friends Pete often relied on to untangle legal and police matters were dead or behind bars. This left him, Kathy and now Dave, sitting in Kathy's apartment, glued to the television set, waiting for people to call back and for something else, ideally not terrible, to happen.

There was little new information circulating on the TV news, though. Local stations only had the bare minimum. "Retired FBI agent brought in for questioning under suspicion" morphed into "ex-FBI agent a suspect in McRyan murder, arrested at his home" in a few hours. Getting in to see Harras would be impossible. Even Jackie would have had trouble swinging that, but she'd have gotten them close. Close enough for Harras to call in a few favors and seal the deal, if he wasn't the guy sitting in a room waiting to be questioned for the thirtieth time by some rookie detective with *frijoles* and *cafecito* stains on his off-the-rack suit.

It was late morning now, and they had slept little, just a few hours before dawn, as they had waited for Dave to arrive. Pete's old friend was cold to him, distant and angry, but trying to hide it. He only spoke to Pete when he had to, if a question or comment was directed at him and there was no way to ignore it. Otherwise, he said everything he needed to say to Kathy. He had a line on Harras' lawyer, a slick Coconut Grove criminal-defense attorney who Harras—and a lot of other paranoid law enforcement types—kept on their "top friends" lists. Guy's name was Edwin Gustines and he'd never met a bottle of hair gel he didn't like. Or so Dave said. As the clock ticked toward noon and the news cycle creaked toward another, sexier story, that was all they had. So they waited.

Kathy's apartment was silent aside from the background noise emanating from the television, which discussed the McRyan assassination in between updates on a new tropical storm named Elizabeth that seemed headed their way, and the occasional clatter from the kitchen when someone shambled in to fix a sandwich or get a drink. *Processing.* That's what Pete had said when Kathy asked him how he was doing. He was processing. Trying to figure out how the nightmare he'd seen unspool in his mind less than twenty-four hours earlier could actually be true. It seemed that no matter how much his life had changed, it still dragged him back to this place, under similar circumstances: tired, homeless, staring into darkness with only Kathy by his side to help navigate it. It would almost sound romantic if it wasn't so dire, like a song by The Smiths you can only bear to listen to every few years.

"I'm sorry we didn't talk," Pete said to Dave, who was seated on Kathy's recliner, checking his phone. Pete was on the couch, his base of operations for what felt like a decade.

No response. Pete tried again.

"I needed some space," he said. "From everything. Miami, Kathy, you, Harras. I had to step back."

"Well, mission fucking accomplished," Dave said, not looking up from his phone. "You did it. Another point goes to insensitive asshole Pete Fernandez. You alienated the only three or four people who seemed to give a fuck about you, even after you alienated an entire city. I'm impressed. But, newsflash, bro? We're all busy. We're all going through some shit. But that's not the way to treat people you call friends."

"You're right," Pete said. "I don't know what else to say. Miami overwhelms you sometimes."

"Yet you came back," Dave said, looking up at Pete for the first time.

"I did," Pete said.

"Kathy told me about you guys," Dave said, clearing his throat, the shift in subject sudden.

"She did?"

"Yeah," Dave said. "I'm surprised it took so long."

"It was a bad idea."

"Why's that?" Dave said. "Would you say that if she was sitting here?"

"We're friends," Pete said. "We shouldn't have turned it into something else."

"Why'd it stop?"

"I wasn't ready to get into anything serious," Pete said, avoiding eye contact. "It was a bad idea."

"Did she agree with you?"

"She was pissed," Pete said. "She's still pissed."

"I see a trend forming when it comes to your former friends," Dave said. "Do you still have feelings for her?"

"I'm not sure. Like I said—"

"You're not ready," Dave said, mimicking Pete's voice. "I heard you. Not for nothing, *amigo*, and I get that we haven't seen each other in a good long while, but when will you be ready?"

"Maybe never."

"Jesus."

"What?" Pete said.

"This martyr thing is a real bummer, man," Dave said, throwing his hands up, the last word dragging out like an exasperated breath. "We all know you. We know you fucked up before. We know you're a drunk and you made big, cosmic mistakes. Why does that mean you can't do anything that'll make you happy? This whole hiding out in

New York, suffering in that Godforsaken cold, not even in fucking Manhattan—Jesus!— but some dead-end town in Rockland of all places. Why not just jump in front of a Metro North train, dude?"

"Kathy's smart, beautiful, and successful," Pete said, counting the compliments off on his fingers, like a diligent scorekeeper. "She can do better than me."

"Maybe she doesn't want to."

"Did she say that?"

Dave shrugged and took a swig from the beer resting on the floor by the chair. It was not too early for him.

"She didn't say anything that overt," Dave said. "You'll have to figure that out for yourself. Y'know, if you're ever ready."

"I need to pick your brain on something," Pete said, changing the subject. He couldn't worry about Kathy now.

"Don't get too cozy, alright?" Dave said. "I'm pissed off at you. I hope that's clear. But I know how much Jackie meant to you, so I'll help. So, shoot."

"What do you know about Iglesia de la Luz?"

Dave let out a quick cough, as if choking on something he hadn't chewed properly.

"Say again?"

"La Iglesia de la Luz," Pete said. "It's a cult or religious group. It was pretty big in Miami in the late eighties, early nineties. I'm trying to figure out if it's still around."

"It's around," Dave said, grabbing his beer and finishing it off. "Yup."

Dave wasn't the type to clam up, which was the first warning sign for Pete. He pressed on.

"I came down here on a case for McRyan—well, for him and his wife. They wanted me to find their son. Normally, I would have passed, but this guy was familiar. I'd seen him before," Pete said. "Do you remember the Patty Morales case? The dead teenager?"

"Right," Pete said. "So, a few days ago, the McRyans are in my office in New York, asking me to find their son, who happens to look just like a guy named Kenny Sampson. Sampson was the guy who popped up, claiming to know the truth about Patty's death—and then disappeared—right before I found her, uh, remains."

"So did you find their son?" Dave asked, more interested now. "What did they want with him? Was he causing trouble for them?"

"I don't know," Pete said, his voice getting lower. "Trevor McRyan got shot before I could figure it out. He's dead. Jackie's dead. This whole thing is spinning out and I'm not sure what to grab onto yet. Something's eating at me about this McRyan thing, and about Patty Morales. There's a thread there that weaves through all these cases, and it might mean looking into this cult, or what's left of it. But I need to know where to start, otherwise we're flying blind."

Dave ran his fingers through his long brown beard. His eyes seemed distant, but Pete knew he was just working things out in his head.

"Well, first suggestion," Dave said. "Don't call it a cult."

Pete laughed. "Got it."

"Iglesia de la Luz was hot shit when we were kids," Dave said, his eyes bouncing around the apartment. "It was the hip thing to do. Rappers, politicians, even one of the original Marlins were members. It was basically Scientology minus the science in Miami. It was all over my high school, even though it was a strict Catholic private school. The head dude—Figueras—was all over TV for a while. He made Jim and Tammy Bakker seem tame. People gave up everything to follow him. Jobs, savings, left their families. The guy drew a crowd, too. I'm talking rallies, marches, big ceremonies in the streets. Sometimes he'd hold these massive revivals way down south, by the Redlands. Had a walk-in church in Little Havana with sermons every night. Packed. He'd do the circuit, too, tour the country and talk about all the right things. His most hardcore followers even hinted that he was divine, a son of God who could heal the sick and see the future. Kind of thing that nowadays would get you torched on social media. People ate it up. He preached love, brotherhood, all the buzzwords. Even the Cuban *viejos* were behind him for a while."

"What's left of the group is in the Keys, right?" Pete asked, trying to compare Dave's version with what Harras told him. "They moved there after Figueras got busted?"

"Yeah," Dave said. "There's a compound further south—Key West, I think. It's a big farm. That's where Figueras and his followers live. And their influence beyond that property is zilch, I hear."

Dave heard a lot. Though just a humble bookstore owner at the moment, Dave had a murky and winding past that connected him to a lot of the Miami underworld's seedier characters. The guy was tapped in, and that connection had helped Pete and Kathy out on numerous occasions.

"Anyway, the thing is, Jackie's half-brother, Roger Morales, and Patty's dad," Pete said, "was part of Iglesia de la Luz."

"That sounds like a clue," Dave said. "Sounds like a lot of work for a detective like you. More than a day or two. You gonna stick around for a bit?"

Pete looked around. The apartment felt smaller.

"Until this gets figured out, yeah," Pete said. "As long as I can get some help."

"I'll help Kathy as much as she needs," Dave said, shrugging. "We can play the rest by ear."

Before Pete could respond, Kathy's cell phone chimed in the other room.

"Your friend is in deep shit," the voice said, squawking out of Kathy's iPhone, the speakerphone's bleating dominating the living room. Dave, Pete and Kathy stood around the coffee table, as if waiting for some kind of divine intervention that would wake them from what was becoming a long, meandering nightmare.

The pitter-patter voice, terse and not wasting a syllable, belonged to Edwin Gustines, Harras' newly minted lawyer. He did not sound optimistic.

"How deep?" Pete asked.

They heard a muffled noise from the other end, then Gustines cleared his throat.

"Look, I can't get into it too much over the phone," he said. "And I don't really have time to meet with his fan club. I'm supposed to be working this case for him, and after just a quick conversation with the police, I'm pretty sure this will require my complete attention."

"We can help you," Kathy said. "We've done stuff like this before."

"Sure, sure, I know who you are," Gustines said. "I also know that when you do 'stuff like this,' people die and things blow up. So, sorry, lady, count me out. The fact is, the cops have evidence—concrete evidence—that they found at my client's place that I now need to explain away. They also found posts from these obscure websites— like, not Facebook, but some secret, dark-web shit—that don't really make your friend seem like he was all there, *tu sabes*? I'll be honest with you, and hey, I have a healthy, well-fed ego, but this shit is gonna be tough for me to overcome. And if it leaks to the press? Your pal is fucked, no matter how much he denies everything—which he is, of course, without any prodding from me. But still, if that comes out, he's guilty before he even steps into a courtroom."

"How is he?" Pete asked.

"How is he? How do you think? You ever faced murder charges? No, wait, let me update that—have you ever faced murder charges that involved the most beloved politician in this swamp since Lawton Chiles took a hike? Deserved or not, people were creaming their pants for this McRyan guy, already talking president and whatever. Stupid shit. Anyway, here's your answer: no, you've never faced that. So, yeah, he's not well. He's an old ex-FBI agent facing the rest of his life in prison for a crime that instantly makes him more hated than Scott Peterson. He's definitely had better days. A future that could see him locked up with a ton of people he's had arrested is not exactly rosy."

"That's it, then?" Kathy said, her voice sounding desperate, almost pleading. "There's nothing we can do?"

"Sure, honey," Gustines said. "You can light a *velita* for Harras and hope we get a wimpy judge and the DA forgets how much evidence they have against him, yeah. That would be helpful."

"Did he ask you to tell us anything?" Pete said. Dave shot him a confused look.

There was a pause on the other line before Gustines spoke again.

"Now that you mention it," Gustines said. Pete heard rustling on the other end, like someone flipping pages on a notebook. "He did, yeah. I almost forgot to tell you. Made little sense to me, and I didn't have time to get an explanation. Anyway, he says to look at Morales.

He says to follow Morales and his trail, that it'll take you to the answer. Who's Morales, anyway? Anyone we can pin the crime on?"

Pete pushed the red button on the phone and ended the call.

CHAPTER EIGHTEEN

Pete slid the flathead screwdriver into the window frame next to the front door of Jackie Cruz's West Kendall townhouse. It was close to three in the morning. The call with Gustines had set the tone for the rest of the day, and by nightfall, Pete couldn't sleep, his mind under attack from visions of Trevor McRyan crumbling into himself, of Jackie's shivering body on the reddening floor. In the middle of the night, after tossing and turning for a few hours, Pete got up and left Kathy's apartment. He didn't want to sit and think of a plan. He didn't want to strategize alternative or potential outcomes. He wanted to do something. He left his phone in the car, parked a few blocks away. This was off the grid.

Jackie used to be Pete's lifesaver—his literal get-out-of-jail-free card. Unlike other, more flush PIs, Pete couldn't afford having a lawyer on retainer, and most of the lawyers he knew wouldn't give him the time of day. But he and Jackie had a history. So, whenever he found himself in a jam, he knew it would just take a call, some pleading, and she'd show up and work her magic. This would not happen tonight. Or ever again.

The window gave and creaked up. Pete pocketed the screwdriver and opened it. He lifted the screen and crawled into the two-story townhouse. She lived in a West Kendall complex called Lakes of the Meadow—a collection of dirt brown three-bedroom Mission-style bungalows with tiled roofs and arches. Just carbon-copy houses sitting in a row. Pete remembered when Jackie bought the place— she'd just landed a bigger job, was finally making some money and wanted to lay down roots. He'd been proud of her. Or tried to be. His mind had been brined by alcohol, but he cared, with the five percent of his brain that could sometimes think about the well-being of others.

He groped around in the darkness—his gloved hands reaching out tentatively to prevent him from knocking anything over. After turning left, he found the stairs that led to Jackie's bedroom and office, the steps he'd wandered through just a few nights before, under very different circumstances. He walked up and made another left into her large bedroom. He dug into his front pocket, pulled out a tiny flashlight and flipped it on. The room was not heavy with knickknacks or decorations—only a few photos of family and a stuffed white tiger on her unmade bed. The dresser was bare aside from a jewelry box and her laptop. He grabbed the computer and slid it into his backpack. Pete could hear Kathy yelling at him in his head. He persisted.

The room smelled slightly of incense and mint. The dresser drawers revealed little beyond what was expected—underwear, socks, bras and a few photos of exes, Pete not included. He moved to the small closet and turned the light on—it was full of dresses, fewer shoes than Pete would have expected and, tucked under a row of business suits, a small metal cabinet. Pete crouched down and tried the door. Locked. He said a quick prayer and pulled out the screwdriver, jamming it into the cabinet's lock—slowly at first but then harder. He heard a crack and the door opened—as if it was letting out a final gasp.

The cabinet was mostly empty. There was a stack of unused folders, a few pens and a tape dispenser sans tape. Pete cleared through the collection of lost office supplies and found something else. Two heavy file folders hidden under a few unopened stacks of copy paper. One was familiar to Pete. It was the same folder Jackie had gone over with him just a few nights prior. He pulled the second file out and started to flip through the pages—medical reports, photos, Post-it notes in Jackie's flowery handwriting, and a few handwritten pages of legal pad paper. The folder was labeled *PM*.

A creaking sound.

Steps on the stairs.

Pete slid both folders into his backpack and walked out of the closet. The footfalls were still coming. Not hesitating. Whoever was in the house expected no one else to be there. He inched toward the far side of the room—which had a small balcony that looked out onto a shared courtyard. He opened the pink, door-length shades to get to the sliding glass doors that opened onto the balcony. Someone was fiddling with the door. The tiny balcony—about a fifth of the size of the bedroom—was surrounded by a short, black iron railing. Pete positioned himself to the right of the balcony doors, trying to avoid being seen, and looped one leg over the railing, making sure he didn't slip. Holding on, he did the same with his other foot.

The balcony door shattered, the glass spraying over Pete, sharp pieces swarming him as the rest of the window crumbled to the floor. Pete had heard nothing before the glass exploded, but all that meant was whoever was in the room had a silencer and no qualms about using it.

Pete crouched and let his feet dangle as he held himself up on the railing, and inched his body down, trying to minimize the size of the jump he'd have to make. After a few moments, he let go and landed on his feet. Hard. Pain shot up his legs, but it didn't feel like anything was broken or bruised too badly. He looked up and saw a tall, built man in a black turtleneck and black jeans to match his black ski mask looking down at him. He had a gun pointed at Pete.

"Drop the bag," the man said, his voice muffled and low.

Pete sprinted forward, under the balcony where the man stood, unleashing a series of expletives. He waited a moment—half expecting to hear a spray of bullets rain down on him from above. But although it was late in the evening, Pete guessed that the man didn't want to draw too much attention to himself. Miami was known for being the kind of town where neighbors closed their blinds and ignored the drama going down at the end of the block, but the residents of Lakes of the Meadow wouldn't ignore gunfire across the way, even if it was muffled by a silencer.

Pete heard the bedroom door close and ran around the corner outside of the townhouse and onto one of the small streets that made up the complex. He could hear steps behind him. He didn't turn around. He cut right, onto a grassy area with some short palms that surrounded a man-made lake and provided some cover. Pete glanced back and saw the man in black hesitate, looking around.

Pete sped down the shore of the lake, his sneakers slapping the moist ground. He was running out of steam. He wasn't used to this kind of workout, and his bag was loaded down with the files. He reached the end of the lake and the winding sidewalk that lead out of the complex to a large intersection. Pete hung a right and after a block found his rental car. He tossed the bag inside and gave himself a moment to look into his rearview mirror. The man was charging toward the car, about half a block away. Pete put the car in drive and sped off. He didn't look back, his foot heavy on the accelerator, the car wheezing as he turned onto the first street he could.

CHAPTER NINETEEN

"**Y**ou're unbelievable."

Kathy sat down across from Pete at the table in her tiny kitchen. The sole window in the room looked out on an alleyway of garbage cans.

She blew on her steaming cup of tea as she stared at Pete. It was close to five in the morning.

"Do you even know what you stole, you maniac?"

Pete stared at the ceiling. He was exhausted. Whatever energy he had disappeared the second he ditched the man with the silencer staking out Jackie's house.

"A bit," he said. "There's a lot to go over. I'd seen a bit of it before with Jackie, but there's another folder that's new to me."

Kathy placed a free hand on Pete's, clenching it for a second before retreating.

"I'm sorry for dragging you into this," Pete said. "Especially with everything—well, with everything that's happened. With us. To you."

Kathy waved him off.

145

"Stop it," she said. "Now's not the time to analyze why you're too stupid to realize how amazing I am."

Kathy got up and filled two glasses with tap water. She set one in front of Pete and returned to her chair.

"So, Roger Morales was part of some weird Miami killer cult," she said. "Iglesia de la Luz. He gets exonerated for the murder of his daughter. Somehow, Harras thinks this might help get him off for murdering McRyan in broad daylight. What else?"

"Jackie suggests the McRyans hire me to work for them to find their son, who she knows is the same guy who was wanted for questioning in the death of her niece," Pete said. "We start to sniff around and McRyan and Jackie end up dead."

"Do you have any way to contact Roger Morales?" Kathy asked. "Does he still live at his old house? I doubt it, mainly because it'd be freakishly weird if he still lived in the house where his daughter's remains were dumped, but hey, people are strange, as loser Jim Morrison sang."

"Hold that thought."

Pete got up and wandered into the living room. He grabbed his backpack and unzipped it, snaking his arm inside. He came back to the kitchen with the heavy folders, letting them drop on the small table. Kathy moved back, away from the table, as if Pete had just spilled a warm drink in front of her.

"Christmas came early?" she said.

Pete sat down and opened the top folder. He pulled out stacks of papers and spread them out on the table, then onto the empty chair to his right. Soon every surface was covered with papers.

"This is Patty's file," she said. "Well, pieces of it. Most of it seems to be from the time after her remains were found."

"Seems to be more than just her case file," Pete said. "The cops were looking at Roger pretty hard, too."

"Is that surprising?"

Kathy looked over Pete's shoulder at one of the documents.

"That's a signed affidavit from Roger's ex-wife," Kathy said. "And it doesn't look like a love letter."

"Patty's mom was adamant that Roger killed their daughter," Pete said. He flipped through a few pages. "This all hit right after her remains were found."

"Yet they didn't have enough to indict him?"

"Apparently not," Pete said.

He moved the affidavit over and reached for another, smaller pile of documents. Handwritten notes on legal paper. He passed a few pages to Kathy and took the top half for himself. They sat in silence for a while, the sounds of the streets interrupting the quiet every now and again. Honking horns, bursts of loud Spanish and the occasional wheeze of a bus slogging by. After spending almost a year in New York, Pete found himself comforted.

"These are dated after the case fizzled out—when they couldn't bring Morales in on charges," Kathy said. "Looks like Jackie was trying to work out alternate scenarios."

"Yeah," Pete said. "She has a list of all the key people the cops questioned or wanted to question—which isn't long. Roger Morales, Kenny Sampson, a.k.a. Stephen McRyan, and it looks like someone else's name was blacked out with a pen."

"Wait, what?" Kathy said, coming over to look at the paper. "How does that work? Were her notes edited?"

"By her, apparently," Pete said. "Jackie must have known of someone that the police were interested in, but she didn't want to risk anyone finding out their name from her notes."

"Do you think she knew she was in trouble?"

"Not sure," Pete said. "The notes are pretty recent—well, they were updated recently. Like, last week."

Pete handed Kathy the page he'd been looking at.

"See the writing? The newer notes are in black and she dated them '2017,' and the black pen crossed-out one is from 2013, when the case went cold a second time."

"Either she didn't want anyone to know about this person, which is weird," Kathy said. "Or maybe she thought there was no way they could be a suspect."

Pete put the notes down and reached over for the stack of interview transcripts. He scanned a few pages before answering.

"There's nothing in the official documents that Jackie had that tell us who was questioned or who they wanted to question, so she must have based her intel on something else—maybe her ex-husband, who was a cop, passed some stuff along," Pete said, "Aside from Morales, I know the police wanted to interview Sampson before he went AWOL. But he's nowhere to be found in the police file, not even as a person of interest or even in a section that's blacked out. That's consistent with what Jackie and I went over when I first got back."

"When you worked this case before," Kathy said, "did you intersect with the cops much? Or was it yanked away from you the second you tripped over where she was dumped?"

"I talked to one detective," Pete said. "Paul Brownstein. He was helpful, because he didn't treat me like a pest, but listened to what I'd figured out. But he still did things on his own terms and didn't much warm to me tagging along."

"Where is he now?"

"He died," Pete said.

"Care to elaborate on that or are we going to devolve to grunts and slaps?"

"I wish I knew more," Pete said. "One day I'm having coffee with the guy, after Jackie was attacked in her driveway. Then I come by the station and they tell me he's gone, died in his sleep."

"May I remind you, dearest Pete, that at the time this cop dropped dead, you were—albeit not officially—a fucking private investigator?" Kathy said with a dry laugh. "Did you not pursue this?"

Pete's jumped back to that moment, years ago, when he got the news that Brownstein was gone. He'd walked into the police station, a dirty, hazy vodka buzz making every step and thought slow and molasses-like, a few days shy of a warm shower and with a week's stubble on his face. He'd been reeling from the big break in the Morales case—the discovery of Patty's remains. He was all but certain it'd put Roger Morales behind bars. Pete had decided to go out, not to celebrate, but to numb himself, to block out the memories of that sweet, pretty girl and where she had ended up.

The bender had taken him from the shiny, neon-soaked corners of South Beach and Coral Gables to a dingy Little Haiti dive bar and then, finally, to his own house, where he'd dusted off a bottle of Belvedere he'd kept in a distant cabinet. The bottle had been his father's. Pedro rarely drank, and if he did, only had one or two. Pete, on the other hand, always drank. He drank to destroy himself, and that night, before he walked into the station, he wanted to obliterate any memory he had of Patty Morales, not caring what else the mushroom cloud of vodka took with it.

So, no, he hadn't pursued it. He'd been falling into a widening abyss before he'd even gotten the news that this detective Pete barely knew—but who'd also shown a microbe of kindness toward him—was dead. Heart attack? Overdose? Suicide? Pete didn't linger to hear the details. He got the gist of it. Paul Brownstein had died in his sleep, which marked another good cop dead while Pete, a drunk piece of shit, kept bumbling along, sticking his nose where it didn't belong and continuing to make things worse for everyone within a hundred-mile radius of him.

"I wasn't in the right headspace for that," Pete said finally.

Kathy had known Pete a long time. She knew his struggles and fears, inasmuch as he could share them with her, a normal person who could have a glass of wine or two and not have them devolve into a weeks-long bender. But as much as people who didn't have a drinking problem wanted to relate or sympathize with an alcoholic, Pete knew that it was impossible for them to truly get what being an addict was like. Pete couldn't expect a normal person to fully grasp that desperate sense of craving and need that could, immediately and without a care, overrule any other facet of a drunk's life. So, this slithering feeling that came with the rush of memory, the dirty, grimy coating of filth that seemed to trickle over him, would not be shaken off—could not go away easily, like a bad mood. The only thing it understood—the dark, virulent and rapacious disease that raged in his mind no matter how much or how little he drank—was despair and oblivion. The disease wanted Pete to drink, it wanted Pete to isolate himself and step away from his life, his friends and his responsibilities. And on that day, years ago, it didn't care about a nice cop. It only cared about any excuse it could muster to unleash an emptiness Pete could not describe to anyone but another alcoholic. A barren feeling that swallowed your hope and left you to die.

I don't deserve to live.

Kathy gave him a kind look and returned her gaze to the stack of papers arrayed in front of her.

Pete grabbed another pile of pages. "These look like Patty's."

"Patty's what?" Kathy asked.

"Medical records," Pete said. He plucked a lime-green Post-it note from the top page. "Well, the coroner's report. Jackie got her hands on these not too long ago."

"So, what killed her?"

"She'd been stabbed multiple times," Pete said, stopping for a second before continuing, letting the fact float between them. "Because the remains were so decayed over time, they could only identify her from dental records and there was no way of noting if she'd been sexually assaulted, but they could confirm that."

"So this poor girl was stabbed to death for doing nothing wrong except staying at school on the weekend to work on a project?" Kathy said. "That's what we're dealing with. A monster."

Kathy was silent for a moment.

"I don't care how long it's been," she said, her voice a sharp whisper. "Whoever this asshole is, he needs to go down, hard."

The late evening morphed into early morning and, thanks to a coffee-fueled second wind, found Pete and Kathy in the same spot at the small kitchen table, sifting through paper as the stereo shuffled through some early Springsteen—*Darkness on the Edge of Town, Born to Run* and *The River* adding to the somber mood.

Pete felt like he was tapped into Jackie's brain—there was a method to the file she'd built, and it all revolved around Patty and exonerating Roger Morales. But why hadn't she shared it when she met Pete, or after they'd met with Kathy? Was she planning to?

The last bit of paperwork to be reviewed was a small stack of stapled pages that consisted of old photocopied *Miami Times* clippings, dating as far back as the late 1980s. Many of the early stories were written by Chaz Bentley. Chaz was Kathy's father—the once-beloved *Miami Times* newspaper columnist who had hired Pete to find Kathy when she was kidnapped. Pete did find her, and in the process exposed the Silent Death, who Chaz had been working for. Chaz became a victim of his own murderous boss, but the traumatic situation had forged a friendship between Pete and Kathy. He owed a lot to the dead, alcoholic newspaperman.

It seemed, according to the first few clippings Pete was scanning over, that La Iglesia de la Luz had been under Chaz's watch for at least a year or two.

Pete slid some of the pages over to Kathy.

"Guess your dad was on the story," Pete said.

She looked them over.

"Yeah, actually, I do remember him talking about this—vaguely," Kathy said. "It was right before my parents got separated. He was having a tough time with it."

"How so?"

"No one was talking," Kathy said. "This cult had permeated every part of the city—I mean, everyone wanted to be part of it. Hell, it was almost fashionable. But no one was talking. It was all so secretive. Eventually, Chaz gave up."

"He just dropped the story?"

"Well, I guess you could put it that way. But it was more like there was no more story to write. You can only report what the facts or your sources tell you."

Pete grabbed the most recent story from the pile—a few years back—written by Ben Wilhoite. Someone who'd probably joined the paper after Pete was fired and climbed up the company's thinning ranks. Pete read the piece—a look back at La Iglesia de la Luz, fifteen years after its heyday. Pete felt his body push back. He was tired. The lines of text were blurring together. He hadn't even cracked open Jackie's laptop. But that might have to wait.

The story itself was standard—few people talked about the group anymore, and the church's leader, Jaime Figueras, had purchased land in the Keys as a final spot for his compound. La Iglesia now clocked in at around twenty members, a steep drop from the thousands that had followed him years before. Pete noticed that Jackie had highlighted two sentences toward the end that discussed where the church was now. Figueras declined to comment for the story. In fact, the story was light on sources—which wasn't a complete surprise. The one name that popped up was Ramon Medrano—a former member of the group who was now living in West Dade and trying to enjoy a quiet life while working security. Pete jotted the name down.

"I am exhausted," Kathy said, dropping the papers she was trying to read and letting out a long, winding yawn. "Brain done. Need sleep."

They both stood, ending up closer than they'd expected. Their eyes moved over each other. Pete felt himself inch toward her.

"You can take the couch," she said, turning away toward her bedroom.

"Sure," he said.

Kathy's bedroom door clicked shut and Pete heard the lock snap, leaving him alone with the morning's flickering light, slipping through the blinds, and his own scattered, uneasy thoughts.

CHAPTER TWENTY

Patty's father worked at El Dorado Furniture in Miami Gardens. If you grew up in Miami, it was likely that you had a sofa or dining room set from El Dorado, a chain of stores sprinkled over South Florida, started by a Cuban fleeing Castro. While the Miami Gardens location wasn't the shiniest or the busiest of the stores, it still adhered to the minimum quality requirements for an El Dorado. And good presentation went far.

Miami Gardens itself was a new city, born out of the construction of I-95, and previously known as Carol City. Incorporated less than twenty years earlier, the city was a mostly black and Hispanic, middle-income area. Still, Pete was surprised to find that Roger Morales, a former hospital administrator who had earned a salary in the six figures, was working as an assistant manager at a furniture store.

Pete had run a quick skiptrace on Morales and had gotten his basic info, a sign that his target wasn't trying to run or hide. Morales lived in a small studio apartment close to his job and seemed to do little else but go to work six days a week and hang out at home. Pete knew what that kind of isolation wrought, at least for him, and hoped Morales had found some peace to mix in with his loneliness and regrets.

The store was near the Palmetto Expressway, off 167th Street and 42nd Avenue. Pete and Kathy pulled into the parking lot, found a space a few rows from the entrance and made their way in. The place was well lit and welcoming, not crowded, and smelled of pine cleaner and coffee.

"Is this where Cubans get their … what do you call them, *pin-pan-puns*?" Kathy said, not looking at Pete.

"I think every Cuban family is just born with one," Pete said, referring to the thin rollaway beds that seemed to be part of every Miami Cuban household, in case guests stayed over, or an uncle or cousin fresh from Cuba needed a mattress before he got settled. It sounded funny now, but was probably essential in the early days after the Castro takeover and even into the current, somewhat inconsistent Cuban thaw. You never knew when someone would need a warm bed, even if it was a pretty uncomfortable one.

Before they made it too far into the expansive store, they were approached by a stocky, tan man with close-cropped black hair. He couldn't have been over forty-five, but looked like he'd lived a rough life—at a quick glance, Pete could tell his nose had been broken and his face was scarred by what had once been severe acne. Perhaps he'd been a boxer or some kind of athlete in his younger days. His nametag read LIONEL OLIVA.

"*¿Hola, como te puedo ayudar?*" he asked, smiling, his white teeth gleaming.

"We're looking for a friend of yours," Kathy said, not bothering to bumble her way through the conversation in Spanish. Lionel nodded, giving himself a second to process this tall, attractive woman cutting through any niceties and, unfortunately for him, any chance at making a decent commission.

"I see, well, who is this friend of mine?" Lionel asked.

"Roger Morales," Pete said. "He works here."

Lionel's eyebrows inched upward, as if he'd heard a salty joke in mixed company.

"Oh, Rogelio," he said. "Yes, he works here, *mi amigo*. But he is not a salesman, no. He is high up, *casi un* manager."

Lionel reverted to Spanglish to cover the words that didn't load for him as fast as he'd like. Pete got the meaning. Roger—or Rogelio—wasn't fully at the top of the ladder just yet, but he wasn't a floor salesman like him.

"Are you sure there's nothing I can help you with first?" he said. "We are having a fantastic sale on loveseats."

"We're here to speak with Roger," Kathy said. "Can you tell him we're here?"

"Yes, yes, *señorita*," Lionel said, lifting his hands up to show deferral. "Let me see if he is available. Can I ask what this is about?"

"His daughter," Pete said.

Lionel nodded then started to move. Before stepping away completely, he turned his gaze to Pete, his eyes thin slits.

"Can I ask your name, *amigo*?"

"Pete Fernandez."

"Ah, I knew it, I knew it," he said with a smile that was now more knowing than warm. "We have a celebrity here in our store. *Qué bien*. This must be very important for you to be back in Miami, after so much time, no?"

Pete didn't respond. He felt a shiver run through him, despite the ninety-degree heat outside.

"How's your *novia*?" Lionel asked, the smile still on his face, wider now.

"I'm not his girl—" Kathy said.

Lionel raised a hand in her direction.

"Not you, *Americanita*," Lionel said. "The policeman's daughter. Maya. Do you miss her? How terrible, what she did, eh? But maybe you don't think it's so bad?"

Lionel stepped closer to Pete, his voice a hushed growl now.

"You know what it's like to kill people, right?" he said, his mouth a few inches from Pete's ear. "Los Enfermos never forget. Especially an *hijo de puta* like you, okay? We see you. We know you are back. We're back, too."

Pete pushed Lionel Oliva away and stepped back, trying to silence the instinct to raise his fists. The move had caused a stir. Some people turned to look at the three of them.

Lionel raised his hands and moved away, still smiling.

"My apologies, *señor*, I slipped and got too close," he said, nodding. "I am wearing new shoes and you know how that is, I hope."

"Where's Morales?" Pete said. He could feel his heart pounding in his chest, a coat of sweat forming on his skin. How foolish he'd been. To traipse back into Miami and think no one would notice or care, that all would be forgotten and he could slip in, fix this one problem and scurry back to New York, like some kind of Cold War spy.

"Roger Morales?" Lionel asked, sliding a finger across his throat. "*No sé, compadre.*"

"Let's get out of here," Kathy said, tugging at Pete's arm. Pete followed, still staring Lionel down.

"So nice to see you, amigos," Lionel said, waving as they sped to the exit. "*Nos vemos pronto.* See you soon and come back again, okay? Maybe we find you that love seat, huh?"

"**S**hit."

"That sums it up," Kathy said, getting behind the wheel, Pete already seated next to her.

Pete checked his phone. Two missed calls. Both from Dave. He tapped his name and put it on speaker.

"We've got a problem," Dave said.

"I think we know," Pete said as Kathy pulled the car out of the lot and toward the Palmetto. "We just ran into one of Los Enfermos in an El Dorado, of all places. He knew we were coming. They know I'm back."

"What? Well, that's bad, but it's not even why I was calling," Dave said, the wind muffling his voice through the phone. "It's about Morales. He's dead."

"That explains our new friend's little hand gesture, I guess," Kathy said. "Those bloodthirsty Cuban gangsters sure are literal."

˷ shook his head, less at Kathy's comment and more at how ˷ɪngs seemed to be falling apart around them. Each time they formed a strategy, it fell apart before they could gain any momentum, as if someone had a copy of their plans as they made them.

"What happened to Morales?" Pete asked.

"Found dead in his home, gunshot blast to the chest," Dave said. "I only know because a buddy of mine is tapped into the Miami Gardens PD and the name jumped out at him. It'll be on the news soon, after they can alert whatever family he's got left."

Not much, Pete thought.

"We have to stay ahead of this, for once," Pete said, as much to himself as to Kathy and Dave. "For whatever reason, someone doesn't want us to find the link between Patty's death, this weird cult, McRyan and what it means for Harras. They took out one of the major chances we had of figuring it all out by gutting Roger Morales."

"A sweeping commentary, indeed," Kathy said. "But what does that mean in terms of actual, you know, work?"

"If we can't find Roger Morales, we have to do the next best thing," Pete said. "Piece his life together and see what it tells us."

CHAPTER TWENTY-ONE

Tere Acevedo lived off South Dixie Highway in Homestead, in a complex named Villa Biscayne. The building's muted peach-and-white color scheme gave the fabricated neighborhood an air of blandness—benign and easy to ignore. The townhouses, designed in a misguided Art Deco homage, all looked identical, down to the tilting needle palm trees on each lawn. The dwellings were new and clean, but somehow felt worn out—floor models snagged for cheap.

"This is nice, for Homestead," Kathy said, taking off her large sunglasses to get a better look at the cookie-cutter development.

"And for someone without a job," Pete said. Tere Acevedo had little work experience, at least none Pete could find. A stay-at-home mom while Roger Morales was around, she'd managed to get by without him just fine, it seemed.

"You should talk," Kathy said with a laugh.

They reached Tere Acevedo's door and hit the buzzer. A muffled voice responded.

"Who's there?"

"Ms. Acevedo?" Pete said, raising his voice to be heard through the door.

"Who's asking?"

"My name is Pete Fernandez, ma'am," he said. "We'd like to talk to you about your husband."

"I remember you. But I don't have a husband," she said, the last word delivered with an extra spoonful of disdain, like she was repeating a particularly nasty profanity.

"You did once," Kathy said. "Roger Morales. He's dead."

The door swung open. Pete took a step back. Tere Acevedo walked out. She was short and stocky, her hair cut close, looking almost painted on her scalp. She also seemed angry.

"Roger is dead? Are you for real?"

"He was shot in his apartment yesterday," Pete said. "I'm sorry to be the one to give you the news."

"I'm surprised you didn't know," Kathy said.

Acevedo pursed her lips and folded her arms, her eyes locking in on Pete and Kathy. She looked more annoyed than sad over the loss of her ex-husband.

"If they tried to reach me, they probably got an old address," she said. "I don't want to be found."

"Yeah, you weren't listed," Pete said. "Took a bit to track you down."

Acevedo rolled her eyes.

"You're with the police now?" she said.

"Private cops," Pete said. "We're trying to figure out what happened to Roger."

"You said he got shot," she said. "That's it. He's dead. What's left to find out? *Se acabó lo que se daba.*"

"Well, there's the matter of who pulled the trigger, but why linger over minor details?" Kathy said.

Acevedo focused her gaze on Kathy.

"Who're you?"

"We're partners," Kathy said. "Are you going to let us in?"

"No, I don't think so," she said, shrugging her shoulders. "You're not actually the police, so why would I? Roger was *un monstruo*. He killed our daughter. My daughter."

"They never brought charges against him," Pete said. "But you were long gone by then anyway, right?"

"You don't know what you're saying, okay?" she said. "I stayed with him for a long time. Much longer than I should have."

"You think he did it, then?" Kathy said.

"I know he did," Acevedo said. "He is—was—a terrible, sick man. A predator."

"Nice house you have here," Pete said, looking around her front porch.

"Thank you," Acevedo said, her tone neutral.

"Can't be cheap to keep up such a nice place."

"Nothing's cheap in Miami anymore," she said.

"How's work going?" Pete asked.

"What?"

"Work?" Pete said. "You must work long hours to pay rent on this townhouse, right? It's not a bargain. It's almost $2,300 a month, from what I could figure out."

Acevedo turned around and walked toward her door. She was done.

"That's it?" Pete said.

"I don't have time for this," Acevedo said, one foot in her apartment, her hand on the door. "Just leave me alone, okay?"

"Do you care about what happened to Roger?" Kathy asked. "Or are they paying you to keep quiet about how you feel, too?"

"Maybe some of your neighbors might be able to help us," Pete said.

Acevedo winced, like a kid bracing for an injection. Then she let out a long breath and spoke. "Come in, *por Dios*."

The inside of Acevedo's townhouse was an orchestra of boxes, half-built furniture and empty rooms. They walked in to what could be a living room and noticed a flight of stairs to their left. Acevedo motioned for them to follow her. They did, turning into another room where a black card table was set up, with mismatched chairs on each side. Acevedo sat down in one and waited for Kathy and Pete to follow suit.

"Okay, you wanted to talk with me. Here I am, let's talk," she said, drumming her fingers on the plastic table. "I don't have a lot of time, either. I have to be somewhere in an hour."

"What can you tell us about your ex-husband?" Pete said, sitting across from her, Kathy taking the seat to his left. The townhouse smelled of spoilt milk and oranges, sweet and nauseating at the same time.

"I told you already," she said. "Roger was a prick—a really, really bad man. He did bad things to our daughter, even before she died. He was sick in the head."

"He abused Patty before she died?" Kathy said.

"Yes, many times," Acevedo said.

"What do you mean?" Pete asked.

Acevedo hesitated for a moment, trying to figure out how to stall.

"I don't want to talk about it," she said, her volume dropping a few notches.

"Quit fucking around," Pete said. He was tired of this half-baked back and forth. His head was throbbing.

"Excuse me?" she said, taken aback. She put her palms on the table and was about to stand up when Pete continued.

"Your husband didn't kill your daughter," Pete said. "You know that. We know that. The police know that. Someone else knows that, too, and doesn't want us to find out the truth. So, tell me one thing, Tere—did you love Patty?"

"Of course I did. She was my world," she said, a tinge of pride in her words mixed with what Pete recognized as regret.

"Then explain something to me," Pete said, his eyes locked on Acevedo. "If you loved that girl so, so damn much, how did you let Roger get away with what you say he did to her?"

She paused and sized Pete up. She bit her lower lip and leaned back in her chair, folding her arms.

"I didn't know it was happening until after Patty died."

"You're lying," Kathy said.

"I don't have to listen to this," Acevedo said, smacking her hand on the table once. The sound was muted and ineffective. She got up.

"I knew your daughter, Ms. Acevedo," Pete said, standing. "She was a special girl. We weren't close friends, but she was the kind of person I admired. She didn't deserve to die the way she did—stabbed to death like a dog. She didn't deserve to have her bones dumped on your front lawn like compost. There are a lot of questions that need to be answered. Don't you want to know what happened to Patty? Don't you care?"

She rushed toward Pete, her face in front of his, her eyes wide and red, her mouth twisted in a pained grimace. Pete expected a swing, or a shove—anything physical to show him how angry Acevedo felt. Instead, she just stopped, her eyes watering, a frozen, frightened expression on her face, like a cornered prisoner with nowhere to run.

"Of course I care," she said, her voice a muffled wail. "I loved her. She was better than any of us. A part of me died when she disappeared."

She drifted off, the words becoming stilted sobs. She stepped back and fell into a free seat.

"What happened to Patty, Tere?" Pete said, his voice low and calm.

She rubbed her eyes, smearing the tears on her face.

"She died," she said, the last word dragging on like a misplaced violin note. "Someone got her. They dumped her at our place like some kind of trash."

"Was Roger in trouble?" Kathy said.

Acevedo looked at her, surprise on her face.

"I can't tell you," she said, her voice quiet, a frantic whisper. "I can't say anything about it. They'll kill me."

"Why?" Pete said.

"Roger made them mad," she said. "He just wouldn't listen. He dug too deep. He had to be difficult, had to be the good guy."

"Who did he make mad?" Pete said.

"He wouldn't go along," she said, turning her face down, as if she were talking to herself, another crazy person on the street whispering nothings into the wind. "He didn't let it go."

"Let what go?" Kathy said. She was getting impatient, leaning over the table.

"I can't say any more," Acevedo said. "Roger is dead. Patty is dead. I'm alone now."

Pete stood up and moved in closer, looming over her.

"Your husband died—blasted in the chest with a shotgun less than a day ago," Pete said, the words coming out in a careful rhythm, like he was reading a prayer—slow and thoughtful. "That's no way for someone to die, in a shitty studio apartment in Miami Gardens, without their family or friends around. Your daughter died that way, too. Punched and kicked and stabbed and battered until she just couldn't live anymore, then dumped in her parents' front yard, years later, her body just broken bones. We're just trying to find out who thought it was okay to put down two of your family like dogs?"

Acevedo didn't respond, her whimpering growing louder as she turned away from Pete.

"You're pathetic," Pete said, straightening up. "We're going to find out who killed Roger and Patty. We're going to find out who's putting you up in this empty apartment. And when we do, you're going to have to come to terms with what you've done—and the devil you sold your soul to."

Pete turned and walked out, Kathy a few steps behind, the sound of Tere Acevedo's pained sobs muffling their footsteps.

CHAPTER
TWENTY-TWO

Homestead Hospital was a ten-minute drive from the Villa Biscayne Apartments, down Kingman Road and over the Turnpike onto Campbell Drive. It was bordered on one side by a few cheap motels and a gaggle of cookie-cutter townhouses on the other. Like most new buildings in Homestead, the hospital sat under a huge coat of pastel paint, surrounded by dwarf palmetto trees and wide stretches of vibrant, green grass and sky-blue lakes. If he didn't know better, Pete would have thought they'd entered a resort instead of a place to get over what ailed you. It was very Miami—dolling up the ugly and sad with pastel colors.

Roger Morales had worked at the hospital for over twenty years—mostly as an administrator, but first as bookkeeper and general assistant in the intensive care unit. The last few years before he was laid off, Roger worked in human resources, vetting employee complaints—usually about long waits, doctor-so-and-so's poor bedside manner and the occasional threat of malpractice. From what

Pete learned, Roger had been well liked and thorough, a quiet man who was fair and discerning.

It was past five o'clock, well after any regular administrative staffers would be around, but Pete and Kathy stepped into the main entrance anyway, following the signs to the ICU.

"Let's start where he did," Pete said as they walked out of the elevator, which deposited them on the third floor. The ICU seemed peaceful—aside from the usual symphony of beeps and low-playing televisions. A few nurses were busy in what appeared to be the main hub on the floor, a cluster of terminals and a front desk. Kathy and Pete approached the nurses' station and were met by a lanky white man, probably in his late forties, with sandy hair and a few days' stubble. He wore blue scrubs, and the tag he wore around his neck signaled he was a registered nurse.

"Can I help you?"

"I hope so," Pete said, looking around. "I was wondering if I could speak to anyone about Roger Morales."

The man's eyes narrowed for a second.

"Roger Morales?" he said. "Are you a cop?"

"Sort of," Kathy said. "We're investigating something related to his death."

"Oh, I see," the man said. He reached out his hand. "I'm Gary Sallis. I work in the ICU most nights."

Pete and Kathy took turns shaking it. They introduced themselves.

"Did you say his death? Roger's dead?" Sallis said, concern in his voice.

"Yes, he was shot and killed yesterday, in his apartment," Pete said.

"Oh jeez, that's terrible," Sallis said, his pasty face losing what little color had been there to begin with. "I knew he was in a bad spot—I mean, all that stuff with his daughter and people thinking he did it. But, damn."

"They never charged him," Kathy said. "From what we know, the case is still open."

Sallis rubbed his chin.

"That makes sense," he said. "I always thought that was a raw deal. Roger was a good man."

"Did you know him well?" Pete said.

"Everyone here did," Sallis said. "He was a big part of the hospital, you know? He kind of dealt with every department."

"He got his start here, too, right?" Pete said.

"Yeah, yeah, he did," Sallis said. "A few years before I got my gig here. He moved up much quicker, I guess."

Sallis let out a dry laugh and smiled to himself.

"Can you tell us anything about Roger?" Pete said. "What was he like? What did he do for fun?"

"Oh, I didn't know him that well," Sallis said. "He was always nice to me, though. Very kind. My car broke down a lot when I first took this job—just a piece-of-shit Datsun—and he'd give me a lift to the bus or sometimes to my apartment. He didn't need to do that. I'll never forget it."

"Can you think of anyone who might have been at odds with him?" Kathy said. Pete could tell she was fighting the urge to whip out her reporter's notebook.

Sallis pondered the question for a moment, his mouth twisting to one side as he processed.

"You know, not really," Sallis said. "I mean, Roger had to deal with a lot of the negatives—when someone thought they didn't get the right care, they'd go to Roger, or if there was a hint that someone was gonna sue, Roger was the first one to deal with it. It was a pretty thankless job, I think."

"Did anyone else here know him at all?" Pete said.

Sallis looked around. By now the other nurses had given the three of them some space and continued with their usual tasks, tending to the patients and bracing for whatever the night's traumas would be. A state of constant waiting until it became frantic trench warfare.

"Nah," Sallis said. "I mean, Roger's been gone for a while. He was let go pretty soon after the stuff with his daughter really hit the press, and that was a while ago. I sometimes feel like the last man standing here, at least from the old guard. It's weird."

"I can imagine," Pete said.

"Do you have any leads about his death? Do you think someone was after Roger?"

"He was living under the radar, working at a furniture store in Miami Gardens and living in a rat-infested apartment down the street. No family, no goals, no waves—but, clearly, someone felt the need to erase him," Pete said. "Someone didn't want him there."

"That's a real shame," Sallis said. "Sad when good people go down like that. What a crummy way to end a life."

"Is there anything else you can tell us about him?" Kathy said. Pete caught her glancing at her watch.

"Roger was a nice guy, but he could be intense about, well, certain things," Sallis said. His head swayed to the left in a slow shrug. "He had his ideas."

"About what?" Pete said.

"Well, like religion. He was very religious," Sallis said.

"Like, born-again Christian style?" Kathy said. "Did he invite you into his Bible study? What?"

Sallis bristled at Kathy's tone, scoffing.

"Well, now, miss, I don't think there's—"

"No, it's fine, there's nothing wrong with being Christian, of course," Pete said. He didn't want to lose the thread.

"Roger wasn't into organized religion," Sallis said. "He was part of this group, this—"

"Cult?" Kathy said.

"I wouldn't say that, you know, I'd hate to disparage any group," Sallis said.

"It's fine," Pete said. "Iglesia de la Luz?"

Sallis shifted his weight from one foot to the other.

"I think that's it—sure," he said.

"What about it?" Pete said. "Was he very involved?"

"He would hand stuff out sometimes," Sallis said. "Tell us about how it saved him and could save us. Nothing too preachy or annoying. Roger, like I said, was a pretty calm, friendly guy. I think this was the only weird thing about him anyone would comment on."

"What'd he say about the church?" Kathy said. "Did he talk about his role?"

"No, nothing like that," Sallis said, waving off Kathy's question. "He would just talk about it, casually. Like, this is what I did over the weekend—I went hiking with my friends from the church, or, hey, I had a fundraiser, yeah, come to the next one. Stuff like that. He'd sometimes go a little deeper, about how it helped him. But it never got pushy or weird."

"That's good, I suppose," Kathy said.

"Yeah, I miss Roger," Sallis said. "All these youngsters around—I feel old. At least with him I had someone to roll my eyes with, you know?"

"What's life without someone to roll your eyes at, right?" Pete said.

Sallis laughed, a soggy, hacking sound. He cleared his throat before looking at his watch.

"Well, I gotta get going," he said. "You never know where the night's gonna take you—might be quiet, or there might be a ten-car pileup on the Turnpike. Got to be ready either way."

"Thanks so much for your time," Kathy said.

"My pleasure," Sallis said, nodding as he backed away. "I hope you find out what happened to Roger."

Kathy moved toward the main hallway. Pete stayed where he was.

"One more thing," Pete said. "If you don't mind me asking."

"Not at all," Sallis said.

"Do you know why Patty Morales was brought here?" Pete said. "After they found her remains? That's what the medical examiner's report said."

"Yeah, yes—the ambulance brought her here," Sallis said. "Roger demanded it—had a forensic anthropologist called in, too. He said Patty had to come here, to this hospital. He wouldn't budge about it, from what I heard."

"Weird to bring remains to a hospital, don't you think?" Pete asked.

Sallis pursed his lips.

"Not really," Sallis said. "As you seem to know, we have a medical examiner, so I imagine they looked at the body, or what was left of it."

"Do you know who was working that night?" Kathy said. "Was anyone questioned by the police?"

"I couldn't tell you," Sallis said. "I wasn't on that night. I would have remembered if I was. But ask our administrators or someone who worked more directly with Roger, if you come back during regular business hours."

Pete nodded. They thanked Sallis for his time and headed back toward the elevator.

"Something's not clicking here," Kathy said as the elevator doors hissed shut. "It feels like there were two Roger Morales running around."

"We have to figure out which one was real," Pete said, staring at their warped reflection in the elevator doors. "And why someone wanted him—and the version of events we were all pushed to believe—gone."

Pete found Lonnie McQueen smoking a cigarette near the front entrance of the Academic II Building of Florida International University's northern branch campus—more formally known as the Biscayne Bay Campus—which housed the school's journalism program, among others. Unlike the better known, bigger main campus in southwest Miami, the BBC always seemed grittier and more urban to Pete. The looming gray buildings and hodge-podge architecture contrasted sharply with the picturesque greenery and tropical Miami weather.

McQueen noticed Pete approaching and dropped the butt at his feet, grinding it into the pavement before kicking it toward the grass. McQueen was in his late fifties but looked to be much older than that, a thick belly pushing out from his worn white long-sleeved shirt and a gleam of sweat covering his dark skin. Pete gave the man a wave as he approached the professor.

"Pete Fernandez, I presume," McQueen said.

"That's me."

"Not every day I get to talk to another *Miami Times* survivor," McQueen said, his white teeth gleaming. "Though I can't say I remember you from the newsroom."

"I worked in sports, mostly," Pete said. "On the desk."

"Ah, right, that explains it. I was on the day side," McQueen said. "You all prepped for the storm?"

Pete gave McQueen a confused look.

"They just upgraded Tropical Storm Elizabeth to a Category 2 hurricane," he said. "Should be even bigger in a few days. Still early, but it looks like it's coming straight for us."

"News to me," Pete said. The weather was the last thing on his mind.

"Alright, alright," McQueen said. "You want to get down to business?"

"Sure."

"Well, let's go," McQueen said, motioning for Pete to follow him into the building. "I doubt you came here to talk storms or to reminisce, right?"

McQueen's office was a claustrophobic space on the third floor of the building—his desk loaded with books, various stacks of paper and an errant potato chip bag. The walls were packed with award certificates and framed newspaper clippings. A photo of a somewhat younger McQueen with his wife and two kids stood sentinel at the far edge of the desk. The office looked a lot like its main resident—rumpled, chaotic, nostalgic and overflowing. McQueen cleared a few folders from one of the two chairs in front of his desk, the other too loaded with stuff to even be considered a viable seat. McQueen nodded to himself as he strode to his own chair. He let out a long, relaxed yawn as he waited for Pete to take his seat, like a cat getting ready for a nap. Then he gave Pete a long look, noticing his black *A Love Supreme* shirt for the first time.

"You a Coltrane fan?" McQueen said. "I dig 'trane. More of an Ornette Coleman man, though. Would've pegged you as an indie rock, Neil Young lover. Maybe some Snoop Dogg for street cred."

"You're mostly right," Pete said. "Trying to embrace jazz in my later years."

McQueen nodded, his gaze growing distant before he pulled himself back to the present.

"You were vague in your call," McQueen said. "So, I have to be honest—part of the reason I'm even taking this meeting is curiosity."

"Oh?"

"I know who you are," he said. "And I know your reputation. I may not be working for a newspaper anymore, but those reporter instincts don't just die off, you feel me? So, why does Pete Fernandez, Miami private investigator, want to talk to an FIU journalism professor who hasn't had a byline in years?"

"We have a—we had, rather—a friend in common," Pete said. "Jackie Cruz. She said I should look you up."

McQueen's eyes closed for a moment.

"That was a tragedy," he said, shaking his head. "Not so much the politician, because I could give two shits about him. They're all corrupt, and I'm not generalizing, I'm talking straight, because I know, okay? That girl was whip-smart. Heart of gold. She would call you on your bullshit before you even know knew it was your bullshit."

Pete waited a beat before continuing, allowing the man to cycle through his grief on his own terms.

"They any closer to finding out who shot her?" McQueen asked. "They think it was that ex-FBI guy, right?"

"They do, but it wasn't him."

"Oh? Is that what you're working on now?"

"Sort of," Pete said. "I'm circling back to something I should have done earlier, and I'm hoping you can help me with it."

McQueen gave Pete a slight, impatient smile. A sign he should get to the point.

"What can you tell me about La Iglesia de la Luz?"

"Shit, son," McQueen said, a wide grin returning to his face. "How much time do you have?"

"**I** don't know much about La Iglesia now," McQueen said, standing up and scanning the jumbled stack of books and papers that littered the shelves behind his desk, "because I tend to lose interest in things when they stop paying me to write about them, and I haven't been the religion writer at the *Times* for quite a while, you see? But I also don't forget, and I learned a lot about that sick crew, most of which I couldn't even write about."

He turned to face Pete, a slim, unmarked DVD case in his hand. He shook it slightly in Pete's direction, as if to say "just wait," then moved to the small TV set at the far corner of his office. He pushed a button on the device and slid the DVD into the TV's tray. As the set read the disc, McQueen returned to his chair and swiveled it to face the screen.

"What's this?" Pete asked.

"It's all you need to know about our friends at the church," McQueen said.

The television screen flickered to life, a rush of static giving way to what looked to Pete like amateur footage shot by a handheld camera. The clip was old, the colors on the screen faded and off. It was dark, too, the dead of night, with some lights visible in the distance. The chatter of a crowd could be heard, and the person filming was getting closer to what could only be described as an event or concert. The audio kicked in, and a rush of live music overtook the small office. The sound was a mix of folk and what Pete could only describe as revival music—he heard gospel singers, twangy guitar, and hands clapping. The footage was shaky and the camera held low.

"'Jesus I Need You,'" McQueen said, as if talking to himself.

"What?"

"That's the hymn," McQueen said, humming a few bars softly. "I shot this video in 1998."

"What is this?" Pete asked, the music continuing in the background.

"Don't be dense," McQueen said. "This is what you're looking for, right? This is La Iglesia de la Luz at its peak. Late nineties. Hottest show in town. This was shot down south, out in the Redlands. One of the last revivals before the shit really got hot around Figueras."

Pete's gaze returned to the small screen as the camera tried to inconspicuously zoom in on a stage. One man stood at center stage, in front of a full band—guitars, drums, and piano—and four female backup singers swaying to the music. He was tall, his hair an oily black, his hands raised up to the sky as his entire body shook to the rhythms coming from the band. Jaime Figueras was a man possessed, his entire being coursing with the electricity of the moment. He was dressed in white from head to toe, a crisp, gleaming *guayabera* and white slacks. It made the man look like a shining star, bursting from the black night.

The camera panned over the crowd in one quick motion, and Pete could tell that this was no small congregation. The crowd had to be in the thousands, and their rapt attention was focused on the man under the spotlights.

As the hymn ended, Figueras stepped to the front of the stage and took the microphone. The crowd responded with a wave of uproarious applause and hooting. They loved this man. The garbled words of an announcer introduced Figueras. Pete couldn't help but be reminded of the last time he saw a charming man manipulate a massive, enthralled throng of people.

The camera wobbled down, glimpsing the small wicker baskets being passed around the crowd, already loaded with piles of singles, fives, tens, and what looked like personal checks. The money machine was already rolling.

The view shunted back toward the stage, Figueras walking across it, waiting for the frenetic cheers to die down.

"Are you feeling God's love today?" Figueras said, his voice confident and booming, as if it didn't even need a microphone to carry his message to the pulsing crowd. "Are you feeling reborn yet?"

His followers responded with a manic flurry of exclamations—"*Sí, Jaime!*" "Yes, father!" "We hear you!"—that Pete could barely decipher. The camera rocked left and right, and Pete heard McQueen curse under his breath on the video, almost dropping the equipment.

"Needless to say, filming was not allowed," McQueen said, running his fingers over his thick goatee. "Watch this, though."

"We are a family, you are my family," Figueras said. "*Mi sagrada familia*, my beloved people. We must stand together to fully feel God's light upon us. I can feel your faith, your love, reaching out to me, pulling us closer. I can feel God flowing through us, making us stronger, more united. We are the chosen, no longer the chosen few, because we are legion, we are an army of God's will … " Figueras paused, pacing around the stage as if trying to speak to each member of the audience individually. "But there are those who would disparage us. Who spread lies. They say we are a cult. That we drink blood. That we have carnal relations outside of marriage. That we hurt our children and sin. But they are the sinners, my brothers and sisters, they are the ones who bask in the darkness and wallow in Satan's sins."

He continued, "The Bible says, 'no man can take my life from me, I sacrifice it voluntarily.' And that is my belief, and that is my action, for I will not sit back and let our fates be decided by others, by evil men sitting back and sucking the very soul from us—taking our money, our homes, our dreams—to pad their bank accounts."

"He sounds desperate," Pete said.

McQueen nodded. "He was feeling the heat," the professor said. "The church is still around today, but was never like this again. In a few years, Figueras would be in hiding and his reputation would be in the garbage. And that's just from the stuff the feds could confirm."

"What do you mean?"

McQueen motioned toward the television.

"Just watch."

Onscreen, Figueras had been joined on stage by an elderly Hispanic woman in a wheelchair, her body frail and thin, almost folding into itself. But her face looked alert, and her gaze followed Figueras' every movement.

"Brothers and sisters, let us look to our very own here, our very own family member, right up on this stage with me," Figueras said, waving his hand in the woman's direction. "This is Ivelise Quiñones, *mis hermanos*. And the world considers her dead."

A gasp echoed from the crowd.

"Not because she is dead, mind you," Figueras said, stepping closer to Quiñones, his free hand on her knobby shoulder. "As you can see, our sister is very much alive. But the powers behind 'modern medicine' have decided she is to die. She is to suffer from cancer and shrivel into nothing because they said so."

McQueen shook his head, befuddled by what was about to unfold even decades after filming it himself.

"Now, Ivelise, we live in doubtful times," Figueras said. "But is it true that I have not met you before, and that I only know of your name and your ailment? Is that true?"

"Y-yes," the older woman said, her voice a rasp. "We have never met before."

"Now, Ivelise, is it true that you are not well? That you are suffering?"

"*Tengo cancer*," she said. "*Estoy muriendo, me falla todo—el cuerpo, la mente.*"

"This woman is falling apart right in front of us, *mi sagrada familia*," Figueras said. "But we will help her. We will help her. We will—with the power of our prayer—we will pull the cancer out from her, rip it from her body, and make her whole again. Will we not?"

The crowd responded with applause.

"Because inside this woman, there is a growth, a malignant thing of darkness," Figueras said. "That growth is looking for a home, a house—a space to fill inside her. But it's gonna leave her body. That tumor is coming out of her. For God never fails."

"This is bizarre," Pete said.

"Keep watching," McQueen said in a hushed tone.

"Rise, Ivelise," Figueras said.

Quiñones gripped the sides of her chair and pushed her shaky frame up, straightening out her brittle legs to reveal a thin, waifish body that looked more like a bag of bones being hoisted up than an actual human being. Her expression was foggy and puzzled, as if she'd walked into the wrong room at a party, the spotlights above the stage pointed at her face. The camera wasn't shaking anymore.

Figueras seemed to spring at the older woman, gripping her face in his hands. He shook her, slowly at first but then with growing intensity, the movement violent but controlled, Quiñones's brittle body making herky-jerky movements as Figueras clutched her. The sounds from the crowd increased—confusion, curiosity, lust, anticipation—as the spectacle continued. A moment later, Figueras stepped back, leaving Quiñones shaking on her own, her face now contorting, as if racked by painful, violent coughs. Figueras took another step back and the older woman collapsed, her knees hitting the stage floor with a thud that could be heard even from McQueen's position in the crowd, followed by her entire body crumbling to the floor. Figueras waved off some of the band members, who'd lingered onstage and were showing signs of concern for the older woman. Though Figueras was not speaking into his mic, Pete could make out some of the guru's words: "Let it be, brother, leave her be."

A few seconds dragged on before Quiñones' body began to spasm. First a leg kicking out, then an arm shooting upward, followed by a shoulder shift—soon her entire body was contorting, as if she were trying to twist herself into a full-form knot in front of the entire congregation. Adding to the strange scene were the guttural, wailing sounds coming from the older woman, as she hacked and wheezed with each movement, until, finally, she was on all fours, her head hanging down, mouth agape, blood dripping onto the stage. Figueras, cautious in his approach, moved closer as Quiñones appeared to be choking, a hand on her throat as her cheeks filled with air, then deflated as a chunk of what seemed like flesh was expelled from her mouth and onto the stage. Exhausted, the woman slid backward, away from the small, red chunk of what could only be described as meat, slick with blood. The camera tried to zoom in on the disgusting display, but it was too far and McQueen's equipment was not hi-tech enough.

"Holy shit," Pete said.

As if he could hear Pete's surprise and it encouraged him to go even further, Figueras walked toward the bloody chunk, ignoring the woman who produced it, and picked it up, gripping it tightly in his hand as it dripped onto the stage below him.

"Be not afraid," he said, yelling now, his voice the only sound, breaking through the shocked silence of his followers. "For we can do what modern man has forsaken."

Figueras motioned toward Quiñones with his mic hand, his other still upraised, droplets of blood streaking down his bare arm and over his white shirt.

"Rise, my sister," he said. "Rise, for you are free of the disease man has thrust upon you. Free of the disease they could not cure. Free of the death sentence they gave you."

Quiñones stood, an unexpected and terrifying spring in her step as she bounded to her feet, blood still caked around her mouth, her eyes now wild with energy and her motions laced with a speed and confidence unimaginable when she was first wheeled onto the stage. This woman seemed decades younger. She moved toward Figueras and enveloped the man in a tight, desperate embrace.

"*Ay, Dios mio, Dios mio*," she said, her words being picked up by Figueras' mic as the cult leader tried to preserve some personal space. "*Estoy bien ... me curaste.*"

Figueras stepped back from Quiñones—who was now prancing on the stage, performing a dance of pure joy and elation that would put even the most innocent child to shame—and spoke into the microphone, the lights dimming to one, sole spotlight focused on him as the band played a series of slow, sluggish chords in the background, ramping up for the next song. Gasps and a general buzzing coming from the crowd.

"Now you see the power I wield, the power I have been granted by God," Figueras said, his hand, still holding the bloody clump, raised to the sky, an offering to his rabid following. "In the name of Jesus Christ, Ivelise, move—walk, run!—for you are healed. You are one with the family, you are overcome by the spirit of God, which has moved through your body..."

Figueras' final words were drowned out by the booming voice of an announcer, heard through the massive speakers set up around the space.

"For she is healed! Healed and free of the cancer that ravaged her body! Thanks to the power of La Iglesia de la Luz, *hermanos y hermanas,* this woman will live to see another day! You saw the miracle, you felt God's power surge through you, and we are all one in his eyes…"

McQueen's camera was jostled, and Pete could hear some indecipherable words on the video before it abruptly cut to black.

"You okay?" McQueen asked. "You were looking pretty green in there."

They were standing outside the professor's office, the bustle of the campus creating a buzz of noise around them as students milled by. Pete turned to face him.

"Yes, I think so. That was something else, though," he said. "What happened after?"

"I got my camera smashed," McQueen said, a slight smile on his face. "I snuck the tape into my jockeys and got out of there, but the camera was destroyed. I got a few bumps and bruises, then some threats in the form of mysterious incidents—tires slashed, apartment broken into, heavy breathing calls and hang-ups. They were not happy, for sure."

McQueen pulled out a cigarette and lit it, blowing a puff of smoke out into the campus' open-air pavilion.

"But you didn't put any of that on paper," Pete said.

"Tried to. Got cut."

"Ever wonder why?"

"I don't have to wonder why," McQueen said, looking past Pete. "The *Times* was scared. They didn't want blowback, so they just reported stuff that was indisputable. The allegations, the innuendo, that was off-limits, even with something like video footage to back it up."

"What else was percolating?" Pete asked, pulling a notepad out of his back pocket. "What were people saying about the church back then?"

"Put your pen away, squire," McQueen said. "I'm not on the record here, and you're not a reporter."

Pete did as the older man said.

"La Iglesia de la Luz wasn't just a support group where people got fooled into giving up a few extras bucks in the hopes of enlightenment," McQueen said. "It was vile. Figueras is a devil, and, believe me, I get the irony in that description. He had people killed. He had a harem of women—some barely teenagers—who looked at him like he was the son of God. And he destroyed their innocence. He manipulated the people around him to do some dark, devious shit, man. And that's just what I know about, based on sources I cultivated for years, people who lived in fear that one day, Figueras would discover they were talking to me and have them killed. He was not someone to be fucked with."

"Must have been frustrating to do all that reporting legwork and have to shelve it."

"Hell yes it was," McQueen said. "I wouldn't call it my life's work, because, knock on wood, I've got some time left on this rock. But it sure as hell would've been my crowning achievement in terms of being a reporter. But that story is long buried."

Pete waited a moment before rolling into his next question.

"How did Roger Morales fit in with the church, then?" Pete asked. "From what I can tell, he wasn't a bad guy, on paper."

"Morales was a believer," McQueen said, shaking his head. "He thought Figueras was the real deal, and he turned a blind eye to a lot of the really sick stuff, most of which Figueras kept behind closed doors—the sex, the money laundering, the bodies. Morales wasn't party to that. He was the go-to boy. He got things done and beat the pavement supporting the church. He was smart, good with numbers, a people person. He opened a lot of doors for la Iglesia. More than Figueras could have gotten on his own. But he was a dupe, for sure."

"What did these kids see in Figueras?" Pete asked. "What made this appealing?"

"Who doesn't want a pipeline to God?" McQueen asked. "Who doesn't want to cut the line? For a few bucks, these people—a lot of them teenagers from poor families or broken homes, who'd never made a decision on their own ever—were part of something. They were part of something special, something different that went against the grain. It fed their teenage independent streaks and also comforted them, gave them warmth. They were taken care of. They got guidance: advice on how to live; access to jobs, cars, school and a sense of family; all for some loyalty. You can't quantify that. Especially if you're a kid who does not understand what it's like to come home and have dinner with a family, get a hug from your father or sleep in the same bed for a few nights in a row. Figueras knew that, and he preyed on these kids—and on the elderly and the adults, too. He lulled them into a sense of peace, made them think they were safe and taken care of, cured if they were sick. But he lied. And he was—and is—a bad motherfucker."

"These sources, former members," Pete said. "Are any still around?"

McQueen sighed and met Pete's eyes.

"Man, I don't know you from a hole in the wall," he said. "I'm happy to talk shit about the church to anyone willing to listen. I'd put that video up on YouTube in a second if I thought it'd get me anywhere, or if I felt like I'd live through the day. But give up a source? I can't do that. These people live in fear for their lives. There are no real former members, okay? There are people who've drifted away, but they're still expected to be loyal to the church. They're still being watched, no matter what they say about the cult fizzling out."

"I've been in your shoes before," Pete said. "I know how to be discreet. I need some help here if I want to figure out who killed our friend Jackie. Who killed Roger Morales's daughter, too. She was barely eighteen when she died. I think it's all connected."

That got McQueen, Pete could tell. The man's face looked stricken—a mixture of anger and resignation that meant he would help Pete, even if it went against his better judgment.

"Check your email in a couple of days," McQueen said. "I'll send someone along if they agree to chat with you. Now get lost, alright?"

CHAPTER TWENTY-THREE

"**Y**ou have no idea what I'm feeling."

Ellen McRyan leaned back on the large, cushy sofa that took up the middle section of her suite at the Biltmore Hotel, another Miami landmark, which, like Vizcaya, was also created in the Mediterranean Revival architectural style, with Moorish and Italian flourishes. The hotel, a fixture of the Miami landscape since the 1920s, had a dreamy, ethereal quality. Its imposing marble columns, lush gardens and 90-foot tower—modeled after one in Spain—made for an elegant and unforgettable piece of Coral Gables. It was a place for celebrations and embracing the city's history—a perfect location for a gubernatorial candidate's campaign kick-off party, after a rousing announcement. But that was not to be.

Pete doubted Ellen McRyan could have foreseen how somber the room would be now when she and her husband first checked in, on the eve of his momentous announcement. Pete noticed an open box of McRyan for Governor signs near an end table.

"And, honestly, I'm not even sure why I'm speaking with you," she said before nodding toward Chadwick, who was hovering by the front door. He came over and freshened up her gin and tonic. "Your friend is the main suspect in the assassination of my husband. Trevor is gone. What am I supposed to do now?"

The last few words came out closer together, as if she was trying to get them out before the next wave of sobs took over. Ellen McRyan had never struck Pete as the type who wept in front of people she barely knew.

The room was dark, a gray pallor hanging over everything despite the luminous day happening outside. It smelled musty and of stale bread. It was doubtful McRyan's widow had left her room in the days since her husband and Jackie Cruz were gunned down.

"I can't express to you how sorry we are," Pete said, trying to choose his words carefully, aware that he and Kathy could be ushered out at the first perceived slight. They sat across from McRyan in two stiff, uncomfortable chairs, as if they were being interviewed for some high-end personal assistant job. But Chadwick already had that gig on lockdown, Pete thought.

"Words mean nothing now," McRyan said, waving off Pete's condolences. "I have to arrange my husband's funeral—in a hurry, mind you, now that this storm is approaching. Not to mention that I still don't know where my son is. I'm not really even sure what we're doing here. Or why we got into this mess, running for governor."

"It seems like your husband had a great chance of winning," Kathy said. "He inspired a lot of people."

McRyan responded with a slurred scoff. She looked like this wasn't her first drink of the early afternoon and certainly wouldn't be her last. Even from his seat, Pete could smell the familiar scent, his head spinning a bit as he inhaled. Pete had been there. But he didn't need a death as an excuse for daytime drinking. No, that had been his standard operating procedure.

"Mrs. McRyan, I'm sorry we even have to bother you at all," Pete said, folding his hands together. "But we need to ask you a few questions if we're ever going to find your son and find out who did this to Trevor."

"Who did this?" she said, her voice rising a notch. "It was that Robert Harras. It's all over the news. He had it in for my husband. He was some kind of whacked-out ex-FBI guy who'd lost his mind doing who-knows-what. The mystery isn't one, my dear. As for my son ... well, I hope he comes home. I hope he sees that his father is dead and that his mommy needs him now."

She whimpered into her handkerchief, wiping her nose before returning her look to Pete and Kathy.

"Well, we obviously think differently," Pete said, trying to be conciliatory but also refusing to ignore the Harras issue—and his innocence. "I think there's something you're not telling us. Something that didn't come up when you hired me to find your son."

"Oh?" she said. "I'm sorry I didn't fill out every form. If I recall, you were quite eager to push us out of your office once we dropped the information on your desk. It didn't really seem like you even wanted this assignment, to be honest. If Ms. Cruz were still alive, I would consider firing you outright. You made zero progress in finding Stephen, and, if anything, put a target on my husband's back."

Pete could feel Kathy tensing up next to him, like a rubber band stretched taut.

"Listen, sympathy can only go so far," Kathy said, her tone flat. "We are sad your husband died. He seemed nice enough, for a politician. That said, we lost a friend, too. Someone who worked for you. We also don't buy this bullshit story that another friend of ours pulled the trigger. He's not that kind of guy. We know him. We've worked cases with him. Anyway, it's too tidy. I don't need to give you a Sirhan Sirhan or Lee Harvey Oswald tutorial, but it's rarely an open-and-shut case when it comes to assassinations like this. So let's put that aside for a moment, okay? There is something you're not telling us, and it involves your son and why he's missing, and it might also involve something called La Iglesia de la Luz. That's not the kind of thing you leave out of a briefing for a potential investigator, yet you did, which makes us think you've got something to hide. I hope we're wrong. And I hope your husband didn't die because he crossed the wrong people. Please clarify this for us and we'll get the fuck out of your way."

Pete heard Chadwick take a few steps toward them.

"That is no way to—" Chadwick said.

"It's fine," McRyan said, shooing him away. He returned to his post. She gave Kathy an appreciative look. "You're a little spitfire, aren't you? It's charming for a few minutes. I have no idea what you're talking about, dear. I don't know what the Iglesia is, or what it would have to do with my husband, if anything. To think you'd bring this up to me, just days after he was slaughtered in front of a massive crowd, on what was supposed to be a crowning moment for him…"

As she drifted off, Pete pulled the sheet of paper from his back pocket. He stood up and handed it to her.

"What is this?" she said, not even looking at the page.

"It's a rough breakdown of campaign contributions," Pete said, taking his seat again. "Well, contributions to your husband's political action committee, Fighting for Florida's Future, which he formed before formally announcing his run. Usually, politicians use those organizations to lay the groundwork for statewide or national campaigns before they officially get in the race, in case something comes up and they have to back out. That way, they still have a platform and means to get their name out there. It's a nifty little loophole."

McRyan's demeanor changed, morphing from standoffish and bothered to what seemed like barely contained panic.

"How did you get this?"

"Remember Ms. Cruz?" Kathy said. "She documented everything. Those files ended up in our hands. She was already concerned about who was funding your husband's unexpected ascension from political obscurity, or at least that's what her notes suggest. I mean, she liked Trevor. We all did. But this document is particularly enlightening, especially when it comes to stuff like motive and money."

"This is absurd," McRyan said. "So many people donated money to my husband, it's impossible to keep track."

"Well, it's kind of the law to keep track," Pete said, trying to step on the brakes a bit with his sarcasm and failing. "But I understand. There are plenty of ways people can donate and it could become overwhelming. But if you look down at the second or third name on that sheet, which, like I said, is a breakdown of major donors, you'll see a group called Sun Trinity Investments. Do you see it?"

McRyan didn't respond, but her eyes were on the sheet.

"That's a shell company, or was, years ago, for La Iglesia de la Luz," Kathy said. "Are you familiar with the group?"

McRyan cleared her throat.

"I know who they are, yes," she said.

McRyan's combative stance was gone. Her shoulders sagged and her body seemed to melt back into the cushions of the plush white couch.

Pete let the silence linger between them. He didn't want to press too hard, not yet. He could feel her shaking a bit, on the edge of a long drop. It was either fall or reach out a hand. He hoped she'd make the right choice.

Pete let his gaze rest on the woman, who seemed to have lived a decade over the last few days.

"Oh, God," she said. "Oh, Trevor. What have we done?"

Chadwick left. Mrs. McRyan didn't want him in the room for what she would share. It was a secret, even to him. But she'd read between the lines of what Pete and Kathy had thrown down: We have this information. If we want, other people can have it, too. Let's play nice.

So, she played nice.

It all went back to Stephen McRyan, their son. What started as youthful rebellion and impishness eventually evolved into a string of minor, but worrisome crimes. Unlike his parents, who spent most of their time up north, tending to their constituents and serving in the state legislature in Tallahassee, Stephen loved Miami. It was home to him. So much so, Mrs. McRyan explained, that at a certain point, his parents decided it was fine for him to relocate there, starting in high school. They set him up with a full-time nanny and enrolled him in a Catholic private high school, Christopher Columbus. They hoped the new, permanent location and new school would help recalibrate their child, who'd evolved from a concern to an actual political liability. That his behavior was not on the radar of local journalists yet was a byproduct of being from a relatively small district in northern Florida and the McRyans' low political profile. When Trevor McRyan inevitably sought higher office, they would need to close the book on their son's misbehavior, or at least pour enough money over it to hide the truth.

What they hadn't expected was that their son would find God, or, some form of him, in the shape of a middle-aged Cuban man named Jaime Figueras. It was the early 1990s and La Iglesia de la Luz was taking its first few jabs in the press and in the court of public opinion, but mostly, the organization still seemed to be the alt-religious group *du jour*, and Ellen and Trevor saw their son's burgeoning interest in the church and its work as a positive more than anything.

"Until Patty Morales died," Pete said, interrupting McRyan's story.

She nodded yes, "until the girl died—that threw things for a loop. That was when the man showed up. Figueras. He had presence, seemed like something more-than. Tall, lanky, a darkness around him. His eyes were pitch-black, his voice was low and clear. He was mesmerizing."

"What did he want?" Pete asked. "Did he offer money?"

"No, not then," McRyan said, "not yet, at least. He told us about our son, and how he was doing so well as a member of his church. *Church?* we thought, how weird. Our Stephen involved in a church."

That was around the time Trevor McRyan began thinking about running for governor, as a long-term plan. The death of the Morales girl—even though Ellen McRyan could never imagine her son being involved in anything like murdering a classmate's girlfriend, which was all she was to Stephen—would hang over them for a long time if it became a story. Somehow, this subject came up easily when the McRyans were talking to Figueras. He promised them it would not come to pass, that the girl's death would be solved in due time and they didn't need to worry about Stephen. He was safe in the church.

"So that was that?" Kathy said.

"No, not exactly," Ellen McRyan said. It was quiet for a while, Trevor became more vocal in the Florida senate, built a name for himself on water cooler issues, and around the time the Patty Morales case—still a disappearance, though few held out hope for her safe return after over a decade—truly went cold, the church faltered and Stephen disappeared. Not that he'd been safely tucked into the bosom of his parents' home before then, to be fair, but Trevor and Ellen had at least kept tabs on him. Or, better said, the church did. But after years of controversies, stop-and-start civil litigation and rumors of criminal cases, the church took what many thought would be a fatal blow—as the once seemingly invincible Figueras went to jail for tax evasion. Not the crime many expected to finally topple the guru, but it happened. A while later, Stephen was gone, on what the McRyans assumed was just an untethered drug bender. They didn't expect it to last years. In fact, the next time they heard from their son, it was not directly, and it was after Figueras had been released and decided to gather his remaining followers and trundle down to the Keys.

"It was when Patty's remains were found," Pete said.

"Yes, that was it, when you found them, right?" she asked.

Pete nodded.

"Stephen wasn't even using his real name anymore," McRyan said with a could-you-believe-it sigh. "Kenny Sampson? What was that about? He was making a hubbub about knowing the truth about Patty's death, our worst nightmare realized, but somehow, the story didn't trickle up north to us."

The connections were not made, McRyan continued. "Kenny Sampson" was just an unknown drifter who might know something and apparently didn't. The heat was on Roger Morales.

"Around that time, when we were hopeful we would be able to find our son and get him some help, we heard from someone at the church."

"Who?" Pete asked.

"A new person," she said, "but he wouldn't name himself. He only spoke by phone and through others. He said the church wasn't gone, and they wanted to help, help us. Help us with Stephen, help us with the campaign and help us to make sure this Patty Morales stuff didn't hurt anything we were doing."

"Help with money, you mean," Kathy said.

"Yes, with money. It wasn't a lot at first," McRyan said, "but then it grew, and eventually we had to form that PAC to build up a little war chest for Trevor. We spent those years crisscrossing the state, putting the money to good use, shaking hands, meeting people, building a platform. We felt momentum but there was still one big nut to crack—one city Trevor had to win over if he was going to have any kind of chance to win the big seat: Miami.

She continued, "Stephen would pop up from time to time, usually drugged out, so we'd give him some money and he'd run off to who-knows-where and we'd be worried but at least he'd be gone and our fingers were crossed that our new church friend would eventually get him under control."

"You couldn't be bothered, I guess," Pete said, but McRyan shrugged.

"We'd tried. We tried a lot. He didn't want our help. He wanted our money. And we settled for that. But just as we were getting our Miami machine in place, with Ms. Cruz's help, our friend from the church called and said we needed to corral our kid, because he had something that belonged to them and it would be terrible for all involved if it got out. He didn't specify what, but he made it clear in no uncertain terms that it would be a major problem for us if we didn't bring Stephen in, and that it was already hurting the church financially. The man said that all the things we'd tried to hide about Stephen, about Patty Morales and about this Kenny Sampson would be out in the open and any chance Trevor had of being governor, or even regaining his own paltry seat in the state senate, would go down the tubes faster than you could say Gary Hart or John Edwards. Can you imagine? We had to find Stephen fast, because we were already speeding along toward announcing Trevor's candidacy, and that would wait for no one."

"Did the church, or your friend there, did they want you to wait?" Kathy asked.

"Oh, yes," McRyan said. "They were mad about it. But we had no choice. You can't announce much later than this. We had to do it now. We needed to be first. We had momentum. We had the money. We needed to let the people know Trevor was the definite front-runner and scare off any super-lefty challengers. So we hired you, on Jackie's suggestion, and just hoped the stars would align. We hoped that you'd do your part, find Stephen, and we could get on with it."

"If you found Stephen, or if I did," Pete said, "what were you going to do with him?"

"Well, get him help," McRyan said. "Get him into a rehab or some kind of facility and make sure our contact got the item he wanted so we could get back to what we wanted."

"What if he wanted Stephen dead? What then?" Pete said. The room was getting warm. Chadwick was back, and had inched closer now. The hot midafternoon sun was on full bore. "What would you do then?" Pete said, pressing, not caring if this lady was about to break because he felt he needed something to break, needed to take this sharp turn to have any hope of solving this case, this case that had morphed and mutated over the years into something bigger, dirtier and deadlier than he'd ever imagined. And it all pointed back to this one girl, this girl he never really got to know but also wanted to save, because in a way, it meant saving himself.

"Then, well, that would be that," McRyan said, her eyes clear, unwavering. "He would die. And we would continue. I believed in my husband. He believed in his cause and we were going to win. If that meant Stephen would be a victim of a greater cause, well, then that was probably for the best. At least he'd have died for something. Instead, his father—Trevor, my Trevor—is dead. Dead because we couldn't stop our own son from ruining everything, like he always did."

"Well, that was something."

"Yeah," Pete said as they waited for the elevator to arrive to take them down to the Biltmore's lobby.

Chadwick, the McRyan's handler, had ushered them out fast after Ellen McRyan's final, jaw-dropping outburst against her own son. Which was fine, they'd been ready to leave. She'd given them enough to go on. But go where, was the question.

Kathy pushed the DOWN button again.

"Where are you?" she asked.

"I'm wondering how quickly we can get our shit together and make it down to the Keys."

CHAPTER TWENTY-FOUR

October 1, 2017
Key West, Florida

The Duval Inn was a tiny bed-and-breakfast off Duval Street near the corner of Angela Street and Josephine Parker Road in Key West. The inn was modest but proud, which evoked the spirit of Key West itself, the island always reeling from or preparing for an unwelcome storm. The Old Town-style house, made of rot-resistant Dade County pine, was both stylish and practical—its antique, wraparound verandas were paired with louvered window shutters. Kathy and Pete's room room was stuffy but comfortable—the furniture was old but well kept and the owner, a fiftysomething woman named Marnie, who looked like she was born with a deep tan, was been friendly enough. It was an affordable spot for a night—or maybe longer.

"This brings back some memories," Kathy said, tossing her overnight bag onto the bed.

Pete didn't respond. He dropped his bag next to the dresser and sat down on the tiny couch across from the bed. A few years back it was right around Duval Street in Key West that Pete had tracked down Kathy after she had been kidnapped and presumed dead. Pete had figured out where she was, loaded her into his friend Mike's Ford Focus and—after a car chase through the backstreets of Key West—escaped to the mainland. Twelve hours later, Kathy was on the run, Mike was dead, and Pete's life had changed forever.

"None of them good," Pete said.

"So, aside from the rantings of a newly minted widow, why are we here again, my dear?" Kathy said. "We have no client. Jackie's still dead. Harras is still in prison, and the guy we thought would help point us in the right direction is sitting in the morgue. Our case is a stack of papers you stole from Jackie's apartment and I don't think she'll be footing the bill for this little jaunt."

Pete put on a black Miami Heat cap and a five-dollar pair of sunglasses they'd bought on the way.

"Iglesia de la Luz is around here somewhere," he said. "So it seems like as good a place as any to start. Everything, from Patty to McRyan to Jackie, points to them."

They made a right as they exited the inn and another right on Duval Street. It was early afternoon and the bar crowds were getting loud and sloppy—as were the patrons. The weather was heavy with humidity and the sidewalks were filling up with tourists, swaying to varying degrees of inebriation as they walked by. Pete closed his eyes for a few seconds. He needed to hit a meeting. He wasn't up for barhopping for information.

Kathy bumped into Pete, holding onto his left shoulder to avoid falling. She righted herself and continued.

"Where to?" she said. "Or are you taking me drinking because you feel bad?"

"Bad about what?"

"About everything," she said, turning to look at him. "This case. How weird you're behaving. That we have zero money. Notice a theme here?"

"It's all my fault?"

"Obviously," she said.

"I don't think now's the time to have a talk about—"

192

"About you and me? Sure," Kathy said, her joking tone taking a darker turn. "Let's table it for a while more. Let's forget that weird moment a few days ago, too. I'll just pretend—"

"We're here," Pete said, turning into an open-air bar that took up a big chunk of the block.

The decor at Willie T's was pure Key West tourist trap. The vibe was casual and clustered, the walls crowded with knickknacks, and photos of the owner with various celebs and local stars as the speakers blasted Aerosmith pleading about how crazy they were for someone. Sports memorabilia—including Miami Dolphins and Marlins banners and pictures—filled out the few spaces left untouched above the handful of big-screen TVs set to whatever games were happening at the moment. Pete thought he heard Kathy say something in response to his abrupt entrance, but he couldn't make it out. He didn't need to know the words to get her tone, though. He took a seat at the bar.

Pete noticed the handful of older men sitting at the bar focus their attention on Kathy as she took the seat next to him. She ignored them, her energy and anger focused on Pete.

"What is this dump?" Kathy said. "Willie T's? Have you been here before?"

"I have," Pete said. "Years ago."

The bartender approached, tossing two cardboard coasters in front of them. She was their age, stocky, with long red hair, no makeup and a tired expression on her face.

"What'll it be?" she said, not meeting their eyes.

"Is Ash around?" Pete said.

The name got her attention for a second. She looked up at Pete.

"Ash?" she said. "Who's asking?"

"My name's Pete Fernandez," Pete said. "And this is my friend Kathy Bentley."

"I'm Gina," she said. "What do you need with Ash?"

"I know him, sort of," Pete said.

Pete had spoken to Ash on the night he found Kathy, years before. It was a tip from Ash that pointed Pete to her. He was hoping the old, brittle local could help again.

"I'll ask him if he wants to see you," Gina said, backing away, wiping her hand with a rag she had hooked on her belt.

"That went well," Kathy said as Gina walked toward the rear of the restaurant.

"It's a gamble."

"So, who is this guy? Who the hell calls themselves Ash?"

"I've met a few, actually," Pete said. "I crossed paths with this guy the last time I was here. I'm—"

Before he could finish, an older, salt-and-pepper-haired man with a thick, nicotine-stained mustache approached. He was wearing a worn-out Willie T's shirt and large glasses. He reeked of tobacco and cheap gin.

"You say you know me?" Ash said, leaning on the bar for support, his face inches from Pete's. He realized his mistake and wove back, trying to stand straight. Gina went to help one of the other customers.

"Yeah, we met a few years back," Pete said. "I came asking about Contreras."

Ash pursed his lips.

"Haven't heard that name in a long time," he said. "Forgot about you, boy."

"Here he is," Kathy said. "In all his boy glory."

Ash gave Kathy a disdainful look.

"Who's the broad?"

"Oh, for fuck's sake," Kathy said.

"She's my partner," Pete said. "We were wondering if you had time to talk."

"What, are you some kind of cop now?" Ash said. "I've got a business to run. I don't have time to chitchat. You haven't even bought a drink."

"I'll take a Diet Coke and she'll take a rum and Coke," Pete said. "How's that?"

"A start."

"I'd prefer a Tanqueray and tonic, actually," Kathy said. "It's too early for rum."

Ash shouted the orders to Gina and turned back to them. Pete put a fifty on the counter.

"This should cover us," Pete said.

Ash hesitated, as if he wanted to be sure he understood Pete's gesture. Once it registered, he snatched up the bill and stuffed it into his pocket.

"No problem," Ash said. "Bring your drinks to the back office. We can talk more there."

Gina brought their beverages over and Pete and Kathy followed Ash as he bobbed and weaved his way through the crowded bar. The rear office was a locker-like crevice next to the men's room. It had enough space for a tiny desk with an aging laptop, two chairs and a few stacks of books and maps. There was a cat calendar on the wall showing off a fat tabby that looked like it'd just taken a roll in the nip. The room was dim and smelled of aftershave and sawdust.

"I'd offer you both a seat, but space is tight, so, deal," Ash said as he took the office chair behind the desk, leaning back to look Pete and Kathy over.

Pete motioned for Kathy to take the remaining seat and leaned against the wall opposite the desk. The room was hot and stuffy; the simple act of breathing seemed like work.

Ash scratched at his bumpy red neck.

"Fifty bucks isn't an unlimited stay here, you got it?" he said. "So ask what you wanna ask and I'll see if I know anything."

"We're looking into La Iglesia de la Luz."

Ash snorted.

"They're long gone," he said.

"Literally or figuratively?" Kathy said.

Ash ran a shaky hand through his curly gray mop of hair.

"I don't care," he said. "They're gone. That whole operation is kaput. Don't you read the news? Kind of detectives are you?"

"We know the operation fizzled," Pete said. "But we also know they have land around here. I want to know where."

"You working for yourself?" Ash said.

"We have a client," Kathy said. "Of sorts."

"Oh yeah?" Ash said. "Why does your client care about a dead cult?"

"Do you know where they are?" Pete said.

Ash got up and closed the door. He turned the knob and made sure it was locked before returning to his seat.

"What's this about?" Ash said. "You know, now that I think on it, you got me into some hot water last time I saw you. Shit, there was a pile-up of cars in front of this place. Cops everywhere. Asking me questions about Contreras. Why should I help you again?"

"Maybe he just gave you fifty reasons to help?" Kathy said.

"Maybe that's not enough?" Ash said.

Pete took another fifty from his wallet and tossed it on the desk in front of Ash. He didn't miss Kathy's scolding look as he backpedaled to the wall.

"Okay, now we're talkin'," Ash said. "Here's the deal—the church is done. Doesn't operate or exist the same way. Whatever they were is past tense."

"What are they now, then?" Pete said.

"It's more like a weird commune than anything," Ash said. "The guy that founded the thing—Figueras—he still runs the show. But they've tried to cut themselves off from the world. They're not interested in, uh, recruiting people."

"How big is their operation?" Kathy said.

"Tiny," Ash said. "Only ten people, twenty tops. The move from Miami down here left them broken and scared. They're marked. This cult wasn't just some quick newsreel, you know? They might as well have defined the term 'bad PR.'"

"How do you know this?" Pete said.

Ash scoffed.

"I've lived down here all my life," he said. "I know all about this town. I can sense when it changes and why. They're cultlike, but they're not a secret society. They also don't live in a bunker. They have to come up for air. Sometimes they even pop in for a drink. Two drinks and they're chatty. Figueras, though, I never see. He's an urban legend almost. But I talk to some of the guys."

"Where can we find their base, for lack of a better term?" Kathy said. She seemed exasperated and exhausted. They were both running on fumes.

"Take Southard Street down, let it turn into Quay Road and then follow Angela Street past the marine sanctuary for a few miles," Ash said. "It'll be on your right, before you get to Fort Taylor's. You can miss it—they don't want to be found. Keep your eyes open. It's really just a bunch of trailers off the side of the road. If you reach the docks, you've gone too far."

Pete started to ask another question but was interrupted by Ash's clearing throat.

"That's it," Ash said. "I got nothing else. Like I said, whatever that group was is gone—dormant, maybe. But they were not to be fucked with twenty years ago. I'm not looking for them to want to fuck with me for talking to some half-baked mall cops."

"Well, you just won the lottery, then," Kathy said, standing up.

"You don't think this is worth a hundred bucks, lady?" Ash said. "You can fuck right off."

"I'm blinded by the bright charms of Señor Ash," Kathy said as they walked out of the bar and onto Duval Street.

"He gave us some info," Pete said, turning back toward the Duval Inn. "You want to drive by and see if we find this mini-compound?"

"I'm not sure what else we can do," she said, "that would still manage to fall under 'working on the case that pays us nothing.' I'd like to have a few drinks and lay out on the beach until my skin turns brown, but somehow that seems slightly unproductive."

"I feel like there are two threads we need to tug at a bit," Pete said. "One is Roger Morales—who he was and what happened to him. Iglesia de la Luz is part of that, maybe Los Enfermos, too."

"What's the other thread?"

"Jackie and McRyan," Pete said. "They're related—but not immediately so. Roger's actions seem to have lead to Patty's death, but how does that tie into the Trevor McRyan and Jackie? If the same person orchestrated all of these killings, what spurred them on to do it? Because the McRyan job wasn't the kind of murder you commit from one day to the next."

"This is true; one must plan how to kill someone to do it, if you want to get away," Kathy said. "Care to elaborate?"

"Whoever did this needed help getting to McRyan," Pete said. "Jackie's not dumb. She took precautions. She advised McRyan to do the same. Whoever killed them knew those precautions and cut through them. They were also gunning for me, not Jackie, if you buy Harras' theory."

"Even the tightest security has flaws," Kathy said. "Everyone makes mistakes."

Pete stopped talking as they reached the Duval Inn's front porch. Marnie, the owner of the establishment, was seated on a comfortable-looking wicker sofa. She seemed to be sleeping soundly, but her eyes fluttered open as Pete and Kathy climbed the first few steps.

"Oh, welcome back," she said. Her voice was soft and soothing, like an adult contemporary DJ working the overnight shift. "Did you have a nice walk?"

"We did," Kathy said. "Though I could do without the crush of tourists."

"Are you a local?" Marnie said. Her tone remained serene.

"I'm from Miami," Kathy said. "Born and raised."

"Well, that's good," she said. "Why don't you sit out here for a bit? This is fine weather for an afternoon cocktail."

Pete and Kathy settled into two chairs across from Marnie. The older woman yelled into the inn.

"George? George, are you around?"

A man in his early twenties with a hipster beard, wearing a long-sleeved plaid shirt and tight black jeans stepped outside. He was overdressed for the Key West heat and it showed. His hair was wet with sweat, his face red.

"Yes, ma'am?"

"Lordy, how many times do I have to mention it's *Marnie*? *Ma'am* makes me feel even older than I know I am, dear. Could you scoot into the kitchen and get us some beverages? Whiskey sour for me." She turned to Kathy and Pete. "What would y'all like?"

"Gin and tonic," Kathy said.

"Water's fine," Pete said.

George nodded and stepped back into the inn.

"He's not from around here," Marnie said.

"He seems like a nice kid," Pete said. "Though he'll melt if he keeps dressing like that."

Marnie laughed—a long, warm laugh. Pete wondered how many afternoon cocktails she'd already knocked back.

"He is a good boy, yes," she said. "He's from the big city. Wanted to get experience running an inn or bed-and-breakfast, so he applied. I told him I don't really need much help. Still, he came."

"There are worse places to work than Key West," Kathy said, smiling.

"This is true," Marnie said. "Are you all here on vacation? Honeymoon, perhaps?"

"He wishes," Kathy said.

George arrived with their drinks, setting them over coasters on a small table between the wicker sofa and the chairs.

"Thank you, George," Marnie said. "That'll be all."

He made a small bow and walked off.

"So why are you here, then?" Marnie asked.

"We're actually private detectives," Pete said. "We're investigating something called La Iglesia de la Luz. Based on our research, they call Key West home now."

"Oh, well, I wasn't expecting that answer," Marnie said. "And here I thought you two were just lovebirds looking for a weekend getaway. I've never met actual private eyes before."

"*Actual* is relative," Kathy said. "We used to work at the *Miami Times*, though not together."

"How long have you owned the inn, Ms.—" Pete said.

"Just call me Marnie," she said. "And it's Missus. Mrs. Marnie Rayburn. My husband died a few years ago. We bought this place together when this was all wide open. No foot-long beers or wet T-shirt contests to speak of."

"You don't sound very enamored with what's happened to the town," Pete said.

"I'm not," Marnie said with a sigh. "But it's the way of the world. It's hard for me to compete with the big chains. But there are still people looking for an authentic experience—and to be treated like a person, not a name on a screen."

"Do you know anything about the church?" Kathy said.

"A little," Marnie said. "Enough to know to keep my distance. I have my hands full with my own problems."

"We've heard that some of the members come up now and again," Pete said.

"Sometimes," Marnie said. "I don't see them that often. They don't wear signs, either. But I've heard they come up for supplies and to cut loose. I do know one of them—man named Ramon Medrano—fairly well. We chat if I see him in town."

Pete felt a buzzing in the back of his head. *Medrano.* The name was familiar—from Jackie's files on Patty Morales.

"He's still a member of the church?" Kathy said.

"I guess so," Marnie said. "I mean, I don't grill him about it. He talks about where he lives from time to time—they have some land near the fort. Not sure how they lucked into that."

"When was the last time you saw him?" Pete said.

"Why, just a little while ago," Marnie said. "He drove in for lunch. Said he was craving some fried fish. I can't imagine he eats all that well where he lives."

"Did he say where he was going?" Pete asked.

"Well, he didn't have to say," she said.

"Why's that?" Kathy asked.

"Because I saw him taking a seat at DJ's Clam Shack," Marnie said with a tinge of surprise, as if everyone should know where to go for fried fish in this town.

"Is that nearby?" Kathy asked.

"It's around the corner, I think," Pete said.

"Yes, it's on the corner of Angela and Duval," Marnie said. "Not even a block away."

Pete got up.

"We'll be back later, Marnie," he said. "Thanks for your help."

"Think nothing of it, dear. The drinks will be here for when you return," she said. "I hope you find Mr. Medrano. He's a nice man, even if he hasn't found the right calling yet."

Kathy followed Pete down the porch steps, the high-pitched, whistling cry of an osprey competing with the inebriated bustle and chaos of the tourists milling around on a muggy Key West afternoon.

DJ's Clam Shack was just that—a shack. The small, hole-in-the-wall restaurant seemed like it'd been around since Key West was founded. The floor creaked as you walked in, the fried fish smell seemed to permeate the entire space, and you couldn't look in any direction without catching a slogan—on a shirt, a sign, or a coaster. The phrases didn't bother trying to keep things classy, either. From *No Money, No Honey* to *Blowjob is better than NO job*, they aimed for the cheap laugh and succeeded most times. Instead of tables, there were stools and benches. The vibe was casual. No shirt and bare feet seemed to be enough to get you a hot plate and cold beer. A beach bum's paradise.

Kathy and Pete arrived after the lunch rush, and three-quarters of the place was cleared. A few drinkers sat near the register, which was located toward the front, at the end of a long counter where people placed their orders. DJ's Clam Shack wasn't a table service kind of joint.

Beyond the flock of sunburnt college kids on their second bucket of Landshark beers, Pete spotted an older man sitting near the back, past the counter. He was finishing off the last bite of a massive lobster roll—shoving the messy chunk of food into his mouth with gusto. He followed that with a long pull from a Corona and a thoughtful wiping of his lips with his already-soiled napkin.

"That's gotta be him," Pete said, walking down past the register and the confused look of the cashier.

"Maybe we should discuss, oh, I don't know, a plan before we corner this guy?" Kathy said in a sharp whisper. Pete ignored her. He stopped in front of the man's table.

"Ramon Medrano?" Pete asked.

The man looked up from the remains of his meal, still chewing that last bite, a bemused expression on his sun-worn face. He was over fifty, chubby but not fat and had the laid-back look of someone who didn't have to shave or shower every day. He swallowed, took another slow sip of his beer and responded.

"Who's asking?" he said.

"I'm Pete Fernandez," Pete said. "This is my friend Kathy Bentley. We were wondering if we could talk to you for a few minutes."

He looked across the small table and nodded. They sat.

"Sure," Medrano said. "I got a little bit of time."

"Sorry to interrupt your lunch," Pete said. He was trying to slow things down and give himself time to think. He'd come on too fast, and wasn't sure what the best approach was for someone like Medrano. Pete had made a tactical error and Medrano knew it, his expression placid and patient, like a spider watching a fly struggle in its web.

"It's fine," Medrano said. "I'm just finishing up. How'd you know to find me here?"

"We asked around," Kathy said. Pete was glad she'd avoided outing Marnie.

"About lil' ol' me?" Medrano said in a put-on, jovial voice. "That's interesting."

Pete didn't see much point in doing this dance for long.

"We're private detectives, Mr. Medrano," Pete said. "We're investigating the death of a man named Roger Morales. Did you know him?"

Medrano didn't flinch at the mention of Morales' name.

"Yeah, I know Roger," he said. "So what? He's dead?"

"He died in Miami a few days ago," Kathy said.

"That's a shame," Medrano said. He'd pulled a toothpick out of his tattered shirt's pocket and poked at his teeth.

"We're looking for more information about Roger, to hopefully figure out what happened to him," Pete said.

"Good luck with that," Medrano said. "Not sure how I can help you."

"How did you know Roger?" Kathy asked. "Did you work with him?"

"You could say that," Medrano said, looking Kathy over. "We were friends for a few years. Then not friends for a while. Haven't spoken to Roger since that business with his dead daughter. Did he blow his brains out?"

"He was murdered," Pete said. "Shot in his apartment."

"*Qué lástima*," Medrano said.

"Do you know anything about a group named Los Enfermos?" Pete asked. He was pushing his luck, and he knew it.

Medrano responded with a terse "No."

"What about La Iglesia de la Luz?" Pete asked.

Medrano said nothing, his bland expression decorated by a distant smile.

"According to our info, you were a member," Kathy said. "Then you quit. Are you back with them now?"

"Seems like you two have been doing your homework on me," Medrano said. "That's funny."

Pete and Kathy shared a concerned glance. He was stonewalling them and not even breaking a sweat.

"Can you tell us anything about Roger? How did you guys get together?" Kathy said. She'd taken Pete's cue. They were going all in.

"I got nothing to say about that," Medrano said. "I don't know you two from Adam. You come here, 'been asking around' about me, and I'm supposed to lean back on the couch and tell you my deepest darkest? Nah. No offense or nothing, it's just not gonna happen."

Medrano stood up, dropping three singles on the small, cluttered table. He guzzled the last bit of his beer and placed the bottle down with a slam. He moved toward the door when Pete got up, putting him face to face with the stout man.

"Ramon, listen," Pete said, trying another tack, "we'd really like to chat with you for a bit longer if you can spare the time."

"I'm sure," Medrano said. "But what are two private dicks doing in the Keys when your body's in Miami? Doesn't make sense. This isn't a good look for me, either. I got places to be. *Nos vemos*."

Medrano wove past Pete and walked out of DJ's without looking back. The door chimes crashed into each other, creating a discordant, uncomfortable sound.

CHAPTER TWENTY-FIVE

"**I** fucked up."

Kathy took another swig from her half-empty Corona and nodded before swallowing. They had settled into Ramon Medrano's old table.

"You took a risk," Kathy said. "And you were wrong."

"It's more than that," Pete said, rubbing the bridge of his nose. "We just tipped off Medrano and the whole group. Now they know we're onto them."

"Yes," Kathy said. "This is true."

"You're not helping," Pete said.

"What would you like me to say? 'Better luck next time, champ'?"

Kathy was not one for consoling speeches or pats on the back. She was direct and honest in a way Pete had always found refreshing. At least when he didn't find it grating. They worked well together because they could read each other. Even when one took a wrong turn, the other was there for support. He was grateful that, despite their time apart and romantic friction, the core of their friendship hadn't washed away.

Pete felt his phone vibrate in his pocket. He pulled it out and checked the display. It was a Miami number, but one Pete didn't recognize. He picked up.

"Pete Fernandez."

"Hey, PI man, it's your buddy's attorney," Edwin Gustines said. "Got a second?"

"Sure."

"Figure you might want an update on your pal Harras, soon to be known permanently as inmate number whatever-the-fuck, if things keep going this way."

Kathy crinkled her nose in Pete's direction, and he mouthed "Gustines" in response. She rolled her eyes and went back to her beer.

"We have a bail hearing soon, so I'm hoping we can at least get him out until the trial, but you never know, especially with a case that's gotten this much press," Gustines said. "Where are you?"

"I'm in Key West," Pete said. "Taking some time off."

"Time off in the Keys a few days before a hurricane hits? That's some bullshit right there, but I don't have time to figure out what you're doing," he said. "I just wanted to let you know that they're officially charging him with McRyan's murder, and the lawyer's—so, two first-degree murder charges."

"I guess I shouldn't be surprised, but shit," Pete said. He felt like his chest was going to explode. "I still can't believe it's happening."

"Oh, it's happening. But let me finish," Gustines said. "Like I mentioned before, they found a bunch of nasty social media postings under a username they tied to his personal computer, ripping on McRyan and his political stance. Of course, a few months ago, McRyan was a blip on the radar, so no one really seemed to care that some nut job with a fake screen name was going off on a nobody from North Florida. But the evidence is bad, and it's gonna hit the news outlets today."

"Harras isn't a killer," Pete said. He was getting frustrated. "He was framed."

"Well, then, my friend, I hope part of your vacation plans down there involve you figuring out who put the frame on this *viejo*," Gustines said. "Because things look pretty dire otherwise. Do you have anything I can work with?"

"Nothing yet," Pete said. "But ask Harras one thing for us and get back to me as soon as you can."

"What?"

"Harras clued me into La Iglesia when I got to Miami—ask him what connections, if any, he's had to this Figueras cult, either as an FBI agent, retired, whatever," Pete said. "It looks like someone with ties to them wanted him and McRyan eliminated."

Kathy got up and walked toward the food counter. She ordered another beer.

"Sure, fine," Gustines said. "So, lemme play a little pretend with you, okay? A little theoretical?"

"I'm all ears."

"I know McRyan was your client," Gustines said. "I'm also going to assume you're not quitting on the case even though he, and his proxy, are dead."

"Theoretically," Pete said.

"Right, theoretically," Gustines said. "So, in that situation, what would you do?"

"Well, I guess Kathy and I would figure out how long we could push forward without a benefactor," Pete said. Kathy returned to the table, her eyes narrowing at the mention of her name—and money.

"And, theoretically, how long would that be?"

"Not very long," Pete said.

"Let's say I open my checkbook and offer to bankroll you two," Gustines said. "In the name of my client."

"Why would you do that?" Pete said, dropping the pretense.

"Because you're the only chance your friend Harras has," Gustines said. "And I don't like to lose. Plus, your buddy's got a nice chunk of change saved. So I'm angry and I have money to burn."

"What are the ground rules?"

"Ground rules?"

"Yeah," Pete said. "Every client has them. What's the mission statement? How often do you want us to check in? What're the parameters?"

"Does this mean you're on board?"

"Of course we are," Pete said. "I'd do it for free, but I think I'd have to talk to my partner first before she agreed to go *gratis*."

Kathy shrugged, only hearing one side of the conversation.

"Do that," Gustines said. The line went dead.

Pete put his phone back in his pocket.

"That sounded promising," Kathy said. Her new beer was half empty. Pete scolded himself for keeping track. He needed a meeting.

"Gustines wants to take us on."

"Take us on?" Kathy said. "That's interesting."

"Yeah," Pete said. "What do you think?"

"Well, I'm no economist, but I think some money is better than no money," Kathy said. "Depending on the strings that are attached to it."

"Agreed."

"And look, I guess you'll find this out eventually if you haven't already," Kathy said, her tone softening and slowing down, "but Robert Harras is not my favorite person in the world. He'll never be. I'm in this to help him because I have this twisted sense of justice that seems to overlap with yours, and because I don't like being shot at, but it isn't because I'm feeling warm and fuzzy about him."

"It's about the baby, right?" Pete said, meeting her eyes.

"You knew?"

"I figured it out," Pete said. "I had a lot of time to myself in New York, a lot of time to think about what went down—with us, before that."

"Well, goodie for you," Kathy said. "Maybe I'll feel like talking about it someday. But that's not going to be today. I did chat with him before you came back to town, though."

"Oh?"

"Yes, it involved some yelling and an awkward hug," she said. "Plus I got to walk out of a crowded restaurant, so it was basically a Kathy Bentley inside-the-park home run of drama."

"That does not sound pleasant for Harras."

"I hope not," she said. "But that's not why I'm bringing it up. He seemed different—scared and anxious. With all the shit going on, I'd completely blanked that we even got together, but he said he needed your help and felt like he was being followed."

"He told me the same thing when I got into town, just a few days before McRyan was shot," Pete said, tapping his fist on the table, the two stories blending together to form one image—of their friend, trying to outrun the shadows chasing him down. But who were they? And what did they want?

"I guess the bigger question is, how does Harras being—well, harassed—fit in with your theory that this weirdo cult is behind it, and probably trying to set it all up well in advance. But maybe we're missing something," she said, finishing her beer, her face flush. "So, let's move forward. Gustines is no slimier than some of the other people we've worked for. Ask him for an advance, send him our expenses and give him our rate."

"What should our rate be?"

"You figure it out, dear. Don't you do it for a living?" she said, standing up. "I would like to take a swim before the sun goes down and then hash out whatever the hell the plan is."

CHAPTER
TWENTY-SIX

The Rusty Anchor Group met in a clubhouse a few blocks from the Duval Inn. To call it a clubhouse was somewhat generous—it consisted of a cluttered room with a wheelchair ramp and a handful of parking spaces surrounding it. The exterior resembled a fancy trailer. But that mattered little. It was a space, and it welcomed recovering alcoholics. From what Pete could tell, the group held meetings a few times a day, every day of the week. The room had probably saved innumerable lives.

The meeting had worked. Pete felt lighter. Clearer. The clutter from the last few weeks had disappeared a bit and the constant buzzing in his head wasn't as loud. He stepped outside of the clubhouse and closed his eyes for a second.

"Good to hear you in there," a low, strained voice said.

Pete opened his eyes. A fiftysomething man with long gray hair and a worn-out blue T-shirt stood next to him, trying to light a cigarette.

"Thanks," Pete said. "What's your name?"

"Sam," the man said. "I've got three days."

"That's a miracle," Pete said. He didn't mean it as a slight—it was a miracle. He felt a surge of joy for the man.

"Don't feel like one," Sam said, puffing smoke out of the side of his mouth. "But it can't get any worse, I guess?"

"My worst day sober was better than my best day drinking," Pete said, looking out on the small parking lot. By now, the cars had moved out and only a few stragglers lingered on the fringe of the clubhouse. "I used to hate that saying, but it turned out to be true."

"How much time do you have?"

"Couple years," Pete said. "Fits and starts before then."

"Yeah, fits and starts," he said. "Couldn't string more'n a week together. Been in and out of these rooms for almost a decade."

"Sometimes it takes a while to click," Pete said. He offered his hand. "I'm Pete."

"Nice to meet you," Sam said, his drawl slow and plodding. "You're not from here, are you?"

"No, I live in New York," Pete said. He felt himself cringe. Saying it out loud felt weird. "But I'm from Miami."

"New York City," Sam said, drawing out the last word. "What brings a city boy down here? Vacation? You didn't come to see the storm, didja?"

"Not really," Pete said. "You live nearby?"

"I've been crashing with friends," Sam said. "But yeah, I'm from here."

"I've only been gone for a little while and I feel like it's a whole new town," Pete said.

"Here or north?"

Pete knew that by "north," the man meant Miami. Key West was its own place, and Miami was a distant metropolis.

"Miami," Pete said. "I feel like I'm behind the curve."

"Places don't wait for you," Sam said, dropping his cigarette butt and crushing it with his heel. "They got better things to do. The Miami you know is gone. Maybe it was never there to begin with."

"That's the truth."

"So, you ain't here on vacation and you don't drink," Sam said. "From the looks of you, you don't go to the beach much either. So, surfing is out. What the hell are you here for?"

"Just poking around."

"You a cop?"

"Private cop," Pete said.

"Shit, that's kind of cool," Sam said.

"You going to a lot of meetings?" Pete said.

"Trying to do a ninety-in-ninety," Sam said, referring to ninety meetings in ninety days, a practice suggested by the program for newcomers. Pete hadn't nailed that his first time around. Or his second. But he'd gotten closer, and it had saved his life.

"How's that going?"

"Three for three so far," Sam said. He patted his shirt pocket but didn't find what he was looking for. "You got a cig?"

"Don't smoke," Pete said. "You hear anything about a church around here?"

"Like a building? Sure, there's a few around."

"No, I mean a group," Pete said. "Like a church group that lives around here. Near the Taylor Fort. Down Angela Street."

Sam looked at his feet and then over at the empty parking lot. The lingering members had left, the only sound coming from the cicadas and the distant traffic.

"We don't talk about them," Sam said.

"How come?"

"You should be careful what you're talking about here, being a stranger," Sam said. "Iglesia de la Luz is not to be discussed. They do not exist."

"But they do," Pete said.

"Not anymore," Sam said. "Let it be, dude. It ain't for you."

Sam started to turn away. "It was nice to meet you," he said. "I hope you figure out what to do next. Be safe."

"Wait," Pete said. "Isn't there anything you can tell me? Right now, all I know is where they're based, but I can't just—"

"Do not go there," Sam said, his eyes wide, mouth agape. "Do not go down there, okay? Just listen to an old man who knows this town.

Leave it be. Go back to Miami, get on a plane, lay down in your New York bed and watch your cable TV and snuggle with your French Bulldog or whatever the fuck. This is not for you to be mucking with."

Pete tried to say something else, but Sam had turned his back on him and started for the street. The sound of the winds as they rustled the swaying palms dominated the quiet, clear night.

Pete opened the glove compartment and took the gun out, sliding it into the holster he'd put on under his black polo. He'd parked the car about a block away from where he expected to find the compound and shut off the engine. He grabbed a long flashlight from under the rental's front passenger seat, took a deep breath and walked out, closing the door.

He didn't get very far.

The guy was big and moved fast. He looked like two shopping carts stacked vertically with a human head on top, a 'roided out creature straight out of an old WWF wrestling video. The guy approached Pete, a snarl taking over his face. He wasn't armed—but he was pissed off.

Pete pulled out his gun, but by then it was too late—the man's giant ham-hand smacked the gun away and knocked Pete to the floor. He fell with a thud, rolling to the right to avoid having the man's massive foot from landing on his face.

"Get out," the man said.

Pete scrambled to his feet, backpedaling in a crouch, his hands up—trying to look over the dark, dirty ground for his gun.

"I don't want any trouble," Pete said.

"You got it, buddy."

The man sprinted at him, but this time Pete was ready for the giant, sidestepping and elbowing him in the back of the head as he stumbled forward. But the man didn't fall. Instead, he popped up and turned, grabbing Pete by the shirt and flinging him into the deserted street. Pete landed on his back on the asphalt, his back skidding away from the man. He didn't get up.

Pete's head spun. He heard the man approach, but couldn't get up. He felt himself being lifted up by his shirt collar. The man's breath—which smelled of over-the-counter mouthwash and uncooked meat—bombarded his face. Pete felt himself lose focus. The large man's mundane features blurred as Pete struggled to stay conscious.

"Why are you here?"

"Put me down and we can chat," Pete said.

The man let go, adding a shove to speed up Pete's drop. He landed hard, rolling backward, before he recovered and stood up, slowly.

"Talk," the man said. "Tell me what you're doing here."

"I'm a detective," Pete said. "Pete Fernandez. I'm looking for La Iglesia de la Luz."

"What for?"

"I need to ask a few questions," Pete said. "Who're you?"

"Pike," the man said. "Call me Pike."

"Got it," Pete said. "So, Pike, do you usually hang out in abandoned lots waiting for people to show up so you can attack them?"

Pike tilted his head, like a wild animal straining to hear something in the distance. Instead of responding, he moved toward Pete, ending with another shove, this one harder and more punch-like, sending Pete into an awkward sitting position on the ground. Pete groaned and leaned back, careful to keep an eye on Pike as he approached again. He also noticed something next to his outstretched hand: his gun.

He grabbed the weapon and scooted back, the gun now pointed at Pike, whose approach was slowed by its appearance.

"I'm going to ask you again, this time in simpler terms you might understand," Pete said. "Who are you?"

Pike grimaced. It was clear he wanted to run at Pete and pound his face bloody, but his remaining brain cells were preventing the attack.

"I could kill you right now," Pike said.

"Not quite," Pete said, waving the gun barrel in Pike's direction. "See this gun? That means I'm in charge. So, let's talk, okay?"

"What do you want?"

"I ask the questions," Pete said. "Who are you? What are you doing here?"

The brain cells lost the battle. Pike made a play, charging toward Pete.

Pete had enough time to angle his shot and go low. The sound of the bullet hitting Pike's knee was followed by a low, guttural yell and a sloppy cracking sound that resembled a full bowl of soup hitting a tile floor. Pike folded on himself, his hands on his bloodied knee, his mouth open in a silent scream.

Pete stayed where he was, gun still on Pike. After a few minutes, the bigger man recovered enough to speak.

"You fucking shot me," Pike said. "My leg."

"Answer my question," Pete said.

"I work here," Pike said, choking back a sob, clutching the bloodied leg, like a star athlete facing a season-ending injury. "I live here."

"Who else is here?"

Before Pike could answer, a ragged blast of sound and force whizzed by them, striking Pete's car parked a few yards away. Pete covered his ears, the gun still in one hand. The shotgun spray obliterated the front passenger side window of Pete's car.

Pete looked past Pike to see a deeply suntanned woman of medium height, with long and curly black hair, worn-out blue jeans and a two-sizes-too-big flannel shirt standing on a small hill. She was holding the shotgun. She was also pointing it at Pete.

"Put the gun down," she said, yelling to make up for the distance.

Pete complied. He dropped the gun at his feet.

"Raise your hands," she said.

Pete did so.

She took a few steps toward them, stopping at Pike and looking him over, keeping the gun on Pete. She was in her mid-forties, a little older than Pike, and Pete was struck by the resemblance. But, unlike Pike, she was an attractive woman, a natural beauty. The air she gave off was rugged and no-nonsense.

"*Comemierda,*" she said to Pike. "It's always amateur hour with you, eh?"

She turned to Pete.

"So tell me, who the hell are you?"

"I'm Pete Fernandez. I'm a private investigator."

"Yeah? What are you investigating here? This is private property."

"Who are you?"

"I don't need to say anything," she said, a blazing glare directed at Pete. "Answer my questions first, then maybe you'll get to keep walking."

"I'm investigating two murders," Pete said. "Both of them point to La Iglesia de la Luz, which I believe is located here."

She let out a dry laugh.

"*Que cojones tienes*, Mr. Pete Fernandez," she said. "To come here and ask questions about La Iglesia. Who sent you?"

"My client is confidential," Pete said.

"Even with a shotgun pointed at you?"

"I'm hoping you're more reasonable than your brother," Pete said.

The comment was a gamble, but it seemed to land—she did a quick double take.

"How'd you know that?"

"It's my job to know things," Pete said.

"Well, *qué chévere*," she said. "Get in your car and get lost. You're lucky that bullet just went through Pike's stupid leg. Otherwise, your face would look like your car window."

Every part of Pete's body said to comply, to just turn around and head back to the inn and, if it wasn't too late, back to New York.

"I just need to ask you a few questions," Pete said.

The lady almost spat up a laugh.

"Are you insane?" she said. "I will kill you if you don't leave. Don't make me count."

"I need to find Figueras," Pete said.

"Guy is stupid," Pike said to his sister, wincing with each word.

"Shut up, Pike," she said before looking at Pete. "Figueras is not here. And even if he was, he doesn't want to talk to you."

"Where can I find him?" Pete said.

"You won't find him."

"Who are you?" Pete said. "Can you at least tell me that?"

"Call me Ana, if you have to call me anything," she said. "But I don't expect to see you ever again."

Pete didn't either. He picked up his gun and backed away, his eyes on her and the shotgun until he reached his car and drove off.

CHAPTER
TWENTY-SEVEN

A few cop cars whizzed by in the opposite direction as Pete pulled off Duval Street and parked next to the inn. He checked himself—for bruises, cuts, or surprise bullet holes—for what felt like the hundredth time. He was fine. He was alive. He looked back at the car and its destroyed window. If that was the biggest injury sustained tonight, he was lucky. He made sure he had his phone, wallet and car keys and walked up the porch steps. He found Kathy stretched out on the wicker couch, Marnie sitting across from her. They were laughing, swaying back and forth at some unheard joke. He wasn't surprised to see a half-empty carafe of some kind of lemonade drink. He doubted it was just lemons and water.

"Oh, you're back," Kathy said, straightening up in her seat a bit. "That was a long one, huh?"

It took Pete a second to remember that he'd only told Kathy he was going to a meeting.

"Yeah, it got more complicated."

Her mood went from jovial to serious.

"What happened?"

"Come, Pete, join us for a beverage," Marnie said, oblivious to Kathy's understanding of the situation.

Pete complied, sitting on the edge of the wicker couch as Kathy scooted over, her eyes still on him, as if she were performing a mental full-body scan for injuries—internal and external.

Marnie offered him a clean glass and the carafe, but Pete waved it off.

"Not up for a drink," he said. He preferred to just sidestep alcohol when it was offered, as opposed to explaining the whys of his sobriety. Pete had realized early on that no one really cared what he was drinking as long as he didn't bum out their own imbibing.

"No better time than now, I say," Marnie said, smiling as the glass neared her lips.

"Marnie, do you know anyone else that lives out there, near Iglesia de la Luz?" Pete said.

She seemed startled by the question.

"You didn't run off and do something silly, did you?"

"I really hope you didn't," Kathy said.

"I guess *silly* is relative," Pete said. "Could you answer my question, Marnie? It'd be a big help."

Marnie took another sip and stared off toward the inn, her eyes losing focus before she looked at Pete.

"It's a good question," she said. "But I'm not sure I should answer it."

"Why's that?"

"Well, listen, I like you two," Marnie said, giving them a wan smile. "I really, truly do. But we have a way of life down here. We have people who were born and raised in Key West. We deal with tourists, visitors, investors, real estate magnates—you name it. Because we have to. But this is home to us. I don't know how I feel about disrupting lives just because you're on some kind of quest."

"Even if it could help solve a murder?" Pete said.

"I guess, if you put it like that, I must seem like a she-devil," Marnie said, taking another sip from her drink.

"It is like that, Marnie," Pete said. "Two men and a woman are dead—just in the last week. Years ago, a teenager was found dead after being missing for years. And all of it points to the people living by that fort. I went there tonight and almost got killed myself."

He ignored Kathy's sharp intake of breath and pressed on.

"I'm lucky I had a gun on me," Pete said. "I'm still surprised I made it back with only a busted rental car window. Now, I get what you're saying—we all want to keep our 'hoods pure, but this is a little more serious than stemming the tide of gentrification."

Marnie sighed.

"I suppose so," she said. "I just hate to bring any more heartache on that place."

"What do you mean?" Kathy asked.

"Their home, their compound," Marnie said. She reached over and topped off her drink. She offered the carafe to Kathy, who declined.

"Who lives there?" Pete said.

"It's not what you think," Marnie said. "It's not some super-secret Waco-like cult. It's not even more than a few dozen people, I'd wager. That man, Medrano, and the Figueras family, seem to be in charge."

"Pike and Ana?" Pete said.

Marnie let out a humorless chuckle.

"You met them, did you?"

"I did," Pete said. "They didn't seem to like me much."

"They're angry," Marnie said. "Years ago, as children, their dad was something close to the messiah. Now, they're the only people who still believe that."

"What's their deal?" Kathy asked. "Are they as insane as their *papi*?"

"Oh, I don't know, they're just around your age," Marnie said. "Pike is a nickname. His real name is Raul. Ana is the older of the two. Their father is ... not well."

"What's wrong with him?" Kathy asked.

"I don't feel like it's my place to say," Marnie said.

"Why stop now?" Pete said. "You were playing coy with us earlier, now you're hemming and hawing a bit when we could really use the info."

Marnie bristled.

"I can do as I please," she said. "If I'm correct, you're sitting on my porch, drinking my drink and staying in my house."

"That's true," Pete said. "And I appreciate the hospitality. I should note that we'll do our best to keep any information you give us confidential."

"It's not that," Marnie said. "Look, I know the church has done wrong. Anyone with half a brain does. When they moved down here, it was like a virus had invaded our bodies. But after some time, they became part of the furniture, part of the town. And it's clear that over time it's stopped being what it once was. It's not even much of anything now. So, I hesitate because I've seen those two children grow up—like savages—but children nonetheless, and I'd hate to add to their grief."

"Do they care for their father? Is he ill?" Kathy said.

"Jaime Figueras hasn't been a functional man for years," Marnie said. "He's been slowly dying for almost as long as I've known him. He couldn't hurt a fly."

"**S**torm comin.'"

The bartender's words rose above the clatter of the crowd as Pete and Kathy settled into a small outside table at the Grand Cafe, a casual dinner joint that was built inside an old Victorian mansion. The place felt comfortable and welcoming, with modern, artsy touches and decorations that blended with the house's aged décor and antique design. It had history, but wasn't afraid to keep up with the times—Key West in a nutshell. The crowd was tapering off as the clock inched toward closing time.

"What's he talking about?" Pete said as he unfolded the cloth napkin and placed it on his lap.

"Well, there's a Category 4 hurricane making its way here, hence the 'storm comin,' lingo," Kathy said. "Where's your brain at?"

"Not here."

They ordered their meals as Paul Desmond's sax kicked in on a Dave Brubeck Quartet song, the mellow jazz tune rising out of the restaurant's exterior speakers like a pleasant mist.

"We have to figure out our next move," Kathy said.

"What have you got?"

"I did some research on Figueras while you were off cowboying," Kathy said.

"I thought you went for a swim?"

"Some people can multitask, little one," Kathy said. "I happen to be able to cyber-stalk people while sipping a daiquiri and taking pool breaks quite effectively. I can even avoid shattered car windows while doing so."

"Why didn't you say anything earlier?"

"I don't know what to make of Marnie," Kathy said.

The food arrived. Kathy dove into her steak while Pete fiddled with his seafood pasta. The night was breezy and mild.

"You don't trust her?" Pete said.

"Do you?" Kathy said, looking up from her plate, a hunk of steak on her fork. "It's nothing personal. I just don't think having two mildly pleasant conversations with someone means I should trust them with my whole heart and soul."

"Fair," Pete said. "What did you get on Figueras?"

"Not just Figueras," Kathy said. "But his brood. Seems his wife died fairly early in the marriage, left him with two young kids to raise—the very pleasant Ana and Raul, or Pike. Ana's actually in good standing around here. She does real estate and manages her father's affairs. Pike, not so much. He's a local thug who's been arrested a half-dozen times for things like drunk and disorderly and minor drug possession. He has no known job beyond being a big oaf."

"What about Daddy Figueras?"

"That's the gray area," Kathy said. "After he moved his operations down here, he went fairly quiet. It was soon after he did a short prison stint and shook off any real, hard time, thanks to his crack legal team. The between-the-lines message I'm getting is that's when he got sick."

"Sick how?"

"Unclear," Kathy said. "I have a few old sources from when I was at the paper that I reached out to, softly, about Figueras. They didn't have much, but they said he went into early retirement about ten years ago."

"Where does Roger Morales fit into this?"

"Also muddy," Kathy said, taking a bite of her baked potato and washing it down with a long sip of red wine. "We know Roger was heavily involved in the church. We also know that Patty Morales' remains were found about four years ago. Then Roger finds his reputation beyond repair, so he's forced into some kind of exile. Then a man with ties to Patty's death—Stephen McRyan aka Kenny Sampson—goes missing with something that belongs to the church, sending the McRyans—and a mysterious church contact—into a panic. Then Trevor McRyan ends up dead, Jackie gets caught in the crossfire—that might have been meant for you. Somehow, the McRyan job gets pinned on Harras, who was in a tizzy for weeks before, thinking he was being watched."

"Figueras is covering his tracks—he doesn't want Patty's true killer found, we knew that."

"We think that's the line," Kathy said. "But if Figueras is incapacitated, like Marnie said, then we have another player involved. Remember, McRyan was dealing with Figueras first, then some invisible 'friend.'"

Pete spread food around his plate. He hadn't eaten much. His thoughts felt scattershot and unfocused, as if the weight and pain from the last few days had decided to settle on him at once, like quick-drying cement. Here he was again, in South Florida, running for his life, desperately trying to unravel a mystery he had no business mucking with.

"I don't know if I can do this again," Pete said. The words spilled out of his mouth before he could think to stop them.

"You think this is easy for me?"

Kathy's eyes seemed far-off and unfocused. The dim lighting of the restaurant gave the entire space a dreamlike veneer. Fast-moving shadows moved and merged into the crowd.

"It's happening again."

"What is?" Kathy said. "Something bad? That's real life. It'd catch us wherever we go. Life is about making the best of things and pushing through the bad. I think you're good at one of those. You can guess which one."

Pete straightened up in his seat.

"I failed this girl, and I tried to move past it without dwelling on it. I buried it in a corner of my mind," Pete said. "I failed Jackie. Now she's dead. I can't even process that yet. Even sober, even with my head sort of put together, I keep fucking stuff up."

"You do, that's accurate," Kathy said, polishing off her glass of wine. "But so what? We all fuck up. Your problems are no more important than mine, or our waiter's, or Marnie's. You think I don't regret going into that bar last year and getting stabbed? And losing my baby? You don't think I regret sleeping with the guy who would have eventually been an old, distant and weird father to that kid, if it got the chance to be born? My whole adult life has been about fucking up and still living. Yours has been about fucking up, avoiding your fuckups, and then doing something for someone else. You're a great person—good-hearted and brave and sometimes smart—but, Jesus Christ, you need to live a little. Give yourself a break. What's that quote from *Shawshank Redemption*? 'Get busy living or get busy dying.' That sums up where you're at."

Pete started to respond but was met with Kathy's raised palm.

"Don't say anything," she said. "Okay? I'd like to get out of here."

"Okay."

"And I'd like to have a nice nightcap somewhere else, somewhere quiet," she said, her eyes watering before she wiped at them. "And sit by the water. And feel the breeze on my face and not think about dead teenagers, murder or cults."

They woke up around ten to the noises of the street—people on their way to the beach or looking to get that first hair of the dog to help get through the day. The blinds let the sun sneak in just enough to wake them. Pete rolled off the small side couch and grabbed a T-shirt from the dresser. He put it on and stood up. Kathy, buried under the covers on the bed, stirred.

"Coffee?" Pete asked.

"If you're just asking, and not offering, then I hate you," she said, sitting up, her voice hoarse from sleep. She was wearing a worn-out Old 97s shirt.

The room's large queen-size bed dominated the space, leaving just enough room for a cherry wood dresser, the small couch and a tall wardrobe near the door. The windows, behind the bed, looked out onto a small parking lot behind the inn.

"Lemme try to fix the whole hate thing," he said, fidgeting with the small coffeemaker on the dresser. Kathy rolled out of bed and moved toward the small closet on the far side of the bedroom and started to change out of Pete's view.

"How's that hangover treating you?" Pete asked, handing her a cup of black coffee.

She grabbed the cup, looking recharged and refreshed after just a change of clothes.

"It's in my rearview, mister holier-than-thou AA monk," she said between gulps. "I paced myself pretty well, if you must know. What's on tap for today, señor?"

Pete didn't respond. He was looking past the bedroom set and out the window. The small parking lot was tucked behind the inn, which wasn't very large itself. There were a handful of parking spaces—a few of which were occupied by guests of the inn. But it was what he saw between two of the cars that caught Pete's attention. A large man, face-down, his body spread out at a weird angle.

"Pete?"

"There's someone out there," Pete said. "Knocked out or passed out."

"Who knew? People drink in Key West," Kathy said.

He grabbed her arm and moved her to face the window.

"No, look," Pete said. "That's worse than just passed out."

"I guess you're right," Kathy said.

Pete hopped into his jeans and shoes as he headed for the door, the *slap-slap* sound of his gift shop sandals following him out.

Outside, the cool breezes of the night before were long gone, replaced by a smothering late-morning humidity that would only get more oppressive as the day progressed. The sun was out, an orange furnace inching up higher in the sky. Pete felt like he was stepping into a steam room with a parka on.

The man hadn't moved and there weren't any signs of a struggle. Pete assumed the worst as they got closer to the fallen body. Pete recognized him immediately. It was Pike, the man-child of Jaime Figueras he'd tangled with the day before. Pete could hear Kathy a few steps behind him. He motioned for her to stay back as he stepped closer.

The large man looked serene—like he'd just dozed off on his way to his car late last night. But Pete noticed he wasn't breathing. He checked for a pulse and found nothing. He stepped back from the body and looked around. Pete wasn't a cop, but he'd seen his fair share of dead bodies and grew up around police. His father built a legendary career on the Miami PD homicide unit while Pete was learning his ABCs. Still, something felt wrong. Pike had managed to change his clothes and tend to his wounded leg after his tangle with Pete, so whatever went down happened late in the evening or early morning while they slept.

"Is he dead?"

Pete turned to face Kathy.

"Yeah," he said. "This is Figueras' kid, Pike."

"The dude you crossed last night?"

They heard a loud, surprised intake of breath and saw Marnie stepping out onto the parking lot. She was wearing an apron over her clothes, her hair tied back, stains from the morning breakfast decorating her clothes.

"Oh my goodness," she said, walking toward them. "Is that Raul Figueras?"

"Looks like it," Pete said. "He's dead."

"Dead? But how?"

Pete knelt down next to the body and placed two fingers on Pike's exposed neck.

"He feels cold, so he was probably here last night," Pete said, standing up. "Maybe he was looking to even the score with me."

"We, we, uh, we have to get him inside," Marnie said, pacing around. With each circle of steps she'd get a bit closer to them and the body. "We can't have him out here like this—the guests, they'll see him ..."

"We have to call the police," Kathy said.

"No, no, we can't do that, no," Marnie said. "It'll cause a scene. I'll lose the inn."

"Marnie," Pete said, placing his hands on her shoulders. "We can't just drag a dead body into the inn. That'd make things even worse. We have to call this in."

"This is my property," she said, staring off, avoiding the dead body on the pavement. "Not yours."

"That's true," Kathy said. "But the cops will come. If not now, eventually. You don't want to explain to them why you thought it might be a good idea to bring a dead man into your place of business. It doesn't really scream *innocent*."

Marnie's shoulders sagged.

"Alright," she said. "Alright."

Pete nodded at Kathy, who took Marnie inside, her arm around the older woman. Pete returned his attention to the dead body. The lot was still quiet—only half past ten. People were still sleeping or enjoying a leisurely breakfast before they wandered to the beach or down Duval. Pete checked Pike's pockets and found a wallet with six singles and a driver's license for Raul Figueras. He found a loose key in his back pants pocket with a piece of tape around the base. Scrawled on the tape was the word "office." Pete pocketed the key and replaced the wallet. He pulled out his phone and sent a quick text. A few moments later Pete was on the street, heading to his car, the squeal of his tires drowned out by the thumping bass of a passing truck's radio.

CHAPTER
TWENTY-EIGHT

October 3, 2017
Key West, Florida

The AM talk station was blathering on about the storm. Hurricane Elizabeth. She was on her way and gaining power. They estimated landfall in four days.

Pete jabbed his finger at the car stereo, turning it off. He pulled out his phone, dialed a newly saved contact and put it on speaker, letting the phone rest on the seat next to him. It rang a few times before someone picked up.

"So, are you in or what?" Gustines said.

"One of the Figueras spawn is dead," Pete said.

"Figueras spawn?"

"Jaime Figueras, the founder of La Iglesia de la Luz, has two kids. One was found behind the inn where Kathy and I are staying."

"How old?"

"Full grown," Pete said. "Hell, he was a giant."

"How long are you two going to be on your honeymoon down there?"

"It's not like that," Pete said, turning the car onto Angela Street. "I have one more thing to do. Then we should probably head back. Did you talk to Harras?"

"Yeah, coming back would be good, especially with the storm," Gustines said. "I talked to Harras, but I can't talk now. I'm about to step in for his bail hearing and everything else takes a back seat to that, sorry. Let me know when you return to civilization."

Gustines cut the line.

Pete pulled the car into a vacant lot next to the area where he'd run into Pike and Ana the night before. In the daylight, it looked less menacing—a desolate, large chunk of land littered with garbage and a few abandoned cars, the ground dead and grassless. The deserted area seemed to stretch for miles, but Pete caught a slight outline closer to the shore. The building looked like a small trailer. He'd missed it the last time, blinded by the pitch-black night and distracted by Pike and his gun-toting sister.

Pete reached the trailer, panting for breath, his shirt coated in sweat. The morning heat had ramped up, going from mild to a full-fledged heat wave in less than an hour. The trailer was large—the size of a nice studio in Brooklyn, Pete thought—but in disrepair. Splotches of rust covered the structure, which looked more like a shed than a living space. Pete rapped on the door, not expecting a response. He didn't hear any movement inside and knocked again.

Nothing. He took out a pair of black leather gloves and slipped them on. He tried the handle. Locked.

He pulled the key he'd found on Pike and pushed it into the lock. No dice.

Pete stepped back from the trailer and scanned the surrounding area. He couldn't see any other buildings or structures around. He cursed under his breath.

He felt his phone vibrating in his pocket and knew it was Kathy—at first, wondering where he was, then mentally hexing him for going without her. He ignored it.

He walked up to the door again, shifted his weight, and rammed his shoulder into the flimsy entranceway. After a few seconds, it gave and Pete was inside. He pulled the door shut behind him. He was immediately struck by the smell—of age, dirt and mildew. The interior of the trailer was an ad hoc office and bedroom, with a tiny cot next to the wall opposite the door and a small table across from it. Or at least that was Pete's guess, as the table was hidden under stacks of paperwork, used cups and garbage. The rest of the space was taken up by boxes, also filled with files and paperwork, a battered two-tiered filing cabinet and a small corner "kitchen" that consisted of a plugged-in microwave and hotplate next to each other on the floor. That's when he saw him.

Kenny Sampson. Stephen McRyan.

It took Pete a moment to recognize the missing son of Trevor McRyan, lying on a ratty rollaway bed. But as he stepped closer, the fallen figure began to resemble the photo that had launched Pete on this journey back to Miami and the thorny branches of his own past.

McRyan wasn't moving much, but even from a distance, Pete could tell he was breathing. He looked ragged. His clothes were torn and streaked with dirt, and his face was covered with scratches and bruises. He wasn't here by choice and had probably been there for a while.

Pete stepped toward him, trying to remain quiet. It didn't work. On his third step, McRyan rolled over, his lazy eyes opening.

"Who the fuck are you?"

"I'm getting you out of here," Pete said.

"Yeah? Good lu—"

The first shot tore open what was once a window, sending glass and debris across the trailer, the sound booming through the flimsy room. Pete fell backward. He rolled away from the hole in the trailer wall and cursed himself for not bringing his gun. He crawled toward the wall opposite the door, his back now to it, and waited. McRyan was now on the floor, no longer relaxed and passed out, but pressed against the ground and on alert, a low whine dribbling out of his mouth.

Another shot came, hitting around the same area. Pete covered his face and brought his head to his knees. He heard a voice but couldn't make out the words, his ears ringing from the two shotgun blasts. He'd lost track of McRyan now. *Was Ana back to finish him off?*

After a few moments, amid the dust and debris created by the shots still drifting down to the ground, the voice spoke again. It was muffled and low, as if the person speaking was trying to hide their identity. *No, not Ana. A man.*

Pete couldn't make out everything said, but he got the gist of it. Whoever was outside was coming inside. With a shotgun.

He got down low and crawled to the other side of the trailer. He reached the file cabinet and tugged. Locked. He tried the key from Pike's pocket and the cabinet popped open. At first glance, the drawer seemed empty. Scooting up a bit, Pete noticed a thick stack of folders, held together by rubber bands, tucked away near the back of the cabinet. He grabbed the folders, unsure how the dusty files would help him when faced with a shotgun-toting thug but curious about what they contained anyway. He could sense McRyan behind him, panting heavily, moaning to himself. Not from pain, but from fear, like a cornered dog, trying to figure out where to run.

"Bad idea, man," McRyan said, his voice coarse and low. "You don't want that stuff. It'll only cause you hurt. Trust me."

Pete ignored him. He held the folders to his chest and inched toward the door, trying to listen for any signs of movement outside. The door swung in, propelled by a kick. A tall man wearing a black ski mask and what Pete guessed was a protective vest over military-style fatigues stepped into the trailer, his eyes covered by large, thick goggles. The man noticed Pete and trained the gun on him, then moved toward McRyan, who was a few feet away from them. Even through the mask, Pete could tell the man hadn't expected to find two men in the trailer.

"You can't have that," the man said to Pete, turning the gun back to him. His voice came out low and warped, like someone yelling through a pile of laundry.

"Who're you?" Pete asked.

"Just do what he says," McRyan said, the words coming out more like a whispered croak than words. "He'll hurt you."

"Drop the files," the man said.

Pete wasn't sure that he'd survive even if he dropped the files, but he wasn't about to test the theory. He put the folders down on the floor.

"Hands up," the man said, motioning with the shotgun. "Both of you." They did as instructed.

"Look, I didn't want to get into a situation," Pete said. The man cut him off.

"Shut the fuck up," the man said. "You break in here, bust through the door, and you say you don't want to get into something? You think I'm stupid?"

Pete hesitated. He thought he recognized the man's voice—though it was muffled a bit, lower than he remembered it. But he didn't have time to think about it, much less place it.

The sound coming from Pete's left resembled a high-pitched yowl, barely human. The masked man wheeled around halfway, pointing the gun in the direction of the noise, an enraged and possibly manic Stephen McRyan. Pete moved forward and sent a sharp kick into the gun-toting man's left shin. There was a low snapping noise, followed by the man's pained scream. He tumbled down, his hands still on the gun, but by then McRyan was on him, punching his face and tossing the weapon aside like a toy.

Pete got up, grabbed the folders and headed for the door. He motioned for McRyan to follow him; the masked man was on the floor, dazed and groaning.

"Come on," Pete said. "We have a lot to talk about."

McRyan seemed frozen in place, his energy spent in the tussle with the masked man. Pete grabbed McRyan by the shoulder, half-dragging him as he sprinted across the vacant lot to the car. Pete tossed the folders and McRyan into the back seat and hit the gas. In the rearview, Pete could see the masked man stumbling out of the wrecked trailer as Pete peeled out onto Angela Street, the tires' screech almost matching McRyan's long, pained wail from the back seat.

CHAPTER TWENTY-NINE

"**G**et in."

Kathy did, hopping into the front passenger seat after tossing their bags in the trunk. Pete stepped on the gas just as Kathy slammed the door shut.

"Whoa, let me at least buckle up first," she said, turning to face Pete, just then noticing the man slumped in the back seat. "Who the fuck is that?"

"That is Stephen McRyan, also known as Kenny Sampson," Pete said, driving down Duval Street, trying to keep it around the speed limit and not having much luck. "I'll tell you more once we get on the highway back to Miami."

He did. McRyan was dead to the world, but Pete watched what he said, mindful to give Kathy a topline version he could expand on later, when they were alone. For now, he had to get off the Keys and back to Miami, hopefully without many people on their tail.

"Marnie is not happy with us, just FYI," Kathy said, looking out onto the water that surrounded the Overseas Highway that became

US 1. "She thinks this whole Pike-being-dead thing is our—well, mostly your—fault. At least my credit card wasn't declined."

"Did the cops show up?"

"They seem to have no idea why Pike dropped dead outside the inn," Kathy said. "So who knows what they're going to do. I managed to get out of there before they questioned the guests. Which reminds me—you really need a tutorial in traveling light. You're a serious overpacker."

"I'm not worried about Marnie," Pete said. "We have bigger problems right now."

"Who cares about the elders, right?" Kathy said, tying her hair back into a ponytail. "Where are we going, exactly? That is my subtle, foot-in-the-door way of asking what the hell the plan is."

Pete slid his right hand down to the floor of the car's back seat and pulled out the thick stack of folders he'd taken from the small trailer. He handed them to Kathy.

"This is the thing you almost got killed for?"

"That's it."

"It could be Publix receipts, for all we know," she said, flipping through it. "Or Pike and Ana's old elementary school attendance awards."

"I haven't spent any time with it, aside from flipping through it for a second," Pete said. "Been under a bit of stress, but it seems to be coded in some way. It's definitely a list of some kind."

"It's a ledger."

The voice sounded more like a broken door hinge than an actual human. Kathy turned to face Stephen McRyan, who was still splayed out in the back seat, his eyes now slits as opposed to scrunched shut.

"Good morning, sunshine," she said.

"A member roll?" Pete asked, looking back at McRyan through the car's central rearview mirror.

"That, but much more, man," McRyan said, between two long coughing jags. "It's the key to everything. Who signed up, what they did, the prices they paid. All the dirt, signed, sealed and delivered. They finally found me, tossed me into that hotbox. They were still deciding what to do with me when you showed up."

"Who is 'they' exactly?" Kathy asked.

McRyan didn't respond. He seemed to be coming out of a deep sleep, his eyes fluttering as he leaned his head back, a low moan escaping his lips.

"Stephen, stay with us, okay?" Pete said, not looking back. "We need to ask you a few questions."

"Ask away," McRyan said. "What've I got to lose, I guess?"

Pete wasn't sure how much runway he had with the guy, who looked like he was entering another dimension.

"Talk to me about the cult, Stephen, the church."

"Shit, man, where do I start?" McRyan said, his head swaying back and forth like some kind of deranged hippie.

"How's the beginning suit you?" Kathy asked. "Like, what made the son of a Florida career politician sign up with this crew of whack jobs?"

McRyan stifled another wave of coughs before responding.

"I was a mess, still am," McRyan said. "My parents didn't want me—didn't give a shit about me or what I did as long as it didn't affect their 'plan' or 'strategic goals,' so I said fuck it and went to Miami, changed my name. I wanted to start over. So innocent, right? So stupid. Like I could escape my past. I was maybe sixteen? I had money, I knew they'd send me more if I needed it, so why not? A friend of mine—well, some guy I met at a party, stoned off my ass—mentioned the church. Said he'd found some kind of serenity listening to this man, Figueras, that his message resonated with him. He'd even spent some time on the church grounds, living and helping, becoming part of the community."

"Who was the friend?" Pete asked. He checked the rearview. McRyan seemed more lucid now.

"Some older guy, I forget his name, but he seemed cool, pretty chill," McRyan said. "I didn't see him again after that, but I went to a meeting—revival, whatever. They did it outside, way down south, like a big festival. Place was packed. And, I dunno, it just felt so ... so real, and not put-on, like everything else. This guy was talking about serious stuff, and he wanted to help people. He wanted to help me, a kid who was basically alone, in this strange city, and he made me feel like I wasn't a piece of shit, you know?"

"Did they know who you were?" Kathy asked, her expression not without empathy. She was no stranger to feeling alienated from the world, or from family.

"Not at first, I don't think. I met with Figueras himself pretty fast and he just said that La Iglesia was a place of love and hard work, where we were all brothers and sisters and we had to be honest with each other," McRyan said, licking his lips. "I didn't think on it too much, to be honest. It felt good to have something to do, to have a place to crash, someone who cared about what I did—where I went to school, who I was hanging out with, if I was eating. All the things my parents dumped on other people if they thought about it at all."

"But eventually your parents did get involved," Pete said.

"Yeah," McRyan said, shrugging. "I got in some trouble and Figueras had to reach out to them, at least that's what he told me. That's when things really changed. When it went from being something that I felt was mine, where I felt like I was part of something, and became something else. I wasn't one of the team anymore, you know? I was treated differently. I got my own room, I got whatever drugs I wanted, I spent time with Figueras directly—and his people, sometimes. And that was nice, trust me, it was good to get fucking hammered on demand, for real—but it showed me that the church was just like everything else, you know?"

"How so?" Kathy asked.

"It was corrupt, it wasn't special, there was no utopia there," McRyan said, leaning forward, his hands on the front seats. Pete could feel his presence behind him, like some kind of swirling, manic energy. "Something had gotten lost in the translation. I got to see the real Iglesia de la Luz and it was fucking toxic. Figueras was no saint, man. He fucked every member of the church that even made eye contact with him. Didn't care about age, either. Guy was a monster. A fiend. He was using the church as a way to collect information on as many people as possible, so, eventually, if it all went south like it did, he'd have a nice little nest egg of intel he could use to keep things going. It was all a blur. The drugs. The sex, the beatings and programming—it was a constant mindfuck. And my own fucking parents left me there. Can you believe that?"

"What about Patty Morales?" Pete asked. This was it. He hoped McRyan stayed lucid long enough to give them something, anything they could use.

"What about her?" he said, his reaction duller, more muted than the feverish release of information that preceded it. "She's dead."

Pete gripped the wheel tighter.

"A few years back you reappeared in Miami," Pete said, hoping the slow and methodical approach might work better. The traffic around them was light and they were making good progress. "You led the police to believe you knew something about the case."

"Nah, I didn't know anything," McRyan said. "I was just tweaking them, fucking around."

The answer came too quick and felt too definitive for Pete.

"Most people don't consider lying to the police 'fucking around,'" Kathy said, whatever sympathy she felt for McRyan melted away. "Either you're a world-class moron who thinks it's funny to interfere with a murder investigation, or you knew something, got scared and backed off. Which was it?"

"You should've asked my parents," McRyan said, a defiant look in his eyes. "They'd tell you what happened—what they made me do."

"Well, we're heading back to pay your dear mom a visit," Pete said, stepping on the gas, checking the odometer. He didn't need to get pulled over now. "We're going to put everything on the table and get some answers."

McRyan let out a creaking laugh.

"Mommy's dead," he said. "They got to her last night. That's what they told me, at least. The guy in the mask. When he brought me a bucket of water to drink from."

Pete and Kathy shared a concerned look.

"They're closing all the loopholes," McRyan said. "Morales, the lawyer, my parents, me—they want anyone who can connect the dots dead. That includes you two, now that you have that book."

"Who's they? Figueras?" Pete asked.

More coughing. "No, no," he said. "Not really. Someone else pulling the strings. But I'm not sure who. He dealt with my parents a lot. Made sure I got a nice little severance package when I bailed on them so I'd come back to the fold, including some bonuses when I needed a fix."

"So you took the ledger as a way to protect yourself?" Kathy asked.

"Only thing I thought I could do to stay alive," he said. "As long as that was missing, they needed me breathing. Not sure what they were planning to do with me now that they found the book."

"What did your parents make you do?" Pete asked. "We've lost whatever they had, in terms of info. Or Roger Morales. Everything he knew is gone. We're just left with some mystery man who might know who killed Patty Morales."

McRyan stiffened a bit at the mention of the girl.

"You're too far into it now, I guess," he said. "If we'd met sooner, I'd have told you to let the whole thing go. Some relics need to stay buried."

"Well, it's a little late for that bit of sage, clichéd advice, pal," Kathy said. "We are in the goddamn thick of it. So anything you can do to help us get out of it would be much appreciated."

McRyan gave her a weak smile.

"Follow the secrets," McRyan said. "Morales is dead, but he didn't live as solitary a life as he wanted people to believe. He had this little cop friend, Cristina something. Not sure if they were fucking or not, but they were definitely more than buddies. She might know something. She'll give you a sense of what his life was like, at least. He was also close to his mom, like a good little Cuban boy."

The traffic was clear and the car was making good time. They'd be in Miami in a few hours.

"Listen," McRyan said. "You've got the one thing La Iglesia wants more than anything—a list of everyone who's ever been a member, from the first Figueras follower to the guy trying to take the head man down. The only way they survive now is by working that list, blackmailing and cajoling current and former members with the threat of revealing their past life in the church. You also just spit in their eye and kicked them in the shin. So I give you points for that alone."

Pete tried to process the new information. Someone was pushing back against Figueras and his failing health. He was clearing the decks of his enemies. This ledger put all that at risk. Did it also reveal who killed Patty? Who framed Harras? Or was it just another false start?

"Um, Pete," Kathy said, her voice shaky.

"What?"

"Did you hear anything about a roadblock?"

"No," Pete said, squinting, trying to look down the highway, not seeing anything but a few specks. *Were those people?*

But as the car got closer, the picture became clearer. The specks were people. Half a dozen, spread out across the Miami-bound lane. Those people had guns. One of the men armed with rifles looked eerily familiar.

"That's Lionel Oliva," Pete said. "Los Enfermos."

"Fuck," Kathy said.

They were about fifty yards from the gunmen when the rifles came up and Pete knew they were in some serious shit.

"Get down as low as you can," Pete said, not looking away from the road. He lined up the car in the lane.

The first bullet whizzed by the driver's-side mirror. Kathy and McRyan started to get down.

"I can't wait until you start, well, turning around," Kathy said, hunching down in the seat, trying to slide into the tight legroom space. "That'd be great."

McRyan was already spread out on the floor of the back seat. Pete crouched down, too, but kept his eyes over the top of the wheel. Another shot, this one off the car's roof. Then another—Pete heard one of the car's headlights pop.

"Yep, whenever you're ready," Kathy said. "I would not mind going back to the Keys right now."

"We can't just keep going—" Pete heard McRyan get up to be heard, his voice loud and frightened. He could smell the man's sweat and stink, like soiled clothes that were left outside in the hot sun. Like a drunk hobo who hadn't seen the inside of a house in years. Then he heard the pop, first the windshield, followed a split second later by a softer, crunchier, wet one as the bullet drove through the front of McRyan's head, sending blood and brains over the back seat. Kathy screamed.

Pete didn't look back. Couldn't look back. He felt wet warmth on his face and neck but he stayed tucked down low, his hands holding the wheel steady and his foot pressing down on the gas as hard as he could.

"Jesus Christ, Pete," Kathy said, curled up under the passenger seat, her eyes wider than he'd ever seen them, trying to make herself even smaller as the tiny car barreled forward. "What are you doing? They blew his head off. We have to turn around."

"No," Pete said. "That's what they expect. They know all our moves. They knew we were down here. They knew we were chasing Stephen McRyan. We have to surprise them. We have to push back."

He allowed himself to glance over the dashboard for a split second and saw the small cluster of gunmen disperse as the car closed in, now about twenty feet from their formation. Oliva was holding his ground, at the peak of the triangle of shooters, but the others, especially the ones in the back, were getting shaky. The window of time they had to dart off the road and live was closing fast. Pete pushed the car harder. He peeked again. Oliva was stepping to the side of the road now, cocking his rifle as the other Enfermos dove for the safety of the highway's narrow shoulder. Another pop and the car swerved and shuddered. The front left tire had been hit, putting the car into a high-speed fishtail that Pete couldn't control. He sat up for a second, knowing he was making himself visible to the men whose one mission was to kill him but also realizing that he had to steer what was left of the rental car before it careened into oncoming traffic.

"Fuck, fuck, fuck," Pete said, screaming each word as he tried to turn the steering wheel back. He slowed the car's spiral enough to stay on land, the useless hunk of metal still hurtling down the Miami-bound lane. He felt the car slam into one of Los Enfermos, followed by a pained scream, the man's body tumbling up the hood and over the roof, before the car stopped. The vehicle had spun around, smoke billowing from the engine. Pete couldn't see the remaining men, but Oliva was back on the road, walking toward them. Pete reached behind his back and pulled out his Glock.

"Pete, no," Kathy said. "No, you can't outshoot these guys. It's stupid. Try not to be stupid for once."

"We have no other way out of this," Pete said as he opened the driver side door and stooped down, gun in hand, letting his eyes peer through the window. Oliva was closing in, rifle pointed at the car. Pete could make out a smile on his face even from this distance.

"*Casi, casi*, Mr. Fernandez," Oliva said. "You almost got away. Now I'm going to ask you and your *novia* to step out of the car with your hands up, and maybe my boss will let you live a little longer."

Fuck this.

Pete leaned left, allowing his head and gun-hand to reveal themselves for a moment. He got a shot off. It went wide, but got Oliva's attention. The older Cuban man crouched in a military shooting stance and fired off two shots—one destroyed the driver's side window, spraying Pete with glass, the shards slicing at his face and neck. The other hit the doorframe, making a loud *thunk* sound and rocking the entire car back. *This is not a long-term solution.*

"I have many, many more bullets," Oliva said, his voice carrying. "I can use as many as you want, *compadre*."

Traffic was slowing on the Keys-bound lane and Pete could see cars stopping close to Oliva on the Miami side. The cops would be here soon—but not soon enough.

Pete snuck another look and noticed that Oliva's men were getting their gumption back, and had reassembled around him, guns raised. Now he was really out of his league. No way his tiny Glock could compete with a handful of high-powered rifles. The car was wrecked. Kathy was unarmed and McRyan was a pile of bloody meat in the back seat. Surrendering now would only guarantee a slower, more torturous death in the next few hours.

Then one of Oliva's men dropped, clutching his knee, his rifle clattering on the hot asphalt. Pete didn't dare keep his head visible.

He heard a series of quick pops. He looked again. Two other men were down—shot. Only Oliva remained, standing up, waving his rifle around trying to figure out who to shoot at.

A black Escalade made a sharp turn from the Keys-bound lane and swerved around in a rough, sloppy U-turn. Oliva didn't have time to react before the car rammed into him at the best speed it could manage, sending the enforcer onto his back in the car's path. A moment later, Oliva was under the car, the large SUV wobbling as it drove over the man. Pete heard a soft, sloshy *splock* sound and looked to see what was left of Oliva's face—a bony red and dark-brown smear on the pavement. The Escalade kept going, making a jagged, nervous turn so the car's tinted driver's side window was a few feet from Pete and his own wrecked car. Pete stood up as the tinted window slid down to reveal the driver.

"Well, what are you waiting for?" Harras said. "Get in."

CHAPTER THIRTY

Marathon, Florida

"Gustines is an asshole, but he's good at his job."

Harras took a long sip of steaming coffee from the Styrofoam cup as he plopped down into a worn-out Island Auto Repair shop lobby chair.

"Not that I'm ungrateful, but," Kathy said, standing across from Harras, "how, upon finally being let out of jail, did you decide, 'Well, let's go *really* kill some people now'?"

Harras shrugged. The ex-FBI agent didn't seem up for verbal sparring with anyone, much less Kathy. They'd pulled into Island Auto Repair in Marathon. It was the best they could find on short notice after a call to Dave. According to him, they trafficked in cash and asked no questions. For a few hundred bucks cash, Harras' bloodied and banged-up Escalade would be in better shape than when he bought it.

"It was pure luck. Gustines told me you were in the Keys," Harras said, looking at Pete. I was heading down to find you after I made bail.

Then I saw the little shootout across the way. It had your signature written all over it."

Pete gave Harras a wan smile. The ride to the repair shop had been fast and harried, leaving little room for a proper catch-up. Pete reported his own car stolen, hoping that'd be enough to at least muddle things, so when it was discovered as part of a deadly shootout on US 1 that involved members of Los Enfermos, no one would bat an eye. Drug deals went sour in Miami all the time, right?

"You saved our asses, that's for sure," Pete said. He placed a hand on the stack of folders that made up the ledger on his lap. "Now we just need to figure out what to do with this, and what we do with the info once we crack the code."

"Did McRyan give you any intel?" Harras said. "Anything useful?"

"He did, actually," Kathy said, returning to her seat next to Pete, not looking at Harras. "He said Roger Morales had a cop friend he may have been dating. She might be privy to some of his secrets. We'd also been meaning to talk to Jackie's mom—also Roger's mom—to see if the family knew anything that might help."

Harras nodded. "What about the McRyans?"

"They're all dead," Pete said. "Stephen said they got to his mother and he went down pretty fast in the car. We didn't get much time to interview him."

"Ellen McRyan was a piece of work, though," Kathy said. "She basically confirmed that someone is trying to usurp Figueras, or has. Someone she and Trevor had been dealing with."

"The church always had factions," Harras said. "From what little I'd figured out, Morales sided with Figueras, until he didn't. That was around the time of Patty's death."

"So there's a third party," Pete said. "Who wanted the group to go a different way."

"And maybe was willing to kill a fellow member's kid to get things going that way," Kathy said.

"Those are the broad strokes," Harras said. "Seems like we're on the same page."

"How does that help your cause?" Pete asked.

"It doesn't," Harras said. "Not yet. We've got a little time before the trial, but I need to lay low. Well, lower than the last few hours."

"From what Dave is hearing, with Oliva dead, Los Enfermos are in a bit of a tailspin," Kathy said. "So that's something."

Pete rubbed his eyes. He ached all over. Since he'd touched down in Miami, his life had gone from a somewhat mundane PI existence to something closer to working on a SWAT team. He wasn't even sure what day it was. Or where he lived anymore. He said a silent prayer and looked up. Harras was standing now, checking his cell phone.

"Car's ready," he said. "Let's get going."

The name Allapattah was taken from the Seminole word for alligator—but the small city didn't resemble the large reptile in any ways Pete could tell. Tucked between Miami's Wynwood art district and below impoverished Liberty City, Allapattah was a home for the displaced: the African Americans bumped over while I-95 was being built, Cubans looking for a home after Castro took over, and myriad Latinos from Central and South America. It was working class—a blue-collar part of town with a thriving garment and textile industry and an active crime rate. It was also not without its share of scars—the fading storefront facades and vacant businesses living proof that while some areas of Miami were thriving and changing, others struggled to keep up. Yet, there were signs of life, as people drifted away from the pricier areas in Miami, setting their sights on cheaper rent and new restaurants, stores or bars. In five years, Allapattah might be the next Wynwood.

The Cruz house was on the corner of NW 27th Street and 15th Avenue, a modest one-story building with chipped beige paint and a lawn that had grown a bit too tall. The car parked in the drive, a beat-up LeBaron, didn't seem like it'd been driven in years.

Pete realized he'd been holding his breath as he pulled in next to the LeBaron. The last time he'd been at the house, four years prior, he'd been in a different mental state.

"You okay?" Kathy asked.

Harras had opted out of this interview, choosing to stick to his script as a murder suspect out on bail, trying to lay low. He'd lent Pete and Kathy his spare car, a nondescript Subaru he'd used on less-than-official stakeouts during his Bureau days, and sent them on their way.

"I think so," Pete said. "Haven't been here in a while."

"If it was before you got your head on straight, I doubt you remember what happened anyway, right?"

"Maybe," Pete said. "I do know I had to tell them their granddaughter was dead."

They got out of the car and walked toward the front door. It opened before they reached the steps.

A well built, sixtysomething man stood in the doorway. Jorge Cruz.

"Mr. Cruz, I'm not sure if you remember me, but—"

"I know you," Cruz said. "Come in with your friend."

The greeting wasn't exactly warm, but Pete took it. They stepped into the small house—its tidy and simple decor gave the place a frozen-in-place feeling, as if, after a certain point, the residents had decided there was little value in keeping up with the times. Cruz motioned toward a patterned brown couch. Pete and Kathy took opposite ends while Cruz pulled up a chair and sat across from them.

"Been a long time," Cruz said.

"It has," Pete said. "Thanks for talking to us. I'm sorry for your loss — Jackie was a friend. Is your wife around?"

"Gisela's still at work, *gracias a Dios*," Cruz said. "She would not want to be here for this. She doesn't talk about these tragedies much if she can help it."

Pete looked around the living room. It was light on photos—and the ones Pete saw were of the couple in younger, more pleasant times. Jackie at her law school graduation. A photo of Roger as a kid. None of Patty.

"You heard about Roger, I'm guessing?" Pete asked. He didn't want to dance around it.

Cruz seemed to cringe.

"Yes, we heard that he died—not all the details, but enough," he said. "We're still dealing with it all, whether we should have a funeral, even. Roger was a good man. We did all we could for him and for Patty. We loved them both."

"He was gunned down a few days ago," Kathy said. "In his apartment in Miami Gardens."

Cruz's gaze was blank.

"We were hoping you could answer a few questions about Roger and Patty for us," Pete said. "If you're up for it."

"Sure," Cruz said. "That's fine."

"Roger is your wife's son from her first marriage, right?" Kathy asked.

Cruz shook his head.

"Yes, that's true," he said. "My wife's first marriage was—well, she didn't talk about it much. The man, her first husband, is dead now. Roger was the only kid she had, and when I came into the picture, Roger was older, in high school. We didn't expect to have any kids of our own, but then Gisela got pregnant and we had our *querida* Jackie. It was the best gift God could have given us."

Cruz's eyes glazed over with a film of tears as he discussed his only daughter.

"Did you get along with Roger?" Pete asked.

Cruz sighed and closed his eyes for a moment.

"I loved Roger like my own son. I told you this."

Cruz's matter-of-fact delivery threw Pete off. He hesitated for a second, allowing Kathy to step in.

"Did you believe the cops when they said he killed Patty?" Kathy asked. "When Pete discovered her remains on his property?"

"At first I did, yes," Cruz said, nodding to himself. "The evidence was there, they said. I had to."

"Did your wife believe her son could do this?" Kathy asked.

"She couldn't accept that Patty was gone," Cruz said. "Her own son being the one who killed her—that just made it worse. Just twisted the knife. She couldn't believe it. She didn't want to. But then they never charged him. They backed off. So we don't know what happened to that little girl. We may never know."

Pete hated conversations like these. Dragging good people through their darkest, most painful moments. It had the intimacy of a confession, without the spiritual release. Instead, they were left to stew in their own sadness.

"So what happened?" Kathy asked. "Why would anyone kill Patty? Was she having trouble?"

"She was a teenager," Cruz said. "Girls always have trouble at that age. Dating the wrong people, staying out too late, talking back. You name it. But in her heart, inside, she was a good girl. She worked hard. Did well in school. Always with extracurricular things. She was a happy kid, even *con esa mama* and a father who was not really paying attention to her. She was *una niña buena*. Always home in time for dinner and always helping out. I don't know why anyone would want to hurt her, much less…"

He stopped himself. He looked around the room, as if he'd just woken from a nightmare and was trying to get his bearings—except the nightmare was real.

"Did Roger have any enemies?" Pete asked. "Anyone who would want him gone?"

"I can't think of anyone," Cruz said, squinting his eyes, as if trying to see further back into the past. "Roger was hardworking. He had his job at the hospital and he had his church. He was dedicated to both. And he had a wife."

"We met his wife," Kathy said.

"She's a, well, she's a *malagradecida*," Cruz said. He let out a humorless laugh. *Ungrateful.*

"She didn't seem keen on speaking with us," Pete said.

"Can't say I'm surprised. Tere was always doing her own thing."

"Do you talk to her much?" Pete asked.

"Gisela does, *de vez en cuando*," Cruz said. "We invite her over for the holidays. Let her know she's loved and part of the family. But I haven't seen her since before … everything."

Kathy cleared her throat.

"She was not very welcoming when we saw her," she said. "And I think that was an understatement. She seems to think Roger did kill Patty. Or someone wants her to say that."

Cruz shook his head. "She's gone astray."

"What do you mean by that, Mr. Cruz?" Pete said.

Cruz looked at Pete, his eyes wary.

"Why're you here?"

"We wanted to talk about Patty—and Roger," Pete said.

"I know that, *mijo*," Cruz said. "But why? Roger's dead. Patty's dead. My own daughter is dead. My daughter you knew and loved and worked for. They're all gone. All that's left are me and my wife, sitting in this old house staring at each other and wondering when it'll be our turn, when God will look down and remember he left us here to suffer. What's the use in digging up the past? Tell me the truth. You owe me that."

Pete looked at Kathy before turning back to Cruz.

"We want to find out who killed Patty," Pete said. "Because whoever did that probably killed your daughter, or ordered it."

A noise came from the door and it creaked open. A small older woman walked in with a few plastic grocery bags on her arms. She looked up and noticed there were people in her living room.

"Oh, well, I didn't know we'd have company over," Gisela Cruz said. She noticed Pete and her light, welcoming mood darkened. "Hello, Mr. Fernandez."

Her husband got up and grabbed the bags from her.

"Pete is here to talk about Patty, *mi amor*," he said, keeping his voice low. "Figured we could chat with him for a little bit and let them be on their way."

Gisela nodded, more to herself than anyone else. She took the seat her husband had vacated as he carried the bags to the kitchen.

"I don't want to talk about this for very long," she said, looking older than she had just a few moments before. "We did the best we could for Patty. She's gone. Now Jackie's gone, too. My heart is empty. I don't have room for more tragedy."

Mr. Cruz returned, kneeling next to his wife and taking her hands in his.

"They know about Roger, Gisela," he said, giving his wife a tender, knowing expression. "Roger was killed in his apartment. Shot."

She bowed her head. The sobs came—slowly at first, but soon they overtook her body, now racked with the desperate sounds that accompany tragedy. Pete looked at his feet.

She composed herself after a few minutes, wiping at her eyes with a tissue offered by her husband.

"I'm sorry," she said. "Roger was my son. No matter what they said he did. He was my baby boy. It's been so hard the last few days."

"We understand, Mrs. Cruz," Kathy said. "And we're sorry for bothering you."

"See, Pete I know—but who are you?" Gisela asked.

"Kathy Bentley. I'm Pete's partner when it comes to—investigations like this."

"But what is there to investigate?" Gisela asked. "Roger is dead. I doubt anyone is going to care what happened to his daughter. Or my daughter."

"We care, ma'am," Pete said. "Because we think they might be tied together."

"Well, I don't see how," Gisela said.

"Did Roger ever talk about an organization called La Iglesia de la Luz?" Kathy asked.

Gisela dimmed her eyes.

"That was his church," Gisela said. "Roger was devoted to that place. Lot of good that did him."

"What do you mean?" Pete asked.

"What do you think?" Gisela said, her eyes picking up a fiery glint as they focused on Pete. "It's suggested that he had something to do with his daughter's death, and his job drops him, then his church wants nothing to do with him. All those years, days, hours, spent at that church for nothing. They left him to rot."

"Were they at odds?" Pete asked.

Gisela nodded to herself, as if confirming a long-held suspicion. "By the time Patty disappeared, Roger wasn't as active in the church as he once was," Gisela said, her words dribbling out, slow and steady.

"Do you know why?" Kathy asked.

"He didn't like how it was going," Gisela said. "He and the main man, what's his name? Figueras. They weren't on the same page anymore. Roger learned some things that concerned him."

"Was he going to leave the church?" Pete asked.

Gisela didn't answer, she closed her eyes and let out a long breath.

"I know this is hard for you," Pete said. "But it could be a great help."

Gisela folded her hands together and waited for Pete to continue.

"After ... all this, with Patty, after her remains," Pete said. "Roger was basically left with nothing. No marriage, no job, no home. How did he cope with that? Was he able to move on? I'd heard he might have—"

Gisela didn't let him finish.

"Roger died a sad and destroyed man," she said, her mouth quivering, tears streaming down her face. "He couldn't recover from losing Patty. We couldn't, either. But yes, he did try to rebuild his life. He was working, he had a home, he was even seeing a nice young lady—"

Jorge moved between Gisela and the couch, as if to signal that their time was up. Pete had pressed too hard. But Gisela's comments about Roger's life seemed to jibe with what McRyan had mentioned on the way back from the Keys.

"I think this has gone on a little too long," Jorge said. "Gisela is tired."

"Did you know anything about Jackie?" Gisela said, her voice muted, as if her husband's body was filtering the sound. "She was good to Patty. Treated her like a daughter. When all that happened."

"When all what happened?" Pete asked. Jackie had never told him about her relationship with Patty beyond the general. By the time Pete found Patty's remains, going backward and analyzing how Jackie felt about her niece seemed irrelevant.

"Nothing, nothing we want to relive," Jorge said.

"Oh, just let me tell them," Gisela said, tapping her husband's hip, signaling for him to move out of the way.

"Patty was thinking about pressing charges against a cop," Gisela said. "Patty had this boyfriend; she dated him for a little while. Really liked him—Danny Castillo, the poor boy who was killed the night she ... " Gisela trailed off. "But she got worried about this boy, didn't trust him anymore. So she ended it. Next thing she knew, this one cop was visiting the house, following her, cornering her at school. It was stalking, but what do you do when your stalker is a cop? He kept asking her to think about her father, think about what his decisions could mean for her. She didn't understand. I didn't understand when she told me, either. I thought it was just another perverted older man, someone who wanted to torment Patty because her father was prominent in this church that fewer people seemed to like. But after Patty died, we mentioned it to the cops and nothing. The whole investigation fizzled out until you found her body, and by then we were too numb from wondering if Roger might have done it to think about this."

"Who was the cop?" Pete asked. "The one that stalked Patty?"

"The man's name was Broussard," Gisela said. "Nelson Broussard."

"You come to the zoo a lot?" Pete asked as he approached the figure lighting a cigarette.

The lanky man stood in the long shadow of ZooMiami's Sumatran Tiger exhibit, the faux-Indonesian structure surrounded by a large moat to keep Satu the tiger safe from gawking tourists, or was it the other way around?

It was a little past four in the afternoon and the park was winding down, families wheeling their safari cycles back to base and various food stands shutting down. Pete had hoped to at least glimpse the giant jungle cat on this unexpected trip to the park, which he'd visited often as a child. But no luck. Satu was staying cool in the shade of the imitation castle his captors had built for him.

"Not a lot, I must admit," Gary Sallis said, the cigarette still dangling from his mouth. "Figured it'd make for a nice, neutral place to talk."

Pete shook his hand. Sallis looked around before continuing. His shirt was sweat-soaked, which wasn't uncommon in Miami, but Pete didn't think it was a byproduct of the heat.

"Thanks for talking to me, I really appreciate it," Sallis said. "I know you're busy and I don't want to waste your time."

"It's fine," Pete said. "You knew Roger, so I'm happy to talk again."

"Look, I know Lonnie McQueen," Sallis said, sticking his hands into his jeans pockets. "He's an old friend. We used to talk a bit back in the day when he was covering the church. And he let slip that you spoke, so I said I knew you and he said that it seemed like you were hitting a big wall. He mentioned you were trying to get in touch with someone who was part of La Iglesia, to get a sense of what it was like."

"I am," Pete said. "Do you know anyone?"

Sallis took a long drag from his cigarette.

"Well, see, that's the thing," he said. "I wasn't entirely on the up-and-up with you and your partner. You guys just, I dunno, kind of caught me off guard, I guess? I was on the spot and at work, so I couldn't really tell the whole story."

Pete gave Roger Morales's former hospital coworker a once-over. The man seemed anxious, on edge and almost desperate. Coming here had not been easy.

"Don't worry about it," Pete said. "If I'd known this is what we were talking about, I would've brought Kathy along, but I just figured you wanted to point me to someone else."

"Yeah, no, I'm the person," Sallis said, tapping his chest. "I mean, Roger and I were both part of the same thing. And look, he got fired, and I should have backed him up more, told our bosses that this thing would've tricked anyone into buying their 'we are all family' bullshit, but I was scared, man. I need this job. I don't have a family, a network to support me. I lose my job, I'm dead, you know? I left the church years ago and I've felt like they've had it out for me since before that."

They walked over to the zoo's in-park rail station and sat down on a bench. The crowds had thinned enough to afford them some privacy, though Pete had already gotten a few "we're closing soon, okay?" stares from the employees milling about.

"Talk to me about the church," Pete said. "What was it like? How'd you get into it?"

"Look, up front, I'm a drug addict, okay? Pills, meth, weed, alcohol," Sallis said, tapping a finger for each vice, counting them off. "Whatever made me feel different, better and not myself, which I felt was a piece of shit, I'd gobble up. I've been sober for almost fifteen years now, but I was a beast when I met Roger. I was on the street, living in a box somewhere downtown. He didn't care. He shook my hand and he didn't have that disgusted, I-hope-I-don't-get-a-disease look most people have plastered on their faces when they touch a homeless person. He treated me like any other man he'd run into. He was doing outreach for the church and he handed me a flyer. Said they were having a gathering—that's what he called it—and asked if I'd like to come. Food, showers, free consultations for stuff like getting an apartment or a car or your license. You know, basic life shit, right? So I said, okay, fine, I'll get a free ride to your party, eat your food, then bail. No skin off my back. I thought I had it all figured out."

"But it wasn't like that?" Pete asked.

"No, it was exactly like that," Sallis said with a laugh. "At least the part where they gave me food, gave me a free medical examination. I took a shower and I got to stand and listen to their guru, this Figueras guy, talk for what felt like three hours. Hell, it might have even been four—the guy could go on, you know? But a funny thing happened on the way to the bus station, as they say—I started really jibing with what this guy was talking about. His message was good. It felt real."

"What was it?"

"Be good to one another, be helpful, be a brother not a boss or competitor or opponent," Sallis said. His words were delivered with more vigor, as the man got into his story. "It felt clear and right, and shit, here was someone trying to help me, trying to pull me out of the gutter and clean me off—like I was a person—instead of ignoring me and treating me like shit when I did pop my head out for a second to face the world. Then I'm going to these gatherings a few times a week. I helped, doing cleanup, making calls for the undocumented people who needed someone who spoke English so they could turn their power on, shit like that. I felt like I was making a difference. Then I reconnect with Roger and he says they need some help at his job, and next thing I know I'm gainfully employed for the first time in forever, using Roger's address as my base. Then I have an apartment. My entire life changed in a few years—and it was all thanks to the church. That will never change, no matter what happened next."

Pete waited, knowing it was better to let Sallis keep going than try to guide him. The park was empty now, and it was only a matter of time before someone came by to usher them out.

"But after the first few years of, you know, me being a drone or some kind of bit player," Sallis said, his voice lowering, becoming more conspiratorial, "things changed. The gatherings were less about Figueras helping or talking about helping us—the little people—and more about him and his power, his connections, how people were out to get him. I mean, there was always some of that, from day one for me, but it was on the back burner. I knew the guy thought he was some kind of son of God, but it always felt like bluster, not what Jaime really thought. But like I said, time passes and the events change. Jaime Figueras changes. Suddenly, he's exorcising demons, he's curing people—people who are paralyzed can suddenly jump, people with cancer yank hunks of tumors out of their fucking bodies—and, look, I don't doubt what those people say or feel, but fuck! That shit felt wrong to me. Like this guy was messing with a power that we, we normal people, shouldn't be fucking with, okay? It was just bad juju, you know?"

Pete stood up and moved his head toward the exit. It was time to head out. Sallis followed.

"What did Roger think of all this?" Pete asked as they walked through the park's turnstile and past the large zoo gift shop. "Was he onboard with the new Figueras?"

"Not at first," Sallis said. "Like I told you before, Roger was really tender-hearted and kind, helped me out a ton, so I feel bad even bringing any of this up."

Pete waited a beat.

"But he changed, too, I can't deny it," Sallis said. "It was really tough to see."

They reached Pete's car and stopped.

"I guess we all kind of accepted that Jaime had this, I dunno, dark side," Sallis said, looking around the expansive parking lot, the sky fading to a soft amber. "He was imperfect. He was our leader, we loved him, we'd probably die for him, but he was doing some things that were, I mean, not cool. Sleeping with members of the church when we knew he was trying to portray himself as holy, taking pills to keep awake, moving the money around, it was just the price we paid for the good Jaime, I guess. But Roger was the rock. He was the guy who kept everything running and tried to keep Jaime in line in terms of his vices. But toward the end there, man, I dunno."

"Gary, I appreciate you coming to talk to me, I really do," Pete said. "But I need something more concrete. Was Roger in on something bad? Tell it to me straight."

"The church had this thing, this document—we called it the Book of Truth," Sallis said. "It had everything. Everything bad you ever did, everything you ever said about someone, every sin you ever committed—in or out of the church—and it kept people accountable. It was in code, but they'd decode bits of it to share with people, to get them involved. So, if you felt low, you'd read that and think, 'Hey, I'm better than that guy,' or if you were fucking up, you got called on the carpet. It's all in there. It was a legend among the regs, the people who just came to the services and weren't fully, I guess, indoctrinated. But it was a real thing. I've seen it. Only glimpses. But everything Roger did is in there. Everything Jaime did and everyone did is in there. You find that, and you have the key to the whole thing—including Roger and what happened to his daughter. I can't say for sure he did anything to her, because I don't know. I do know that he changed toward the end, before she even disappeared. It was getting harder and harder to tell him and Jaime apart."

Pete pulled out his car keys.

"Look, this took a turn I wasn't expecting," Pete said, opening the front door of Harras' loaner car. "Do you want to take a ride and talk to me and my partner somewhere else? We have some documents that you might be able to help us figure out."

"Man, I don't know," Sallis said, shaking his head. "I felt bad dancing between the raindrops with you and the lady earlier. That's why I called. But having a formal meeting, going over documents. That's … that's not what I want to do. I don't want to relive those days anymore, okay? I've got to move on sometime. I hope I gave you something to work with."

Pete nodded. He could see the man felt conflicted but also relieved to be nearing the end of their conversation. It had taken a toll on him. He made a note to circle back to him, though. Gary Sallis had more stories to tell. Pete was sure of it.

"Fair enough," Pete said, sliding into the driver's seat. "Any parting advice?"

Sallis leaned over the doorframe, his body hovering over Pete.

"Watch your back," Sallis said. "La Iglesia is everywhere."

CHAPTER THIRTY-ONE

"**D**oesn't ring a bell," Harras said, sipping his cafecito. "Sure he was Miami PD?"

"That's what Jackie's parents told us," Pete said.

They were sitting at an outside table at Palacio de los Jugos—literally translated to Juice Palace—a Coral Way eatery that featured some of the best Cuban food in town besides the aforementioned juices. The décor was loud and carnivalesque, but it had struck Pete as the right spot to lay low. The crowd was noisy and the place seemed to be bustling, which Pete hoped would help camouflage him, along with the dark shades and Montreal Expos cap he was wearing.

"This is weird," Harras said.

"What is?"

"This," Harras said, motioning to Pete with his chin. "Take those stupid shades off. What the fuck are we doing here anyway? This isn't how I'd like to spend my time before I'm sent to prison, you know? I mean, the food here is fine, but could we have picked one closer to my house, at least?"

"I don't know if you remember," Pete said, "but it was made clear to me—and Kathy—that we were not welcome in our hometown. Los Enfermos are not nice people. Remember that shootout on US 1? So much for them being gone, right?"

"I remember alright," Harras said. "I was the one who saved both your asses. But I get it. So, tell me about this Broussard guy. The Cruzes think he followed the Morales kid around? And?"

"They said he was stalking Patty," Pete said, finishing off the last *croqueta de jamon* on his plate. "And it all started right after she broke it off with the Castillo kid."

"Again," Harras said. "So what? I don't mean to squash your Eureka moment, but I'm not seeing it."

Pete pulled out a heavy manila envelope, pushed their plates aside, and dropped it on the small table.

"This might help."

"The stuff you stole from the Figueras compound?" Harras said, eyeing the envelope. "Have you cracked the code yet?"

"Not yet. But Stephen McRyan thought this was the golden key before he got killed. Said it was more than just a list of names—it itemized everything. I spoke to a former member who basically corroborated that, too. They called it the Book of Truths—some kind of weird accountability system. I bet we find Broussard, or some link to him, in here."

"Go on."

"I think we may discover that Broussard was somehow tied into Iglesia de la Luz," Pete said.

Pete knew they were getting close. You could always tell by just how antsy people got—and by "antsy," he meant how many people were shooting at them. It left Pete in a state of high anxiety, knowing that the brushes with death would become more frequent and intense the longer it took for him and Kathy to get to the truth. It didn't help that, while he felt like the case was moving in the right direction, he still had no definite answers. He needed results, fast.

"So the cult was unhappy with Roger Morales. And you think Figueras wanted to get to Morales through his daughter, by way of Broussard?"

"And it seems like they set Roger up," Pete said. "So maybe Broussard had a hand in it."

"A name on a member roll means only so much," Harras said. "What other evidence can you get?"

"Not sure yet," Pete said. "But Gisela Cruz says that Roger and Figueras had a falling out a little while before Patty died."

"How so?"

"It jibes with what Roger Morales's ex suggested," Pete said. "That Roger learned something about La Iglesia that created problems for him. Maybe he realized his boss was a fraud? It was tough for me to buy Figueras after I dug into some of the stuff the church was doing."

"What do you mean?"

"I hooked up with the *Times*' old religion reporter," Pete said, remembering the disturbing video he'd watched in McQueen's stuffy office. "He talked me through some things and showed me a few clips from when the church was buzzing. He also passed my info to a former member, who corroborated a lot of stuff and seemed to point at Roger pretty heavily."

"Those clips are some scary shit, eh?"

"That's an understatement," Pete said, a sour taste coating his mouth as his mind replayed the final minutes of the video. "It was terrifying."

"So Roger was on the outs with Figueras and someone wanted to put the heat on him," Harras said. "Okay, where do you go with that? I don't have to tell you we don't have a ton of time to figure this one out."

"McRyan mentioned a few things I want to follow up on," Pete said. "I need to retrace Roger Morales' last few months. I think that's where we'll find an answer."

Harras pushed his empty espresso cup away.

"Not bad," he said. "You're getting better at this."

"Doesn't mean shit if I can't figure out these documents," Pete said. "Or who killed Patty and Jackie."

"Lemme borrow the ledger," Harras said. "See if anyone on the federal side can crack it."

Pete slid the envelope over to Harras.

"Just don't let their fingers get too sticky," Pete said.

"I'll keep you posted," Harras said, putting the documents into his rucksack. "Where are you setting up shop now?"

"Crashing on Kathy's couch, avoiding public places or hotels if I can help it," Pete said. "Trying to keep costs low."

"Appreciate you going on the cheap while I pick up the tab."

"I feel weird asking you for money," Pete said. "Your pension can't be that good."

"Just don't stay at the Eden Roc and we'll be okay," Harras said with a laugh. "What else you got?"

"I'm getting nothing on Pike," Pete said. "Seems like he just dropped dead outside of that inn."

"Key West cops seem okay with the idea that the guy was wandering around, drunk, and just fell on his face and died," Harras said. "Nice and easy."

"Did they find anything in his system?"

"The kid drank worse than you ever did," Harras said. "A few times over. So, yeah. There was alcohol in his system. But there weren't any other signs of a struggle or him falling and hurting himself. Seems like he just dropped dead asleep, emphasis on the 'dead' part."

"He just ended up where Kathy and I were staying?"

"If you believe the cops."

"That's always worked out well for me," Pete said, downing the last of his *cafecito* as he stood up. "What's your deal?"

"Just meeting with Gustines and trying to put a defense together," Harras said, dropping two twenties on the table. "They really did a job on me."

"We'll figure this out," Pete said. "I'm not letting you go to prison."

"That's kind of you."

"Stay in touch."

"I sure hope so, seeing as how you work for me now," Harras said. "I'll call if I get anything on this ledger."

Cristina Soto was tired. She let the grocery bag drop to her feet as she tried to find her house keys. It was close to nine in the evening and all she wanted to do was get inside, put the food away, feed her dog and relax for a few hours. She was owed at least that, she thought—at least a few hours away from work. Away from desk duty. Away from the angry stares and awkward silences.

She yanked out her key chain and slid the right key into the front door lock. Before she could turn it, she heard footsteps behind her. She wheeled around. There was a man a few feet away, waiting at the bottom of the steps that led up to her fourth-floor downtown apartment, like a delivery guy trying to figure out how to find a specific apartment. She lived off North Miami Avenue—close enough to everything and high up enough to ignore the world if she wanted to. This stranger was not playing along with her goal.

"Can I help you?"

The guy seemed nice enough—decent-looking, a little underdressed and not threatening. Cristina had an eye for these things. She was a cop. She'd dealt with the entire spectrum, from the drugged-out homeless guy screaming on the Grove to the white-collar businessman with a dead prostitute in his suite. She got fed lines of shit 24/7. "I have no idea how that gun got here." … "I haven't had anything to drink, miss." … "Are you even a cop?" She'd heard lies from the best, so she was tuned into bullshitters. This guy didn't seem like one. Yet.

"Are you Cristina Soto?" the man said. He was polite, but his manners couldn't hide his tone. Cop? Not possible. They would've called Cristina if something had come up, or taken her aside at work. She was in hot water, but she knew how hot. This guy wasn't Internal Affairs. Nah, he wasn't a cop. But he was close.

"Who's asking?"

The man took a hesitant step forward.

"I'm Pete Fernandez," he started.

"Wait, I know you," Cristina said. "You're that PI. Thought you were gone."

"I'm back."

"You know how much shit I'd get into if my bosses knew I was talking to you?"

"It's important," Pete said. "I just need a few minutes of your time."

"For what?" she said.

"To talk about Roger Morales."

Cristina saw her evening of relaxation slipping away. She motioned for Pete to follow her inside.

Pete waited for her to drop her bags and offer him a seat before he started rolling. It'd taken him the better part of the morning to figure out where Soto lived, and he was now down a few favors. But Jack, his old Miami sponsor and an ex-cop, had known people downtown, and after an extended game of telephone, he was able to find the right office. Jack let him go with only a mild query about his recent meeting attendance. A few calls to the right office finally got Pete a full name. With her name, Pete could track down an address. With her address, Pete could find Cristina Soto. She wasn't what Pete expected—around his age, with a relaxed demeanor and soft features. He noticed the resemblance right away—the dark, heavy-lidded eyes and long dark hair, and the pale skin. Had Patty Morales lived, Pete thought, she would have looked a lot like Cristina Soto. As he'd planned his visit, Pete had worried he'd end up with a steel-eyed cop's cop. Someone who had no interest in blurring the lines or speaking out of turn to a private investigator with a rep for tearing down the police. Maybe it was the weariness that allowed Cristina to set aside regulations and talk to him.

She lived in a tiny studio high-rise apartment. The kind of space that looked more like a hotel than a home. Even the personal touches Pete saw—the Pearl Jam *Binaural* poster above the couch and the shelves loaded with paranormal romances and self-help books—did little to make it feel like a unique place, a personal space.

She settled in a chair across from the small love seat.

"I'm not going to offer you a drink because I don't plan on having you here for very long," she said, her eyes dimming.

"That's fine," Pete said, sitting down. "I'll keep it short."

"And I'm not answering anything that'll get me fired."

"That's the last thing I want."

"You could give a shit."

"You knew Roger Morales?" Pete asked, pressing on.

"Not exactly."

Pete paused.

"Let me rephrase that," Pete said. "Did you spend time with Roger Morales?"

"Like I said, not exactly."

"Can you help me be more exact?"

"What's in it for me?"

"I'm trying to find out who killed him."

"Okay," she said. "My mom knew his mom. Some *viejitas,* lunch group. They'd get together and have mojitos until they couldn't drive once a week. Roger's mom told mine about his problems. My mom, because she can't keep her nose out of anyone else's business, let Gisela know I was a cop—not a detective, nothing fancy. But a cop. I walked a beat. So she told her I could meet with Roger, give him some advice to help him get back on his feet after ... Honestly, I think she was just trying to set me up with a single guy. She didn't care he was suspected in the murder of his own fucking daughter. I'm not supposed to do that—meet with people like Roger and help them. But my mom doesn't know where to stop. She'll offer up my time like it never runs out. By the time I was talking to Roger's mom, I'd basically agreed to marry the guy, sight unseen. I'm a sucker."

"So, this was recent? Can you tell me anything about him? About what he was doing after he was cleared of the charges?"

Cristina pursed her lips.

"Shit, Roger was a nice man," she said. "You get a bunch of bad guys and women—people you know are just chomping at the bit to get thrown in jail or some kind of institution. I almost didn't know what to do with myself when I was talking to Roger. He was just a good man."

"A good man believed to have murdered his daughter."

"But he didn't," Cristina said. "Nothing the cops did could make him guilty."

She winced. She'd said too much.

"Did they want him to be guilty?"

"Roger thought so," she said. "He thought he was getting gamed. He'd pissed off the wrong person and now they were trying to get him."

"But why would Miami PD want him in jail?"

"Not all of Miami PD."

"Some?"

"Right," she said. "Roger felt like someone wanted him eliminated."

"The church?"

"Church?"

"Roger was involved in something called La Iglesia de la Luz," Pete said. "It was big in the nineties and before. Their guru, Jaime Figueras, went down on a minor charge a while back, then moved the whole operation to the Keys. Around that time, Roger fell out with him and suddenly things went south for him."

Cristina's stare was blank. She wasn't impressed by Pete's info.

"Look, all I knew was that Roger was a good guy. I liked him. We went out a few times. It was nice. Next thing I know, my job finds out I'm hanging around this dude, this guy they're desperate to put in jail for killing his kid, and I'm an outcast. I'm on desk duty. No one talks to me, no one explains why," she said, clasping her hands together. "And that's fine. I know I fucked up. But I wouldn't have done it for any piece-of-shit con. Roger wasn't guilty. I tried to help him get back on his feet. Now he's dead and I've got one foot out the door."

"What was he like?" Pete asked. "When you were together?"

"He was happy," she said. "We didn't take it all too seriously, you know? He was older than me, almost like a dad-type figure, but my *papi* left us when I wasn't even walking, so maybe I have some of my own issues to deal with." She let out a dry laugh. "But he was nice to me. Took me out. It got deep pretty fast. I'm not gonna lie, I thought I was going a little nuts, falling for this dude suddenly. But it felt nice. I fell in love with him."

Pete swallowed. The bright overhead light blanketed them both, like a flickering spotlight in a police interrogation room. He felt Cristina's eyes hammering him—waiting for the conversation to end, despite her clear desire to unburden herself about Roger and their relationship.

"Have they figured out who killed him?"

"What?"

"Roger Morales was shot to death in his apartment," Pete said. "Like a common thug. Who did it?"

"Did someone hire you to investigate his murder?"

"It's part of a case I'm working on," Pete said. "I think you can figure it out from there."

"I hadn't talked to Roger in a few days," she said. "He said he wanted to touch base with some old contacts and maybe get a business going. He was bored of working furniture sales. Can't blame the guy. He was smart. Professor-smart, you know? He was better than selling furniture at El Dorado, you know? But then I didn't hear from him. That's all he said about it. He had to meet with someone he knew from back in the day."

"He didn't say who?"

"I'm not even sure I'd tell you if I knew," she said, standing up. "I'm not even sure why you're here. What you hope to accomplish. I'm sad Roger died like that—after we'd started to get to know each other. But that's life. It ain't fair and people sometimes taste something good and it gets taken away. I think you should leave now."

Pete stood up.

"Get too close to the truth?"

"What?"

"You were fine about chatting with me until I asked about his murder," Pete said. "What did I miss?"

Cristina walked down the short hallway that led to the front door.

"I have nothing else to say to you."

"Look, I know you were friends with Roger, more than friends," Pete said, standing close to her, the door inches away. "Help me figure out what happened to him. To his daughter. Someone is out there killing people and they need to be brought in."

Cristina looked down at her feet.

"Help me help Roger," Pete said.

Cristina looked up at him, her eyes watery and red.

"Just leave."

The realization hit Pete fast—like a splash of cold water, frigid and eye opening.

"You set him up."

"What?"

"You set up that meeting," Pete said. "You got him killed."

"Get the fuck out of here," Cristina said, reaching for the door. Pete slammed a hand on it, holding it shut, his eyes still on Cristina.

"Why else would you risk your job to help a guy like him? What would a young, attractive girl like you see in a washed-up old man?" Pete said. "You're not a bleeding heart. I did my research. You're a career desk-jockey on the brink of being fired. Did you think I came in here blind?"

Cristina let out a short, detached laugh.

"Blind enough."

Pete heard the door swing open. He turned around and found the end of a shotgun pointed at his head. Ana Figueras was on the other side, a smirk on her worn face.

"Surprise."

PART IV: BAD BLOOD

CHAPTER THIRTY-TWO

Pete was on a bed.

His head felt clogged—his thoughts slow and cottony. His forehead pounded as he tried to get up. That's when Pete realized his hands were tied above his head, the thin white rope woven through the metal bed frame. The room was dank and dim. A tiny window to his left let in some light. He could hear the staccato beat of rain outside. He looked himself over. He felt a warm liquid on his lips and tasted coppery blood. Everything ached. He remembered the gun being pointed at him after Cristina's betrayal. He remembered being led into the back seat of a black car. A bag tossed over his head. Then nothing. Blackout.

The room was bare aside from the bed, a small table to Pete's right and a beat-up chest of drawers on the opposite wall. The only exit was to Pete's left—a door that was surely locked. He guessed it was morning, but that was only based on the light coming in through the crack in the blinds. Pete let out a jagged cough and winced.

The door swung open and a figure stood in the doorway. Pete tried to make it out, but the darkness made that impossible. The man was big and not in a hurry to come inside.

"He's awake," the man said, and stepped back, closing the door behind him. Pete heard the soft click of a lock.

Pete tugged at his restraints. They were tight and he didn't have the strength to get any traction. He let his head drop back onto the mattress and closed his eyes.

The door opened again and another shape walked in—smaller, sleeker. By the time the light from the window caught the figure as it approached, Pete knew it was Ana Figueras. She sat at the foot of the bed, her expression Mona Lisa flat. The figure from before walked in, too. Ramon Medrano—the Iglesia flunky who stonewalled Pete and Kathy in the Keys. So much for not knowing about the church.

He had a snide smirk on his face. Pete longed for the chance to knock it off with an elbow or suitably blunt object. The visual made Pete smile despite the piledriver-like pain in his head.

"Something funny?" Ana said.

"Not really," Pete said. His words came out like a throat clearing, ragged and broken. "Nice place."

"Only the best for our five-star guests," she said, no sign of humor in her voice.

"Why am I here?"

"You have something of mine," she said. "Something of ours."

Medrano stepped in, closing the door behind him.

"You keep doing dumb shit," Medrano said. "You and *la Americanita* can't just leave it alone, eh? Gotta poke one more time?"

"You'll have to forgive me, I'm trying to get over what seems to be a nasty concussion," Pete said, turning his head to face Medrano. "Can you let me know what you want, and maybe we can suss something out? As much as I love having guns pointed at me, or being beaten into unconsciousness, I can't say I'm a fan of being taken on an unwilling vacation. I have to draw the line somewhere."

Medrano let out a hissing sound and looked at Ana. She was in charge.

"The files," she said. "Where are they?"

"I don't know what you're talking about," Pete said.

"Bullshit," she said. "We saw you take them. When you invaded what you thought was our ranch. Did you really think we'd tell everyone in town where we live?"

"I didn't really think about it one way or the other," Pete said. He pulled on his wrists, then looked at Medrano. "Can you cut me loose? I have this weird feeling I'm at the dentist and it's just not doing wonders for my conversational skills."

Medrano looked at Ana. She nodded and Medrano untied him. Pete got up—too fast, his head swirling a bit. He waited a few moments for the world to right itself.

"Thanks," he said.

"Where are the files?"

"The FBI have them," Pete said.

Ana took in a quick breath.

"You'd better be lying," she said. "Otherwise, this is going to be over a lot quicker than we thought."

"Told you this guy was an idiot," Medrano said. "Came up to me in broad daylight asking about us. Asking about *him*. Like he was talking about a Marlins game."

"No one talks about the Marlins anymore," Pete said.

She slapped him, a fast, pointed strike. Pete grabbed his face, and felt his cheek begin to redden from the blow. Her eyes were aflame with anger. She'd moved closer to him. He could smell the grass and sand on her. She looked wired, nervous. She didn't want Pete here anymore than he wanted to be there. It was a desperation move.

"You have no idea what's happening. Do you really think it's just us against you? That we even care about what you're doing? And what, my brother just dropped dead asleep?" she said, her voice shaking. "We're all just fodder here, trying to survive. You know nothing, Goddammit."

She got up and paced around the room, eyes on Pete. Medrano stuck to his post by the front of the bed.

"Why don't you enlighten me?"

"Listen, *papa*, this isn't as easy as you want it to be," Medrano said, stepping in front of Ana. "Okay? I know you want this to be you against us, but we just want to be left alone. Now, we can't be quiet because you went through our shit. Now our shit is public. That's bad."

Pete rubbed his hands, trying to get the circulation going again.

"You know what I want?" Pete said. "I want to find out who killed Patty Morales. I want to figure out who killed Roger Morales. I also want to know who killed my friend Jackie Cruz and the man she worked for, and his wife and their son. That's all. I don't care about your whacked-out cult, okay? I could give a shit. But I do give a shit about these murders. I'm not going to drop that. If it means blowing what's left of this operation down, I don't care."

The door opened, followed by a quick gasp from Ana. Pete looked up and saw a man—or what once was a man—enter the space, leaning heavily on a metal walker, his thin, wasted body sagging down, as if melting, his gray hair and deep wrinkles almost folding over his face. Pete knew Jaime Figueras wasn't over seventy, but this person could pass for a century. Pete wasn't even sure the man was moving until he heard the squeak of the walker's rubber legs as they slid toward the room.

"¿Papi, pero qué haces?" Ana said, rushing to him. "¿Estás loco? La doctora Vigil te ordenó descansar."

The old man ignored his daughter and inched his walker forward. He stopped and raised a thin, branchlike hand toward Pete, his mouth agape. A hollow, chime-like sound escaped his dry, chapped lips.

"You," Figueras said. "You have my books. The Book of Truths, my book …"

He trailed off. He leaned into his walker and lurched forward, suddenly wracked with a long, creaking coughing fit. When he finished he lifted his head and glared at Pete anew.

"Everything I built is in those books," Figueras said. "I thought they were lost, but they're not. You have them. I need them back, I need to rebuild. I'm the chosen one. It is God's will that I rejoin my people now, in these dark, savage times."

"Lost?" Pete said. "I took them from you. From your compound."

"That's what you don't understand," Ana said, clutching her father, giving him some added support. He looked winded, like a fading boxer who stayed in the ring ten rounds too many. "The ledger was stolen. What you found is ours, but it wasn't in our possession."

"So whoever had your book also had control of Trevor McRyan?" Pete asked. "You're not even in control of your own operation, are you?"

Pete saw the shame consume Figueras' face. A once-proud man reduced to begging and threatening to try and reactivate a cult most had written off years ago. Figueras swayed. Ana reached for him, but he waved her off.

"There was a time, *hijo*," Figueras said. "When I was the most loved and most feared man in Miami, in South Florida. I would preach to thousands. First in my church, then in fields, then in stadiums. They would come to me, they would ask to be healed. I would bless them. I would cure them—cancer, AIDS, paralysis. I had the touch of God. I am a piece of God. I was so close then—so close to building a bridge to heaven. I can do it again. We will start again ..."

Pete saw Medrano lunging for Figueras and rolled off the bed, landing in a crouch. He winced as he hit the floor and tried to ignore the sharp knives of pain stabbing his ribs. Medrano moved fast, and in a few quick motions Ana was shoved aside and Figueras was hunched over, clutching his stomach. Medrano stepped back, the blade he'd kept hidden now slick with Figueras' dark red blood. The older man seemed to fold into himself, muttering something Pete couldn't make out. Ana was screaming now, a potent mix of anger and fear. Figueras toppled to the floor with a *thunk* as his body and walker hit the carpet. Pete was certain he was dead.

Medrano shifted his focus to Ana now, waving the knife in her direction as she took a few steps back—her eyes wild.

"*Traidor*," she said, her voice low and guttural. "He loved you like a son, and this is how you repay him? Judas."

Medrano didn't respond. He took another step forward—holding the knife in front of him. There was only a wall behind Ana. Pete looked and saw the open door. Just a hop and a skip over Jaime Figueras' dead body. It would be easy.

Too easy.

Pete straightened up and pivoted around the bed. The dive was sloppy and wouldn't have gotten him a Major League tryout, but it got the job done, his body toppling into Medrano's legs and sending the man forward. Pete landed hard and heard Medrano do the same, the man's face slamming into the floor as he gave a prolonged groan of surprise. He heard Medrano's knife bounce away. Pete got up and faced Medrano, who'd recovered from the tackle, his eyes scouring the floor for his knife, momentarily forgetting Ana. He charged Pete.

Pete sidestepped the rush, using his own momentum to shove Medrano toward Ana as she leapt at him, the knife now in her hand. The larger man fell on the woman, and they became a tangle of curses, elbows and legs. Somehow, Ana managed to flip Medrano over and position herself above him, struggling to gain traction in the fight. Pete had bought himself twenty seconds. Maybe half a minute. He watched as Ana grappled with Medrano, one hand clutching his hair, her other hand bringing the knife to his throat and slicing across, blood pulsing out in a slow waterfall. The knife came down again. And again.

Pete left the room and locked the door handle as he closed it. He'd bought himself another minute. Ana would have to give chase, but he wasn't sure she would. He needed to find his way out, though. The hallway was dark and empty. There was a door at the end of the hall, leading to a wider room. He opened the door and saw he was in a small one-story house, empty but for a few pieces of furniture—a table and three or four chairs, some food wrappers and a tiny radio on the floor. A car engine turned off outside. Someone was approaching the door. He heard Ana's frantic footsteps behind him. She was out.

The front door swung open. Kathy stood on the other side. Soaked from the rain, holding a gun—a desperate, panicked look on her face.

"We have to go."

They lost a few seconds starting up the car before Ana Figueras reached them. Pete didn't ask how Kathy had found him. Not yet. They had to leave.

Pete let himself breathe once he got a better sense of where they were—not the Keys, as he'd surmised while bound in the room. Not

Miami, even. Kathy pulled onto the Coconut Creek Expressway, checking her mirrors every minute or so to make sure they weren't being followed, the gun resting on her shaking lap. She shoved a cigarette in her mouth and tried to light it before cursing and tossing it out the window.

"Thank you," Pete said.

"You're lucky I check my voicemail," Kathy said, wiping at her eyes. Pete wasn't sure if it was rain or she'd been crying. He didn't ask.

"That girl set you up pretty well," she said, turning onto the Turnpike, checking the rearview one more time. "It was too easy."

"I should have known."

"She folded fast," Kathy said. "It's amazing what a loaded gun can do to tip the scales of a conversation."

Pete tried to laugh, but let out a quick sob instead. He was spent.

Kathy reached over and grabbed Pete's hand. She squeezed it for a second, returning her grip to the steering wheel.

"How do you feel?" she said.

"Like I got run over by a few buses before being thrown into a ditch," Pete said.

"Could be worse, then," she said, smiling for the first time.

"Standard hangover, if we're grading on a curve."

"Your bags are in the trunk," she said. "I packed my things, too. My apartment's too visible. Harras—our new, benevolent sponsor and a permanent asshole—wants us to stay with him until we find some new, less obvious digs."

"He's really taking this seriously," Pete said.

"When have you known him to take anything casually?" she asked.

Pete closed his eyes for a second, tried to push past the pulsing pain in his head to get to some kind of clarity. He needed a meeting. He needed a break from the case. He was wearing down and he hadn't fully processed how much of a bullet he'd just dodged.

"Did you learn anything of value while hanging out with your inbred friends?" Kathy said.

"I saw Jaime Figueras."

"What?" Kathy asked. "What did he say? How did he look?"

"First, he looked almost dead," Pete said. "Then he looked definitely dead."

"You saw him die?"

"Medrano took him out—guess he was working as some kind of deep plant in the Figueras camp," Pete said before taking a long sip from the water bottle Kathy had in the car's central cupholder. "Then Ana sliced Medrano's throat. Odds were I would've been next. You saved my life."

"Add it to your tab, I guess."

"They seem as confused about the ledger as we are," Pete said. "I don't think we stole it from Figueras. Someone else had it."

"That's interesting," she said. "Did they have any info on who this mystery person might be?"

"I didn't get that far," Pete said.

Kathy pulled into the lot next to Harras' apartment building—a recently built cluster of condos off Biscayne. As she finished parking the car, Pete leaned over, his mouth close to hers. She pulled back, fast. The space between them was mere inches, but it felt like miles to Pete in that moment.

"Are you high?" she said. "What are you doing?"

"No, I—" Pate said, his words jamming up in his throat. He'd acted on impulse, feeling raw and near death, gravitating to the one comfort he could find. Now he felt stupid and out of line.

"Look, Pete, I'm glad you're okay," she said, her breath warm on his face. "It would have been a pain to organize your funeral. But I don't think we should ... do this kissing thing now. Or until this is over. Until we figure out what we want."

"I mean, this is what I want," Pete said, settling back into his chair. "I don't want to miss this chance anymore."

"Pete," she said, placing a hand on his face. "I don't want to be your adrenaline fuck, okay? Or kiss, or whatever. If we both feel the same way when the dust has settled, then, well, maybe it's something. But I'm tired of falling into things because it's exciting and all the bells are going off. That hurts too much and I'm tired of going from these big highs to feeling like I should die. It's not sustainable. We tried this once before and you couldn't handle it. I'm not a well you can just come back to."

"You're right," Pete said. "I'm sorry."

"Stop apologizing, you psycho. You almost died. I get it. But for now, let's go see what our pal Harras has in mind for us, yeah? There's also a hurricane about to hit any second now," she said, stepping out of the car. "It's like we're getting the band together except we've all slept with each other. Very Fleetwood Mac. With lots of rain."

Pete waited a moment, his hand on the door latch. He looked up at the main rearview mirror and saw Kathy trying to open the trunk, her hair blowing in the wind. He felt a dull ache in his chest as he stepped out into the hot Miami afternoon.

CHAPTER THIRTY-THREE

"**H**ope you're ready for this storm," Harras said. "Also, you were right."

"Don't give him a big head," Kathy said to Harras as they stepped into his spacious condo. She didn't look at the older man as she wove in, a duffel bag hung over her shoulder.

"What am I right about?" Pete said, following his partner in.

Harras hefted a heavy manila envelope in Pete's direction.

"This is much more than just a ledger," he said. "It's a detailed list of everyone and anyone who's been a member of La Iglesia de la Luz since its inception, not to mention explicit details of everything they ever did as members, and even before. And I don't mean what yoga classes they attended. Some dark reading. Lots of heads would roll if this became public. There's a lot of power in here."

"There's a lot of power in my stomach," Kathy said. "Is there anything to eat here? I'm assuming we're not rationing food yet."

Harras motioned toward the kitchen next to the living room. She dropped her bag and left the two men alone. Harras moved toward the couch and placed the ledger onto the nearby coffee table. Pete stood across from him.

"Glad you're alive," Harras said.

"Barely."

"Where would you be without her?" Harras said, as if reading Pete's thoughts from a few minutes before.

"Dead, a few times over," Pete said. He glanced at the ledger. "What else is in those pages?"

"It's a ton of information," Harras said, rubbing the bridge of his nose. "A lot of it is just juicy—cops, ex-ballplayers, D-list celebs. You can picture the church badgering them for money with this hanging over their heads. The McRyans are here, too."

"We expected that."

"Right, and I haven't read through the entire roster yet," Harras said, pulling the ledger out and opening it on the table. "But there's more. I knew this Broussard name was weird. I don't think I know every cop that ever served in Miami, but the name fell flat. I asked around, and nothing. Yet he's on this list as a card-carrying member."

"Possible you just didn't know him?"

"Very," Harras said. "But possible none of my contacts knew him either? Less so."

Pete's phone vibrated in his pocket. Dave. He picked up.

"Hey."

"You got a minute?" Dave asked. He sounded muffled. Like he was calling from a tunnel.

"Sure, shoot."

"Things are getting hot out here, man," Dave said. "And I don't mean this storm. I'm not sure what you guys are up to, but it's setting off a lot of alarm bells. I'm hearing weird shit from people out there."

"Could you be any vaguer?"

Kathy walked back in, one hand in a bag of Cape Cod potato chips. She looked at Harras, who responded with a shrug.

"Just ... I dunno," Dave said. "Just cool down what you're doing. People are out and looking for you guys, okay? Watch your back."

"What are you talking about?"

"Are you guys safe?" Dave asked, changing the subject. "Hunkering down for a while? Supposed to hit early tomorrow."

"Yeah," Pete said. "Harras is putting us up until the storm passes. Are you? Where are you setting up?"

The line went dead.

They got to work. The three of them set up shop in Harras' dining room, which was wide and seemed to have been used sparingly over the years. They spread out chunks of the ledger—translated into English by Harras' FBI pals—and pages from the Patty Morales files that Pete taken from Jackie's apartment. Kathy sat at the end of the long table, Jackie's old laptop open, typing. Pete was at the other end, scanning a few pages. Harras left the room to brew some coffee.

"Remind me what we're looking for, dear."

"Someone wanted Patty's death to point to Roger Morales—because Roger discovered that the church he'd dedicated his life to wasn't all that it was cracked up to be," Pete said, "that same person wanted Roger out of the picture when it came to the church. That same person had the McRyans in his pocket because he exerted some kind of control over their wayward son."

"Until the son got his hands on this," she said, tapping her finger on a ledger page. "The money train for our dear faded cult."

"Right," Pete said. "And this person is probably the one who killed the McRyans—all three of them—and Jackie, trying to get me. But that gets us no closer to figuring out who it is."

"It also doesn't help that these files don't seem to have much on, well, the leaders of the organization," Kathy said, flipping through a stack of pages. "Kind of convenient to keep your sins out of a book used to blackmail your followers."

"There's some stuff on Sallis, about a drug bust in the eighties, but nothing on Morales or Figueras that I can see," Pete said. "I don't think this is a dead end—we still have a ton of stuff to go through. But it's not a slam dunk."

Kathy took a long sip from her vodka cranberry. "You're right, which means we won't be able to solve this tonight."

"You calling it a night already?" Pete said, looking up from his screen.

"I doubt I'll be able to sleep," she said. "But I'm going to try before the storm starts, and I'm spending the rest of the wee hours in the bathroom praying the building isn't blown away. Why, do you plan on dozing while the eye of the storm waddles by?"

Pete didn't answer. Kathy closed her laptop and walked toward him, giving him a peck on the cheek before wrapping him in a tight hug.

"I'm sure I'll see you later, when the true howling wind starts," she said, her face close to his, their mouths a few inches apart. "Don't stay up too late, okay?"

"I'll try."

She walked down the hall toward Harras's guest room.

"Never a dull moment for you, huh?"

Pete looked up and saw Harras, holding a mug of coffee. He passed it to Pete and leaned on the table.

"Anything yet?" he asked.

Pete shook his head.

"Nothing concrete," Pete said. "I feel like we have the broad strokes, but that's not enough."

"Talk me through it," the older detective said as he took the seat next to Pete.

"Jaime Figueras ran La Iglesia de la Luz for a long time," Pete said. "In that time, some factions formed. One, I think, was run by Figueras' right-hand guy, Roger Morales. The other was run by someone else. Someone who wanted the top spot. So that meant taking Morales out, especially after Morales figured out something bad—maybe some of the stuff in this ledger. The first strike was stalking Patty Morales in 1998, via that cop, Broussard. But then things escalated and Patty was killed. But even that wasn't enough. Morales is still involved in the church. Figueras maybe told the guy to cool off, step back. But then Figueras loses some power, maybe this is where he gets sick— around the time Jackie has me re-investigating Patty's disappearance. Maybe this guy gets wind of that, leads me to Morales and then he dumps Patty's remains. The charges don't stick, but Morales is done.

His marriage is over, his job drops him—he's a pariah. His wife even starts getting paid to bad-mouth him. At the same time, this person is also trying to cultivate the McRyans—helping finance their campaign and also using their son as bait, because what better way to get your cult back on its feet than by having the governor in your pocket? So, he starts paying off the estranged kid when he bubbles up and puts his dad's political career at risk. But Stephen is under enough control that this guy can torment the McRyans to do what he wants. Except it's not them he should worry about. Stephen manages to get his hands on the one thing that's actually been bringing money into the church in the interim. The ledger—the Book of Truths, as Figueras called it. Without the ledger, the money dries up, so it makes it imperative to find Stephen McRyan. So the man puts the screws on the parents. Find your kid, find my book, or it's over. They took it to mean the campaign was over. But our guy meant over as in, 'you're dead.' And whoever this guy is, he's not just some suit with a boner for money. He has connections."

"How so?"

"He's tapped into the Miami underworld enough that he can point what's left of Los Enfermos to me," Pete said, tapping his chest. "He can manipulate Broussard, a cop, into doing his bidding. He's no lightweight, and he's using everything he's got to box us out."

Pete hit the heel of his hand against the table.

"What?" Harras asked.

"I'm missing something," Pete said. "I can see it, right in front of me, but it's not clear yet. Fuck."

Harras stood up.

"I'll leave you alone," he said. "I know what you're dealing with. But look at it this way—we're gonna be in this apartment for a while with this storm coming, so take your time. Clear your head. Find the links and follow them back."

Pete nodded. Harras placed a hand on his shoulder.

"I'm glad you're back," he said. "Don't think I'd get out of this mess without your help."

"Don't thank me yet."

Harras nodded and walked toward his bedroom.

Pete waited until he heard the door click shut. He reached for his phone and scrolled through his recent email until he found the note from Lonnie McQueen. The email didn't have a subject and consisted of a line of text, a name and a number: "Here's the contact I promised." Pete's thoughts spun around the solitary sentence and its implications. But he didn't have time to dwell on it for too long.

He tapped the phone number next to the name, Hannah A. She picked up on the first ring.

"Hello?"

"I'm Lonnie's friend," Pete said. "He gave me your number."

"And?"

"He said you might have something I could use," Pete said, watching his words, aware that a minor slip could end the call in seconds.

"I don't do phone," she said. "Text me your email and I'll send you what I have. The rest is up to you."

"Okay," Pete said. "Thanks. I appreciate your help—"

She'd already hung up. Pete couldn't blame the woman, who'd experienced who-knows-what level of grief and pain at the hands of La Iglesia, for not wanting to revisit it. He just hoped Lonnie's lead wasn't coming too late.

He sent Hannah A. a text and waited in front of his laptop, his Gmail account open. A few minutes passed. He stood up, stretched and paced around the dining room. As he slid back into his seat, he noticed a new message, the bold black text like a small beacon in the night. He clicked. The email was empty aside from an attachment: ForLonniesFriend.pdf.

He clicked on the file and downloaded it. It didn't take long for Pete to realize what he was looking at. The first image was a photo of a thick black book. It had a glossy cover which featured a long film reel unspooling and the words *Lights, Camera, Action!* emblazoned on the front in embossed, cursive letters. Under the title, it said AQUILA CLASS OF 1998. It was Pete's high school yearbook. Well, not his exactly. That copy had been lost in a fire that had destroyed his father's house a few years back. A fire caused by a madman looking to murder him and Kathy. This electronic copy was clean—no long, scribbled notes from friends he'd never see again, littered with "xoxo" or "K.I.T.!" or "I didn't know you very well, but …"-style messages. But Lonnie's contact had sent him this file for a reason, and it was yanking him back in time, to the days when he was just an awkward teenager with a crush, spiraling out of control after a disastrous moment, trying to figure out what to do with himself. Not much had changed. But Pete owed it to Patty Morales to decipher why this file was in front of him, and what it revealed about her last night alive.

He clicked to the next image in the PDF and noticed it wasn't a complete scan of the book—that would probably be too big a file to email, he mused. The subsequent page took Pete to the back of the yearbook—a large photo spread. The two pages were dominated by a massive headline over a senior headshot of Patty: REMEMBERING PATTY MORALES. Pete recalled the discussions that preceded the spread's addition to the book. Patty wasn't dead, some of the school administrators said, meaning an "in memoriam" style spotlight was a bad idea. It didn't help that the girl had disappeared under mysterious circumstances, following a murder on school grounds. But logic won out—though the two pages had to be purchased as advertising. Thanks to an anonymous buyer, though, that issue had been resolved. Pete had never figured out who laid down the cash to purchase the spread. Some mysteries—and good deeds—were best left unsolved.

Under Patty's enlarged headshot was a generic paragraph outlining Patty's accomplishments, her hobbies—"Patricia loved sports, writing and watching *Friends* … " Pete wasn't sure what information he was supposed to glean from this book he'd pored over numerous times over the years. But Pete hadn't been himself for a long time, and his half-baked investigation into Patty's disappearance four years ago had been sloppy at best, a drunken joke at worst. Now he could look at the evidence with more clarity, and hopefully find a sliver of truth he'd missed.

Pete scrolled over the candid photos that covered the remaining space and zeroed in on one, off to the lower left. Patty, hand-in-hand with a tall, dark-haired boy with a scowl on his face. They were outside, at a football game. Though the pictures were in black and white, Pete knew she was wearing the school colors, purple and white, on her T-shirt, a massive eagle head under the SOUTHWEST HIGH SCHOOL logo. Sadly, football was not one of the Southwest Eagles' better sports. *Had they even won a game that year?* Pete wondered. The picture bothered him. The caption read: "Patty with Columbus student Daniel Castillo, who was killèd the night of her disappearance."

Pete leaned back from the book. Danny Castillo. He remembered the kid. He had everything, or seemed to. Quarterback of the Columbus football team. Tall, handsome, sulky in an attractive, River Phoenix way. Pete had seen him a few times and had instantly hated him. He was the guy dating the girl Pete pined for. Typical, egotistical young male behavior, Pete thought. Like he owned Patty. *You haven't learned much since,* he thought, his mind flipping back to earlier in the day, shoving his face in front of Kathy like her willingness was just a *fait accompli.* The words of the program rang in his head: Progress, not perfection.

He remembered cheering aloud when he heard Patty and Danny had broken up, as if that meant he'd have a chance in hell with her. He never thought it would end up with both Danny and Patty dead, Patty's remains sprinkled over her father's front yard for Pete to find years later, drunk off his ass, reeking of cheap vodka and shame. Pathetic. But now he had a chance to right that wrong, to close the loop and find out what happened to this girl—for Jackie and for himself.

Pete closed the file and opened a new tab on his browser. He typed a few words into Google and leaned over to pull a stack of pages from the ledger toward him. He checked the screen. It was an old *Miami Times* story, written by Darryl Forges. Pete didn't recognize the byline. Castillo wasn't even the sole lead in his own murder story: "*SW Dade Teen Found Dead, Another Missing.*" It was interesting to read something that was written in the immediate aftermath of the crime. Had Patty done it? Was she on the run? Those questions, though not the key one, would be answered eventually. But at that moment, anything was possible. He scanned the story, loaded with quotes from the police and plenty of overwritten filler. Then he found it. It seemed like a joke at first—a trick of the light, or a byproduct of tired eyes and delirious thinking. But no, there it was.

Pete felt like he couldn't breathe. *Not possible.*

He turned to the ledger and flipped through the pages. He found the names: CASTILLO, DANIEL, SR.; CASTILLO, ANTONIA. He went back to the story.

"Motherfucker," Pete said under his breath.

The discovery that Danny Castillo's parents were members of the church should have been enough, but that bit of information was minuscule in comparison to what the rest of the story revealed to Pete. The fringes of his mind still buzzed with the idea. It had to be a mistake. A typo. He clicked on Forges' byline and discovered the reporter had been part of the team covering the Morales case in its early days, and so had written a handful of pieces immediately following the girl's disappearance, along with Kathy's dad, Chaz Bentley. Another headline jumped out at Pete: "*Murdered Columbus teen's friends ask: What about Danny?*"

The story wasn't anything new: friends or family of a victim overshadowed by another element of the crime bemoan the lack of attention paid to their loved one. But Pete wasn't thinking about that now. He wasn't thinking about kinds of newspaper stories and puff pieces and color-heavy features crafted to show the "human side" of Miami. No, he'd homed in on two names Forges quoted in his rambling, award-angling piece. Two names that belonged to friends and classmates of Danny Castillo. Two boys who were now men. The two people who discovered their dear friend Danny murdered in the halls of Southwest High—not mentioned anywhere else: police reports, follow-up coverage, witness accounts. Nowhere.

Pete felt a big puzzle piece, the kind that blended in with the others, inconspicuous and oddly shaped, click into place, allowing him to figure out what he was looking at.

One name didn't surprise him. The other name Pete couldn't believe was there, in black and white.

The first was Kenny Sampson.

CHAPTER THIRTY-FOUR

Pete left a note on Kathy's door. His request was simple, and he knew she'd be able to handle it fast. He hoped. It was already nasty outside. The outer bands of Elizabeth were pelting the Miami shore and Pete had maybe half an hour to get where he needed to go.

At least the streets are empty.

Pete flicked his high beams on and tried to make out the road between wiper blade swipes. He drove the loaner car west.

He dialed Harras' cell.

"Where the fuck are you?"

"Gotta handle something," Pete said.

"In the middle of a storm?' Harras said. "It's a Category 4. Get back here, you moron. Anything you need to do can wait."

"No, it can't," Pete said. "I don't have a lot of time, so answer one question for me."

"Shoot."

"When you asked your pals about Broussard," Pete said. "How'd you describe him?"

Harras waited a moment before responding.

"Same way the Morales girl described him to her parents," he said slowly, trying to figure out Pete's game. "Older, thin, salt-and-pepper hair, friendly but with some menace."

"Can you put together a list of the cops or other people you asked about him?" Pete said. The wind was getting louder, the rain slapping against the car. He felt the vehicle shudder as he turned onto Bird Road.

"Sure," Harras said. "But what for?"

"Compare the list to the ledger," Pete said. He was almost yelling now, trying to have his words heard over the storm. "Call me back, okay?"

He didn't get a response.

The connection was gone. He knew what Harras would find. But he needed to be sure. He parked the car in the strip mall lot and slipped the raincoat hood over his head. He dropped his phone into his pocket and reached for the glove compartment. He pulled out the Glock and checked it. Loaded. He got out of the car and hooked the gun on his waistband, behind him. He gripped the car as a burst of wet wind walloped him. When it slowed, he walked toward the store. The lights were on and Pete could see a figure standing inside, looking out.

The Book Bin sign flickered off as Pete approached.

CHAPTER THIRTY-FIVE

The bells made their familiar chime as Pete walked into the used bookstore that had been a second home to him for years. The space he'd once called an office had been little more than a closet, but had hosted some of his darkest moments: his final falling out with his ex-fiancée Emily, his desperate return to the bottle when he thought she was dead, taken by a serial killer looking to get back at Pete. But the space had also been a launching pad of sorts. A place for him to rebuild. Redefine. The small room had offered him a chance at redemption.

"I guess it was only a matter of time," Dave said, stepping into the store's main foyer, next to the front desk, past the massive, overstocked bookshelves.

"I don't want to be right about this," Pete said. His voice was shaking, not from the storm.

"Are you arresting me, Pete?" Dave asked. He looked at ease, almost resigned.

"Talk to me," Pete said, taking a step toward his friend. "I can help you."

"I don't need your help, man," Dave said. "You're not my friend. You made that clear when you ran off. After all I'd done for you. Saved your life who knows how many times. Then you pack up, disappear. Like I never existed. Now you want to come back and dredge all this up like some kind of avenging angel? Fuck you."

The winds were getting louder now. Pete could hear a distant crashing sound. The store's windows were bending back, being pushed in by the 130 mile-per-hour gusts. And this was only the beginning.

"I didn't want to believe it," Pete said. "I mean, Dave Mendoza is a pretty common name. So, I pushed it out of my head. And even if it was true, that you, Dave, the guy I loved like a brother, were buddies with the kid found murdered the night Patty Morales died …"

Pete wasn't able to finish. Dave let loose with a rage-fueled scream and lunged toward him, grabbing him and swinging him onto the table, banging his head against the cash register, sending bookmarks, greeting cards and other knickknacks flying. Dave pulled him up and slammed him back down. Pete's vision flickered.

"Like a brother?" Dave said, screaming into Pete's face, his eyes red-rimmed, his mouth contorted into a pained grimace. "You don't know me at all. You never wanted to know me. I was just the guy you called when you got in trouble. Well, guess what, Pete? I had to call someone when I was in trouble, way back then. I needed help then. Where were you?"

"Why didn't you tell me?" Pete said, a trickle of blood sliding down his chin. He was seeing double, his head lolling forward as Dave loosened his grip and stepped back. "Why didn't you tell me you knew Danny Castillo? What are you hiding?"

"Everything," Dave said, the words a hiss. "You don't know what you're dealing with."

Pete took a step forward, straightened up, and fell to his knees, his brain swimming. He gripped the sides of his head and looked up at his friend. Still his friend. Dave had to have an explanation. He had to.

"Why ... ?"

"Just tell him, Dave."

The voice boomed from the back of the store, bouncing off the shelves and paper and coming through to Pete like a crowbar to the face. He knew the voice. He should have known the owner of the voice would be here.

Dave wheeled to his right, shock on his face as Gary Sallis stepped into the crowded front area. Roger Morales's former hospital colleague seemed relaxed, his clothes hanging loosely off him, like a beach bum out for a stroll before a nice seafood dinner. But most beach bums didn't carry .44 Magnums in their right hands. Sallis reached Dave and pointed the handgun at Pete.

"Hi, Pete," Sallis said. "Been a bit."

Pete didn't respond.

"Well, since we last spoke," he said. "Since you last saw me. But I've seen you, buddy. Man, have I ever. You are one annoying piece of work, you know that? You and that dumb bitch."

"Detective Broussard, I presume," Pete said, looking up to meet Sallis' eyes.

"Bingo, buddy," Sallis said, flicking the gun in Pete's direction. "You aren't as bad at this as people say, you know? You might have a career at this PI business, if you keep your chin up and work hard. Or, wait. No. That won't fly."

Sallis pushed the gun's hammer back and stepped toward Pete.

"Hope you brought what's mine," Sallis said.

"The ledger?" Pete said, his eyes following Sallis as he paced in front of him. "The Book of Truths? That's safely tucked away where you won't find it. How much of what you told me was true, Sallis? Or were you just trying to get a bead on the ledger?"

Sallis gave Pete a disingenuous smile.

"More truth than fiction, believe it or not," he said. "But I leave that to you to figure out."

Pete turned to look at his friend, Dave's expression anxious and on edge.

shy? Come on, tell him, Dave, don't keep your
~~~an,"~~ Sallis said, a vile grin dominating his face,
te. "Your pal here was one of us, Pete. He saw
a while, at least. From the early days, you see?
~~~us~~ parents didn't just get rich from blood, sweat
~~~, no sir.~~ They bought in. Invested. And they made bank
along with Jaime and the other leaders. But then things got rough.
Money wasn't flowing as fast. Controversy and all that. Jaime was a
fallen messiah. He hadn't even gotten sick yet, but I knew it was time
for a change. Time for new leadership. It was my time." Sallis patted
his chest with his free hand. "But that fucking brown-noser Morales
saw through me. He knew what I was after. Kept whispering that into
Jaime's ear. Then he got wind of the real Jaime, the Jaime that liked to
get hopped up on Benzies and fuck his apostles. The Jaime who sent
teenagers to kill people. The Jaime who blackmailed politicians and
cops to get what he wanted. Roger got itchy and scared, talked about
going to the cops, being 'true' to himself. That couldn't stand. I would
not sit there and let that buttoned-up piece of shit ruin it all because
he couldn't grow a pair, couldn't make his own move. It was time to
do something. And, boy, did I know where to hit Roger Morales. I
knew his weak spot. His world. I figure, lemme start pestering his
pretty little girl. Threats. Ratchet up the tension, you know? Make
her feel unsafe. Figured that'd do just fine, maybe Roger would even
resign from the church and be on his way. But no, not quite. So, when
I hit a wall with that Morales bitch, when I couldn't put enough of a
scare into her, I knew we had to step it up. We had to make a fucking
statement, man. Leaders don't just whimper and ask politely to be
put in charge, Pete. You must know that, right? No, we step the fuck
up, man. We make moves. And so, when I asked a few of my most
favorite boys, including little Stephen McRyan and your buddy here,
chubster supreme Dave Mendoza, to beat the shit out of Patty's little
fuck buddy, well, they went above and beyond."

"Stop it," Dave said. "I didn't kill him."

Pete could barely hear his complaint, as the winds picked up even
more force outside the store. Pete's head throbbed. He was still reeling
from the tussle with Dave. He couldn't sit for long, though, he knew.

Sallis turned to face Dave for the first time.

"Oh, I'm sorry," Sallis said. "Am I telling it wrong? Did you to break the news to your friend? Did you want to tell him t. 'Wow, me and Stevie, we got so fucking excited beating the shit ou of Danny that we, hell, just shot the guy a few times. So sorry, Mr. Sallis, I know you told us to just beat him up, but, if anything, we're overachievers. And hell, sure, you told us to leave the girl alone, but when we made him call her it just seemed oh-so right, and then she saw us so, well, gee, it didn't leave us much choice—'"

Before Sallis could finish, there was the sound of shattering glass followed by darkness as the block lost power.

CHAPTER THIRTY-SIX

Pete lunged forward, arms outstretched, and rammed into Sallis, sending them both back into shelves loaded with used paperbacks and hardcovers. Pete heard Sallis curse in surprise. The shelves made a booming sound as they hit the floor and Pete rolled to his right as they toppled into each other, a short—but heavy—set of dominos. He got to his feet and heard Sallis scrambling to do the same. A bolt of lightning lit up the Miami sky and cut through the thrashing wind. He glimpsed Sallis, still on the floor, groping around for his gun. He saw Dave standing by the register, unaffected by Pete's dive.

"Run," Dave said.

Pete did.

He made it a few feet outside when the wind slammed him backward. Pete gripped the doorframe, holding himself up. He heard the rustling of paper and the creaking of furniture as Hurricane Elizabeth's winds swept into the store, finding new space for their fury. He pushed himself forward and ran into the wet, dark night.

Pete was soaked in seconds, the parking lot a swirl of rain, debris and thrashing wind. The trees bent in awkward positions and it seemed to Pete, as he squinted through splashes of whipping water, that the buildings themselves were swaying ever so slightly.

But he didn't have time to marvel at Mother Nature. He pivoted toward his car. He felt in his pockets and came up empty. Where were his keys? Lost in the tussle? *Fuck.* He had no choice. He had to run. Pete started down Bird Road. That was when he heard the gunshot, cutting through the din of the storm and meaning only one person would walk out of the Book Bin alive tonight—Dave or Sallis.

He didn't have time to look back. Pete sped down the strip mall's empty storefront row, catching glimpses of boarded-up windows, overturned furniture and swirling debris. The whole area looked like someone had picked up the street and shaken it with the carelessness of a toddler playing with a dollhouse.

Pete felt the bullet whizz by his head and crash into one of the strip mall's faded beige pillars as he hopped down into the parking lot behind a Checkers hamburger spot. The second bullet hit near his feet, sending bits of asphalt up toward Pete, making him jump a few steps forward. Still, he didn't look back. He couldn't. But he knew Sallis was closing on him.

Pete made a left at the end of the fast food restaurant and leaned his back against the wall. He grabbed the gun that was still tucked behind him and checked it. He leaned out an inch and tried to see through the torrential rain and wind. All he could make out was a tall, slow-moving figure heading toward him, as if there wasn't a care in the world, just a local out for a late-evening stroll. Pete rolled out into the open and fired two shots, but felt his arms move, jostled by the wind, and knew they were off. Sallis didn't even seem to flinch. He kept walking toward Pete.

Pete pivoted, his feet pushing off the wet pavement and crossing SW 107th Avenue. Then he felt his shoulder hurtle forward, almost as if on its own, and he fell along with it, his body slamming into the wet ground. The pain came next, annihilating whatever cushion the surprise and adrenaline gave him. His entire right arm felt like it was on fire, tingling and screaming. He wasn't sure if the shot had gone through him and he wasn't able to take a second to figure it out. He rolled onto his back and looked up. Sallis was still coming, the winds dancing around him, the rain turning his gray hair a wet, dark color and his footsteps splashing closer to Pete.

I can't get up, Pete thought. He tried to lean forward, to prop himself in a sitting position first, so he could try to stand, but his body refused. The pain was too much. Sallis was a few yards away now, the Magnum raised and pointed at Pete. The rain didn't even feel like a storm anymore—it was something stronger. Like the world coming apart.

"Oh wow, you don't look so good," Sallis said. He was standing over Pete now, his shadow giving Pete's downed figure some cover from the rains smothering them both. The streets were empty. No cars on the road. No passersby to scream to. *This is it.*

It was bound to happen. He'd been through so much—survived things that even the most trained professionals couldn't evade. Serial killers. Murderous drug gangs. Rifle-toting assassins and his own self-destructive habits. If he was being honest with himself—and what better time to try that than now, on the last stop before oblivion—he had to admit he'd been trying to kill himself since he took the first drink. The rest was just the story of how he died. Even over the past few years, he'd shambled forward, no longer drunk-dead, but barely alive, a sober zombie trying to learn how to exist in this strange, raw world and not having much luck.

Pete's mind was a flurry of sharp images and visceral memories, moments rushing through his mental camera. His father's look of shame as he picked him up from the police station. Emily on the night he proposed. The call, letting him know his father was gone. The spiraling, euphoric void that came with each drunken blackout, always stronger, lingering longer than the one before. An exploding car. Blood dripping from his mouth behind a dingy Gables bar. His father's house ablaze. Cradling Kathy's crumpled body, a bleeding gash through her midsection. So much pain. So much destruction in such a short time.

Pete lifted his head up and met Sallis' dark, unflinching eyes.

"I gotta tell you, bud," Sallis said, yelling the words, trying to communicate over the booming winds and rain. "I wasn't sure we'd get here. You kept slipping right through my hands. First the McRyan thing, then the Keys, then our little zoo chat—hell, I thought you'd be halfway to the beach in your car by now. Guess your luck just ran out, Mr. Pete Fucking Fernandez, eh?"

Waiting to die. But had that been it? Had he just been biding time after a fateful decision to spiral into darkness?

No.

Pete lashed out, his left leg shunting forward and connecting with Sallis' shin. A wet, muted cracking sound signaled success. Sallis' surprised moan confirmed it. Pete rolled left, his arm sending waves of pain up to his brain with every second it took to move away. He wasn't sure how he found the energy to sit up, much less the energy to stand, but he did. He wanted to live, Pete realized. He wanted to not only live, but he wanted to live for something. For himself. *To live*, he thought. *I want to live.*

He pointed his Glock at Sallis, on the floor, looking like a wet pile of garbage. The roles reversed.

"You piece of shit," Sallis said, clutching his leg, which was now twisted at an unnatural angle. Sallis' head bobbed left and right, looking for his fallen weapon.

Pete took a step forward, holding the gun with his good hand. He could barely see Sallis now, his eyes coated with rainwater, the sky an unnatural gray-black color. He tried to take another step, but felt himself lifted, the wind sending him back, the full force of his body landing on his limp arm, a desperate, primal scream escaping from his lips without a thought as he watched his gun clatter away.

Sallis stood, his weight shifted onto his uninjured leg, giving him a zombie-like gait as he stepped toward Pete. He leaned forward and scooped up Pete's gun without missing a beat, as if he'd lived his whole life favoring a leg. Pete saw this in spurts, his mind blinking in and out from the pain in his arm, which he could no longer move. He felt, more than saw, the tall, angry man approach him. He saw Sallis lift the gun—his father's gun. The irony wasn't lost on Pete, even now, as everything zoomed past his mind's eye. Pete felt his body spasm, splayed out on the side of the road, his face buried in grass and dirt, his entire form twisted up like a newborn baby trying to go back from where it came. He closed his eyes.

"You know what they say," Sallis said. "Fool me once—"

A gunshot burst through the bluster of the storm and Pete closed his eyes, bracing himself for the destruction and nothingness that would come from Sallis' gun.

But Pete felt nothing, aside from the rain and wind already assaulting him from all sides.

He opened his eyes in time to see Sallis, the top of his skull no longer where it should've been, crumple to the ground with a wet, sloppy *splack*.

In Sallis' place was someone Pete never thought he'd see alive again.

"Dave," Pete said, unable to speak louder than a whisper.

Dave skidded toward him, his knees sliding on the wet pavement as he tried to lean down toward Pete.

"I told you to run, man," Dave said, yelling into Pete's face, his eyes red and brimming, his shirt torn and caked with dirt, his left shoulder coated by a spreading stain of blood. "Why didn't you run?"

Pete reached up a shaking, battered hand. Dave clasped it and helped him to his feet.

CHAPTER THIRTY-SEVEN

Jackie Cruz's funeral, delayed by the storm, had been well attended—a mix of family, political luminaries, friends and police. Pete winced for the millionth time as the tight suit jacket rubbed against his bad shoulder. The doctors said it might never heal right, but the shot had been clean and, aside from some major blood loss, he'd been lucky.

Lucky didn't cover it.

Harras, Kathy and Pete walked toward the black Escalade after Jackie's burial. She'd been buried near Patty's final resting place. Dave, on the advice of his new attorney Gustines, was keeping a low profile until his role in the Patty Morales case was cleared up to the liking of the Miami PD. Pete wasn't optimistic the process would be short or painless, especially since Dave had two strikes against him: a long rap sheet and his friendship with notorious cop-baiter Pete Fernandez. Dave's family was also ensnared in the fallout from Sallis' death. Dave's parents—former members of La Iglesia—now found their lives engulfed by the media shitstorm that followed the revelation of

Patty Morales' murderers and their ties to a cult most of Miami had considered a footnote in the city's criminal history.

Harras pushed a button on his keys and the car unlocked. He held the back seat driver side door open for them.

"Surprised the press didn't storm this one," he said.

"They're past it now, sadly. Jackie's old news," Kathy said. "They're chasing the sexier angles."

Kathy slid into the car and Pete followed, Harras getting behind the wheel.

"I can't shake the feeling we will never get the full story here," Pete said, as much to himself as to his friends. "I haven't had a minute to talk with Dave since he took out Sallis, and I'm not sure I will anytime soon. And while I know Dave trafficked in some bad stuff before, I can't buy him murdering an innocent girl. But I don't know."

"We're never going to get the full picture, no," Harras said. "That doesn't happen in the real world. But the facts law enforcement gathered, based on what you told them, are pretty tight. When you asked me about the people I'd checked with on Broussard, I went back to the ledger. Your hunch was right—they were all on there."

"Broussard was a fake," Pete said. "I didn't know Sallis was Sallis then, but I knew whoever we were chasing was posing as a cop and was the man threatening Patty."

Harras pulled the car onto Caballero Woodlawn's winding internal roads and drove toward SW Eighth Street.

"Miami PD confirmed Dave's parents—and Dave, too, albeit to a lesser degree—were members in good standing in La Iglesia," Harras said. "Had been for years. Loyal to Figueras but one of the first major donors to side with the Sallis faction. When Sallis decided it was time to move on Morales, to eliminate him as a threat, it made sense that he turned to his biggest benefactors."

"And to his private psycho, Stephen McRyan," Kathy said, leaning her head on the window, her eyes distant.

"Or Kenny Sampson," Pete said. "It's just—Dave. Jesus. To have that secret inside him for so long. I knew he'd done some bad things before, but—"

"It explains Jackie's notes, too," Kathy said. "Even she couldn't believe it. Or doubted it enough to strike out his name."

"It also explains how Sampson's name disappeared from the police files," Pete said. "Sallis used his influence over some of these cops to tweak the file, as if Sampson never existed. But I'm still floored that Dave didn't just tell us this was going on. We could have helped him."

"It's messy," Harras said. "Maybe he thought he'd moved past it? Who knows. There were no signs he was still an active member. At least not until very recently. But a lot of that can point to Sallis, who made a name for himself using former members' identities against them. That was why the ledger was so valuable. It was a phonebook of people Sallis could circle back to and threaten with outing. If you were a member of La Iglesia de la Luz years ago, the last thing you wanted was to have that info out in the open now, for the world to judge you in real time on social media, twenty-four hours a day."

"You think he blackmailed Dave?" Kathy asked.

"I'm pretty sure he did," Harras said, looking back at Kathy. "Maybe even got some intel on us as the investigation was happening. Los Enfermos knew you were in the Keys, Ana Figueras knew you were visiting Cristina Soto—though, based on the ledger, Soto was at least a fringe member, maybe not completely looped in on who you were—but she was in on it to some degree. Either way, someone was funneling info to La Iglesia, had to be. My guess is Dave, though I doubt he was happy doing it. But it felt like they knew what we were doing before we did."

Pete shook his head. He didn't want to think about it, to dwell on his friend putting their lives at risk to avoid his own shame.

"I realize we're dealing with murder and cults and lots of bad, bad stuff," Kathy said. "But it is kind of funny that the one piece of the world Sallis or La Iglesia couldn't control or scrub was your high school yearbook. I mean, that was the only way you were able to find out that Danny Castillo was pals with Dave and Stephen McRyan, right?"

"Exactly. The only reason anyone even cared about Stephen McRyan was because McRyan was flaunting his info to the press, otherwise his name appears nowhere. I'm sure that rankled Sallis,'" Pete said. "What a devious guy."

"Yeah, Sallis was a piece of work, too, once we got to dig into him. Not a zealot like Figueras but evil in his own way, driven by money and a sharp sense of revenge," Harras said. "After the story broke, the hospital inventoried everything he did, from the time he took the job until today. The results weren't pretty. Missing chemicals, equipment, you name it. The guy had built his own little med-lab in his apartment, and he wasn't working on a cure for cancer, I'll tell you that much. Guy cooked up his own little poison pill—a cocktail of untraceable chemicals that could kill, but wouldn't show up on an autopsy unless you were looking for it."

"He wanted the ledger," Pete said. "That was his main goal. If he couldn't run the church, he'd at least be able to get rich from the information in that book. That's why he popped up again pretending to be Lonnie McQueen's contact—to confirm I still had it and figure out a way to get it. And I took the bait, like an idiot."

"Any of us would have," Harras said. "From the way you made it sound, Sallis said all the right things and tried to point you toward Roger being the bad guy."

"Yeah, which backfired, but it got me distracted enough to ignore him," Pete said, shaking his head at his mistake. "Roger Morales actually was a good man—and if I'm piecing it all together correctly, he was an actual believer, not a twisted megalomaniac like Figueras or an opportunist like Sallis. When he realized that his guru might be abusing his power, he asked questions—the opposite of what Sallis hoped I would believe. That was why Sallis was pressuring him, on Figueras' orders, but also as part of his own bigger plan. Sallis wanted to be in charge."

"And he knew that would come easier if he pitted Morales and Figueras against each other," Kathy said. "It worked, too. For a while. He even had his own little spy in the Figueras camp with Medrano, who Sallis recruited after he originally quit years back. And the medical connection explains Pike, too. He looked like he was taking a deep, pleasant nap, but he was dead."

"Sallis tracked him down after you ran into him—he probably freaked after you clashed with Pike, worried the big lunk said too much," Harras said. "Must've drugged him at some point, but the giant was so strong he almost fought off the meds."

"He got as far as the parking lot next to our room," Kathy said. "Pretty impressive. But not far enough."

"Sallis' drug know-how explains Brownstein dying in his sleep, too," Pete said.

"The cop you dealt with the first time around?" Harras asked. "He was good police."

"Yeah, I mean, the cause of his death is uncertain, but I know Miami PD is looking into it," Pete said.

Harras turned the car onto Eighth Street and headed toward Le Jeune.

"One more dose of Cuban food before you hit the road," Harras said, changing the subject as he pulled the car into the restaurant's parking lot. A quick *cafecito* at Versailles would do everyone some good, Pete thought.

As they walked toward the restaurant's entrance, Pete felt his phone vibrate in his pocket. He pulled it out. Once he noticed the display, he stepped back from Harras and Kathy.

"I have to take this," he said.

Kathy raised an eyebrow but said nothing. Harras shrugged and kept walking. When they were out of earshot, Pete tapped the phone and picked up the call.

"Dave," Pete said. "Talk to me."

"I'm going to assume you haven't decided what's next," Kathy said as Pete dragged his luggage toward the Delta terminal at Miami International Airport.

It was midday on a Tuesday, meaning the MIA crowds were obnoxious but not rage inducing. Pete was a few hours early. He knew this would be a delicate goodbye.

He turned to face his friend. They were both bone-tired. Even two shots of *cafecito* couldn't revive them after the last few weeks.

Pete's injured arm was in a sling, still a few weeks from being even somewhat useful. But physical pains aside, he'd never felt better. Clearer.

"I'm coming back," he said.

"Oh?" Kathy asked. "That was not what I expected."

"I was running away from my problems when I went north," Pete said. "Coming back here, facing that, helped me. Losing people I cared about—Jackie, Dave, too, in a way—reminded me that I should make the best of the time I do have left with people I care about. Sounds hokey, I know."

"No, not at all," Kathy said. "Not at all, for once."

"Plus, now that Harras isn't going to jail," Pete said, "who's going to keep you from killing him?"

"No one can stop that," she said with a smile.

The Harras aspect of it all had been the slowest to resolve. He was still facing two murder charges in the deaths of Trevor McRyan and Jackie Cruz. But thanks to some deft detective work and a thorough search of Sallis' apartment and storage units, detectives found a cache of plans, weapons and hacking tools that made it clear he'd been the one who pulled the trigger and had also coordinated some of his followers to slap Harras with the rap.

"You never said anything about my note," Pete said.

"The illegible piece of paper you slid under my door before you went careening into oblivion during a hurricane?" Kathy said. "I got it. I read it, too. But you're alive and you didn't need me to finish solving your case for you, so I didn't think there was a point in revisiting it."

"You don't seem surprised that I did solve it."

"It's just funny how you keep getting underestimated," Kathy said. "I mean, this guy Sallis took Harras off the board first, thinking he was the main threat. By the time he noticed you, it was too late."

"Bringing in what was left of Los Enfermos took me by surprise," Pete said.

"I think it took them by surprise, too," Kathy said. "Talk about 'not ready for primetime.' It's got to feel good to kick them in the face once more, I'd imagine."

"Would feel better if Jackie was alive," Pete said. "I let her down."

Kathy leaned in and gave Pete a tight squeeze, her cheek on his.

"Of course it would," she said, her mouth next to his ear. "But here we are."

She moved back, her hands on his shoulders, trying to avoid the injured area.

They looked at each other and Pete knew this would be his last chance to bring it up, crowded airport or not.

"What do we do now?"

"Do now?" she asked. "You get on a plane, pack up your shit and come back. The couch awaits you."

The couch.

"What about you and me, I mean?"

She pursed her lips and tried to reel back the long sigh that Pete knew was coming.

"I can't decide anything now," she said. "I don't even know when I'm going to see you again. Or what your plans are. Or what my plans are. We've been through all this shit and I'd like to sit down and breathe for a few days. I mean, if your worst-case scenario is we're friends and partners, things can't be so bad, right?"

Pete felt his face warm up. He had expected this response. That didn't make it sting less. This whole "engaging with his emotions" thing was something he'd have to get used to. He made a mental note to call Albert once he got back to New York.

"What?" she asked.

"Just give it to me straight," Pete said. "So I'm not holding out some weird hope because you just want to be nice. It's fine."

Kathy's breath came out in a rush.

"Oh, okay," she said, her usual dollop of sarcasm missing from her voice. "This sounds so trite, and you know I do love you, but … how do I say this? I feel like you need to figure yourself out. And I'm not here to do that for you. God knows I have my own load of baggage to deal with. So, I'd rather say no, it's not happening now—or, ever, really, instead of dangling this out like a carrot. I want you to come back because we're partners and family and I think we work well together, not because you're hoping that we'll get naked again soon. I don't know if that makes sense, but it's how I feel, and I don't think it's going to change. I want to keep working together and helping people, but the rest just felt, I dunno, weird. Nice, but weird. Can we do that? Can we just be partners? I'm tired of feeling weird around you."

He stuck out his hand. Kathy took it.

"Partners," he said.

"Forever, I guess."

CHAPTER THIRTY-EIGHT

October 11, 1998
Miami, Florida

"**D**ave, help me!" Patty said, her scream echoing through the empty halls. "Danny's dying!"

She was crouched down, her face close to Danny's, his breathing ragged and fading. She felt her hands slick with his blood as she tried to put some pressure on what—*the gunshot wound?*—she thought was his main injury. That's when she'd seen his friend Dave. His sidekick. Danny DeVito to his Arnold Schwarzenegger. Funny, always friendly, chubby—good ol' Dave. She liked him. Felt they'd become close while she and Danny did whatever they were doing. But now everything had been turned upside down, and Danny was dying, Dave was looking at her like some kind of lost dog and she was covered in blood when she should have been walking outside to get in her car and go home.

Dave turned away from her, his hands shaking. He was looking down the hall, in a direction Patty's gaze couldn't follow.

"She's here," Dave said, voice quivering. "She came."

"Who are you talking to?" Patty asked. She could feel Danny's body, hollowing out as his last breaths left him. It was going to be too late. *Why was Dave just standing there?*

Then she saw him, and she knew she was in trouble. His long shadow appeared before he did, and a cold sweat spread over her as she saw Kenny Sampson take his place next to Dave. The familiar shape jutting out of his back pocket confirmed to Patty just how dire things had become. *A gun.*

For everything good about Dave—his sense of humor, his kindness, the warmth he had showed Patty, even after she broke things off with Danny—there was something bad, dirty and evil in Kenny. From the moment they'd met, when he'd stormed into Danny's room one lazy afternoon, interrupting them and not seeming the least bit embarrassed, Patty knew Kenny was *not right.* He was a spoiled rich kid who'd been suspended for bashing another kid's face into some lockers at Columbus, and he had followed up the suspension by tracking the kid to his house and continuing the assault, leaving the poor guy with a broken nose and two busted ribs. Patty wasn't sure what strings were pulled to keep him at the all-boys private school, but he had survived. And for some reason, Danny looked up to him, their shared experience on the football team building a bond Patty had major issues trying to understand.

But that was all in the past now. Old news. She was here, sitting on the dirty floor of her high school cradling her ex-boyfriend's head as he died, and Kenny Sampson was lurking, his eyes sliding over to meet her, a savage, terrifying grin on his face and a gun in his pocket. Patty admitted she knew little about this boy, this young man who was more keg of dynamite than teenager. But what she knew chilled her insides. He was angry, violent and probably whacked out on who knows what. Patty needed to get out of here—fast.

"Patty, Patty, Patty," Kenny said, walking past Dave, stopping a few feet from the stairwell and his friend, who she was certain was dead.

Oh fuck, he's dead, in my arms.

"You don't look so good," he said. "Danny doesn't look like he's doing well either."

"He needs help," Patty said. "He's in trouble. We have to get him to a hospital."

"Yeah," he said, looking away for a moment before returning his gaze to her. "That's not gonna happen. Dave and I have a job to do. I think we went a little too far, you know, with Danny, so I think we have to keep going if we're going to cover our asses, you get me?"

No. No. Nonononononono ...

"Come on, Kenny," Dave said, his voice a feeble whimper. He was begging him. "Let's just go. She won't talk."

"Be quiet, you fat piece of shit," Kenny said, the words snapping at Dave. "You're not in charge here. We do as we're told. Gary said mess him up. We messed—"

"He's dead," Patty said, surprised at her own calm delivery. "You killed him. And I know you did it and I'll tell them it was this Gary person who made you do it, I'll—"

Dave shook his head, muttering under his breath. He was shivering, going into some kind of shock.

"See, that was the wrong thing to say. Very, very wrong," Kenny said, moving toward her. She heard a clicking sound and noticed the knife in his hand, the blade out, the hilt twirling around as he walked, that goddamn smile still on his face. "Now we know what we have to do, Patty. Because we can't have you talking, and this thing, this way we're going to make you hurt, it might be more than we were asked to do, but it'll send a message. To you, your daddy, the church—"

"Just finish it," a voice said. A deep, older voice, from down the hall, getting closer. "You know what we have to do now, Stephen."

She noticed Kenny react and was surprised to see something close to fear in his eyes, an expression he covered fast with bluster and bravado, but one that Patty saw regardless. Dave was now on the floor, his head in his hands, lost to the world.

"W-who was that?" Patty said as she stood up, leaving Danny's lifeless body behind and taking a few steps back, though she knew there wasn't anywhere to run to.

Stephen?

If she sped up the stairs, they'd catch her eventually. She couldn't get past them. Her best bet was to scream.

But she never got the chance.

Kenny moved like a snake in sand, his left arm jutting forward, the knife slicing into her midsection—deep—and across. She felt warmth cover her belly and she fell forward, and then that same deep, slashing sensation cut across her neck. She reached for it, felt her hands slip over her throat, she was choking—

On my own blood.

Her knees hit the floor, stained and coated by decades of students walking to and from class, her friends, her enemies, her teachers and her—

But not anymore.

She tried to open her mouth, to let a sound, any kind of sound, escape her lips but all she tasted was blood, and all she felt was the burning pain where Kenny had slashed her and all she saw was his blood-spattered, toothy grin.

She wanted to run.

CHAPTER THIRTY-NINE

October 15, 2017
New York City, New York

Spring Valley would have to wait.

Pete didn't think he could have survived New York City if he was still an active alcoholic. Even now, with a few years of sobriety under his belt, he felt a soft, subtle tingling of familiarity as he stepped into the bar. Like any other city, New York had its share of trendy, obnoxious and crowded hot spots. It also had a wide stretch of dark, cool and comforting bars. The ones with the jukeboxes that seemed to play your favorite songs back-to-back. Where the bartender poured your signature drink as you walked in. Without hipsters or scenesters and with just enough regulars to make it feel like familiar territory, but not so many so that you couldn't get loaded and not care.

I need a meeting.

Iggy's was the kind of place that made Pete want to tour his early drinking days, when he could knock back a few beers and enjoy the company of friends or a date and all the alcohol would do was loosen him up and make his jokes land and his charms rise to the top. He was not up for a tour of the later times, the dark days—when every drink was the first step toward a dirty, shivering blackout and often ended with him at the bottom of a literal or proverbial ditch—lost, confused and ashamed. By the end of his run, the black times far surpassed the good moments. But it's funny how one's brain worked—the pleasant memories seemed to pop up faster, like some kind of nostalgic self-preservation.

Iggy's, on Ludlow and Rivington, was the kind of place you could miss if you weren't looking for it, nestled between a taco joint and a Comfort Inn—small, unpretentious and pretty forgettable—the perfect place to have a few beers alone if you didn't want to be found. The bar's dim lighting synched up well with the Modern Lovers playing on the sound system. But Pete didn't dwell on the distractions. He was here for something else. Someone else.

He'd called in a favor with an old friend—Kathleen Stone, a private investigator Pete had worked a Manhattan case with years before. He'd made a handful of private detective contacts in the business over the last few years—Ash McKenna, Jackson Donne, Gabriella Giovanni—but few encounters were as memorable as the week he'd spent investigating a high-stakes Broadway murder with Stone. He didn't have time to look her up, though. He just needed a lead, and she helped track it for him. His unexpected phone conversation with Dave had pointed him to Manhattan's Lower East Side. He just wasn't sure where, exactly. That's where Kat came in.

"I've got an address," she'd said, skipping any pleasantries when she'd called him less than a day before. "Not sure how long it'll be good. Hell, it's an Irish dive bar, so it's already not good. Anyway, I'm told he spends a lot of time there."

Pete didn't want to risk losing the lead. He thanked her for her help.

"Took me less than an hour, so don't sweat it," she'd said.

Pete hopped into the first cab he could snag at JFK after arriving from Miami. He'd lost one of his best friends and finally put Patty Morales to rest. But the case wasn't closed. Not yet.

Iggy's was empty. Not a surprise, considering it was late in the afternoon. The bartender, a stocky dude who looked like a washed-out frat bro who'd discovered the power of hydroponic weed, was scrolling through his cell phone. Pete rapped on the bar with his knuckles. The bartender looked up.

"Yo," he said. "You Kat's friend?"

"Yeah. He here?" Pete asked.

The bartender pointed toward the back seating area, near the far wall and by the jukebox, which consisted of a few booths and a handful of high-top tables and stools.

Pete slid into the booth with his backpack on the seat next to him. Across from Pete sat a man wearing a frumpy Members Only jacket and a black Yankees cap over his tousled gray hair and scraggly salt-and-pepper beard. He looked up at Pete.

"Guess it was bound to happen," Chadwick said. The McRyan's former fixer gave Pete a look loaded with resignation and, perhaps, a bit of relief.

"Don't try anything stupid," Pete said.

Chadwick shrugged and popped a fry into his mouth from the mostly empty plate in front of him.

"I had a good run," he said. "Good life. Time to pay the piper, I guess."

"You're a piece of shit."

"Did you come all this way to insult me, oh great detective?" Chadwick said, a weary grin on his lips. "I don't think so. Say your piece. Tell me where to go, and I'll lawyer up and this conversation will have never happened."

Pete sighed.

"Don't try to record this, either," Chadwick said, the grin still lingering. "I don't give a shit if New York is one-party consent or not."

Pete leapt over the table dividing the booth and gripped Chadwick by the jacket, pulling the older man over the ketchup-soaked plate and knocking his half-empty pint glass of beer onto the floor.

"Hey, what the fuck?"

"Listen, because I'm only going to say this once," Pete said, the words tumbling out of his mouth in a hushed tone loaded with menace. "I don't give a fuck about what happens to you after I walk away from this table. I don't care if you go to jail. I don't care if you walk into the street and get hit by a truck. I don't care if you go to whatever dive motel you're staying in and shove a gun into your mouth. I do not care. But I do care about the truth, and you owe me that much."

He let go of Chadwick and watched the older man flop back into his seat.

"Fucking psycho," he said under his breath, straightening up his jacket.

"Patty Morales," Pete said. "What happened?"

"You don't need me to tell you that," Chadwick said. "She was killed. Sallis had the McRyan kid and your friend Dave do it, though they went too far. Well, Stephen did. Fucking nutcase. Your pal Dave was a pussy—he didn't want to push it past a few punches. But McRyan didn't stop. Sallis just wanted them to rough up her boyfriend. Then McRyan went overboard, shot and killed Castillo and then the girl. Mendoza bailed, went off the grid for a long time. Sallis hid the body and dumped it on Morales's property as a final 'Fuck you.' Sallis wanted Morales out when it came to the church. That's what finally did it. For a while, at least. Then you started poking around and he had to just kill the sad sack."

"That's not the truth," Pete said. "Not the whole truth."

Chadwick leaned back in his seat.

"After a while of doing this, you get a good sense for bullshit," Pete said. "It's instinctual, really. Your head tingles when things are just a little off. A little wonky. Dave Mendoza was—is—my friend. I know he did bad shit before. Ran drugs. Sold guns. Knew bad people. He has a dark past. But people can change. They can move beyond their mistakes and fix themselves, if they want to. It's difficult—but it's possible. You can move past the darkness and try to figure out why you're here, why you're alive, and why you should keep going. I think Dave did that a while ago. Before I figured it out, or started to. So, when Sallis told me that it was Dave and McRyan—or Sampson, whatever—who killed Patty and her ex, something didn't play right for me. I think Sallis played on the shame Dave felt over his part in it—keeping the secret, helping to hide the evidence, whatever he did end up doing under the thrall of the church and Sallis and his parents—but Dave's not a killer. And while McRyan could be, it still left me wondering. There was a big missing piece. And whenever I'm left wondering about something like that, about where a chunk of the story has gone, I ask myself—who benefits? Who had the means to do it, would be able to get away with it and earn from it? It wasn't Dave Mendoza. It wasn't Stephen McRyan. They're both dead. But you're very much alive."

"Bingo."

Pete put his hands on the grimy table, palms down.

"You were there, weren't you?"

"I was everywhere," Chadwick said, his eyebrows popping up. "I was the cleanup guy, literally and figuratively. Do you really think Mendoza and Sampson could handle this alone? You should have seen the mess they made …"

Pete closed his eyes and let his mind dance around a calming prayer. He had to get what he came here for, and Chadwick admitting to being a part of Patty's murder was just a piece of it.

"What about the McRyans?"

"What about them?" Chadwick asked, incredulous. "Once Sallis knew they were important, that they were of value to the church, he knew he needed someone on them full-time. Then, lo and behold, they find me—eminently qualified to be exactly what they need: a bagman. Someone to do the dirty work and keep tabs on their screwball kid. The truth was, I kept tabs on them, too. For Sallis. I was his number two. I did the dirty work, followed his big picture. I don't wince when it comes to blood or breaking a few bones to get what you need done. I'm a believer, too. La Iglesia gave me a home when no one else would. But they got soft when Figueras faltered. Hell, even before then. Sallis was the leader we needed. I'd do anything for him. I regret nothing."

Pete pulled the Glock from his backpack and pointed it at Chadwick's head. His hands didn't shake. His eyes didn't twitch. He'd envisioned this moment. Longed for it. His finger rested on the trigger. He licked his lips. Chadwick's hands went up, his expression stunned.

"Vizcaya," Pete said. "That was you. I read your file. You're a certified long-range shooter. Graduated from the Army sniper school. You took out McRyan and Jackie."

"I'm a soldier, and my general was Gary Sallis," Chadwick said, his face blank, like a serviceman parroting back his orders. "Trevor McRyan was a liability. His son put everything we were working toward at risk and McRyan and his wife thought they could cut us off and ignore what was owed. Your bitch friend was a nuisance—using her connection to the McRyans to bring you in to meddle in what we were—"

The bullet tore through Chadwick's arm, the sound echoing through the empty bar. The older man let out a surprised and pained yelp as his right hand clutched at the wound, trying to stop the blood that was bubbling out of it. Chadwick's body shook—a combination of pain and surprise.

"You—you fucking shot me," he said, looking at his destroyed arm, the limb dangling at an odd, disturbing angle. Chadwick's words dribbled out of him, shaky and sporadic. "You fucking shot me."

"There are a few more bullets in the gun, too, you son of a bitch," Pete said, still pointing the gun across the table. "That's for Jackie. Piss me off, and you'll get another one, this time between the shoulders, understand? Do as I say, and maybe you'll just have one useless arm instead of a dead body."

Chadwick nodded, wincing as he moved. He looked pale and clammy. His right hand was coated with red, sleek with his own blood. His breathing was ragged. He needed an ambulance. Pete thought he heard footsteps from behind him running toward the exit. The bartender. He didn't blame the guy.

"Take your free hand and pull out your cell phone," Pete said. "Do it slowly. Dial 9-1-1. Tell them you've been shot. Where you are. Nothing else."

Chadwick nodded and did as he was told, the small iPhone clattering on the table, his bloodied fingers tapping a code into the display. Pete slid a card toward Chadwick. It was a simple white business card with a name and newspaper logo.

"While you wait, I want you to call this number. I want you to talk to the person on the other line—my partner, Kathy Bentley. Tell her everything," Pete continued. "You will tell her the truth. The whole truth. On the record. If you don't, I'll find out. Then I'll find you. This will be out tomorrow, for everyone to read."

Chadwick coughed. Red spittle hit the table. He was losing a lot of blood. Pete wasn't sure how serious the gunshot wound was. He didn't care. If Chadwick died tonight, he still had enough time to do what Pete asked. He could give a shit about the rest.

"When the medics come for you, tell them you killed Trevor McRyan," Pete said. "Tell them you should be in jail. Lawyer up if you need to. But they'll know what to do once you say that. Do you understand me?"

Chadwick's head lolled to the left, as good a confirmation as Pete could expect, considering the guy was probably bleeding out. Pete grabbed his backpack and stood up. He pushed the phone toward Chadwick, the gun in his other hand.

"Make that call."

Chadwick dialed.

Pete stepped back. He turned around and walked out.

CHAPTER FORTY

October 16, 2017
Spring Valley, NY

Pete knew something was wrong the second he got out of his car. He was addled and sleep-deprived from the day. He'd strung together a few hours of sleep at his old house, which felt dusty and strange to him, even though he'd only been gone for a short while. He'd called Kathy as he reached Grand Central Station. The conversation had been short. "It's done," she'd said. He had clicked off and used his phone to hit *The New Tropic*'s website. For once, the lifestyle newsletter had become a venue for breaking news, and for at least the next twenty-four hours, Miami's remaining traditional media outlets would be scrambling to catch up with their scoop, penned by former *Times* local columnist Kathy Bentley: *"'I Killed Trevor McRyan': Ex-Army Sniper Admits to Major Role in Assassination of Former Boss."*

Had the scoop not been so entangled in the death of one of his closest friends, Pete might have cracked a smile at having one-upped their former workplace.

That momentary victory felt like it'd happened years ago as he slammed the driver side door shut behind him.

The woman standing in front of the offices of Fernandez Investigations was a cop, no doubt. But why she was here, in front of an office Pete hadn't occupied in what felt like months, was anybody's guess. He kept his luggage in the trunk and walked over.

"Pete Fernandez?" the woman asked, watching him approach.

"That's me."

She flashed a badge. FBI.

"Amanda Chopp," she said. "Organized Crime Unit. Been waiting for you to show your face."

Pete shrugged.

"Had business in Miami," he said. "Can we step inside?"

She nodded and waited for Pete to unlock the door. The waiting room smelled musty and stale. He propped the door open to let some of the air in.

"Sorry, been gone for a bit."

"Yeah, I heard about your adventures down south," she said, not smiling. "You're a professional pain in the ass to people like me, it seems."

"Not by design," Pete said, trying to keep it light. Chopp was about his height, with short black hair and impeccably dressed. As they walked down the hall toward his office, he tried to figure out what this might be about and kept drawing a giant blank.

"I don't want to waste your time or mine," she said, walking behind Pete. "Do you recognize this woman?"

Pete turned around, his face almost hitting the large photograph Chopp held up. It wasn't what he expected—a mug shot or murder scene. It was a casual shot, probably lifted from the person's social media pages or something searchable on the web. Pete knew the woman in question, too.

"Yes, that's Jen Ferris," Pete said. "I know her. Is she okay?"

Chopp brought her arm back down and shook her head.

"No, she's dead," Chopp said. "She was found outside of her place of employment—a strip club named—"

"I know the place," Pete said. He was trying to process what the agent was saying. His head spun. He'd just gotten back here and already felt like he was on his way down another rabbit hole.

"How well did you know Ms. Ferris?"

"We were friends," Pete said. *More than friends, but less than lovers.* He flashed back to Jen's sad eyes, both hurt and defiant at the same time.

He covered his face with his good hand. He could feel his eyes reddening, then watering. He wondered if he would've reacted in the same way if Chopp had broken the news to him before the last few weeks. It didn't matter. What mattered was what he was feeling now: a dull, pulsing ache in his chest that cropped up after Jackie's murder and had only gotten more powerful and painful with the news that Jen Ferris was gone. He was mourning both of them.

I should have done something.

Pete knew the thought was foolish. No one could be in two places at once. But the logic didn't trump the hurt, and that's all he felt, less than a day after coming back to New York, to his adopted home. He tried to collect himself, wiping roughly at his eyes, letting out a rough cough that provided some smokescreen for the sob he felt inside him.

"I'm sorry for your loss," Chopp said, not sounding all that sorry. "My understanding is you did work for her before you disappeared?"

"I didn't disappear."

"Not what people around here say," Chopp said, a tone of derision in her voice. "But okay. What kind of work were you doing for her? And, please, let's skip the client confidentiality bit, huh? She's dead. Any info you may have might help us figure out who did this to her."

Pete swallowed. They were still standing in the hallway leading up to his office but he wasn't sure he could move. He leaned against the wall and faced Chopp.

"She'd asked me to find her father," he said. "We were—we were more than just friends, I guess."

"Older guy fucking a stripper he was friends with," Chopp said, trying to prevent her eyes from rolling too far back. "How novel. Tell me about her father. Same Doug Ferris that runs numbers for the DeCalvacantes?"

"No idea," Pete said. "She just said he'd disappeared and she was worried about him. She said he ran a few grocery stores in Tarrytown."

"Right, well, he did a little more than that," Chopp said, shrugging her shoulders. "My intel tells me he got a lead on a big score—a life-changing one. The kind you do once and never have to do anything else again. Except, when you're in the mob—made or not, Ferris being the latter since he wasn't a full-blooded Italian—you don't get dibs on those scores solo. You have to funnel the info up. Cut your bosses in. Ferris didn't do that. Instead, he booked, made the score and hid the cash. Or so we think."

"But why'd they go after his daughter and not him?"

"Oh, they got him," Chopp said. She pulled out a notebook from her back pocket and flipped a few pages. "He was shot and killed in Suffern, outside of some dirtbag motel. They went after her because it seems like daddy told his little girl where the cash was, hoping she'd skip town and make a new life for herself if he couldn't."

Pete blinked. *Welcome back to New York.*

"Do you need a few minutes?"

"No," Pete said. "What do you want from me?"

"I need more than a quick chat in this shitty hallway, Fernandez," Chopp said. "I need to know about your search for Ferris and about what you recall from the last few times you spoke to his daughter. We're trying to get the assholes who did this, and in case you haven't seen *Goodfellas* or *The Sopranos*, mobsters are fantastic at committing murders and not getting arrested for them."

Chopp started to follow Pete into his office. That's when he noticed the figure standing in the doorway. Fat Vinnie Salerno stepped into the hall, a gun pointed at Pete and Chopp.

"Hey there, Agent Chopp, how are ya?" Salerno said. "Just wanted to see if I could join this little chat of yours. See, my boss and me, we're real curious about Doug's little score. Curious enough to make you both talk for a while."

Chopp reached for her gun but stopped. She wasn't that fast. Pete's gun was collecting dust in his checked bag, in the trunk of his car.

"You spend more time in this office than I do," Pete said to Salerno.

"Shut the fuck up," Salerno said, a sneer dominating his puffy face. "Where's the money? I know you met with the girl before you bounced south. Not a coincidence, I don't think, neither."

"Listen, Salerno—" Chopp said, but her words were interrupted by a gunshot. Pete shifted to his left, his ears ringing. He turned to see the FBI agent on the ground, a growing red dot on her forehead. Dead.

"Jesus," Pete said. "What the hell, man?"

"No, you listen, kid," Salerno said. That's when Pete noticed the desperation in the gangster's voice. The sheen of sweat over his face and his disheveled, rumpled look. Like someone living out of a suitcase. Someone on the run.

"Wait—you're after it, too," Pete said. "You guys don't just kill FBI agents. That'd get you in some hot water with the other bosses and the law. You've gone rogue, eh? You're trying to do the same thing Ferris did?"

Salerno had the gun pointed at Pete now. He licked his lips.

"You got one chance to stay alive, maybe," Salerno said. His gun hand was shaking, either from nerves or he was hopped up on something. That'd explain the sweats, too. "Tell me where Ferris stashed the money and I'll be on my way. That's it. Any other choice and it's done. You got us good last time. That won't happen twice."

Pete jumped at the mobster, gripping Salerno's gun hand. He felt the weight of the rogue gangster pushing back on him, like being buried alive. Whatever advantage Pete got by surprise was soon destroyed by the sheer power of the bigger man. Pete couldn't compete, one arm in a sling, his entire body spent from the last few weeks. He felt himself being pushed down, the gun pointed up but inching back, the barrel arcing toward Pete's face. *I want to live.*

"Fucking nut job," Salerno said, spitting the words out as he forced Pete to bend back against his strength.

Pete felt an opening and took it, kicking out with his left leg and trying to connect with Salerno's midsection.

He missed.

The kick left Pete off-balance against Salerno's power, knocking him onto the floor, the wind rushing out as the big *mafioso* stepped over him. He felt his arm shriek with a familiar pain and knew he wouldn't be able to overpower this man. Pete's vision blurred and his backside felt like it was shattered, the pain charging out in every direction, making it impossible to even think of moving.

"Goodnight, asshole," Salerno said, between gasping breaths. Then the click of a hammer. The gun moving closer, aligning with Pete's fallen body. A loud, ungodly sound followed by a seeping, spreading blackness.

I want to live.

THE END

ACKNOWLEDGMENTS

In many ways, *Blackout* serves as the culmination of the first part of the Pete Fernandez series. For three books, we've seen Pete pull himself out of the gutter and fight back the demons of alcoholism while also getting his footing as a PI, and even solve a few cases. It was time for those two threads to come crashing together and force Pete to face a crossroads many recovering addicts also struggle with: Once you've cleaned up and straightened out your life, how do you proceed? How do you make up for the mistakes you've made, or the regrets that haunt you?

I wanted to explore Pete's teenage days, following his arrest (first mentioned in *Silent City*) for trying to rob a bodega, and show that, like many alcoholics and addicts, his symptoms were present long before he took his first drink. I also wanted to weave a cold case through the various major stages of Pete's life, showing how his evolution allowed him to face it and solve it. He has traveled from rebellious and resentful teenager to distraught blackout drunk to sober but not yet recovered alcoholic. While some of the earlier books dealt with his father's cold cases and helped Pete come to terms with his relationship with his dad, who died too soon, *Blackout* was about putting a mirror to Pete, and showing him his own failures, and seeing how he'd respond. It's up to you whether or not I succeeded.

The case of Patty Morales was partially inspired by the sad tale of Shannon Melendi, a student who attended Southwest Miami High School years before I walked its halls. Melendi was murdered while attending college out of state, though the case remained unsolved for some time. The Melendi case consumed the community and also directly affected many of my friends and teachers at Southwest, leaving a lasting impression on me. When I was thinking of what to write next, the idea of exploring a case similar to Melendi's—a Miami true-crime tale that spanned decades and captured the attention of the city—became an idea I couldn't let go of. Although the story in this book is completely fictional and the Melendi case sadly real, I did spend some time revisiting the details of her story, and that time proved to be invaluable in the writing of *Blackout*.

Before writing the book, I spent a great deal of time reading about topics that interested me that I thought might play a part in the creation of the novel that would become Blackout: cults, unsolved murders, high-profile political assassinations and unusual serial killers. Each of the following books was influential to my work in different ways, and all proved to be obsessive reads that I'd recommend to anyone looking for engaging true crime/nonfiction. Jeff Guinn's *The Road to Jonestown*, which tells the disturbing story of Peoples Temple founder Jim Jones, was an eye-opening history of a volatile, charismatic and very relevant figure. Guinn's descriptions of the inner workings of the church and of Jones' own tactics were inspirational when it came to *Blackout*. *Midnight in Peking* by Paul French, set in the final years of Old China and involving the murder of a young girl, gave me a lot of food for thought in terms of a long-running murder mystery and the plight of the victim's father. Charles Graeber's *The Good Nurse*, which recounted the story of a hospital employee who became one of the most prolific serial killers in history, helped mold my vision for *Blackout*'s main villain, the smooth-talking Gary Sallis. Thanks should also go out to Selwyn Raab's massive mafia history, *Five Families*, John Christian and William Turner's well-researched (and controversial) *The Assassination of Robert F. Kennedy*, and Jim Marrs' *Crossfire: The Plot to Kill Kennedy*.

Also, if *Blackout* leaves you longing for more cult-y fiction, you should check out Stephen King's *Revival*, Emma Cline's *The Girls*, and Ivy Pochoda's *Wonder Valley*, three very different books that resonated with me in the last few months of revisions.

There were many people who helped get this book from concept to finished novel, and I can't praise them enough. First up, I'd like to take a minute to thank my editor (and founder/publisher of Polis Books), Jason Pinter, for being a tireless advocate for Pete and this series. Your support, guidance and friendship have been invaluable.

Thanks to my agent, Dara Hyde, for her sage advice, spot-on feedback, honesty and general support. These books wouldn't exist without you.

To the handful of friends and family who took time out of their busy schedules to read various drafts of this novel and gave important and valuable notes, or to provide advice and help along the way, I can't begin to thank you. But I will anyway. Huge thanks to Paul Steinfeld, Meg Wilhoite, Elizabeth Keenan-Penagos, Angel Luis Colon, Dave White, Amanda di Bartolomeo, Hansel Castro, Sean Tuohy, Andrea Vigil, Rebekah Monson and the crew at *The New Tropic*, Phoebe Flowers, Miranda Mulligan, Austin Trunick, Christian Font and Justin Aclin.

To the fellow crime writers and crime fiction supporters who've shared a kind word, bit of advice or some support over the years, I thank you. The mystery fiction community is a wonderful tribe and I'm lucky to be a part of it.

I'm grateful to Erin Mitchell for her friendship and her indefatigable PR and marketing support.

I owe many thanks to my mother-in-law, Isabel Stein, for her superb copy and content editing skills. She's been with Pete since the beginning and has made sure the books I turn in are much better than what I started out with.

I'm also forever in awe of my dear friends, fellow authors and artists, my great colleagues at Archie Comics and my family.

I'm especially lucky and grateful to have my wife Eva, who remains my first and best reader, and our son Guillermo in my life. I would be nothing without their love, support and understanding.

Thanks for reading.
Alex Segura
Queens, New York
January 21, 2018

AVAILABLE NOW FROM ALEX SEGURA AND POLIS BOOKS

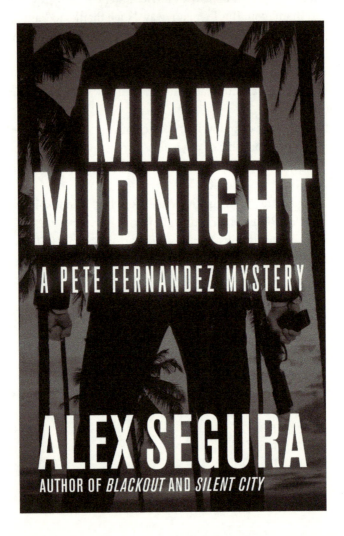

MIAMI MIDNIGHT

A PETE FERNANDEZ MYSTERY

ALEX SEGURA

AUTHOR OF *BLACKOUT* AND *SILENT CITY*

"A FANTASTIC NOIR WITH A COMPLEX AND VERY HUMAN HERO IN PETE FERNANDEZ. MY TAKEAWAY: MORE BOOKS SHOULD BE SET IN MIAMI AND MORE NOVELS SHOULD BE WRITTEN BY ALEX SEGURA." —LISA LUTZ, BESTSELLING AUTHOR OF *THE PASSENGER* AND *THE SWALLOWS*